PRAISE FOR

At the Water's Edge

"[A]n utterly winning story . . . full of riveting scenes and poetic justice."

—*The Miami Herald*

"Riveting . . . gripping . . . Gruen's beautiful setting and deeply sympathetic characters ensure a memorable read for new and returning fans alike."

—*Publishers Weekly*

"Superbly researched and far too easily devoured, this is a truly enthralling love story."

—*The Scotsman*

"I devoured this book. Sara Gruen has proven herself, once again, to be one of America's most compelling storytellers. You might be tempted to rush to get to the answers at the end—but don't, or you'll miss the delectable journey that is Gruen's prose."

—KATHRYN STOCKETT, *New York Times* bestselling author of *The Help*

"Compelling . . . a heartwarming story about life, and the places it can potentially take you."

—*InStyle*

"If I needed a reminder why I am such a fan of Sara Gruen's books, her latest novel provides plenty. Unique in its setting and scope, this impeccably researched historical fiction is full of the gorgeous prose I've come to expect from this author. And even after the final page, its message still resonates with me: The monsters we seek may be right in front of us. In fact, the only fault I can find with this book is that I've already finished it."

—JODI PICOULT, *New York Times* bestselling author of *Leaving Time*

"*At the Water's Edge* skillfully transports us to a small, tenacious Scottish village in the grip of war, and into the heart of Madeline Hyde, a woman who is a stranger to herself until forces convene to rock her awake. Sara Gruen is a wizard at capturing the essence of her historical setting, and does so here in spades, but it's Maddie's unexpected transformation that grounds and drives the novel. As her husband and best friend search the surface of the Loch, desperate for a sign of the elusive creature, Maddie learns to plumb her own depths, and comes fully alive to the world around her. Magical."

—PAULA MCLAIN, *New York Times* bestselling author of *The Paris Wife*

"[Gruen] combines historical fiction, romance, and fable to good effect, and her narrative description is often sublime. . . . This ambitious novel is a natural for the book-club set."

—*Booklist*

"Terrific characters and attention to detail made this moving, suspenseful novel by the author of *Water for Elephants* stand out."

—*Woman & Home*

"*At the Water's Edge* is a rich, beautiful novel. Elegantly written and compulsively readable, it is at once a gripping love story, a profound examination of the effects of war on ordinary women, and a compelling portrait of female friendship. While delving into powerful themes, Sara Gruen never loses sight of what matters: her characters. This story of one privileged young woman, coming of age in a time of impossible upheaval and terrible choices, will keep you riveted until the very last page."

—KRISTIN HANNAH, *New York Times* bestselling author of *The Nightingale*

"Intoxicating . . . Sara Gruen has an exquisite eye for detail, and she evokes the haunted—and haunting—Scottish landscape with her signature passion, freshness, and scope. Atmospheric and gritty, the compelling tale of Madeline's struggle to redefine herself in a world gone mad will linger long after you turn the final page. I love this marvelous, marvelous book."

—JOSHILYN JACKSON, *New York Times* and *USA Today* bestselling author of *Someone Else's Love Story*

"Lively, colorful and gritty."

—*Sainsbury's Magazine*

BY SARA GRUEN

Riding Lessons

Flying Changes

Water for Elephants

Ape House

At the Water's Edge

At the Water's Edge

At the Water's Edge

A NOVEL

Sara Gruen

SPIEGEL & GRAU

NEW YORK

At the Water's Edge is a work of fiction. Names, characters, places, and incidents are the products of the author's imagination or are used fictitiously. Any resemblance to actual events, locales, or persons, living or dead, is entirely coincidental.

2015 Spiegel & Grau Trade Paperback Edition

Copyright © 2015 by Sara Gruen
Reading group guide copyright © 2015 by Penguin Random House LLC

Published in the United States by Spiegel & Grau, an imprint of Random House, a division of Penguin Random House LLC, New York.

SPIEGEL & GRAU and the HOUSE colophon are registered trademarks of Penguin Random House LLC.
RANDOM HOUSE READER'S CIRCLE & Design is a registered trademark of Penguin Random House LLC.

Originally published in hardcover in the United States by Spiegel & Grau, an imprint of Random House, a division of Penguin Random House LLC, in 2015.

Interview between Sara Gruen and Brandi Megan Granett contained within the Reader's Guide originally appeared on HuffingtonPost.com on May 6, 2015, and is reprinted here with permission.

Library of Congress Cataloging-in-Publication Data

Gruen, Sara.
At the water's edge: a novel/Sara Gruen.
pages; cm
ISBN 978-0-385-52324-0
eBook ISBN 978-0-8129-9789-7
Fathers and sons—Fiction. 2. Socialites—Fiction 3. Loch Ness monster—Fiction.
Title.
PS3607.R696A94.2015
813'.6—dc23   2014027470

Printed in the United States of America on acid-free paper

spiegelandgrau.com
randomhousereaderscircle.com

2 4 6 8 9 7 5 3 1

Book design by Caroline Cunningham

For Bob,

'S tusa gràdh mo bheatha

One Crow for sorrow,

Two Crows for mirth,

Three Crows for a wedding,

Four Crows for a birth,

Five Crows for silver,

Six Crows for gold,

Seven for a secret, never to be told.

At the Water's Edge

Prologue

Drumnadrochit, February 28, 1942

AGNES MÀIRI GRANT,
INFANT DAUGHTER OF ANGUS AND MÀIRI GRANT
JANUARY 14TH, 1942

CAPT. ANGUS DUNCAN GRANT,
BELOVED HUSBAND OF MÀIRI
APRIL 2ND, 1909–JANUARY , 1942

T he headstone was modest and hewn of black granite,
granite being one of the few things never in short supply
in Glenurquhart, even during the present difficulty.

Màiri visited the tiny swell of earth that covered her daughter's coffin every day, watching as it flattened. Archie the Stone-
cutter had said it might be months before they could put up the
stone with the frost so hard upon them, but the coffin was so
small the leveling was accomplished in just a few weeks.

No sooner was the stone up than Màiri got the telegram
about Angus and had Archie take it away again. Archie had

wanted to wait until the date of death was verified, but Màiri needed it done then, to have a place to mourn them both at once, and Archie could not say no. He chiseled Angus's name beneath his daughter's and left some room to add the day of the month when they learned it. An addition for an absence, because Angus—unlike the wee bairn—was not beneath it and almost certainly never would be.

There were just the two of them in the churchyard when Archie returned the headstone. He was a strong man, heaving a piece of granite around like that.

A shadow flashed over her, and she looked up. A single crow circled high above the graves, never seeming to move its wings.

One Crow for sorrow,

It was joined by another, and then two more.

Two Crows for mirth,

Three Crows for a wedding,

Four Crows for a birth

Archie removed his hat and twisted it in his hands.

"If there's anything Morag and I can do, anything at all . . ."

Màiri tried to smile, and succeeded only in producing a half-choked sob. She pulled a handkerchief from her pocket and pressed it to her mouth.

Archie paused as though he wanted to say more. Eventually he replaced his hat and said, "Well then. I'll be off." He nodded firmly and trudged back to his van.

It was Willie the Postie who had delivered the telegram, on Valentine's Day no less, a month to the day after the birth. Màiri had been pulling a pint behind the bar when Anna came, ashen-faced, whispering that Willie was on the doorstep, and would not come inside. Willie was a regular, so Màiri knew from that very moment, before she even approached the door and saw his face. His hooded eyes stared into hers, and then drifted down to the envelope in his hands. He turned it a couple of times, as though wondering whether to give it to her, whether *not* giving it to her would make the thing it contained not true. The wind caught it a couple of times, flicking it this way and that. When he finally handed it to her, he offered it up as gently as a new-hatched chick. She opened it, turned it right side up, and let her eyes scan the purple date stamp—February 14th, 1942—added by Willie himself not half an hour before, and then

MRS MAIRI GRANT 6 HIGH ROAD DRUM INVERNESS-SHIRE
DEEPLY REGRET TO INFORM THAT YOUR HUSBAND CAPTN
ANGUS D GRANT SEAFORTH HRS 4TH BTN 179994 IS
MISSING PRESUMED KILLED ON WAR SERVICE JAN 1
1942 LETTER WITH DETAILS TO FOLLOW

She took in only three things: Angus, killed, the date. And they were enough.

"I'm sorry, Màiri," Willie said in a near whisper. "Especially so soon after . . ." His voice trailed off. He blinked, and his eyes drifted down, pausing briefly on her belly before coming to rest again on his hands.

She could not reply. She closed the door quietly, walked past the hushed locals and into the kitchen. There she leaned against the wall, clutching her empty womb with one hand and the piece of paper that had brought Angus's death in the other. For it did seem as though it was the paper that brought his death rather than simply the news of it. He had been dead for more than six weeks, and she hadn't known.

In the time between the arrival of the telegram and the return of the headstone with Angus's name on it, Màiri had begun to blame Willie. Why had he chosen to hand her the telegram? She had seen his hesitation. He would have been complicit in what, at worst, would have been a lie of omission, especially if it meant she could believe that Angus was still out there somewhere. Even if he was doing things she couldn't comprehend, things that might change him in the terrible ways the men who had already been sent home had been changed, she could believe he was alive and therefore fixable, for surely there was nothing she couldn't love him through once he came home.

They had lied to her about the baby, and she had let them.

Since she had first felt the baby quicken, she was keenly aware of its every movement. For months, she had watched in wonderment as little braes poked up from her belly, pushing their way across—an elbow, or perhaps a knee—a subterranean force that constantly rearranged the landscape of her flesh. Was it a boy, or a wee girl? Whichever it was, it already had strong opinions. She remembered the moment it occurred to her that it had been hours since she felt it move, on Hogmanay, of all days. At midnight, precisely when Ian Mackintosh struck in his pipes to form the first chord of "Auld Lang Syne" and seconds before corresponding shots rang out from the doorway of Donnie Maclean, Màiri began poking her belly, trying to wake it, for they said that unborn babes slept. She yelled at it, screamed at it, and finally, realizing, wrapped her arms around it and wept. Thirteen days later, her pains started.

Her memories of the birth were vague, for the midwife had given her bitter tea mixed with white powder, and the doctor held ether over her nose and mouth at regular intervals, putting her under completely at the end. They told her the baby had lived a few minutes, long enough to be baptized. Their lie became her lie, and that was what went on the headstone. In truth, she'd probably lost both child and husband on the same date.

The promised letter never arrived. Where had he died? *How* had he died? Without the dreaded details, she had only her imagination—her terrible imagination—and while she wished she couldn't fathom what his last moments might have been, she could, with distinct and agonizing precision, in a million different ways. Please God that they were moments indeed, and not hours or days.

The murder of crows descended in a noisy fluster, settling in a row on the stone wall, huddling into themselves, their blue-black feathers puffed and their heads tucked in as though they'd pulled up their coat collars. They stared accusingly, miserably, but without their usual commentary. Màiri counted them twice.

Seven for a secret, never to be told.

She knew then that she would never know the details, would never know what had happened.

A bone-chilling wind stirred the fallen leaves until they formed cyclones that danced among the graves. Màiri crouched and fingered the names of her child and husband in the black stone.

Agnes.

Angus.

A third of the stone was still blank, at the bottom. There was room for one more name, one more set of dates, and these would be accurate.

She stood without taking her eyes off the stone. She wiped her eyes and nose on the handkerchief, and kept it in her hand as she wrapped her arms around herself and walked through the black iron gate, leaving it swinging. She headed toward the inn, except when she got to the crossroad, she turned left instead of going straight.

A light snow began to fall, but despite her bare head and legs she trudged right past the Farquhars' croft. She'd have been welcome there, as well as at the McKenzies', where she could see the fire glowing orange through the window, but on she went, teeth chattering, hands and shins numb.

Eventually the castle rose on her left, its majestic and ruined battlements like so many broken teeth against the leaden sky. She had played within its walls as a child, and knew which rooms remained whole, where you had to watch your footing, where the best hiding places were, where the courting couples went. She and Angus had been among them.

The snow was heavier now, falling in clumps that collected and melted on her hair. Her ears were past stinging. She pulled her sleeves over her frozen hands and pinched them shut with her fingertips. Through the gatehouse, past the kiln, pushing through the long grass and scrub gorse, bracken, and thistles, straight to the Water Gate.

She paused at the top, staring at the blackness of the loch. Thousands of tiny whitecaps danced on its surface, seeming to move in the opposite direction of the water beneath them. It was said that the loch contained more water than all the other bodies of water not just in Scotland but also in England and Wales combined, and it held other things as well. She had been warned away from it her entire life, for its depth came quickly, its coldness was fierce, and the Kelpie lay in wait.

She picked her way sideways down the slope, letting her icy fingers out of her sleeves to hold up the hem of her coat.

When she reached the bottom, the water lapped around the soles of her shoes. The edge of the loch looked seductively shallow, slipping over the gravel and back into itself. She took a step forward, gasping as the water flooded her shoes, so cold, so cold, and yet it had never frozen, not once in recorded history. Another step, another gasp. Bits of peat swirled in the water around her ankles, circling her legs, beckoning her forth. Another step, and this time she stumbled, finding herself knee-deep. Her wool coat floated, an absurd umbrella, first resisting and finally wicking water, pulling her deeper. She looked back at the landing, suddenly desperate. If only she had a hat, she could throw it back onto the thorny gorse. If she'd had anything that would float, maybe they'd think it was an accident and let her be buried with her daughter. Maybe they'd think the Kelpie took her. And then she remembered that the loch never gave up its dead, so she spread her arms wide and embraced it.

Chapter One

Scottish Highlands, January 14, 1945

"Oh God, make him pull over," I said as the car slung around yet another curve in almost total darkness.

It had been nearly four hours since we'd left the naval base at Aultbea, and we'd been careening from checkpoint to checkpoint since. I truly believe those were the only times the driver used the brakes. At the last checkpoint, I was copiously sick, narrowly missing the guard's boots. He didn't even bother checking our papers, just lifted the red and white pole and waved us on with a look of disgust.

"Driver! Pull over," said Ellis, who was sitting in the backseat between Hank and me.

"I'm afraid there is no 'over,'" the driver said in a thick Highland accent, his *R*'s rolling magnificently. He came to a stop in the middle of the road.

It was true. If I stepped outside the car I would be ankle-deep in thorny vegetation and mud, not that it would have done any more to destroy my clothes and shoes. From head to toe I was steeped in sulfur and cordite and the stench of fear. My stockings were mere cobwebs stretched around my legs, and my scarlet nails were broken and peeling. I hadn't had my hair done since the day before we'd sailed from the shipyard in Philadelphia. I had never been in such a state.

I leaned out the open door and gagged while Ellis rubbed my back. Wet snow collected on the top of my head.

I sat up again and pulled the door shut. "I'm sorry. I'm finished. Do you think you can take those things off the headlights? I think it would be better if I could see what's coming." I was referring to the slotted metal plates our one-eyed driver had clipped on before we'd left the base. They limited visibility to about three feet ahead of us.

"Can't," he called back cheerfully. "It's the Blackout." As he cranked up through the gears, my head lurched back and forth. I leaned over and cradled my face in my hands.

Ellis patted my shoulder. "We should be nearly there. Do you think fresh air would help?"

I sat up and let my head flop against the back of the torn leather seat. Ellis reached across and rolled the window down a crack. I turned toward the cold air and closed my eyes.

"Hank, can you *please* put out your cigarette?"

He didn't answer, but a whoosh of frigid air let me know he had tossed it out the window.

"Thank you," I said weakly.

Twenty minutes later, when the car finally came to a stop and the driver cut the engine, I was so desperate for solid ground I spilled out before the driver could get his own door open, never mind mine. I landed on my knees.

"Maddie!" Ellis said in alarm.

"I'm all right," I said.

There was a fast-moving cloud cover under a nearly full moon, and by its light I first laid eyes on our unlikely destination.

I climbed to my feet and reeled away from the car, thinking I might be sick again. My legs propelled me toward the building, spinning ever faster. I crashed into the wall, then slid down until I was crouching against it.

In the distance, a sheep bleated.

To say that I wished I wasn't there would be a ludicrous understatement, but I'd only ever had the illusion of choice:

We have to do this, Hank had said. *It's for Ellis.*

To refuse would have been tantamount to betrayal, an act of calculated cruelty. And so, because of my husband's war with his father and their insane obsession with a mythical monster, we'd crossed the Atlantic at the very same time a real madman, a real monster, was attempting to take over the world for his own reasons of ego and pride.

I would have given anything to go back two weeks, to the beginning of the New Year's Eve party, and script the whole thing differently.

Chapter Two

Rittenhouse Square, Philadelphia, December 31, 1944

"*Five! Four! Three! Two!*"

The word "one" had already formed on our lips, but before it could slide off there was an explosion overhead. As screams rose around us, I pitched myself against Ellis, tossing champagne over both of us. He threw an arm protectively around my head and didn't spill a drop.

When the screams petered out, I heard a tinkling above us, like glass breaking, along with an ominous groaning. I peeked out from my position against Ellis's chest.

"What the hell?" said Hank, without a hint of surprise. I think he was the only person in the room who hadn't jumped.

All eyes turned upward. Thirty feet above us, a massive chandelier swung on its silver-plated chain, throwing shimmering prisms across the walls and floor. It was as if a rainbow had burst into a million pieces, which were now dancing across the marble, silks, and damask. We watched, transfixed. I glanced nervously at Ellis's face, and then back at the ceiling.

An enormous cork landed next to General Pew, our host at what was easily the most anticipated party of the year, bouncing outrageously like a bloated mushroom. A split second later a single crystal the size of a quail's egg fell from the sky and dropped smack into his cocktail, all but emptying it. He stared, bemused and tipsy, then calmly took out his handkerchief and dabbed his jacket.

As everyone burst into laughter, I noticed a footman in old-fashioned knee breeches perched near the top of a stepladder, pallid, motionless, struggling to contain the biggest bottle of champagne I'd ever seen. On the marble table in front of him was a structure of glasses arranged so that if someone poured continuously into the top one, they would eventually all be filled. As a rush of bubbles cascaded over the sides of the bottle and into the footman's sleeves, he stared in white-faced horror at Mrs. Pew.

Hank assessed the situation and apparently took pity on the fellow. He raised his glass, as well as his other hand, and with the flair and flourish of a ringmaster boomed, *"One! Happy New Year!"*

The orchestra struck up "Auld Lang Syne." General Pew conducted with his empty glass, and Mrs. Pew beamed at his side—not only was her party a smashing success, but it now had a comic anecdote people would speak of for years.

Should auld acquaintance be forgot, and never brought to mind

Should auld acquaintance be forgot, and old lang syne...

Those who knew the words sang along. I had refreshed my memory that afternoon in order to be ready for the big moment, but when cork met crystal, the lyrics were knocked straight out of my brain. By the time we got to running about slopes and picking daisies fine, I gave up and joined Ellis and Hank in la-la-la'ing our way through the rest.

They waved their glasses in solidarity with General Pew, their free arms looped around my waist. At the end, Ellis leaned in to kiss me.

Hank looked to one side, then the other, and appeared baffled.

"Hmm. I seem to have misplaced my date. What *have* I done with her?"

"What you *haven't* done is marry her," I said and then snorted, nearly expelling champagne through my nose. I had sipped my way through at least four glasses on an empty stomach and was feeling bold.

His mouth opened in mock offense, but even he couldn't pretend ignorance about Violet's growing desperation at the seemingly endless nature of their courtship.

"Did she actually leave?" he said, scanning the room a little more seriously.

"I'm not sure," I said. "I haven't seen her in a while."

"Then who will give me my New Year's kiss?" he asked, looking bereft.

"Oh, come here, you big lug." I stood on tiptoe and planted a kiss on his cheek. "You've always got us. And we don't even require a ring."

Ellis threw us an amused side eye and motioned to Hank that he should wipe my lipstick off his cheek.

Beyond him, the footman was still balanced on the second to highest rung of the stepladder. He was bent at the waist, trying to aim the bottle at the top glass, and had gone from pale to purple with the effort. His mouth was pressed into a grim line. I looked around to see if reinforcements were coming and didn't see any.

"Ellis? I think he needs help," I said, tilting my head in the footman's direction.

Ellis glanced over. "You're right," he said, handing me his glass. "Hank? Shall we?"

"Do you really think she's left?" Hank said wistfully, his lips hovering near the edge of his glass. "She was a vision tonight. That dress was the color of the gloaming, the sequins jealous stars in the galaxy of her night, but nothing, *nothing* could compare to the milky skin of her—"

"Boys! Concentrate!" I said.

Hank snapped back to life. "What?"

"Maddie thinks that man needs help," said Ellis.

"That thing's enormous," I said. "I don't think he can hold it on his own."

"I should think not. That's a Balthazar," said Ellis.

"That's not a Balthazar," Hank said. "That's a Nebuchadnez-zar."

The footman's arms were quaking. He began pouring but missed. Champagne fell between the glasses, splashing onto the table and floor. His gloves and sleeves were saturated.

"Uh-oh," said Hank.

"Uh-oh indeed," said Ellis. "Mrs. Pew will *not* be pleased."

"I rather suspect Mrs. Pew is never pleased," Hank said.

Rivulets of sweat ran down the footman's forehead. It was plain to see that he was going to fall forward, right onto the glasses. I looked to Mrs. Pew for help, but she had disappeared. I tried to signal the General, but he was holding court with a replenished cocktail.

I dug my elbow into Ellis's side.

"Go!" I said urgently. "Go help him."

"Who's she talking about?" said Hank.

I glared at him, and then some more, until he remembered.

"Oh! Of course." He tried to hand me his glass, but I was already holding two. He set his on the floor and yanked his lapels in a businesslike manner, but before he and Ellis could mobilize, help arrived in the form of other servants bearing four smaller but still very large bottles, and three more stepladders. Mrs. Pew glided in behind them to make sure all was under control.

"Now *those* are Balthazars," said Hank, with a knowing nod. He retrieved his drink from the floor and drained it.

"No. Those are Jeroboams," said Ellis.

"I think I know my champagne," said Hank.

"And I don't?"

"I think you're both wrong. Those are Ebenezers," I said.

That stopped them.

I broke into tipsy giggles. "Ebenezer? Get it? Christmas? The holidays? Oh never mind. Someone get me another. I spilled mine."

"Yes. On *me*," said Ellis.

Hank spun around and set his glass on the tray of a passing waiter. He clapped his hands. "All right, who's up for a snowball fight?"

We toppled outside and made snow angels right there in front of the Pews' home and all the cars and liveried drivers that were lined up waiting for guests. I gathered one snowball and managed to land it on Ellis's chest before screeching and running back inside.

In the vast foyer, Ellis helped brush the snow off my back and hair. Hank hung his jacket over my bare shoulders, and the two of them guided me to a trio of ornate, embroidered chairs near a roaring fire. Hank, who had had the presence of mind to grab my mink stole on the way back in, shook it off and draped it over the edge of the rosewood table in front of us. Ellis went in search of hot toddies, and I peeled off my gloves, which were stained and soaked.

"God, look at me," I said, gazing down at myself. "I'm a mess."

My silk dress and shoes were ruined. I tried in vain to smooth out the water spots, and checked quickly to make sure I still had both earrings. The gloves were of no consequence, but I hoped the stole could be saved. If not, I'd succeeded in destroying my entire outfit.

"You're not a mess. You're magnificent," said Hank.

"Well, I *was*," I lamented.

I'd spent the afternoon at Salon Antoine having my hair and makeup done, and had eaten almost nothing for two days before so my dress would drape properly. It was a beautiful pomegranate-red silk, the same material as my shoes. It matched my ruby engagement ring, and all of it set off my green eyes. Ellis had given me the dress and shoes a few days earlier, and before the party I had presented myself to him like a flamenco dancer, twirling so the skirt would take flight. He professed his delight, but I felt a familiar pang of sorrow as I tried, yet again, to imagine exactly what he was seeing. My husband was profoundly color-blind, so to him my ensemble must have been a combination of grays. I wondered which ones, and how many variations there were, and whether they had different depths. I couldn't imagine a world without color.

Hank dropped into a chair, leaving one leg dangling over its arm. He pulled his bow tie open and undid his cuffs and collar. He looked like a half-drowned Clark Gable.

I shivered into his jacket, holding it closed from the inside.

Hank patted his chest and sides. He stopped suddenly and lifted an eyebrow.

"Oh!" I said, realizing what he was looking for. I retrieved the cigarette case from his inside pocket and handed it to him. He flipped it open and held it out in offering. I shook my head. He took a cigarette for himself and snapped the case shut.

"So, how about it then?" he said, his eyes glistening playfully. "Shall we go get us a monster?"

"Sure," I said, waving my hand. "We'll hop on the next liner." It was what I always said when the topic came up, which was often, and always after boatloads of booze. It was our little game.

"I think getting away would do Ellis good. He seems depressed."

"Ellis isn't depressed," I said. "You just want to escape Violet's clutches."

"I do not," he protested.

"You didn't even notice when she left tonight!"

Hank cocked his head and nodded, conceding the point. "I suppose I should send flowers."

"First thing in the morning," I said.

He nodded. "Absolutely. At the crack of noon. Scout's honor."

"*And* I think you should marry her. You need civilizing, and I need a female friend. I have only you and Ellis."

He clutched a hand to his heart, mortally wounded. "What are we, chopped liver?"

"Only the finest foie gras. Seriously, though. How long are you going to make her wait?"

"I'm not sure. I don't know if I'm ready to be civilized yet. But when I am, Violet can have the honors. She can pick a mean set of china."

As I set my drink down, I caught another glimpse of my dress and shoes. "I think maybe *I* need civilizing. Will you just marry her already?"

"What is this, an ambush?" He tapped the cigarette against the top of the case and put it between his lips. A servant appeared from nowhere to light it.

"Mm, thanks," Hank said, inhaling. He leaned back and let smoke drift from his mouth to his nose in a swirling white ribbon that he re-inhaled. He called this maneuver the "Irish Waterfall."

"If I do marry her, Ellis and I won't have a hope, because you girls will gang up on us."

"We won't be able to," I said. "The distribution will be equal."

"They're never equal between the sexes. You already gang up on Ellis and me all by yourself."

"I do not!"

"You're ganging up on me right now, at this very minute,

single-handedly baiting the marriage trap. I tell you, it's the ultimate female conspiracy. You're all in on it. Personally, I can't see what all the fuss is about."

Ellis returned, followed by a waiter who set steaming crystal glasses with handles on the table in front of us. Ellis flopped into a chair.

Hank set his cigarette in an ashtray and picked up his toddy. He blew steam from the surface and took a cautious sip. "So, Ellis, our darling girl here was just saying we should go on a trip," he said. "Find us a plesiosaur."

"Sure she was," said Ellis.

"She was. She has it all planned out," said Hank. "Tell him, Maddie."

"You're drunk," I said, laughing.

"That is true, I will admit," said Hank, "but I still think we should do it." He ground the cigarette out so hard its snuffed end splayed like a spent bullet. "We've been talking about it for years. Let's do it. I'm serious."

"No you're not," I said.

Hank once again clasped his heart. "What's happened to you, Maddie? Don't tell me you've lost your sense of adventure. Has Violet been civilizing you in secret?"

"No, of course not. You haven't given her the chance. But we can't go now. Liners haven't run since the *Athenia* went down."

I realized I'd made it sound like it had spontaneously sprung a leak, when in reality it had been torpedoed by a German U-boat with 1,100 civilians on board.

"Where there's a will, there's a way," said Hank, nodding sagely. He sipped the toddy again, then peered into it accusingly. "Hmmmm. Think I prefer whiskey after all. Back in a minute. Ellis, talk to your wife. Clearly she's picking up bad habits."

He launched himself from his chair, and for a moment

looked like he might topple over. He clutched the back of Ellis's chair while he regained his balance and finally wafted off, drifting like a butterfly.

Ellis and I sat in relative silence, within a bubble created by the chatter and laughter of other people.

He slid slowly down in his chair until it must have looked empty from behind. His eyes were glassy, and he'd turned a bit gray.

My own ears buzzed from the champagne. I lifted both hands to investigate my hair, and discovered the curls on one side had come undone and were clinging to my neck. Reaching further around, I realized that the diamond hair comb given to me by my mother-in-law was missing. I felt a stab of panic. It had been a gift on our wedding day, a rare moment of compassion shown me by a woman who had made no secret of not wanting me to marry her son, but was nonetheless moved to give it to me seconds before Hank walked me down the aisle.

"I think we should do it," Ellis said.

"Sure," I said gaily. "We'll just hop on the next—"

"I mean it," he said sharply.

I looked up, startled by his tone. He was grinding his jaw. I wasn't sure exactly when it had happened, but his mood had shifted. We were no longer playing a game.

He looked at me in irritation. "What? Why shouldn't we?"

"Because of the war," I said gently.

"Carpe diem, and all that crap. The war is part of the adventure. God knows I'm not getting near it any other way. Neither is Hank, for that matter." He raked a hand through his hair, leaving a swath of it standing on end. He leaned in closer and narrowed his eyes. "You do know what they call us, don't you?" he said. " 'FFers.' "

He and Hank were the only 4Fers in the room. I wondered if someone had slighted him when he'd gone to find drinks.

Hank took his flat-footedness in stride, as he did most

things, but being given 4F status had devastated Ellis. His color blindness had gone undetected until he tried to enlist and was rejected. He'd tried a second time at a different location and was turned down again. Although it was clearly not his fault, he was right that people judged, and I knew how this chipped at him. It was relentless and unspoken, so he couldn't even defend himself. His own father, a veteran of the Great War, had treated him with undisguised revulsion since hearing the news. This injustice was made all the more painful because we lived with my in-laws, who had perversely removed any chance at escape. Two days after the attack on Pearl Harbor, they cut Ellis's allowance by two thirds. My mother-in-law broke it to us in the drawing room before dinner, announcing with smug satisfaction that she was sure we'd be pleased to know that until "this terrible business was over" the money would be going toward war bonds. Strictly speaking, that may have been where the money was going, but it was perfectly clear that the real motive was punishing Ellis. His mother was exacting revenge because he'd dared to marry me, and his father—well, we weren't exactly sure. Either he didn't believe that Ellis was color-blind, or he couldn't forgive him for it. The nightmarish result was that we were forced to live under the constant scrutiny of people we'd come to think of as our captors.

"You know how hard it is," he went on, "with everyone staring at me, wondering why I'm not serving."

"They don't stare—"

"Don't patronize me! You know perfectly well they do!"

His outburst caused everyone to turn and look.

Ellis waved an angry hand at them. "See?"

He glanced fiercely around. To a person, they turned away, their scandalized expressions trained elsewhere. Conversations resumed, but in dampened tones.

Ellis locked eyes with me. "I know I look perfectly healthy," he continued, his voice under taut control. "My own father thinks I'm a coward, for Christ's sake. I need to prove myself. To him, to them, to *me*. Of all people, I thought you'd understand."

"Darling, I do understand," I said.

"But do you?" he asked, his mouth stretching into a bitter smile.

"Of course," I said, and I did, although at that moment I would have said anything to calm him down. He'd been drinking hard liquor since early afternoon, and I knew things could degenerate quickly. The carefully averted faces of those around us already portended a very unpleasant beginning to the new year.

My mother-in-law, who had missed the party because of a migraine, would surely start receiving reports of our behavior by noon. I could only imagine how she'd react when she found out I'd lost the hair comb. I resolved to telephone the next day and throw myself on Mrs. Pew's mercy. If the comb had come out in the snow, it was probably gone forever, but if it had fallen down the back of a sofa, it might turn up.

Ellis watched me closely, the fire dancing in his eyes. After a few seconds, his angry mask melted into an expression of sad relief. He leaned sideways to pat my knee and almost fell out of his chair.

"That's my girl," he said, struggling upright. "Always up for adventure. You're not like the other girls, you know. There's not an ounce of fun in them. That's why Hank won't marry Violet, of course. He's holding out for another you. Only there isn't one. I've got the one and only."

"Who the whatty-what now?" said Hank, appearing from nowhere and crashing back into his chair. "Over here!" he barked, snapping his fingers above his head. A waiter set more drinks on the table in front of us. Hank turned back to Ellis. "Is she trying to marry me off again? I swear there's an echo in here."

"No. She's agreed. We're going to Scotland."

Hank's eyes popped open. "Really?" He looked at me for confirmation.

I didn't think I'd agreed, per se, at least not after I realized we weren't just joking, but since I'd managed to defuse the bomb and perhaps even save the evening, I decided to play along.

"Sure," I said, gesturing grandly. "Why not?"

Chapter Three

The next morning, I was startled awake by the telephone ringing in the downstairs hallway. It was exactly nine o'clock, which was the very earliest time considered civilized. I clutched the covers to my chin, paralyzed, as Pemberton, the butler, summoned my mother-in-law. I heard her determined footsteps, then her muffled voice, rising and falling in surprised waves.

I was entirely wretched—my head pounded, my stomach was sour, and it was quite possible that I was still drunk. While I remembered much of the night before, there were moments I couldn't recall, like getting home. The realization that I'd passed the point of being tipsy had come over me quite suddenly—I remembered being acutely aware that it was time to call it a night, but I did not remember leaving, much less the ride home. I had no idea how many—or few—hours I'd been in bed.

My ruined dress lay in a limp heap in the middle of the carpet, looking for all the world like a length of intestine. My shoes were nearby, one of them missing a heel. The white stole was flung over the edge of my polished mahogany dressing table, the fur spiked and dirty. I'd dropped my strand of pearls in front of my jewelry box, and both earrings, cushion-cut rubies surrounded by diamonds, were nearby but not together. A very large champagne cork was planted squarely between them. I checked my finger for my ring and then, with a sickening feeling of vertigo, remembered the hair comb. I burrowed my face into my pillow and pulled its edges over my ears.

At noon, the housemaid knocked gently on the door, then opened it a crack.

"I'm sorry, Emily. I'm not feeling up to breakfast," I said, my voice muffled by the pillow.

"I've brought Alka-Seltzer and gingersnaps," she replied, which made my stomach twist again. It meant that not only had we wakened the entire house when we returned, but also that our condition had been obvious.

"Put it on the table," I said, rolling to face the opposite wall. I didn't want her to see me. I'd fallen into bed without even removing my makeup, as evidenced by the streaks of mascara on my pillowcase. "Thank you, Emily."

"Of course, Mrs. Hyde."

She stayed longer than I expected, and when she left, I saw that she'd taken the dress, shoes, and mink with her.

The telephone rang sporadically throughout the day. With each call, my mother-in-law's voice became a little more resolute until finally it was brittle and hard. I shrank further under the covers with every conversation.

At nearly six thirty, Ellis staggered into my room. He was still in his pajamas. His robe was open, its sash dragging on the floor behind him.

"Dear God, what a night," he said, scrubbing his eyes with his fists. "I'm a bit green about the gills. I could use an eye-opener. How about you?"

I suppressed a retch.

"Are you all right?" he asked, coming closer. His face was drawn, and there were dark semicircles beneath his eyes. I didn't even want to know how I looked—Ellis had at least made it into his pajamas; I was still in my slip.

"Not really," I said. "Look what Emily brought on my breakfast tray."

He glanced over and guffawed.

"It's not funny," I said. "It means they're all gossiping about us in the kitchen. And I lost your mother's hair comb."

"Oh," he said vaguely.

"Ellis, *I lost the hair comb.*"

When the gravity of this sank in, he sat on the edge of the bed and the last of his color drained.

"What am I going to do?" I said, curling into a ball.

He took a deep breath and thought. After a few seconds, he slapped his thighs with resolve and said, "Well. You'll have to telephone the Pews and tell them to be on the lookout, that's all."

"I was going to. But I can't."

"Why not?"

"For one thing, I can't get near the telephone. Your mother's been on it all day. God only knows what she's heard. And anyway, I can't call Mrs. Pew. I can't face her, not even over the telephone."

"Why?"

"Because we were *tight*! We rolled around in the street!"

"Everyone was tight."

"Yes, but not like us," I said miserably. I sat up and cradled my head in my hands. "I don't even remember leaving. Do you?"

"Not really." He got up and walked to my dressing table. "When did you get this?" he asked, picking up the cork.

"I haven't a clue," I replied.

On the main floor, the telephone rang yet again, and I cowered. Ellis came back to the bed and took my hand. This time, when Pemberton fetched my mother-in-law, her footsteps were brisk and she spoke in punctuated bursts. After a few minutes, she went silent again, and the silence was ominous, rolling through the house like waves of poisonous gas.

Ellis looked at my clock. "She'll come up to dress for dinner in a few minutes. You can call then."

"Come with me?" I whispered, clutching his hand.

"Of course," he said. "Do you want one of your heart pills?"

"No, I'll be all right," I said.

"Do you mind if I . . . ?" He let the question trail off.

"Of course not. Help yourself."

At ten to seven, forty minutes before we were expected in the drawing room for cocktails, we crept downstairs, both of us in our robes, glancing nervously at each other and hiding behind corners until we ascertained that nobody was around. I felt like a child sneaking down to eavesdrop on a party for grown-ups.

I telephoned Mrs. Pew and sheepishly asked if she would please keep an eye out for my hair comb. After a slight pause, she said curtly that yes, she would. *As she had told me last night.*

When I hung up, I turned wordlessly to Ellis, who pulled me into his arms.

"Hush, my darling," he said, pressing my head to his chest. "This too shall pass."

At seven thirty, we met at the top of the stairs. I had bathed and repaired my hair as best I could in the available time. I had also put on a touch of lipstick and rouge, since my face was so devoid of color as to be nearly transparent, and dabbed some eau de toilette behind my ears. Ellis had nicked himself shaving, and there were comb marks in his wet hair.

"Ready?" he said.

"Absolutely not. You?"

"Courage, my dear," he said, offering his arm. I curled my icy fingers in the crook of his elbow.

As Ellis and I entered the drawing room, my father-in-law, Colonel Whitney Hyde, raised his face and aimed it at the grandfather clock. He was leaning against the mantel, right next to a delicate cage hanging from an elaborate floor stand. The canary within was the color of orange sorbet, a plump, smooth ovoid with a short fan of a tail, chocolate spots for eyes, and a sweet beak. He was almost too perfect to be real, and not once had he sung during my four-year tenure in this house, even as his quarters were reduced to help him concentrate.

My mother-in-law, Edith Stone Hyde, sat perched on the edge of a silk jacquard chair the color of a robin's egg, Louis XIV style. Her gray eyes latched onto us the moment we entered the room.

Ellis crossed the carpet briskly and kissed her cheek. "Happy New Year, Mother," he said. "I hope you're feeling better."

"Yes, Happy New Year," I added, stepping forward.

She turned her gaze on me and I stopped in my tracks. Her jaw was set, her eyes unblinking. Over by the mantel, the ends of the Colonel's mustache twitched. The canary fluttered from its perch to the side of the cage and clung there, its fleshless toes and translucent claws wrapped around the bars.

Tick, tock went the clock. I thought my knees might go out from under me.

"Better ... Hmmm ... Am I feeling better ..." She spoke slowly, clearly, mulling the words. Her brow furrowed ever so slightly. She drummed her fingers on the arm of the chair, starting with her smallest finger and going up, twice, and then reversing the order. The rhythm was that of a horse cantering. The pause felt interminable.

She looked suddenly up at Ellis. "Are you referring to my migraine?"

"Of course," Ellis said emphatically. "We know how you suffer."

"Do you? How kind of you. Both of you."

Tick, tock.

Ellis straightened his spine and his tie and went to the sideboard to pour drinks. Whiskeys for the men, sherries for the ladies. He delivered his mother's, then his father's, and then brought ours over.

"Tell me, how was the party?" his mother said, gazing at the delicate crystal glass she held in her lap. Her voice was completely without inflection.

"It was quite an event," Ellis said, too loudly, too enthusiastically. "The Pews certainly do things right. An orchestra, endless champagne, never-ending trays of delicious tidbits. You'd never know there was a war going on. She asked after you, by the way. Was very sorry to hear you weren't feeling well. And the funniest thing happened at the stroke of midnight—did you hear? People will be talking about it for years."

The Colonel harrumphed and tossed back his whiskey. The canary jumped from one side of its cage to the other.

"I've heard rather a lot," my mother-in-law said coldly, still staring into her glass. Her eyes shifted deliberately to me.

The blood rose to my cheeks.

"So, there we all were," Ellis continued bravely, "counting down to midnight, when all of a sudden there was a positively *huge* explosion. Well, even though we're a continent away from the action, you can imagine what we thought! We nearly—"

"*Silence!*" roared the Colonel, spinning to face us. His cheeks and bulbous nose had gone purple. His jowls trembled with rage.

I recoiled and clutched Ellis's arm. Even my mother-in-law jumped, although she regained her composure almost immediately.

In our set, battles were won by sliding a dagger coolly in the back, or by the quiet turn of a screw. People crumpled under the weight of an indrawn sigh or a carefully chosen phrase. Yelling was simply not done.

The Colonel slammed his empty glass down on the mantel. "Do you think we're fools? Do you think we haven't heard all about the *real* highlight of the party? What people will *really* be talking about for years? About your *disgraceful*, your *depraved* . . . your . . . *contemptible* behavior?"

What happened next was a blur of insults and rage. Apparently we had done more than just get drunk and make fools of ourselves, and apparently Ellis's moment of temper had not been his worst misdeed. Apparently, he had also crowed loudly about our decision to go monster hunting and "show the old man up," stridently proclaiming his intentions even as Hank was using a foot to shove him into the back of the car.

The Colonel and Ellis closed in on each other across the enormous silk carpet, pointing fingers and trying to outshout each other. The Colonel accused us of going out of our way to try to embarrass him, as well as being loathsome degenerates and generally useless members of society, and Ellis argued that there was nothing he *could* do, and for that matter the Colonel did nothing either. What exactly did his father expect him to do? Take up a trade?

My mother-in-law sat silently, serenely, with a queerly calm look on her face. Her knees and ankles were pressed together in ladylike fashion, tilted slightly to the side. She held her unsipped sherry by the stem, her eyes widening with delight at particularly good tilts. Then, without warning, she snapped.

The Colonel had just accused Ellis of conveniently coming down with color blindness the moment his country needed him, the cowardice of which had caused him—his *father* and a *veteran*—the greatest personal shame of his life, when Edith Stone Hyde swiveled to face her husband, bug-eyed with fury.

"How *dare* you speak of my son like that!"

To my knowledge, she had never raised her voice before in her life, and it was shocking. She continued in a strained but shrill tone that quavered with righteous indignation—Ellis could no more help being color-blind than other unfortunates could help having clubfeet, *didn't he realize*, and the color blindness, *by the way*, hadn't come from *her* side of the family. And speaking of genetics, she blamed *her* (and here she actually flung out an arm and pointed at me) for Ellis's downfall. An unbalanced harlot *just like her mother*.

"Now see here! That's my wife you're talking about!" Ellis shouted.

"She was no harlot!" the Colonel boomed.

For two, maybe three seconds, there wasn't a sound in the room but the ticking of the clock and the flapping of the canary, which had been driven to outright panic. It was a haze of pale orange, banging against the sides of its cage and sending out bursts of tiny, downy feathers.

Ellis and I looked at each other, aghast.

"Oh, really?" my mother-in-law said calmly. "Then what, exactly, was she, dear?"

The Colonel moved his mouth as though to answer, but nothing came out.

"It's all right. I always suspected. I saw the way you used to look at her," my mother-in-law continued. Her eyes burned brightly with the indignity of it all. "At least you weren't foolish enough to run off with her."

I was almost compelled to defend the Colonel, to point out that *everybody* had looked at my mother that way—they couldn't help themselves—but knew better than to open my mouth.

My mother-in-law turned suddenly to Ellis.

"And *you*—I warned you. As embarrassing as it was, I probably could have tolerated it if you'd just wanted to carouse, to sow some wild oats, but no, despite all the other very suitable matches you could have made, you snuck off to marry"—she paused, pursing her lips and shaking her head quickly as she decided what to call me—"*this*. And I was right. The apple doesn't fall far from the tree. It's positively shameful the way the two of you and that beastly Boyd fellow carry on. I despair of the grandchildren. Although, frankly, I've nearly lost hope in that regard. Perhaps it's just as well." She sighed and went calm again, smoothing her forehead and staring into the distance to revel in her victory. She'd successfully dressed down every other person in the room and thought it was now over: game, set, match.

She was wrong. Had she looked, she'd have noticed that Ellis was turning a brilliant shade of crimson that rose from the base of his neck, spread beneath his blond hair, and went all the way to the tips of his ears.

"Let's talk about shame, shall we?" he said quietly, ferociously. "There's absolutely nothing that I—or Maddie, or anyone else—could do to bring further shame upon this family. You"—his voice rose in a crescendo until he was shouting again, pointing his glass at his father and shaking it, sloshing whiskey onto the carpet—"shamed all of us beyond redemption the moment you faked those pictures!"

The ensuing silence was horrifying. My mother-in-law's mouth opened into a surprised *O*. The small crystal glass she'd been holding slipped to the floor and shattered.

Tick, tock went the clock.

This is the story as I'd heard it:

In May 1933, an article appeared in a Scottish newspaper that made headlines around the world. A businessman (university-educated, the reporter was careful to point out) and his wife were motoring along the newly built A82 on the north side of Loch Ness when they spotted a whale-size animal thrashing in otherwise perfectly calm water. Letters to the editor followed describing similar incidents, and the journalist himself, who happened to be a water bailiff, claimed to have personally seen the "Kelpie" no fewer than sixteen times. Another couple reported that something "resembling a prehistoric monster" had slithered across the road in front of their vehicle with a sheep in its mouth. A rash of other sightings followed, sparking a worldwide craze.

The Colonel, who had been fascinated since boyhood by cryptozoology, and sea serpents in particular, came down with a full-blown case of "Nessie Mania." He followed the stories with increasing restlessness, clipping newspaper articles and making sketches based on the descriptions therein. He had retired from the military, and idleness did not suit him. He'd largely filled the void with big game hunting in Africa, but by then he found it unsatisfying. His trophy room was run of the mill. Who didn't have a zebra skin hanging on the wall, a mounted rhinoceros head, or an elephant foot umbrella stand? Even the posed, snarling lion was passé.

When the first published photograph of the monster, taken by a man named Hugh Gray, was denounced by skeptics as being the blurred image of a swimming dog, the Colonel was so incensed he announced he was going to Scotland to prove the monster's existence personally.

He prevailed upon the hospitality of his second cousin, the Laird of Craig Gairbh, whose estate was near the shores of the loch, and in a matter of weeks had taken multiple photographs that showed the curved neck and head of a sea serpent emerging from the water.

The pictures were published to widespread acclaim on both sides of the Atlantic, and the Colonel's triumphant return to the United States was marked with great fanfare. Reporters flocked to the house, stories ran in all the major newspapers, and he was generally regarded as a hero. He took to wearing estate tweeds around town, which made him instantly recognizable as the celebrity he was, and joked, in a faux British accent, that his only regret was not being able to mount the head in his trophy room, explaining that since Scotland Yard itself had requested he not harm the beast, it would have been in bad form to do so. The height of the frenzy was when he appeared in a newsreel that played before *It Happened One Night*, the biggest movie of the year.

Like Icarus, he flew too close to the sun. It wasn't long before the *Daily Mail* published an article suggesting that the size of the wake was wrong and making the scandalous accusation that the Colonel had photographed a floating model. Next came allegations of photographic trickery—so-called experts claimed the photographs had been touched up and then rephotographed, citing slightly different angles and shadows, variations in the reflections. Because the Colonel had processed his own film, he was unable to defend himself.

The Colonel swore by the veracity of his photos and expressed outrage that his honor was being called into question precisely because he'd been honorable enough to defer to the request from Scotland Yard. If he'd just gone ahead and shot the beast—and he'd brought his elephant rifle with him for that very purpose—no one would be able to deny his claims.

The final nail in the coffin of public opinion was when Marmaduke Wetherell, a big game hunter who had been on safari with the Colonel several times, arrived at the loch with a cadre of reporters declaring that he was going to prove once and for all that the monster existed, and then promptly falsified monster tracks using an ashtray made from the foot of a hippo—a hippo that the Colonel himself had taken down in Rhodesia.

Reporters and their impudent questions were no longer welcome. The Colonel gave up his tweeds and his accent. The sketches and newspaper clippings, so carefully glued into Moroccan leather scrapbooks, disappeared. By the time I came into Ellis's life, the subject was taboo, and preserving the Colonel's dignity paramount.

Of course, what was taboo to the rest of the world was anything but to our little trio, especially when the Colonel was acting particularly accusatory about Ellis's inability to serve.

It was Hank who came up with the idea of us finding the monster ourselves. It was a brilliant mechanism for blowing off steam that allowed Ellis to poke merciless fun at the Colonel, imagine himself triumphing where his father had failed, while simultaneously proving that he was as red-blooded as any man at the Front. It was a harmless fantasy, a whimsy we trotted out and embellished regularly, usually at the end of a long night of drinking, but never within anyone else's earshot—at least, not before the New Year's Eve party.

Ellis swallowed loudly beside me. My mother-in-law remained frozen to her seat, her fingers and mouth still open, the crystal sherry glass in shards at her feet.

The Colonel's face was tinged with blue, like the skin of a ripe plum, and for a moment I thought he might be having a stroke. He lifted a quivering finger and pointed at the door.

"Get out," he said in a strange, hollow voice. "Pemberton will send your things."

Ellis shook his head in confusion. "What do you mean? To where?"

The Colonel turned his back to us, resting one elbow on the mantel, posing.

"To where?" Ellis asked with increasing desperation. "Where are we supposed to go?"

The Colonel's stiff back and complete lack of response made it clear that wherever we went, it was of no concern to him.

Chapter Four

Ellis directed the chauffeur to the Society Hill Hotel on Chestnut Street. On the surface it looked fine: the façade and public areas were up to par, but our suite was faded and shabby and had only one bedroom. However, it was what we could afford on Ellis's reduced allowance.

Ellis bought a bottle of whiskey from the lobby bar while the clerk was checking us in and began downing it as soon as we got upstairs.

I understood his desperation. If the Colonel cut his allowance completely, we'd be destitute. Regrettably, it was a very real possibility.

Ellis's crime against his father was twofold, and the parts were equally grievous. He had been caught railing against the Colonel behind his back, and then had accused him of fraud to his face. I didn't think the Colonel was capable of forgiving either separately, but together they were exponentially worse.

As we waited for our things to arrive, Ellis paced and drank, analyzing and reanalyzing what had just happened and generally working himself into a lather. At one point, when he allowed as to how he wouldn't have lost his temper if he hadn't been driven to defend me, I thought he was unfairly trying to shift the blame to me and said so, pointing out that I hadn't uttered a word throughout the entire fiasco.

He stopped and looked at me, both pained and surprised.

"My God," he said. "That's not what I meant at all. Of course it's not your fault. You did absolutely nothing. Her attack on you was completely gratuitous."

"It's all right," I said. "She didn't say anything everyone else wasn't already thinking."

"It's not all right, and I will never forgive her. Neither should you."

I hoped he would change his mind, because his mother was currently our only hope of returning to grace. Although she demonstrated her affection in strange ways, her whole world revolved around Ellis and, to a lesser degree, in torturing me. Without us, her life would be a void. I was entirely sure that she was already attempting to intercede, but I'd never seen the Colonel in such a state and I wasn't sanguine about her chances.

Appealing to my own father was pointless. When I wrote to tell him that Ellis and I had eloped, I'd expected him to be upset and wasn't surprised when he didn't respond right away. It was months before it dawned on me that he wasn't going to. I'd seen him only once since, although we lived less than two miles apart. He was crossing the street, and when he saw me, he pretended he hadn't and turned the other way. From overheard fragments of conversation, I gathered his activities revolved almost exclusively around the Corinthian Yacht Club, allowing him to avoid contact with the fairer sex altogether.

At some point after midnight, I managed to convince Ellis that our things weren't on their way and we should just go to bed. Neither of us had so much as an overnight bag.

While the room was stuffy, it was also drafty. Ellis called me a "blanket hog," accusing me of repeatedly rolling away with the covers, at which point he'd grab them back and leave me exposed. After a few rounds of tug-of-war, which started out in good fun but deteriorated quickly, we ended up facing opposite directions on the edges of the bed with neither one of us adequately covered.

I lay awake worrying. When Ellis finally fell asleep, he snored so loudly I had to hold a pillow over my head, pressing it against my ears. There was an odd smell, sort of earthy and minerally. For the rest of the night, all I could think about was how many heads had lain on those pillows before my own.

We were roused by an understated yet insistent rapping at the door.

"Dear God," croaked Ellis. "What time is it?"

I peered at the radium-painted clock beside me. "Nearly seven."

"The sun's not even up," he complained.

After a few more minutes of intermittent knocking, I mumbled, "You'd better get it. They're not going away."

He sighed irritably, then shouted, *"Coming!"*

He switched on the lamp and rolled out of bed, yanking the chenille bedspread off as though he were doing the tablecloth trick. He wrapped it around his shoulders and stomped away, slamming the bedroom door behind him.

I had a fair indication of what was going on because of the shuffles, bangs, and clunks. It went on for nearly ten minutes.

When Ellis returned, he wadded up the bedspread and tossed it onto my legs. As he flopped back into bed, I tried to straighten it.

"Our things, I presume?" I asked.

"Our every worldly belonging, from the looks of it. Six carts' worth. We're going to have to turn sideways to get to the door."

I tried not to panic—the Colonel would have given the order before he retired for the night, when his anger was still fresh—but a queasy feeling settled in the pit of my stomach anyway.

"I don't suppose you have any idea where your pills might have ended up?" Ellis asked.

"Would you like me to have a look?"

"Never mind," he said miserably. "It's all right."

The lamp was still on, so I went to the front room.

The floor was almost entirely covered by trunks and suit-cases. Emily, Pemberton, and the others must have been up all night packing.

I found my cosmetics case on a low table, along with my hatboxes. To my relief, it was organized immaculately, the pill bottle tucked discreetly under its tray. Poor Emily—we'd cost her at least two nights' sleep, which my mother-in-law would certainly not consider an excuse if her daytime duties suffered.

I handed the bottle to Ellis and sat beside him. He propped himself up on an elbow, shook two pills into his hand, and swallowed them dry. Then he fell back onto his pillow.

"Thank you, darling. I'm a little on edge," he said.

"I know. Me too."

"Let's try to get back to sleep. In the morning—in the *real* morning—I'm going to have the largest goddamned lobster in the city brought up to us, along with a mountain of potato salad. Caviar, too. They can skip the plates and just bring forks."

I made my way back to my side of the bed. When I crawled under the covers, Ellis switched off the lamp. We found our-selves much closer together than we had been before. He rolled onto his side and threw an arm across my waist.

"Well, what do you know," he said. "Maybe there are enough blankets after all."

.   .   .

In the early evening, the concierge called to tell us that Hank was waiting for us in the lobby bar.

Ellis and I were no longer speaking, a result of my suggestion that he talk to his mother and try to pave the way for a truce. We rode the elevator in silence.

The boys drank bourbon sidecars, and I ordered a gin fizz. A few drinks in, as Ellis and I took turns recounting the disastrous repercussions of the party, the freeze began to thaw. Soon, we were finishing each other's sentences and apologizing with our eyes. We were in the same mess, facing the same consequences. Although I was willing to capitulate sooner, it was just a tactical difference. We were upset with our situation, not each other.

I reached my foot out under the table and ran it lightly down his calf. His eyes brightened, and the edges of his mouth lifted into a smile.

"I'm still trying to wrap my head around the idea of your mother shouting," said Hank. "Are you sure it was your mother? The same Edith Stone Hyde I've known all these years?"

"The very one. And it was more like a hooting," said Ellis. "An overtaxed owl."

"A broken-down woodwind," I added. "Frail, yet screechy."

"I'd have paid good money to see that," said Hank, lighting a cigarette.

"I wish I'd known," said Ellis. "I'd have offered you my seat."

"Do you really think the Colonel and your mother had an affair?" Hank asked, blowing a series of smoke rings.

"Of course not," I said. "My gorgon of a mother-in-law extrapolated that because at some point she caught him looking at her, which I'm sure he did. Everybody did."

"Yes, but he also defended her," Hank pointed out. "To his wife."

"So maybe he carried a little torch for her," I said, "which still means nothing, because who didn't? She had that effect on people."

"Not your father," Hank continued. "I never did understand why she married him. She could have had anybody she liked. Gorgeous, pedigreed, a bank account the size of Montana . . . I can't imagine why she allowed herself to get hitched to an old fart like your father."

"She wasn't pedigreed," I said, throwing him a dirty look. Hank knew perfectly well that my mother had married up.

Hank looked outraged. "Of course she was pedigreed . . . *in the Levee District!*" He broke down, cackling at his own joke.

"Ha ha," I said flatly.

"No offense, darling girl. Money is its own pedigree. But back on topic, what if it's true? Maybe that's why your mother-in-law was so hell-bent against the two of you getting married. *Maybe*," he said, waving his cigarette in circles, "you're brother and sister."

Ellis and I burst into simultaneous groans of disgust.

"Hank, that's not even remotely funny! Please. My mother did *not* have an affair with the Colonel."

"How can you be so sure?" Hank went on. "Maybe that's the reason your mother-in-law encouraged him to go monster hunting. To get him out of harm's way, so to speak."

"I'm sure she just wanted him out of the way, period," I said. "She probably packed his bags. She probably booked his passage."

"You're both forgetting that it was his idea," said Ellis. "He couldn't get out of there fast enough. I'm surprised he didn't leave a Colonel-shaped hole in the front door on the way out. Can hardly blame him, though."

"She *is* a trial," I said.

"She's worse than that," said Ellis, looking suddenly grim.

Hank leaned back in his chair and cocked an eyebrow. He

looked first at Ellis, and then at me. "Your drinks are empty. Let me remedy that." He snapped his fingers over his head until he got the attention of the bartender, then pointed at the glasses.

Ellis stared into his depleted drink, poking the ice cubes with his swizzle stick.

"So," Hank said, rubbing his hands together. "Given the circumstances, I think you'll be even more pleased to hear my news."

"Unless you're about to tell me my father dropped dead, I highly doubt it," Ellis said without looking up.

The waiter delivered fresh drinks. Ellis pulled his toward him, picked up the new swizzle stick, and went back to stabbing ice.

"Maddie, darling?" Hank said expectantly.

I sighed before dutifully asking, "What news?"

"I've found us passage."

"Passage to where?" I asked in the same disinterested voice.

I knew full well what he was talking about, and was trying to convey that I didn't want to play, and was quite sure that Ellis didn't either.

"You know," Hank said with a coy smile.

I went for the direct approach. "Hank, we're not in the mood right now. That's what got us into this pickle in the first place."

"Then get in the mood. We leave in three days."

I put my drink down and took stock of his demeanor. He was deadpan, yet clearly pleased with himself.

"You're not serious," I said.

"I'm in absolute earnest," he replied.

"But it's impossible. There are no liners running."

"Connections, Maddie, connections," he said with a flourish. "We're going on a Liberty ship. The SS *Mallory*, a freighter taking supplies. It's part of a convoy. And speaking of supplies, stock up on cigarettes and stockings, both nylon and silk. International currency, if you will."

His continued straight face began to worry me.

"Hank, this isn't funny."

"It's not meant to be."

"We can't cross the Atlantic during the war——"

"We'll be perfectly safe. We're going to the Highlands. That's where they sent the evacuated children from the cities, for God's sake."

I turned to Ellis. He'd abandoned the ice, and was now pushing the ashtray back and forth.

"Darling, say something," I pleaded.

"Don't we need papers, or something?" he asked.

"Arranged for them too," Hank said brightly. "And a sixteen-millimeter Cine-Kodak movie camera. After we get our footage of the monster, we'll send the reel directly to Eastman Kodak and have them develop it. Voilà—would-be naysayers won't have a nay to say. We'll make history. We'll be famous."

After a moment of silent stammering, I managed to ask, "And what does Violet think about this?"

Violet was nothing if not sensible. She didn't even approve when we pulled entirely harmless pranks, like hiding someone's yacht in the wrong slip, or turning the racquet club's pool water purple. She'd sent an apology after we had General Pew's sailboat moved around to the back of his house, even though she wasn't there when the crime was committed.

"No idea. She's off doing something or other," said Hank. "Rolling bandages or the like."

"You haven't told her," I said in disbelief.

"Not yet," said Hank, sipping his drink. "I figured one day of misery was preferable to three."

"She'll never agree to it."

"I don't expect her to."

"Hank, she's expecting you to *propose*. You can't just abandon her."

"I will propose, just as soon as we get back. Frankly, I'm getting a little worried that she's rubbing off on you. I was hoping it would work the other way around."

"Hank's right," said Ellis, still pushing the ashtray around. "You used to like adventures."

"I do like adventures, but sailing into the war is hardly an adventure!"

"Then think of it as a scientific excursion," Hank said calmly. "Honestly, Maddie. We'll be perfectly safe. You can't imagine I would even suggest it if I weren't completely sure of that, and Freddie certainly wouldn't have arranged it."

"Freddie?" I said with growing despair. "What's Freddie got to do with this?"

"He's the one who made the arrangements, of course."

While I was trying to wrap my head around Freddie's involvement in all this, Hank looked deep into my eyes.

"Maddie, darling girl. This is my last hurrah, my final bit of craziness before donning the ball and chain. And since my particular ball and chain seems intent on civilizing me, surely you wouldn't deny me this one final caper?"

"Why don't we come up with something that won't get us blown to pieces? And who's to say that I won't rub off on Violet after all? When the war ends, we'll force her to come with us. I'll buy a pair of hip waders and bag the monster myself— heck, I'll buy a pair for Violet and drag her kicking and screaming into the loch with me. Won't that be a sight?"

Hank leaned forward and pressed two fingers against my lips.

"Shhh," he said. "We have to do this. It's for Ellis."

Ellis looked suddenly up. The fire was back in his eyes. "Let's do it. Let's fucking do it. It fixes everything."

"What? What does it fix?" I asked.

"Everything," he repeated.

I could see there was no arguing with him—at least not there, and certainly not in front of Hank.

"I'll have one of those cigarettes," I said, bobbing my foot under the table and glaring at the rows of glittering bottles behind the bar.

In a flash, Hank had the case open and extended. I let him hold it there for a few seconds longer than was comfortable, then grabbed one.

Hank leaned forward, completely cool, and flicked his lighter, a sterling silver Dunhill with a clock on its side. I sucked a few times, enough to get the thing lit, then pushed my chair back and marched toward the bank of elevators, letting my heels clack noisily on the marble. I ditched the cigarette in the first available ashtray because I hated cigarettes, which both Hank and Ellis knew. Asking for one was a statement. Ellis was supposed to follow me back to our suite. Instead, he stayed in the lobby bar with Hank.

I paced the room, trying to persuade myself that this was a joke, that Hank was just pulling our legs, but every instinct told me otherwise. He'd worked out too many details, and if it was a prank, he wouldn't have let it go on after he saw Ellis's reaction—unless they were in on it together, but that seemed even less plausible. They hadn't had a moment alone to plan.

I just wanted everything to go back to normal, but the only way that could happen would be if we found a solution that let both the Colonel and Ellis emerge with their dignities intact. Collective amnesia would have been an option if the accusations had been limited to the drawing room, where the only witness was the canary, but they hadn't. The Colonel had been disgraced in public.

The part that frightened me most, that made me think

Hank really had made solid plans, was his mention of Freddie. If anyone could manage such arrangements, it was Freddie Stillman, whose father was an admiral, but it was beyond me why he'd lift a finger to help. The four of us had been close friends, a quartet instead of a trio, during one blissful summer in Bar Harbor, Maine, until I rejected his completely unexpected proposal, and probably not as sensitively as I should have. Ten days later, I eloped with Ellis, and we hadn't exchanged a word since. That was four and a half years ago.

I was surprised that Hank was still in touch with him, especially since it was rumored that Freddie had set his sights on Violet before Hank rolled through and swept her off her feet.

Ellis returned hours later, entirely smashed, and confirmed my fears. This was no prank, and he was absolutely determined that we were going to go.

I pointed out, as gently as I could, what I'd hoped was obvious: that it made no sense whatsoever to throw ourselves into the middle of an ocean crawling with U-boats on a quest to find a monster that probably didn't even exist, especially as a way of proving his worth to people who were too ignorant to realize he was as honorable as any of them. We knew the truth. *I* knew the truth. It would be difficult, but together we could withstand the scrutiny until the war ended.

Ellis turned on me with such ferocity I almost didn't recognize him.

Of course there was a monster, he said. Only an idiot would think there wasn't a monster. Never mind all the sightings and photographs, including his own father's—which, by the way, were still the best of the lot—Scotland Yard itself had confirmed the beast's existence when they asked the Colonel not to harm it.

Even as he continued shouting at me, waving his arms

around the tiny, luggage-filled room, even as I absorbed that he
had essentially called me an idiot, what really caught my attention was that he'd done a complete about-face regarding his
father's pictures.

I tried to process this as Ellis pointed at the wallpaper, which
was curling at the corners, at the water stains on the ceiling, as
he wiped his finger along the windowsill and then held it up so
I could inspect the grime. I wondered if he'd believed his father
all along and, if so, why he'd made such a terrible accusation
the night before—never mind the things he'd said as we left
the party.

I hadn't uttered a word since my initial plea, but he continued his tirade as though I were arguing with him.

Did I really want to live in this dump, sitting around like
hostages, waiting to see if the Colonel was going to cut off his
allowance completely? And what if he did? What then? Did I
think it was all right to act like Scott Lyons, running tabs up to
the hilt and then skipping out, moving from hotel to hotel?
Because he certainly didn't.

We were going to Scotland, it was our only option, and we
would not set foot on this continent again until he had found
the monster the Colonel had faked.

He stopped, red and sweaty, huffing and puffing and waiting for me to challenge him, but my brain was stuck on the fact
that he'd flip-flopped on the subject of his father yet again, and
all in a matter of seconds.

I had witnessed firsthand how badly society treated Ellis—
particularly his own father—and was well aware of the toll it
was taking. For four years, I'd stood by helplessly as the happy,
confident young man I'd met in Bar Harbor eroded into the
bitter, suspicious man currently raging in front of me, a man
who constantly believed people were giving him dirty looks
and whispering behind his back, a man who was increasingly
irritated by my Pollyannaish platitudes because he recognized

them for what they were. But because I'd watched this devolution happen in dribbles and bits, I hadn't realized until that moment that he'd already been pushed beyond his limits. What was currently at stake was his entire self-worth.

Hank was right. Ellis needed this.

I crossed the half dozen feet that divided us and put my arms around him, pressing my face to his chest. After a moment of shocked hesitation, he put his arms around me, too, and a few seconds after that, I felt him relax.

"I'm so sorry, my darling, I don't know what came over me," he said.

"It's okay," I said.

"I should never have spoken to you like that. It's inexcusable. You did absolutely nothing wrong."

"I understand, darling. It's okay."

"Oh God, Maddie," he said, breathing into my ear. "Hank's right. They broke the mold when they made you. I can't imagine what I did to deserve you."

For a moment, as absurd as it was, I thought he might want to make love, but from his chest movements, I could tell he was starting to cry. I held him even tighter.

If finding the monster was what it was going to take to make Ellis feel whole again, then so be it. I just hoped there was a monster to be found.

And so, three days later, we sailed into the Battle of the Atlantic.

Chapter Five

I saw my first rat before we set sail.

Although our cabins were in the officers' quarters, there were only two and they were tiny, so Ellis and I had to share a very small bed—a bunk, really—which would have made sleeping impossible even if the engine that powered the rudder wasn't immediately beneath us. There was a small washbasin in the cabin, but the bath facilities were shared. I was the only woman on board, so I had to wash myself at the sink. I was also so sick I couldn't keep so much as a cracker down.

When I wasn't hanging my face over the sink trying not to throw up, I was lying on the bunk with my arms wrapped around my stomach, doing my best to stare into the distance, which in this case meant trying to focus on some point beyond the cabin wall, which was altogether too close.

The day before we were supposed to land at the naval base in Scotland, German U-boats caught up with one of the other ships in the convoy and torpedoed her. We circled back to pull men out of the water, which was so slick with fuel it was actually on fire. The Germans were still there, of course, and we could feel the depth charges, which pitched us about until I feared capsizing and splitting up in equal parts. Unsecured items flew across the room. The electricity flickered on and off, and the cabin was so full of smoke I couldn't breathe without choking. The handkerchiefs I held over my nose and mouth came away the color of lead. Ellis took pills by the handful— he'd refilled my prescription before we left, getting a great many more than usual since he didn't know how long we were going to be away, and the quantities he consumed alarmed me.

When the torpedoes came, Hank shrank into a corner with a bottle of whiskey, saying that if he was going to die, he might as well die drunk. I shrieked each time a deck gun fired. Ellis put his life belt on and wanted me to do the same, but I couldn't. Having something bulky strapped around my middle impeded my breathing and increased my panic, and besides, what possible difference could it make? If the ship went down, the Germans wouldn't pluck us from the water, and even if they did, the poor men the SS *Mallory* had managed to save were grievously burned and likely to die anyway.

I flew into a tear-filled rage: I threw an alarm clock at Hank, who ducked it wordlessly and lit another cigarette. I pounded Ellis's chest and told him he had tossed us into the middle of a war because his father was a stubborn, stupid, irascible old man, and now, because of him, we were going to be killed. I said I hoped the Colonel dropped dead in his House of Testoni shoes, preferably upon hearing that we had all been blown up, because he was a fraudulent, egomaniacal blowhard without so much as a drop of compassion for anyone else on this earth, including—and especially—his own son. I declared Edith Stone Hyde a self-righteous, bitter old cow, and said I hoped she survived deep into a lonely old age so she could reap the rewards of her treatment of us and its fatal consequences. I told Ellis that the second we hit solid ground, I was turning around and taking the next boat out of there, although even as

I said it, I knew I would never willingly get on another ship. I told him that *he* was the idiot, and that his—and his father's—stupid obsession with a stupid monster was going to be the end of us all, and if he could come up with a stupider reason to die, I'd really like to know what that was.

Ellis's nonreaction was almost more frightening than the torpedoes, because I realized that he, too, thought we were going to die. And then I felt guilty and cried in his arms.

When we finally reached land, it was dusk. For the last couple of days, I'd been worried we might be changing ships rather than docking, because everyone kept referring to our destination as the HMS *Helicon*, but apparently that was a code name for the Aultbea Naval Base.

I was so desperate to get off the ship that I staggered on deck while the wounded were still being unloaded. Ellis followed me, but at the sight of the burned men, turned and went back below.

Some of the men no longer looked human—scorched and misshapen, their flesh melted like candle wax. Their agonized moans were terrible to hear, but even more horrifying were the silent ones.

One looked me in the eyes as he was carried past, his head bobbing slightly in time with the steps of the men bearing the stretcher. His face and neck were blackened, his mouth open and lipless, exposing crowded teeth that made me think of a parrot fish. I hated myself immediately for the comparison. His eyes were hazel, and his arms ended in white bandages just below the elbows. His peeling scalp was a mottled combination of purple and black, his ears so charred I knew there was no hope of saving them.

He held my gaze until I turned in shame, leaning my forehead against the salty white paint of the exterior wall. I pressed my eyes shut. If I'd had the strength to go back down to the cabin I would have, but I didn't. Instead, I kept my eyes closed and held my hands over my ears. Although I managed to block out most sounds, I could do nothing about the vibration of footsteps on the deck. I was excruciatingly aware of each ruined life being carried past. God only knew how these men's lives would be changed, if they even survived. I tried not to think of their mothers, wives, and sweethearts.

When we were finally allowed to disembark, I stumbled down the gangplank and onto the dock. My knees gave out, and if Hank hadn't been there to catch me, I'd have gone off the edge. Everything in my vision was jerking back and forth. I couldn't even tell which way was up.

"Jesus Christ, Maddie," he said. "You almost fell in the soup. Are you all right?"

"I don't know," I said. My voice was hoarse. "I feel like I'm still on the ship."

Ellis took my other elbow, and together they led me off the dock. I stretched out an arm and leaned against a white-painted lamppost. The curb at my feet was also white.

"Maddie? Are you okay?" said Ellis.

Before I could answer, a man in a wool greatcoat and hat approached us. He was tall and broad-shouldered, with red cheeks, black leather gloves, and an eye patch. His one eye alternated between Ellis and Hank. "Henry Boyd?"

"That's me," said Hank, lighting a cigarette.

"Well, I knew it was one of you," the man said in a melodious accent, leaving us to interpret the wherefores. "I'll be driving you, then. Where are your things?"

"Still on board. The porters are back there somewhere," said Hank, waving vaguely toward the ship.

The man laughed. "I'm your driver, not your lackey."

Hank raised his eyebrows in surprise, but the man put his hands in his pockets, spun on his heels, and began to whistle.

His earlobe and part of the cartilage was missing on the same side as the eye patch. A thick scar ran up his neck and disappeared beneath his ginger hair.

Ellis whispered, "I think you're supposed to tip him."

"Freddie said it was all taken care of," Hank said.

"Apparently it's not," Ellis murmured.

"Well, somebody do *something*!" I cried.

Hank cleared his throat to get the man's attention. "I don't suppose I could make it worth your while . . ."

"Oh, aye," said the man, in a firm but cheery voice. "I wouldn't say no to a wee minding."

When our trunks and suitcases had finally been identified, collected, and loaded—a feat of engineering that resulted in an ungainly mountain of luggage strapped to the roof and trunk of the car—our driver raised his one visible eyebrow and glanced at Ellis's waist. "I don't think you'll be needing that anymore," he said.

Ellis looked down. He was still wearing his life belt. He turned away, fumbling as he unfastened it, and let it drop at the base of a lamppost. I felt his shame acutely.

The driver opened the rear door of the car and motioned for me to get in. A soiled blanket covered the seat.

"Slide on over then," he said. He winked at me. I think.

Ellis got in after me. Hank took one look at the blanket before walking to the front of the car. He stood by the passenger door, waiting for the driver to open it.

"Well, are you going to get in, or aren't you?" said the driver, jerking his chin toward the rear.

Finally, reluctantly, Hank came around back. Ellis frowned and shifted to the middle seat. Hank got in beside him.

"Right, then," said the driver. He shut our door, climbed into the driver's seat, and resumed whistling.

Chapter Six

After four hours and twenty minutes of utter, stomach-roiling misery, with the driver leaning maliciously into hairpin curves despite (or perhaps because of) having to stop no fewer than six times so I could lean out of the back of the car and be sick, he came to a stop and announced we'd reached our destination.

"Here we are then," he said cheerfully, shutting off the engine. "Home, sweet home."

I glanced outside. It wasn't clear to me we'd arrived anywhere.

My stomach began churning again, and I couldn't wait for the driver to come around and let me out, although he was obviously in no rush to do anything. I fumbled with the handle, yanking it back and forth before finally realizing it twisted. When I flung the door outward, I went with it, landing on my knees in the gravel.

"Maddie!" Ellis cried.

"I'm all right," I said, still grasping the door handle. I looked up, through the strands of hair that had fallen over my face. The clouds shifted to expose the moon, and in its light I saw our destination.

It was a squat, gray building in pebble-and-dash, with heavy black shutters on the windows of both floors. A wooden sign hung over the entrance, creaking in the wind:

THE FRASER ARMS
Proprietor A. W. Ross
Licensed to Serve Beer and Spirits
Good Food, Rooms
Est. 1547

My queasiness rose in urgent waves, and while I couldn't believe there was anything left for me to expel, I hauled myself upright and staggered toward a half barrel of frostbitten pansies by the front door. I crashed into the wall instead, hitting first with my open palms and then my left cheek. I stayed there for a moment, my face flattened against the pebbled surface.

"Maddie? Are you all right?" Ellis asked from somewhere behind me.

"I'm fine," I said.

"You don't look fine."

I turned and slid down the wall, my coat and hair scraping against the embedded stones until I was resting on my heels.

Snow collected on my exposed knees. Somewhere in the distance a sheep bleated.

"Maddie?"

"I'm fine," I said again.

I watched as Ellis and Hank climbed out of the car, regarding them with something akin to loathing.

Ellis took a few steps toward the building and read the sign. He raised his eyebrows and looked back at Hank.

"*This* is where we're staying?"

"So it would appear," said Hank.

"It looks like a pile of rubble," said Ellis. "Or one of those long communal mud houses. From, you know, Arizona or wherever."

"What were you expecting, the Waldorf-Astoria?" Hank asked. "You knew we were going to be roughing it. Think of it as a field camp."

Ellis harrumphed. "That would be putting it kindly."

"Where's your sense of adventure?"

"Somewhere in the ship's latrine, I suspect," said Ellis. "I suppose Freddie chose this dump."

"Of course."

"He might as well have sent us to a cave."

Ellis stepped forward and rapped on the door. He waited maybe half a minute, then rapped again. Almost immediately after, he began thumping it with his fist.

The door swung open, and Ellis leapt to the side as a huge man in striped blue pajama bottoms and an undershirt burst forth. He was tall, broad, and densely muscled. His black hair stuck up in tufts, his beard was wild, and he was barefoot. He came to a stop, ran his eyes over Ellis and Hank, then peered around them to get a look at the car.

"And what are you wanting, at this time of night?" he demanded.

"We need rooms," Hank said around the edges of an unlit cigarette. He flicked the top of his lighter open, but before he could get it lit, the man's hand shot forward and snapped it shut.

"You canna smoke outside!" he said incredulously.

After a shocked pause—the man had reached within inches of his face—Hank said, "Why not?"

"The Blackout. Are you daft?"

Hank slipped both the lighter and cigarette into his pocket.

"Americans, are you?" the man continued.

"That we are," said Hank.

"Where's your commanding officer?"

"We're not being billeted. We're private citizens," said Hank.

"In that case, you can take yourselves elsewhere." The man turned his head to the left and spat. Had he turned to the right, he would have seen me.

"I believe it's all been arranged," Hank said. "Does the name Frederick Stillman ring a bell?"

"Not so much as a tinkle. Get on with you, then. Leave me in peace." He turned away, clearly planning to leave us on the side of the road.

I choked back a sob. If I didn't end up in a bed after everything we'd been through, I didn't think I wanted to survive at all.

"Wait," said Hank quickly. "You have no rooms?"

"I didn't say that," the man said. "Do you know what bloody time it is?"

Hank and Ellis exchanged glances.

"Of course," said Ellis. "We're sorry about that. Perhaps we could make it worth your while."

The man grunted. "Spoken like a toff. I've no truck with the likes o' you. Off you go." He shooed them away with the back of his hand.

From just past the car, the driver snorted.

"Please," Ellis said quickly. "The journey was rough, and my wife—she's unwell."

The man stopped. "Your *what?*" he said slowly.

Ellis inclined his head in my direction.

The man turned and saw me crouched against the wall. He studied me for a moment, then looked back at Ellis.

"You've dragged a woman across the Atlantic during a war, then? Are you completely off your head?"

Ellis's expression went dark, but he said nothing.

The man's eyes flitted briefly skyward. He shook his head.

"Fine. You can stay the night, but it's only on account of your wife. And hurry up getting that kit inside or I'll have the warden around for the Blackout. *Again.* And if I do, I'll not be the one paying the fine, mark my words."

"Sure, sure. Of course," said Hank. "Say, can you do me a favor and send out the porter?"

The man responded with a single bark of laughter and went inside.

"Huh," said Hank. "I guess there's no porter."

"And this surprises you because . . . ?" said Ellis.

Hank looked back at the car, whose suspension was significantly lowered by the weight of our belongings.

Ellis came to me and held out his hands. As he pulled me to my feet, he said, "Go inside, find a seat, and make that brute bring you something to drink. We'll be in as soon as we've got this mess sorted out."

I let myself in. The heavy wooden door groaned in both directions, and when it clicked shut, I glanced around self-consciously.

There was no sign of the bearded man, although he'd left a kerosene lamp on a long wooden bar to my left. Glossy beer spigots ran down its length: McEwan's, Younger's, Mackeson, and Guinness, along with a few I couldn't make out. One had a cardboard sign hanging around it declaring it temporarily unavailable.

The lamplight flickered off the bottles on the shelves behind the bar, reflected and amplified by the mirror behind them. It looked for all the world like there was an identical, inverted room just beyond, and for a moment I wondered if I was in the wrong one.

There were a number of tables and chairs in front of the bar, and a wireless in a chest-high console against the far wall. The ceiling was low and supported by thick, dark beams, and the floor consisted of huge slabs of stone. The walls were plastered, and even by the dim light of the lamp's flame, I could make out the faint raised edges of the trowel tracks. Thick black material covered the windows, and it dawned on me that the white-painted lampposts and curbs I'd seen in Aultbea were to help cars navigate at night during the Blackout.

To the right was a large stone fireplace with an assortment of stuffed and mismatched furniture arranged in front of it. Victorian, from the looks of it—a couch and two wing chairs positioned across from each other on a threadbare Oriental carpet, separated by a low, heavy table. The contents of the grate were covered by an even layer of ash, but still cast a faint orange glow.

I made my way to the couch and perched on the very edge of it, holding my numb fingers toward the embers. They smelled like smoked dirt, and the logs stacked off to the side were not wood. I had no idea what they were. They were rectangular and striated, and looked like gigantic Cadbury Flake bars, the much-coveted treat sent by the British grandmother of one of my classmates.

A dog with scruffy gray fur rose from nowhere, materializing directly beside me. I stiffened. It was enormously tall, and thin as a greyhound, with the same rounded back and scooped abdomen. It stared at me, its dark eyes mournful, its tail curled between its legs.

"Don't worry. He'll do you no harm."

The bearded man had come through a doorway behind the bar. He picked up the lamp, crossed the room, and set a glass of something fizzy on the table in front of me.

The low ceiling accentuated his height, but he would have been imposing in any circumstances. His eyes were an unlikely and startling blue under eyebrows as unruly as his beard. He remained barefoot and robeless, and apparently unbothered by it.

"You've had a rough journey then?"

"Yes." I reached up instinctively to check my hair, although since I could see myself from the chest down, I had a fair idea of how I looked.

He nodded at the glass. "Ginger beer. To settle your stomach."

"Thank you," I said. "That's very kind."

I felt his eyes upon me. After a beat of silence, he said, "I suppose you've heard there's a war."

A familiar bristle ran up the back of my neck. I turned to see if Ellis was within earshot, but he and Hank were still outside, beyond the closed door, having a heated discussion with the driver.

"I have, yes."

"Your husband and his friend look able-bodied enough."

"My husband and his colleague are here to perform scientific research," I said.

The man threw his head back and laughed. "Of course. Monster hunters. Absolutely brilliant. And here I was thinking you were war tourists."

He set the lamp on the table and waved at a board of keys behind the bar. "You can take two and three, or four and five, or two and six for that matter. It makes no difference to me. And be quick about it. I'll not have you wasting my paraffin."

I was emboldened. I'd never met a man so rude.

"Surely you mean kerosene," I said.

"I think I know what I mean," he said, turning to leave.

"Wait," I said quickly. "Don't you want to know our names?"

"Not particularly. What I want is to be in bed." He slapped his thigh. "Conall, *thig a seo!*"

The dog went to his side, and they slipped into the shadows behind the bar.

I was still staring at the place they'd disappeared when Hank and Ellis lurched through the front door, carrying a trunk between them. They dropped it on the worn flagstones and looked around.

"Where's the light switch?" Ellis said, squinting as he searched the walls.

"I don't think there is one," I said.

I watched Ellis's eyes as he scanned the various lamps and sconces around the room. They were all topped by glass globes—oil lamps, every one.

"Are you kidding me? There's no electricity?"

"I don't think so," I said.

His eyes glommed onto the radio. "What about that?"

"Maybe it runs on batteries. I don't know," I said. "Isn't the driver going to help you with the luggage?"

"He took off," said Hank. "Left everything in the drive-way."

"You could have just tipped him again," Ellis said.

"I believe it was your turn," Hank said.

Ellis glared at him.

"What? It's only money," Hank said. "Anyway, it doesn't matter now. He's gone, and we need help. Where's that charming Scotsman?"

"I'm pretty sure he went back to bed," I said.

"But we need help. Did you see where he went?" said Hank, craning his neck. His eyes lit on the doorway behind the bar.

"Hank, please. Just leave him alone."

Chapter Seven

"Good Lord, Maddie—what did you pack? I told you to bring stockings, not gold bullion," said Hank, dragging one of my suitcases behind him and letting it bang against each step.

"Just some essentials," I said.

I was at the top of the stairwell, holding the lamp as Hank and Ellis brought up our luggage. I was freezing and queasy, and the lamp swung accordingly. I was terrified I'd trip and set the carpet on fire.

"Along with anchors and anvils, apparently," said Hank, dropping the suitcase and wiping his hands.

Ellis came up behind him with two hatboxes.

"That's everything," he said.

"Not really," said Hank. "We still have to get it into the rooms. I don't know why Maddie wouldn't just let me rouse Paul Bunyan."

"She doesn't like to discomfit the staff," said Ellis.

"Why ever not?" asked Hank, looking at me with surprise. "Isn't that what staff is for?"

"Well, I would say so, yes," said Ellis.

"It's still not too late to get him, you know," said Hank.

"Yes it is," I said crossly. "He said we could take any of rooms two through six, so can we please just do that and go to bed?"

"All right, darling girl," said Hank, glancing up the row of doors. "I was merely pointing out that it would be faster if we had help. No need to work up a lather."

I wobbled toward a hall table so I could ditch the lamp. I was as dizzy as the moment I'd gotten off the ship. If I hadn't known it was impossible, I'd have sworn the building itself was swaying.

"Why do you suppose room one is off limits?" said Hank.

I turned around to find him trying the locked door. "Hank, stop! For Heaven's sake. Somebody's probably asleep in there, and every other room is available."

He continued to jiggle the knob. "But what if this is the room I want? What if it's the only one with a decent bath——"

The door swung inward, tearing the knob from Hank's hand. He took a long step backward as a striking young woman with red hair burst into the hallway wielding a fire iron.

"And what the hell are you wanting?" she shouted in a thick accent. Her hair was tied into curls with scraps of cloth, and she was wearing a heavy white nightgown. She planted herself in front of Hank, grasping the poker with both hands.

"Henry Winston Boyd," Hank replied without missing a beat. He held out his hand. "The fourth. And you?"

She turned her head and bellowed down the hall. "Angus! *ANGUS!*"

Hank took a step backward, hands up in surrender. "No, wait. We're fellow guests. We've just arrived. See?" He gestured toward our luggage, which was scattered up and down the hallway.

She assessed it, ran her eyes over Ellis and me, and finally settled back on Hank. She stepped right up to him, brandishing the iron in his face.

"I'm no guest," she said, slanting her eyes accusingly. "I'm Meg, and I'm not on the clock until tomorrow evening. So I'll not be doing anything for you until then—and that goes for all of you." She returned to her room and slammed the door.

After a beat of silence, Hank said, "I think she likes me."

"Just pick a room," said Ellis.

"No, really. I think she does."

The rooms were cramped and depressing: each had a dresser with a mirror hanging above it, a narrow bed with two night-stands, and beyond that, a small sitting area with a lumpy chair, fireplace, and a single blacked-out window. The wallpaper was faded Victorian, the rugs threadbare.

Hank chose room two, while Ellis and I took five and six respectively. Although Hank didn't spell out why he'd chosen that particular room, it wasn't hard to figure out.

Despite everything we'd just been through, he was plotting a romantic conquest. I was already incensed on Violet's behalf—I was pretty sure Hank never *had* told her we were leaving—but at that moment I was close to outrage. Then it occurred to me that maybe Hank didn't think a dalliance with Meg would count as an infidelity. Perhaps he simply felt entitled, that he had the *droit du seigneur* over servants.

Various rumors followed Hank around, including one about a pregnant kitchen maid his mother had tried, unsuccessfully, to frame for stealing, and who disappeared shortly thereafter, presumably with a large sum of money. The highlight of the story had always been how Hank's mother had stashed an entire set of Georgian silver in the girl's room and then called the police. The actual cause of the situation was glossed over, dismissed with the vague explanation that "boys will be boys." In the narrative, the maid herself never quite seemed real to me, nor did the child. I wondered now if either ever crossed Hank's mind.

"I'm going to lie down," I said, leaving the men to deal with the luggage.

My room was the final one on the left. I lit the candle on the dresser and fell on the bed, shoes and all, waiting for them to bring in my things.

"The door at the end we thought was a closet?" said Hank, dragging in a trunk. "It's a bathroom. Thank God."

"Shared!" came Ellis's voice from the hallway.

"With running water!" Hank called back. He looked at me and winked. "Wait for it," he whispered, holding a finger to his lips. "Wait . . . Any second now . . ."

Out in the hallway, Ellis mumbled something inaudible.

Hank laughed uproariously. "He always gets the last word. Or so he thinks. Anyway, the bathroom. It's indoors, and it's right next to you, you lucky thing."

As much as I felt like collapsing, I had to at least get the soot off my face and scour my teeth. I revived myself enough to dig through my luggage and find what I needed—no easy task, since I'd undone all of Emily's good work in my panic to consolidate for the trip. We'd been warned that our storage space on the freighter was limited—an irony if I'd ever heard one, since the ship's raison d'être was storage. In the end, I'd found myself throwing things in randomly, frantically, sure that whatever I didn't bring would turn out to be vitally important.

As I left my room, I banged into the corner of the dresser so hard I cried out, and a horrible thought struck me. What if the waves never did stop? What if I was going to be like that forever?

When I returned from the bathroom, Ellis was at the far end of my room, poking the empty grate with a fire iron.

"Empty, of course, and the radiators are off. A class act all around. No electricity, one bathroom, no heat. I'm going to get some wood, or coal, or dung, or whatever it is they're burning downstairs."

"Please don't," I said. "The fellow who let us in seems sensitive about fuel."

"So what? I can see my breath." He presented his profile and exhaled, loosing a gossamer wisp of vapor.

"I'll be fine," I said. "There are lots of blankets. And I can always wear my robe to bed."

"Are you sure? I don't mind dealing with Blackbeard."

"Yes. I'm sure. Anyway, we'd probably burn the place down."

Ellis cracked a slow smile. "You mean like Hamlet House?"

During our honeymoon in Key West, an unattended cigar of Ellis's had nearly caused a catastrophe at an historic painted lady we'd nicknamed Hamlet House because the Prince of Denmark was a fellow guest. The prince, along with everyone else, was forced to change hotels, but since no one was hurt, the incident became funny in the retelling, a part of Ellis's and my shared repertoire, a story we trotted out at parties.

I knew that by bringing it up, he was trying to stir a fond memory and make things better between us, but what he didn't realize was that remembering the fire in Key West just made me think of the horribly burned men I'd seen carried off the ship only a few hours earlier.

"Yes, like Hamlet House," I said.

"We didn't burn it down. Merely scorched a few rooms," he said whimsically.

I climbed into bed and shuddered.

Ellis furrowed his brow, then set the poker in its stand and came to my side.

We'd made a fragile peace after finally outrunning the U-boats, a truce that consisted mostly of giving each other as much space as possible in a situation where there simply wasn't any, and talking only when absolutely necessary. But that didn't mean my breakdown on the ship hadn't happened, or that I wasn't aware of how horrifyingly quickly proximity had bred contempt, or that I wasn't still terrified and furious about being dragged along on this half-baked escapade. It was the stupidest and most dangerous thing we'd ever done.

It was also pointless. I'd realized it the moment the driver commented on the life belt that remained around Ellis's waist, and again when the bearded man asked why he and Hank weren't serving, and I knew that it would keep happening. The very thing we'd tried to escape had followed us across the Atlantic.

I opened my eyes and found Ellis staring down at me, his misery obvious. I knew he wanted comfort, a sign that things would go back to normal between us, but I couldn't give it to him. I just couldn't.

"Please, Ellis. I don't mean to be harsh, but I'm completely and absolutely desperate for sleep . . ."

His lips stretched into a sad line. "Of course. I know you're exhausted."

He leaned over to kiss my forehead, and in that instant my resentment shattered, leaving behind an awful, piercing regret.

No one had put a gun to my head and forced me to board the ship. I bore as much blame for my predicament as anyone else. He and Hank may have told me that nothing would happen to us, but I was the one who'd chosen to believe them.

"Ellis," I said, as he turned to go. "I'm sorry."

"About what?" he asked, stopping.

"The things I said."

He laughed quietly. "Which ones?"

"All of them. I was just so frightened."

He came back and sat on the edge of the bed. "No need to apologize. I just hadn't realized I was married to quite such a firecracker."

He laid a hand on my cheek, and my eyes welled up. I hoped I was wrong about how people over here would perceive him, but if I was not, I hoped I could somehow protect him from their judgment, make him unaware, or better yet, not care.

"I wasn't myself," I said.

"None of us was, my darling."

"Except Hank," I said, sniffling. "Hank was himself the entire time."

"Ah yes. Dear old Hank. Ever the pill," he said, getting up. "Speaking of which, do you think you need one?"

"No, I'm all right."

That was my cue to offer him one, and I would have, except that I had no idea where they were and didn't have the energy to look.

"Sleep tight, my darling. Tomorrow, Hank and I will find a decent hotel, and then all you'll have to worry about is regaining your strength."

He picked up the candle and went to the door. I rolled to face him.

"Ellis," I said as he stepped into the hallway, "this feeling of still being at sea—do you think it's normal?"

He paused before answering. "Perfectly," he said. "It will be gone in the morning. You'll see." He closed the door.

As I lay in bed, I could no more stop the waves than escape the images and sounds of the wounded being marched down the gangplank, one after the other, in a seemingly endless line.

Chapter Eight

I woke up to the sound of a bloodcurdling scream, and it was a few seconds before I realized it was coming from my own throat. My eyes sprang open, but it made no difference. None. The black was impenetrable, the pitching violent.

The engine wasn't running. Why wasn't the engine running?

Even if the whooshing in my head had been shrill enough to drown out the sound of the turbines, nothing would have been able to disguise the vibration. The thrum had been relentless—rattling brains, teeth, and eardrums, just like the propellers of a plane—and its absence was terrifying.

I'd been dreaming that the SS *Mallory* took a direct hit, but now I realized it wasn't a dream. The cabin rocked madly, almost as though the freighter was turning, rotating like a corkscrew as it slid below the surface.

"Ellis?" I cried out. *"Ellis?"*

I felt the blanket on either side of me, but he wasn't there, which meant he was lying injured somewhere on the floor, thrown on impact. I had to find him fast, because the cabin had tilted so drastically I wasn't sure how much longer I'd be able to find the door.

I slapped the surface and edges of the bunk, hoping to identify which direction I was facing, and hoping Hank was trying to find his way to us as well, because I didn't think I could drag Ellis out on my own.

When my hands hit a wooden headboard, I was momentarily confused. When I found a bedside table with a lace runner, I fell onto my back, gasping with relief.

I wasn't on the SS *Mallory*. I was in a bed in a hotel room in Drumnadrochit, and the motion was all in my head.

I reached over and felt my way across the bedside table, seeking the candle before remembering that Ellis had taken it with him the night before. I got to my feet, thinking that if I could just find the dresser, I could then find the door. I had taken only a couple of steps when my foot landed on something and twisted out from under me. I fell on my hands and knees.

The door opened, and a female figure was suddenly in the doorway with light pouring in around her.

"Mrs. Pennypacker? Is everything all right?" she asked.

I blinked at her, wondering why she'd just addressed me by my mother's name.

"My Lord!" She rushed over to help me up. "What's happened? Are you all right?"

"Yes, thank you," I said. "I seem to have tripped over a shoe, of all things."

Now that the light was no longer behind her, I could see that she was about my age, with a sturdy frame, pleasant expression, and thick auburn hair swept into a snood. She had a smattering of freckles, and her face was browned by the sun.

"Shall I get your husband?" she asked, looking at me with concern.

"No, thank you," I said. "I just need a minute to get oriented. When I woke up I wasn't quite sure where I was, and

then . . ." I waved a hand at the carpet, which was strewn with
the things I'd taken out while searching for my nightgown and
toothbrush. "Well, I was in a bit of a rush to get to bed last
night, and this morning I couldn't see where I was going."

"It's the Blackout curtains," she said, nodding decisively
and walking past to the window. "They're that dark you can't
see a thing, although I suppose that's the point."

She braced her fingertips on the inside edges of the window
casing and coaxed out a solid square frame covered with black
material. Light flooded the room.

"That's better, isn't it?" she said, setting the frame on the
floor.

Strips of tape crisscrossed the panes of glass. After a second's
confusion, I realized they were in case of a bomb blast.

"Yes, thank you," I said, trying to suppress my alarm. "Is
that a wooden frame? I've always thought Blackout curtains
were actual curtains."

"Aye. We use traditional curtains too, but then you have to
pin the cloth all the way around so no light can get past. This
contraption is much easier on the fingers. Angus made them
after the last time we got fined—twelve shillings it was, all
because Old Donnie had the temerity to push the curtain aside
for a wee moment to see if it was still raining. *And* the warden
is a Wee Free, *and* he's not from the glen, so there was no getting around that, I can tell you. Twelve shillings! That's more
than a day's wages for a shopkeeper!" she said indignantly,
catching my eye to make sure I understood.

I nodded emphatically.

"Now these," she continued, "you could put the sun itself
right behind them and not one ray would get through. Angus
stretched the material tight, and then painted the whole thing
with black epoxy rubber." She leaned over to tap its surface.
"That's like a drum, that is."

"Is Angus the one with the beard?"

"Aye."

"And he's the handyman?"

She laughed. "I should think not. He runs the place!"

A. W. Ross.

It made perfect sense but hadn't even occurred to me, an assumption based entirely on appearance. I caught sight of myself in the mirror and felt ridiculous for judging. I looked like I'd been dragged backward through a hedge.

The ceiling began spinning again, and I dropped onto the edge of the bed.

"You've gone pale as a potato crust," said the girl, coming closer to inspect me. "Shall I bring up some tea?"

"No, I'll be fine. I'm still a bit dizzy from the ship, strangely enough," I said.

"Aye," she said, nodding gravely. "I've heard of that. People getting stuck like that."

A jolt of fear ran through me, even as I arranged my face into a smile.

"Don't worry," I said. "My husband and I sail all the time. I probably just have a bit of a cold—you know, an ear thing. It will pass. Speaking of my husband, is he up yet?"

"He's been downstairs this half hour."

"Will you please let him know I'll be down in a few minutes? I need a moment to pull myself together."

She glanced at my luggage. "Well, with this lot that shouldn't be hard. I should think you could start your own shop, if you wanted to. If you change your mind about having your tea upstairs, just give me a shout."

"I'm sorry, what's your name again?" I asked, knowing perfectly well she hadn't yet told me.

"Anna. Anna McKenzie."

.   .   .

After Anna left, I remained on the bed, looking into the mirror from a distance of five or six feet. The face that stared back at me was haggard, almost unrecognizable. It was also jerking back and forth. I looked at the doorknob, a seam in the wallpaper, a shoe on the floor. Everything I tried to focus on did the same.

I was well aware of my tendency to become consumed by thoughts and knew I had to put what she'd said out of my mind. I'd been back on solid ground less than a day, which was nowhere near long enough to begin to panic. The seas had been so rough, and I'd been so ill, it made perfect sense that my vertigo would take time to resolve. At home, though, I'd probably have slipped off to see a specialist just to put my mind at ease.

If I told Ellis what was going on, he would have suggested I take a pill, and while they were probably designed for moments exactly like this, I had staunchly refused to let a single one cross my lips from the moment they'd been prescribed.

Because of my mother, people were always looking for cracks in my façade, waiting—even hoping—for me to return to type. My mother-in-law's shocking proclamation on New Year's Day was the first time anyone had been quite so explicit, at least to my face, but I knew what everyone thought of me, and I refused to prove them right. The ridiculous thing was that only I knew I didn't take the pills, so I wasn't really proving anything to anyone except myself. Ellis found them calming, so my prescription was filled often enough to satisfy Edith Stone Hyde, who rifled shamelessly through my things when I wasn't there.

The clock was ticking and Hank and Ellis were waiting downstairs, so I concentrated on the job at hand.

Ellis put great stock in my looks, teasing me that my only job in life was to be the prettiest girl in the room. I had always thought I was perfectly adept at doing my own hair and makeup, but apparently Ellis thought otherwise, and immediately after our marriage placed me in the hands of professionals.

I dug through my suitcases and trunks, collecting my "lotions and potions," as Ellis called them, and lined them up on the dresser. At home, he liked to open the jars and sniff the contents, asking the price and purpose of each (the more expensive, the better).

One time, I'd come into my room and found him at my dressing table with his face half made up. He let me finish the job, and then, for a lark, he donned my Oriental robe, wrapped his head in a peacock blue scarf, and tossed a feather boa around his shoulders.

Emily was entirely nonplussed when she brought up the petit fours and I introduced her to Aunt Esmée. She gawped as I explained that Esmée was a long-lost relation and a *teensy* bit eccentric. After she left, we howled, wishing there was a way we could get Hank involved. We drank whiskey from teacups, and Aunt Esmée read my fortune, which involved a long journey and great wealth. I asked if there was anyone tall, dark, and handsome in my future, and she informed me that my destiny involved a man who was tall, *blond*, and handsome—as well as already beneath my nose.

I leaned toward the mirror to have a closer look, tilting my face back and forth. The trip had taken a toll on my complexion, and my left cheek had thin red lines running across it from when I'd smashed into the outside wall. I looked as though a cat had taken a swipe at me.

I patched and spackled as best I could. In the end, it was clear I'd used a heavy hand, but my face turned out better than I expected. My hair, however, was a different story.

I usually wore it parted to the side, with a wave that swept across my forehead, then up and over my ears before landing in a cascade of curls at the nape of my neck. This was courtesy of Lana, the hair savant at Salon Antoine, who set my hair twice a week. She would cover my head in rollers and put me under the dryer to "cook," while someone else touched up my manicure. When the rollers were out, Lana would coax and pat my hair into submission, spray it until it was as hard and shiny as glass, and send me on my way.

Between appointments, all I had to do was make sure I replaced any bobby pins that came out and wear a hairnet to bed. If it was necessary to smooth the surface, I was instructed to use a soft-bristled hairbrush with caution, but if anything went wrong that I couldn't fix—especially with the curls—I was to go back at once.

Consequently, I hadn't done my own hair in four years and had no idea what to do with the stringy mess that sat atop my head.

In honor of Aunt Esmée, I wrapped a turban around it, pinned a garnet brooch to the front, and went to join my husband.

I kept a hand on the wall to steady myself as I went downstairs, and paused at the bottom to get my balance.

The fire was burning brightly, and the Blackout curtains—or frames—had been pulled out and stacked in a corner. The downstairs windows were also taped, and posters on either side of the radio warned that "Loose Lips Sink Ships" and "Careless Talk Costs Lives."

Another flicker of fear ran through me.

Ellis and Hank were at one of the tables, poring over an Ordnance map with several logbooks lying open. A duffel bag, tripod, and various other pieces of equipment were on the floor, and they had their coats and hats thrown over an empty chair.

Hank watched as I wobbled over, and I hoped he wouldn't have time to come up with a joke about sea legs.

"Look who's up!" he said brightly.

Ellis stood and pulled out a chair.

"Good morning, sleepyhead," he said, kissing my cheek. "Or should I say afternoon?"

I smiled weakly and sat.

"You obviously got your beauty sleep," he said, pushing my chair in and sitting back down. "You look positively radiant."

"It's just a bit of paint," I said. "You two look busy. What are you up to?"

"A little strategizing," he said. "Thought we'd scope out the area on foot, maybe rent a boat. If there's time, we might walk over to the castle."

"Don't forget the newspaper," said Hank.

"Yes, we're going to place an advertisement to find people who've had encounters. Help us establish a pattern. When and where the thing arises, weather conditions, et cetera."

"I thought we were changing hotels," I said, glancing at the equipment on the floor. "Or are we going to send for our things later?"

"Yes. Well, neither, actually," said Ellis. "There don't seem to be any other hotels. Hank took an early morning walk, and the village is the size of a flea. The girl in the kitchen says the next closest hotel is two and a half miles away, but it's full of billeted soldiers, and anyway, it doesn't sound any better than this. Apparently there's no electricity in the entire glen."

I looked around to make sure we were alone. "But what if the landlord doesn't let us stay?"

"It turns out Blackbeard is much friendlier in the morning," Ellis said. "Well, 'much' may be putting it a bit strongly, but we've officially checked in for a stay of indeterminate length, so don't worry your pretty little head for another second." He reached over and play-pinched my cheek.

For the first time, I noticed their plates. There was a pale rectangular slab on each, gray and slightly gelatinous. "What is that?"

"Porridge," Hank said brightly, poking it with his fork. "Apparently they pour leftover porridge into a drawer and cut slices off it when it sets. Waste not, want not."

"You're both in very good moods," I said.

"Of course!" said Ellis, spreading his hands. "We're here, aren't we?"

"Excuse me, Mrs. Pennypacker," said Anna, appearing at my side.

My mother's name again. I shot Ellis a look, but he was watching as Anna slid a small bowl of steaming porridge in front of me, along with a cup of creamy milk.

"I'll be right back with your tea," she said.

"Well, would you look at that," said Hank. "Virgin porridge. Aren't you special."

I stared at it. "I don't think I can eat. My stomach's still iffy."

"You have to," said Ellis. "You're thin as a rail."

"Please. That's how you like me," I said.

"Yes, but if you get too thin your face will suffer."

I looked up, horrified, wondering if he was saying it already had. I was still trying to decipher his expression when Anna returned with a cup of tea.

"I brought a wee bit of sugar, ma'am," she said, setting it in front of me. There were two cubes on the edge of the saucer.

Hank glanced up from his map. "Her tea's stronger, too. I sense favoritism."

"And rightly so," said Ellis. "She needs it."

The back of my throat tightened. So much for my being "positively radiant." I picked up the milk to pour on my porridge.

Anna sucked her breath through her teeth, and I halted with the bowl in midair.

"If you don't mind my saying, ma'am, that's not the best way of going about that. Pouring the milk all over it," she tutted. "It's just not right."

"Don't you have something else?" Ellis said testily. "Ham? Eggs? A steak? My wife is poorly. She needs protein."

Anna drew her shoulders back. "We do not, Mr. Pennypacker. Those particular items are rationed, and we weren't expecting guests. And for your information, milk and sugar are rationed as well—I only brought them out because I thought Mrs. Pennypacker could use a little perking up, what with her motion sickness and all."

"Thank you," I said. "That's very kind of you."

"Fine. Never mind," said Ellis, pulling the logbook toward him. When she didn't leave, he threw her an irritated glance and flicked the backs of his fingers toward her. "I said that's all."

She folded her arms and glowered at him. "No, you did not. You said 'Never mind.' And I don't suppose you've given your ration books to Angus."

"No," said Ellis, without looking at her.

"Oh, aye," she replied on an intake of breath. "Well, I can't do any better for you until you do, and I'll have you know it's a criminal offense to waste food, so get that down you or I'll be forced to call the warden." She lifted her chin and sailed around the bar and through to the back.

Ellis looked agog at Hank. Then he broke into giggles.

"I told you she wasn't all there," he said.

Hank nodded. "She does seem a few sandwiches short."

"You needn't have been so rude," I said. "She's very nice, and she was about to show me, if you hadn't interrupted."

Ellis looked stunned. "Show you what? How to eat porridge? It's *porridge*. You eat it."

"Oh, never mind," I said.

Ellis stared at me. "Shall I call her back?"

"No. I'm fine," I said. "But perhaps you can explain why, exactly, she thinks I'm my mother?"

Ellis laughed, and Hank nearly spat tea out of his nose.

"You're not your mother—thank God," said Ellis, after they'd collected themselves. "But I did sign us in using your maiden name."

"And why is that?"

"My father wasn't terrifically popular around here after the *Daily Mail* fiasco. But don't worry. When we find the monster, we'll come clean." He held his hands up and framed an imaginary headline: "Son of Colonel Whitney Hyde Catches Loch Ness Monster; Hailed as Hero."

"Say, Hero, think we can get back to work?" said Hank, stuffing his napkin under the edge of his plate. He circled an area on the map with his finger. "Since this area is the epicenter of the sightings, I think we should start at Temple Pier, then either walk or row to the . . ."

As Hank prattled on, I considered the two bowls in front of me. If you didn't put the milk in the porridge, surely you didn't put the porridge in the milk? I dipped my spoon in the porridge, looked at the bowl of milk, felt stupid, and gave up.

I put one of the sugar cubes on my teaspoon and lowered it slowly into the cup, watching the brown seep upward, evenly, irrevocably.

Chapter Nine

Hank and Ellis seemed almost relieved when I told them I wasn't going to join them. I would have been offended if I didn't know I couldn't walk straight.

They gathered their things and left in a whirlwind of activity. I hadn't seen Ellis this energized since the summer I'd met him. At the last second, Hank leaned over the table, grabbed his porridge, and gamely chomped it down. Then he ate Ellis's as well, saying he wasn't keen on "being frog-marched to the clink, at least not over a slab of drawer porridge." Ellis kissed my cheek and implored me to eat my own porridge in whatever fashion I saw fit, and to make sure the staff looked after me. And then they were gone.

I had planned on asking Anna to draw me a bath, but after threatening to call the warden she never returned. I began to think she'd left the building.

I found my way up the stairs, grasping the rail and stopping several times. At one point I thought I was going to fall backward, and sat on the step until it passed.

There was a black line painted around the inside of the

bathtub, about five inches up, which I assumed was a guide to how deep the water should be, but no matter what the temperature of the water, there wouldn't be enough to warm a person up. I decided it was a suggestion rather than a rule, put in the rubber plug, and turned the taps on full. I left them running while I went to my room.

When I returned and tried to step into the bath, I discovered that the water coming out of both faucets was icy.

By the time I got my clothes back on and rushed down to the grate, my teeth were chattering.

The fire gave off a fearsome heat, and I couldn't seem to find the right distance from it—too close, and my shins and cheeks stung, too far and I got chilled through. At one point, my toes were burning and my heels were freezing all at the same time. I was cold, dizzy, queasy, and filthy. It was hard to imagine being more miserable.

There was a newspaper on the low table, but when I tried to read, the words swam on the page. I gave up almost immediately, left it open on my lap, and gazed into the fire. Its movement masked that of my eyes, and was the most helpful thing yet in making me feel steady.

The chimney stones were charred, and the fire, part coal and part mysterious other, hissed and cracked and occasionally let off an unlikely whistle. As I watched, a glowing red ember shot out, landed on the carpet, and immediately turned black. A pair of brown utility shoes, thick wool socks, and reddened shins appeared right where it had landed.

Anna was standing beside me, holding a plate and a steaming cup. She put them on the table in front of me.

"I couldn't help but notice you didn't eat your porridge, probably on account of not knowing how." She glanced behind her and added, "I slipped a wee dram into the tea. I thought it might help, as I also couldn't help but notice that you're still a bit wobbly."

The plate held a coddled egg and a few slices of golden fried potato. Moments before, my stomach had been doing flips, but I was suddenly ravenous.

"But I thought eggs were rationed?" I said, glancing up.

"Aye, and butter, too, but we've hens and a cow at the croft. I nipped back and told Mhàthair—that's my mother—that you were feeling poorly, and she said to give you this. She's also the midwife, so she knows such things. She says you're to start with the tea."

"Thank you. That's very kind. Please send her my regards."

Anna lingered, and then said, "Is it really the monster your husband is after? My cousin Donald's seen it, you know."

I looked up. "He has?"

"Aye, and his parents, too," she said, nodding gravely. "My Aunt Aldie and Uncle John were driving home from Inverness when they thought they saw a bunch of ducks fighting in the water near Abriachan, but when they got closer they realized it was an animal—a black beast the size of a whale—rolling, and plunging, and generally causing a right *stramash*." She illustrated with her hands.

"What happened then?"

"Nothing," she said simply. "It swam off."

"And your cousin?"

She shrugged. "There's not much to tell. He was a fisherman. Something happened one day when he was out on the loch, and he hasn't set foot on a boat since. And neither will he discuss it."

"What about your aunt? Do you think your aunt will discuss it?"

"I should think she'd blather your ear off, given the opportunity. Why don't you invite her for a *strupag*? And Mrs. Pennypacker? You were on the right track. You put the porridge on the spoon and then you dip the spoon in the milk. It keeps the porridge hot."

"I'm sorry I didn't eat it," I said. "Is it really a criminal offense to waste food?"

"Aye, several years since. But don't worry, the milk will go into the soup, and your porridge went into the drawer. Conall was that pleased to lick the bowl he wagged his tail. Do you think you'll be needing anything else? Only I need to get back to the croft. You might not think there's much to do in January, but you'd be wrong. There's clearing stones, cutting turnip for the sheep, the milking, oh, it goes on and on . . ." She stared into the distance and sighed.

"There's just one thing," I said. "I'd love to have a bath, but there's no hot water."

"There will be in about twenty minutes. I heard you banging around up there, so I lit the boiler. I'll take up some Lux flakes as well. You're only supposed to run the bath up to the line, but I think maybe this once you might run it deeper."

I couldn't take offense—she'd seen me moments after I'd quite literally fallen out of bed.

"I'm off then. Meg will be back from the sawmill around four. Now get that down you," she said, nodding authoritatively. "I've seen bigger kneecaps on a sparrow, and if Mhàthair hears you didn't finish up that tea, it's the castor oil she'll be sending next."

Although the tea itself tasted like boiled twigs—I supposed it was ersatz—the "wee dram" helped so much that after my bath I lay down to have a rest. I was surprised to find myself drifting off, because I was excited. I couldn't wait to tell Ellis about Anna's relatives.

Several hours later, I floated out of my nap to the buzz of conversation and laughter rising from the main floor. I was surprised by the number of voices, since I knew we were the only staying guests, and decided the inn must also be a pub. I lit the candle, which Anna had replaced, and looked at my watch. It was evening, and I was hungry again. I hadn't had a proper meal since I left the States.

You're thin as a rail, Ellis had said.

I've seen bigger kneecaps on a sparrow, Anna had said.

I let my hands explore my belly—the hipbones that protruded sharply, the concave area between, the rib cage that loomed above.

Oh, Madeline. We really have to do something, my mother had said.

I was twelve and at first had no idea what she was talking about. I'd stepped out from behind the striped canvas of the changing tent on the beach at Bar Harbor and was breathless at the deep blue of the sky and even deeper blue of the ocean, at the laughter and shrieking of the children who played at the edges of the lapping surf, at the seagulls swooping and diving. I turned, alarmed at her tone. She shook her head sadly, but her eyes were hard. She pressed her lips into a thin line as she surveyed the parts of me that made me most self-conscious. They were the parts that were filling out but were not yet curvy. I was merely pudgy. I'd never felt a deeper shame in my life.

She'd have approved now, I thought, stretching my legs out. With my ankles and knees touching, my thighs never met. And then I thought, No, she wouldn't. No matter what I did or who I became, she would never have approved.

Hank's and Ellis's rooms were empty, so I headed downstairs. I assumed they'd returned, discovered I was asleep, and gone down for drinks. I was eager to tell them what I'd learned, sure they'd be pleased with me. Perhaps with the right type of persuasion, even Cousin Donald would tell his story.

As I stepped out of the shadow at the bottom of the stairwell, everyone fell silent. Hank and Ellis were nowhere to be seen, and other than Meg, I was the only woman in the room.

There were a dozen or so burly young men wearing khaki uniforms sitting at the tables, and about six older men in civilian clothes perched on stools at the bar. Every one of them was looking at me.

I girded myself, feeling the men's eyes upon me, and hoping they wouldn't think I was drunk as I made my way to the couch. Conall stared from his place by the hearth. He didn't raise his head, but his eyes darted and his whiskered brows twitched as I approached. At the end, when I sank onto the couch, I realized I'd only been slightly off-balance. I further realized that I had taken the stairs without incident, and then, with some alarm, that what I had thought was ersatz tea was almost certainly medicinal. While I wasn't happy about being dosed without my consent, I couldn't deny it had helped.

Meg was behind the bar, her hair carefully arranged in a cascade of red curls. I remembered the bits of rag tied in her hair the night before, and wondered if I could figure out how to do that. My own hair, still damp from my bath, was back under a turban.

Her periwinkle dress hugged her figure, and her lips and fingernails were scarlet. It was hard to believe she worked at a sawmill. She looked like a redheaded Hedy Lamarr. If she was at all open to Hank's advances, she didn't stand a chance. Hank would never be serious about a barmaid. He was so slippery he could barely bring himself to be serious about Violet. I had to find a moment to warn Hank off, and wished I'd said something that very first night.

"Can I get you something, Mrs. Pennypacker?" she called over. "A half pint? Or perhaps a sherry?"

"Nothing right now, thank you," I said, and at the sound of my voice the men exchanged glances. I didn't blame them—

surely they were wondering how and why an American woman had materialized in their midst. A hot flush rose to my cheeks.

A young man sitting at a table with a glass of beer called out in an accent as flat and un-Scottish as my own, "Canadian or American?" and I found myself staring back with equal surprise.

Before I could answer, the front door opened and an elderly man came in, leaning on a walking stick.

He said to the room in general, "There's rain in it today."

"Aye, Donnie, that there is," said Meg from behind the bar. "A hauf and a hauf, is it?"

"Just a pint of heavy." He made his way to the last empty barstool.

She pulled a glass from beneath the counter and held it under a beer spigot. "There's game pie tonight," she said, "so you can keep your ration book in your pocket."

"Oh, that's grand, Meg," he said. He began to struggle out of his coat.

"Can I give you a hand?" she said, coming around to help.

"I'm in need of one, Meg, surely I am," he said, chuckling at his own joke. His empty sleeve was pinned up against his shirt. As Meg took his coat away, he climbed onto the stool. He raised his glass and turned toward the room. "*Slàinte!*" he said.

"*Slàinte!*" Everyone, young and old, lifted his glass.

At that moment, Ellis and Hank burst through the door, cheeks ruddy with the cold, coats and hats wet.

"—so if the ad runs on Friday," Ellis said, "we could potentially start getting responses on Tuesday. Meanwhile, we can revisit . . . the . . ." His voice petered out when he realized he was the center of attention.

Hank let his hands drop to his sides, clenching and unclenching his fingers like a cowboy ready to draw. Behind the bar, Meg picked up a cloth and began to wipe down the counter.

Our black-bearded landlord appeared in the doorway that led to the back, wearing a heavy ribbed sweater in dark olive.

After a silence that seemed interminable, Old Donnie set his glass down and slid off his stool. He picked up his stick and hobbled slowly over.

Tap, tap, tap, tap.

He stopped directly in front of Ellis. He was shorter by a whole head. He looked Ellis up and then down, and then up again, the skin of his neck stretching like a turtle's as he strained to see Ellis's face.

"You favor your father," he finally said.

"I beg your pardon?" said Ellis, draining of color.

"The monster hunter. From 'thirty-four. I'm not that addled yet." The broken capillaries in his face darkened. A fleck of spittle flew from his lips.

Meg's eyebrows darted up, and she glanced at Ellis. Then she resumed wiping the counter.

"Now, Donnie," she said. "Come take a seat and I'll get your pie."

He ignored her. "I suppose it's the monster you're after, is it? Or are you going to float a balloon and take a snapshot like your old man?"

Ellis's face went from pale to purple in a split second.

The old man spun and hurried toward his coat, his gnarled stick banging on the flagstones. "I'll no be staying where this *bastart* is."

"Did he just say what I think he did?" Ellis said. "Did he just call me a bastard?"

"If he wasn't a cripple, I'd knock his block off," said Hank.

"Your mammie's his wife, then, is she?" said Old Donnie. "Only rumor has it he was an awful one for the *houghmagandy*."

"Now, Donnie," Meg said, sharply this time. "There's no call for that. Come have your pie."

"You'll excuse the language, but there's no other way to get to it," the old man said indignantly. "The pathetic *creutair*, trying to make *strìopaichean* of honest girls up at the Big House, and not a shred of decency. And I don't suppose anyone will help me with my coat." This last was delivered as a statement, although he set his stick against the bar and straightened up, waiting.

Mr. Ross had been studying Ellis since Donnie's initial proclamation, but now he came around the bar and helped the old man into his coat. Donnie picked up his stick and stomped dramatically to the door before turning and declaring, "I'll not be darkening your door again, Angus. Not while this one's in residence."

Several seconds after the door closed behind him, someone said, "Well, I suppose Rhona won't mind not having to come collect him at the end of an evening." A swell of laughter rose, and the men returned to their conversations.

Meg came around the bar and put the radio on, fiddling with the lit dial until she first found Radio Luxembourg, with "Lord Haw-Haw" announcing in a perfect English accent, *"Germany calling! Germany calling!"*

She switched to static immediately, then moved the dial around until she finally found Bing Crosby, crooning about moonbeams and stars.

Ellis, whose face had finally settled on a terrible shade of gray, came and sat next to me.

"And that, my dear, is precisely why I used your maiden name," he said through gritted teeth.

Our landlord was once again studying him.

Chapter Ten

Ellis maintained a cool, silent façade through dinner, and excused himself immediately after. When I rose to go with him, he told me firmly to stay and enjoy my sherry.

I didn't want to stay, and there was certainly no enjoying to be done—all I could think about was what we'd do if we were given the boot for lying—but I knew he wanted me to remain behind and try to save face. I lasted only a quarter of an hour. When I left, Hank was grinding his teeth and white-knuckling his whiskey.

I knocked on Ellis's door.

"Go away!"

"It's me," I said, speaking into the crack. "Please let me in."

He barked something about not being fit for human company.

I went to my own room, hoping he'd change his mind and come to me. When the rest of the house had shut down and my candle had burned to a nub, I gave up and went to bed.

I lay on my back in the dark under a mountain of blankets listening to the rain pound the roof. I was wearing my two heaviest nightgowns but was still so cold I was dabbing my nose nonstop.

I had never heard the words *striopaichean* or *houghmagandy* before but deduced from the context that the former was what my mother-in-law believed my mother to be, and the latter was the activity that defined her as such.

I'd long thought of the Colonel as an irritating blowhard, but it had never occurred to me that he might also be a lecher. The mere thought of the Colonel making overtures to hapless young girls was horrifying. The pasty skin, the jiggling belly, the mustache yellowed by tobacco—

I hadn't noticed it before, but if Ellis were bald, forty years older, sixty pounds heavier, and had an alcoholic nose, he would look very much like the Colonel.

No wonder Ellis hadn't felt fit for human company. Learning that he was going to age like the Colonel must have been a terrible blow, yet there was no denying it, since Old Donnie had identified him as the Colonel's son the first time he laid eyes on him. But there were ways of delaying the transformation with diet and exercise—even hairpieces, if necessary—and there was time to worry about that later. We had a more immediate problem to address.

I flipped back the covers and fumbled in the dark for the matches, lighting my last inch of candle.

A moment later, I was in the hallway, standing outside his door. As I raised my hand to knock, the door to Meg's room clicked open and a heavy-shouldered figure slipped out.

I jumped backward, muffling a gasp.

The man was tall and had prominent ears, but by candlelight I couldn't see much else. He glanced at me, turned up his coat collar, and slipped into the inky black of the stairwell. I rapped quickly on Ellis's door.

"Ellis! Ellis!" I said urgently, looking down the hallway. "Let me in!"

A moment later the door opened and his face appeared in the crack. "What's the matter? Is it your heart? Do you need a pill?"

"No, I'm fine," I said, irritated that he'd automatically jumped to that conclusion.

"You didn't sound fine."

I glanced one last time down the hall and decided not to say anything about the man leaving Meg's room.

"I am. I'm fine," I said, "but we need to talk."

"About what?"

"You *know* what. Can I please come in? I'd rather not do this in the hallway."

After a flicker of hesitation, he held the door open. By the light of my candle, I saw that his room was in roughly the same condition as mine, with his belongings strewn all over the floor.

"Watch your step," he said, sweeping his hand toward the mess.

I made my way to the bed and set the candle on the table. When I climbed under the covers, Ellis said, "What are you doing?"

I felt like he'd kicked me in the stomach. "I'm just getting warm. Don't worry. I won't stay."

He exhaled through puffed cheeks and ran a hand through his hair. Finally, he closed the door and walked to the far side of the bed. He lay on top of the covers with his arms over his chest, stiff as a slab of marble.

"You could at least have brought me a pill," he said.

"I can go get one."

"Never mind," he said.

A few minutes later, when it became apparent he wasn't going to address the issue at hand, or any other, I asked, "What are we going to do?"

"What do you mean?"

"Where are we going to go? We can't stay here."

"Of course we can. Why wouldn't we?"

"Because we checked in under a fake name."

Ellis exploded, sitting bolt upright and slamming his fists on the quilt so hard I recoiled. "It's *not* a fake name. It's your *maiden* name, as I explained to you earlier, so what, exactly, is your point?"

"My point is that I'm terrified we're going to be tossed out onto the street!" I said in a harsh whisper. "And I'm sorry you're upset, but you have no right to take it out on me. None of this is my fault."

"So it's my fault, is it?"

"Well, *I* certainly didn't do anything."

The wind howled down the chimney. The window rattled in its pane.

"I'm sorry about the old man tonight," I said. "The whole thing was dreadful."

Ellis was suddenly yelling again: "I've half a mind to have him arrested! It's slander and libel and God only knows what else, making ridiculous, groundless accusations against someone who's not even here to defend himself. My father would *never, ever*—"

"I know!" I said, interrupting him in a whisper, hoping that it would encourage him to lower his tone. I laid a hand on his arm. "I know."

In fact I did not know. Was he incensed about the accusations of womanizing, or the accusations of fakery? Or because he, himself, had been caught in a lie?

The rain picked up and changed direction, battering the glass like someone was flinging buckets of nails against it. Water dripped sporadically down the chimney and onto the grate, an occasional heavy *plonk*.

Ellis lay back down.

I was infinitely sorry I'd come and was about to climb from

the bed when he suddenly rolled to face me, catching me off guard.

"Well," he said, "to answer your question, I certainly hope we can stay. There isn't anywhere else to go."

"Maybe we can move to the estate? I'm a little surprised we didn't go there in the first place."

"I rather suspect they got their fill of Hydes back in 'thirty-four, don't you?"

"Oh, I don't know. Your father is hardly the first man to try it on with a servant. Anyway, you're family."

He laughed wryly. "I'm a second cousin once removed. And no, even if they would have had us, which is highly unlikely, the point is moot. Apparently the house and grounds are crawling with soldiers."

"It was requisitioned? Where's the family?"

"No idea," he said. "It's not as though we've exchanged Christmas cards over the years."

He laid an arm across me, and I realized we were making up.

"So what did you do today?" he asked.

"Mostly I rested, but I've got exciting news—three of Anna's relatives have seen the monster, and at least two are willing to talk to us."

"Who?"

"Anna. The girl who served us breakfast."

"Hmm," he said. "How interesting."

"I thought you'd be pleased," I said. "Maybe even excited."

"Oh, I am. I'll definitely follow up," he said. "How's the dizziness? Do you think you'll be able to come with us tomorrow?"

"It's much better, and I'd love to," I said.

"Good. We could use your sharp eyes." He wriggled his way under the covers. "Aren't you going to put out the candle?"

I realized he was inviting me to stay.

I blew out the flame and rolled toward him.

A few minutes later, a soft rumbling began in the back of his throat, and before long he fell onto his back. The snoring grew louder. I lay awake for what seemed like forever, blinking into the dark.

I tried to remember the last time we made love, and could not.

I thought about the man leaving Meg's room, and hoped she was being careful. If Hank got her into trouble, her reputation might be ruined, but she'd end up well off, at least by the time I was finished with Hank. If a regular workingman got her into a predicament—well, I just hoped he'd marry her, and that they really were in love.

In the morning, Ellis was gone. He had removed the Blackout frame, so I woke to daylight. It was almost ten o'clock, early by my standards.

Downstairs, Anna was scrubbing the windows with a wad of newspaper. An earthenware jug labeled DISTILLED VINEGAR sat on a nearby table. She had a plain cotton kerchief tied around her hair, knotted on top, in stark contrast to the bright Hermès scarf that was tied similarly around mine.

She glanced at me and turned away immediately.

"Good morning, Mrs. Hyde," she said pointedly.

"Good morning," I said, slithering into the nearest chair. It was only then that I registered the absence of Hank and Ellis.

Anna was watching from the corner of her eye.

"They've gone out," she said, attacking the window with renewed vigor. "They said to tell you they'll be back tomorrow."

I sat up, panicked. "What? Where did they go?"

"Inverness, apparently," she said.

"Where's that? And why?"

"It's fourteen miles up the road. And for what reason, I would not know," she said, setting the wad of newspaper on the sill and wiping her hands on her apron.

"They didn't leave a note or anything?"

"Not to my knowledge."

"Do you know if they cleared up the . . . confusion?" I asked, wincing at the final word.

She turned and glared at me, planting her hands on her hips. "Do you mean about using a fake name? You'll have to ask Angus about that."

I was struck through with terror. If the landlord made me leave, what was I supposed to do? Where was I supposed to go?

"Any chance you've brought your ration book down?" Anna continued. "Only I can't help but notice that not one of you has handed one in, even though I mentioned it yesterday, and you were *supposed* to do it the moment you checked in. Although I suppose if you'll be going elsewhere, it doesn't much matter."

"I'm not sure where Ellis put them," I said weakly. "I'll have a look in a bit."

Anna kept her hands on her hips, staring at me with grave suspicion. I dropped my gaze into my lap.

"I'll get your breakfast then, shall I?" she said, before stomping past.

I put my elbows on the table and dropped my head into my hands. I couldn't believe Ellis would do this to me. There had to be some mistake.

Breakfast was a slab of drawer porridge and decidedly weak tea, with no milk or sugar. Anna dropped them in front of me with a clatter and went back to the window.

"Bacon, butter, sugar, milk—it doesn't grow on trees, you know," she said, as though continuing a conversation.

My hands were back in my lap. I started picking at the chips in my nail polish.

"Or eggs. Or margarine. Or tea," Anna continued. She surveyed the wad of newspaper in her hand and dropped it on the table. She crumpled up a fresh sheet, tipped the mouth of the jug against it, and slammed the jug back down.

"I suppose tea does grow on trees, but not around here." She nodded toward my cup. "I've reused leaves for that," she said.

For about fifteen seconds I thought maybe she was finished.

"I suppose I could make you a beetroot sandwich in the meantime, although I don't suppose National Loaf is up to your usual standards. Neeps, tatties, onions. Porridge, certainly—but no milk, mind you. I might be able to find a tablet or two of saccharine. And I don't suppose you've got a gas mask, have you?" She glanced quickly at me, intuited the answer, and sighed grievously. "I thought not. You're supposed to carry one at all times. You can get a fine for that. And I don't suppose the mustard gas will know the difference between you and a normal person." She curled her lips on the last two words.

I finally looked up from my lap. "Anna, I'm sorry. I don't know what to say."

"Oh, aye. I'm not sure I'd believe it anyway."

She might as well have slapped me.

Mr. Ross came through from the back, wearing the same sweater as the day before, pants of the same dark olive, and heavy black boots. It looked like a military outfit, although there were no badges or any other identifying information on it. He stopped momentarily at the sight of me, then continued as though I didn't exist, going to the till and removing cash. He flipped through a large ledger book, making occasional notes with a pencil. With a start, I noticed that the first two joints of his right index finger were missing.

Anna turned her attention back to the window.

"Shall I correct the spelling in the register?" he said without looking up.

My relief was so great I clapped a hand to my mouth.

"I'll take that as a yes?"

"Yes," I said, barely managing to speak. "Thank you."

It was more than enough that he wasn't turning me out. He had no reason whatever to preserve my dignity, and this simple act of kindness caused my throat to constrict.

"Right then." He slapped his thigh. "Conall, *trobhad*!" The tall dog trotted around the corner of the bar, and the two of them left.

"You're very lucky is all I have to say," said Anna.

My innards twisted into a knot, and my hands and heart fluttered so badly I couldn't even consider lifting a fork, never mind a teacup. I pushed my chair back so hard it screeched against the floor and bolted upstairs, abandoning my breakfast.

"I've half a mind to call the warden for that!" Anna shouted after me.

I turned the lock on the inside of my room and leaned against the door, hyperventilating. My heart was racing so hard I thought I might actually keel over. If I did, it would not be the first time.

The first time had been when I was having lunch at the Acorn Club with my mother-in-law and five of her friends, including Mrs. Pew.

My marriage was not quite four months old, at a time when I still deluded myself that my mother-in-law's gift of the hair comb indicated that she might eventually come to accept me, perhaps even grow fond of me. The ladies were discussing the despicable attack on Pearl Harbor, and saying that despite previous reservations, they now agreed wholeheartedly with the President's decision to become involved. I mentioned the sinking of the *Athenia* and suggested that we might have gotten involved then, given the number of Americans on board. My remark was met with silence.

After a long, pregnant pause, my mother-in-law said, "You are, of course, entitled to your opinion, dear. Although I, personally, wouldn't *dream* of second-guessing the President." She clapped her bejeweled hand to her bosom, letting her eyes flutter as she warbled the word "dream."

As the telltale heat rose in my cheeks, she continued, praising the club for reducing its seven-course luncheon to five in the name of the war effort. She encouraged the other ladies to chip in, telling them that she, herself, had instructed the kitchen staff to donate cans, as well as whatever pots and pans they weren't using regularly. There was a flurry of regret from all of them that they couldn't do more, especially from such a distance, followed by a discussion of the surprising results of Ellis's attempts to enlist.

"A complete shock, I can tell you," said my mother-in-law. "Imagine, all these years, and we had no clue. I suppose it explains why he's crashed so many cars—he can't tell if the light is red or green. He's terribly upset, but there's nothing to be done. Whitney, of course, is beside himself."

There were murmurs of sympathy for both Ellis and the Colonel before Mrs. Pew leaned in conspiratorially to say, "Of course, there are those who *arranged* to be turned down."

"Do you mean . . . ?" said another in hushed tones. Instead of filling in the blank, she let her eyes flit across the room to where Hank's mother was having lunch with her own friends.

Mrs. Pew blinked heavily to confirm. The other ladies went wide-eyed, the thrill of their double-cross palpable.

"Absolutely shameful. Flat-footed, indeed."

"Nothing a pair of good boots wouldn't fix."

"That one's been trouble from the word go," said my mother-in-law. "It's somewhere in the blood, even if his mother *is* a Wanamaker." She lowered her voice even further. "I wish Ellis would keep his distance, but of course he's never paid attention to a word I say."

I was staring at the shrimp and avocado on the fine china in front of me when it hit me that she had almost certainly said those very same things of me, to these very women, perhaps at this very table.

The hair comb hadn't been a peace offering. I had no idea what it signified, or why they had invited me to lunch, but by then I was entirely sure there was a motive.

I remember staring at the glass bowl of salad dressing, the flute of champagne with lines of bubbles rising from tiny, random geysers on the sides. I remember realizing that I had gone still for so long they were looking at me, and that I should pick up my fork, but could not, because I knew I would drop it. Someone addressed me, but it was impossible to hear over the buzzing in my ears. Then I couldn't catch my breath. I wasn't aware of sliding from my chair, but was certainly aware of being the center of attention while lying on the carpet looking up at a circle of concerned faces. And who could forget the embarrassing ride in the ambulance, its siren blaring?

A number of consultations followed, culminating in a visit by a doctor brought in from New York, who took my pulse, listened to my heart, and asked me extensive questions about my family.

"I see, I see," he kept saying, studying me over the top of his wire-rimmed glasses.

Eventually, he folded the glasses and slid them into his breast pocket. Then he informed me—right in front of Ellis and his mother—that I suffered from a nervous ailment. He prescribed nerve pills, and said I was to avoid excitement at all costs.

My mother-in-law gasped.

"Does this mean she can't . . . ? Does this mean there will never be . . . ?"

The doctor watched as she turned various shades of red.

"Ahh," he said, figuring it out. "No. She can tolerate a reasonable amount of marital relations. It's more a matter of avoiding mental excitement. Such a condition is not unexpected, given the maternal history."

He packed his bag and put on his hat.

"Wait!" said my mother-in-law, leaping to her feet. She glanced at me, prone in the bed. "When you say this is not unexpected, do you mean such conditions run in families?"

After a slight pause, the doctor said, "Not always. Remember that each generation is diluted, and any children of this marriage will have only one grandparent who was, well, how shall I put this? Not quite our kind."

Edith Stone Hyde let out a cry and sank back into her chair.

My nervous ailment immediately became a heart ailment, and although I rarely felt grateful to my mother-in-law, I did admire how quickly she'd taken it upon herself to rediagnose me—particularly as it maintained at least the illusion of distance between me and my own mother.

My mother was a famous beauty, with sea-green eyes, a button nose, and Cupid's bow lips that parted over teeth like pearls. In some women, perfect features do not add up to an exquisite whole, but in my mother the sum effect was so stunning that when she married my father, a Proper Philadelphian, society seemed willing to overlook that her father was an entrepreneur who dabbled in burlesque (revised for historical purposes as vaudeville) and married one of its stars, and that her grandfather was a rumored robber baron with connections to Tammany Hall. Her family had a fortune; his family had a name. The arrangement was not all that unusual.

I was aware from my earliest memory that my mother was miserable, although the sheer magnitude and artistry of it took years to sink in. It ran through her like rot.

To the outside world, she presented meekness and long-suffering, subtly conveying that my father was a tyrant and I—well, I was defiant at best, and quite possibly criminally malicious, a situation she found even more heartbreaking than my father's cruelty. She was incredibly nuanced—all it took was a sigh, a slight misting of the eye, or an almost imperceptible pause for everyone to understand the depth of her anguish and how nobly she bore it.

She was excellent at reading a room, and when the atmosphere was not right for garnering sympathy, she was witty and engaging, the center of attention, but never in an obvious way. She'd run a finger up and down the stem of her wineglass slowly, repeatedly, or cross her legs and move her foot in deliberate circles, drawing attention to her exquisitely turned ankle. It was impossible to look away. She entranced men and women alike.

At home, she sulked with extravagance, and I learned early that silence was anything but peaceful. She was always upset about some slight, real or imagined, and more than capable of creating a full-blown crisis out of thin air.

I tried to go unnoticed, but inevitably we came together over the dinner table. I never knew if her displeasure was going to be directed at my father or me. When I was the offender, dinner passed with icy silences and withering looks. I rarely knew what I'd done wrong, but even if I did, I wouldn't have dared mount a defense. Instead, I shrank into myself. On those nights, I got to eat, although she scrutinized every morsel that went into my mouth, as well as how it got there.

On the nights my father was in her crosshairs, the choreography was very different. Her contemptuous looks and snide remarks progressed to masterfully crafted barbs, which he would ignore until they ripened into cutting sarcasm, which he would also ignore. She would then, her eyes brimming with tears, wonder aloud why we both delighted in torturing her so, at which point my father would say something precise and le-

thal, usually to the effect that no one was forcing her to stay—
she needn't feel obliged on his account—and she would flee the
table weeping.

My father would continue to eat as though nothing had
happened, so it fell to me to fix things. I'd abandon my food and
trudge upstairs to her locked bedroom, my dread increasing
with every step. It always took some negotiating, but eventually
she'd let me in and I'd sit on the bed as she regaled me with the
ways her life was a wasteland. My father was capriciously cruel
and incapable of empathy, she'd tell me. She would have left
him years ago, except that he'd sworn she'd never see me again,
had even threatened to have her committed to an insane asy-
lum, and did I know what happened in such places? She'd given
up every chance of happiness for my sake, out of pure maternal
love, although I was clearly ungrateful. But she supposed she
had herself to blame for that. I took after my father. I could
hardly be blamed for my miserable genes, and since I was there
anyway, would I be a dear and fetch her a pill?

Twenty minutes after running away from Anna and the drawer
porridge, my heart showed no signs of slowing down.

I was slumped against the back of my door, still gasping for
air. My hands and feet tingled, the edges of my vision sparkled.

I hated that I'd been prescribed nerve pills—hated that
anyone had seen any kind of parallel between my mother and
me—and although it filled me with self-loathing, I found myself crawling to my luggage and digging through it, throwing
dresses, slips, scarves, and even shoes over my shoulder in my
search for the brown glass bottle that I knew held relief.

I found the pills and swallowed one, swigging water straight
from the pitcher to get it down. I lay on the bed and waited.
After a few minutes, a comforting fog began to settle over me,

and I understood, in a way that frightened me, why Ellis and my mother were so fond of them.

I sat up and looked around me. My room was a mess. I'd been living out of my luggage since our arrival, taking for granted that at some point my hanging things would magically be hung, the rest folded neatly in drawers, and my empty trunks and suitcases stored. I realized quite suddenly that this was not going to happen.

After I put everything away, I made my bed, although it was painfully clear that it was an amateur effort. I tugged the corners and patted the surface, but my adjustments only succeeded in pulling it further askew. I decided to quit before completely unmaking it again.

I had run out of things to do. I had some crossword puzzles, a murder mystery, and a handful of books about the monster that Ellis had instructed me to read, but reading was out of the question—not because of dizziness this time, but because my brain was dulled.

I walked to the window and looked out.

The sky was bright, although a solid cloud the color of graphite loomed in the distance. The row houses across the street were a combination of white stucco and pink limestone, with wide brick chimneys. Beyond the houses were hills dotted with sheep, and fields defined by rows of trees. In the far distance were even higher hills, uniformly brown where they weren't forested, their peaks obscured by cloud.

The cold was insidious, and eventually I pulled a quilt from my badly made bed and draped it around my shoulders. I settled into the chair.

Perhaps Anna had misunderstood. Perhaps Ellis and Hank had just gone on a day trip. Perhaps they were finding a new hotel.

I heard footsteps in the hallway, and from the sound of

doors opening and shutting and water running at the end of the hall, I gathered Anna was making up the other rooms. A few minutes after she went back downstairs I heard—and felt—a door close. I went to the window and watched her ride down the street on a dark bicycle with a big wicker basket, her coattails billowing behind her.

Chapter Eleven

I found myself gripping the windowsill, light-headed and weak. The feeling came over me without warning—my brow was suddenly pricked by sweat, and I realized I was going to either faint or be sick. At first I thought it was a reaction to the pill, then recognized it as hunger. The showdown with Old Donnie the night before had left me unable to do anything but pick at my dinner, and other than the egg and few slices of potato Anna had given me the previous day, I'd eaten virtually nothing since we'd left the States.

I'd felt this way before, in my early teen years, and knew that if I didn't eat something very soon I'd collapse. Because there wasn't even anyone around to find me, I had no choice but to go to the kitchen and scrounge. I would find the drawer porridge and take just a small slice, the slice intended for my breakfast, to mitigate my crime as much as possible.

Halfway down the stairs, I was hit by the aroma of roasting meat. It smelled so good my mouth watered, and it almost brought me to tears—Anna had made it very clear what my diet would consist of until I produced a ration book.

The front room was empty, so I slipped behind the bar. I was pretty sure I was alone in the building but paused at the doorway anyway, listening for signs of life. I heard nothing and went through.

The kitchen was larger than I expected, as well as bright. The walls were whitewashed, and the doors and window trim were cornflower blue. Copper pots, pans, and ladles hung from hooks over a sturdy table in the center of the room. A large black stove emanated a gorgeous amount of heat, as well as the heavenly aroma. There was a pantry on one side of the room, and in the opposite wall—quite literally—was a bed. It was completely recessed, with paneled wooden doors that slid on a track. They were currently open, showing bedclothes much more neatly arranged than my own. I supposed it was where Mr. Ross slept.

I marveled at the contents of the pantry—jar upon jar of preserved red cabbage, pickled beetroot, gherkins, marmalade, loganberry preserves, Oxo cubes, Polo and Worcestershire sauces, baskets of onions, turnips, and potatoes, enormous earthenware jugs of vinegar with spouts, canisters labeled TEA, RAISINS, and SUGAR—it went on and on, and I could see even more behind the glass doors of cupboards.

It was the basket of apples I couldn't resist. A bushel basket, full to overflowing. Most of the apples were individually wrapped in newspaper, but a few lay exposed on top, shiny, round, and beautiful. I felt like Snow White, or maybe even Eve; but all thoughts of virtue and drawer porridge fell away when I laid eyes on that fruit.

I was in the act of lifting one to my lips when a female voice spoke from behind me.

"Find what you're looking for?"

I jumped and spun around, simultaneously dropping my hand and curling my wrist, hiding the apple behind my thigh.

Meg was standing just inside the back door, wearing a thick

olive-colored coat and matching cap. She had a cardboard box labeled ANTI-GAS RESPIRATOR slung over her shoulder by a length of string, which she set on a chair by the door. She put her hands on her hips and looked at me.

"Can I help you with something?"

"No, thank you. I was just . . ."

I swallowed hard and clutched the apple.

Her eyes ran down the length of my arm. Then she looked me in the face. After a pause of three or four beats she turned around and took off her coat, laying it over the back of the chair. "When you have a minute, Angus wants me to show you the Anderson shelter."

She removed her cap and fiddled with her hairpins, keeping her back to me. I realized she was giving me time to either pocket or return the apple.

I leaned into the pantry and placed it gently on top of the others. "Shall I get my coat?"

"You can if you want, but I'm not taking mine. We won't be but a minute," she said. "He just wants you to know where it is so you can find it in the dark. The Blackout, you know. Can't even use a torch to cross the yard. Although to be fair, using a torch during an air raid would probably not be the very best idea."

Despite the pill, my heart tripped.

The Anderson shelter was out back, beyond a large vegetable garden. Except for a few rows of sturdy cabbages and chard, the garden was covered in straw.

The shelter looked like an enormous discarded tin can, half-swallowed in dirt and sporting a thin layer of anemic sod. Moss clung to the sides, and a thick piece of burlap hung over the opening.

"So here it is," said Meg, lifting the flap. "You can go in if

you like, but there's not much to see. Just remember there are
a couple of steps down and two bunks at the back. We've got
torches and bedding, in case we have to spend the night. Keep
your coat and shoes handy. Bedding or not, you'll be wanting
them. I've got a siren suit myself. You pull it on over everything, zip it up, and off you go. Have you got any clothing cou-
pons left?"

I shook my head wordlessly.

"Well, never mind. I can get my hands on a pattern if you
want to make one, although you'd have to come up with the
material."

Although it was just past four, the sky had turned the jew-
eled blue of twilight, and I shivered in a sudden gust of wind.

"That's that then," said Meg. "Let's get inside."

She headed back, walking quickly. I broke into a jog to
catch up.

"Make sure you come down for dinner tonight," she said.
"We've a lovely haunch."

"I can't have any," I said, utterly miserable. "I haven't got a
ration book."

"You needn't worry. It's venison."

"Venison isn't rationed?" Hope sprang up like a bird taking
flight.

"They can't ration what they don't know about," Meg said,
"and Angus isn't one to let people starve."

"You don't mean he poached it?" I was aghast the second
the words rolled off my tongue.

"I said no such thing," Meg said emphatically. "But even if
he did—which I did not imply in any way—the taking of a
deer is a righteous theft. He used to be the gamekeeper at Craig
Gairbh, you know."

"Why did he leave?"

"He joined up. And of course, by the time he came back,

the old laird had offered up the house and grounds to the military for the duration of the war. His son was killed, and the laird thought that was the least he could do, since he was too old to fight himself. He was a real warrior himself, back in the day. So for the moment, there's no need for a gamekeeper. At any rate, the only difference between then and now is the title."

"Was he the gamekeeper in 'thirty-four?" I asked.

She glanced over her shoulder and cocked an eyebrow. "That he was."

Which meant he had been there for all of the Colonel's shenanigans, and making it all the more remarkable that he was letting me stay.

When we reached the building, Meg held the door open and let me go in first.

"It wasn't my idea," I said weakly. "I mean, the name thing."

"Oh, aye," Meg replied, nodding. "From what I gather, your husband doesn't consult you about a number of things. I don't suppose you'll help with the Blackout curtains, will you? Only it's getting dark already and I haven't even started the neeps and tatties."

"Sure," I said. Although I was taken aback, it didn't even occur to me to say no.

"Make sure they're nice and tight. Even a sliver of light will get us a fine. Or bombed." She glanced at my face and laughed. "It's just gallows humor."

"Yes, of course," I said, turning to leave.

"Wait a minute."

She went to the pantry and came back, lifting my right hand and planting an apple in it.

I stared at it, nearly speechless with gratitude. "Thank you."

She picked up my other hand and inspected my nails. "You

look like you've been lifting tatties. I'll fix that for you tomorrow. 'Beauty is your Duty,' you know. Keep the fellows' spirits up. And what's going on under that scarf of yours, anyway?"

"Nothing good," I said, clutching the apple so tightly I pierced its skin. "Maybe you could show me how to set my hair with rags sometime."

"Certainly. If you can stand sleeping on them, you can use my rollers." She looked at me critically and nodded. "You have a natural head for victory curls. Go on then—I have to finish up dinner, as well as make myself presentable."

I ate the apple down to a tiny nubbin, leaving the stem and seeds hanging by a fibrous ribbon of core, but it didn't make so much as a dent in my hunger. I hated the idea of going down to dinner on my own, but since Ellis and Hank had left me no choice, I did.

The barstools and tables were taken up by the same men as the night before (with the notable exception of Old Donnie), but this time none of them paid any attention when I joined Conall by the fire. Almost immediately, Meg set an enormous plate of food in front of me.

The venison roast was well done, brown through and through, and served with rowanberry jelly and an ample heap of mashed potatoes and turnips.

I was dizzy with food-lust. I glanced around to make sure there was still no one looking, then ate. It was a struggle to keep to a civilized speed.

The dog, who was once again lying between the end of the couch and the fire, watched with intense interest until I scraped the plate clean, then heaved a disappointed sigh. I'd wanted to slip him a couple of tiny bits while I was eating, but Mr. Ross was behind the bar and occasionally glanced over. He did not strike me as the type to spoil a dog, and I was trying to be unobtrusive. I didn't want to do anything to make him change his mind about letting me stay.

When Meg came for my plate, she brought a glass of beer, telling me it would "build my blood." I'd never had beer before—our crowd considered it lowbrow—and I sipped it with apprehension. It was not unpleasant, and contributed to the warm glow I felt from finally having a full stomach.

It was the only thing I felt warm about. Every time the door opened, I couldn't help looking, hoping it was Ellis and Hank, but it never was, and I began to accept that they really had left me without two nickels to rub together, no ration book, and no explanation.

I wasn't trying to eavesdrop, but since I was alone, I couldn't help overhearing bits and pieces of conversation.

The young men who occupied the tables belonged to a military lumberjack unit, the Canadian Forestry Corps, which had been deployed to supply the British army's endless need for wood, and Meg—who, in the name of duty, had donned a swing skirt, painted her lips red, and once again drawn lines up the backs of her legs—worked with them during the day. The local men were older, several of them bearing obvious scars and injuries, presumably from the Great War. They sat on stools at the bar chatting with each other and paying no attention whatsoever to either the Canadian lumberjacks or me.

At ten minutes to nine, Meg turned on the wireless to let the tubes warm up. When the chimes of Big Ben announced the nightly broadcast, everyone fell silent.

The Red Army was advancing in south Poland despite intense fighting and were now only fifty-five miles from German soil. In one battle alone, they had killed more than three thousand German soldiers and destroyed forty-one of their tanks. In Budapest, during three days of fighting, they had captured 360 blocks of buildings and taken forty-seven hundred prisoners. On all fronts, 147 German tanks had been destroyed and sixty of their planes shot down. And in four days Franklin D. Roosevelt would be sworn into office for the fourth time.

Despite undisputed progress on the Front, my satiated contentment collapsed into unfathomable depression.

In Philadelphia, the war had seemed a million miles away. It was certainly discussed and debated, but it was essentially an academic exercise, conducted over cocktails, or lunch at the club. It felt like theoretical men fighting a theoretical war, and after Ellis was excluded from service we avoided the topic altogether out of concern for his feelings.

Experiencing the U-boat attack and witnessing the terrible injuries of the men who'd been pulled from the sea's flaming surface had thoroughly shredded any sense of detachment I might have had, but I was still having trouble comprehending the notion of three thousand dead in a single afternoon—and that was just enemy soldiers. I'd heard of death counts at least that large many times over during the course of the war, but until that moment, while sitting in a room full of uniformed men and aged veterans, I don't think I truly understood the human toll.

In bed, with my hair in Meg's rollers and my face slathered in cold cream, I had a sudden longing for Ellis, which was utterly ludicrous given that he was directly responsible for my current dilemma. Then I realized that homesickness was the real culprit. The mention of President Roosevelt had set it off.

I wanted to be in my bedroom in Philadelphia, before New Year's Eve, before any of this. I wanted to be safe, even if it meant enduring countless more years of Edith Stone Hyde.

Instead, I was alone in a building full of strangers in a foreign country—during a war, no less. If I disappeared, I doubted anyone would notice, never mind care. At home, at least my mother-in-law would notice if I disappeared—she might rejoice, but she'd notice.

I thought of Violet, and wondered if she hated me before realizing that yes, of course she hated me. All she'd know was that I'd been brought along and she'd been left behind. I wondered what she'd think if she knew I'd trade places with her in an instant.

It then dawned on me that if Hank really hadn't told Violet about our so-called adventure, the only person on earth who knew where we were was Freddie. When Ellis's parents eventually investigated, they'd see that Ellis had emptied his bank account and that we'd left most of our belongings in storage at the hotel, but then the trail would grow cold.

If Hank and Ellis never came back, it was absolutely true that no one would notice if I disappeared.

Chapter Twelve

Anna was mopping when I got downstairs the next morning. Without a word, she leaned the mop against the wall and went through to the kitchen. Breakfast was a piece of gray, mealy toast and another cup of tea made from recycled leaves, unceremoniously delivered.

Since I didn't have anything else to do, I brought a book down to read by the fire, a murder mystery called *Died in the Wool*. The title had seemed a lark when I packed it for the trip, but judging from Anna's expression, she didn't agree.

After I settled into the chair, she mopped all around me, sloshing the gray water noisily in the bucket and wringing the rope mop quite clearly as a substitute for my neck. Finally, she rolled up the carpet so she could clean directly in front of me, all but asking me to lift my feet.

It was almost a relief when she planted her hands on her hips and said, "Surely you're not going to waste another day?"

I closed my book and waited.

"Here's Meg and me both working at least sixteen hours a day, her at the sawmill, me at the croft, and then taking turns catering to the likes of you, and there's you spending your days lolling about by the fire waiting for your meals to be brought and your bed to be made."

I moved my mouth, but nothing came out.

"Why don't you knit some socks for the soldiers, or at least blanket squares?" she asked accusingly.

"I can't. I don't know how to knit."

"Well, *that's* a surprise."

I set the book on the table. "Anna, I don't know what you want me to do."

"There's a war going on, but apparently it's all fun and games for you lot. I can't imagine what you're even doing here."

Neither could I.

When Anna went back to mopping, I got my coat.

After finding the post office and enduring withering looks from the postman, whose fiery and unruly brows looked like caterpillars glued to his face, I sent the following telegram:

DR ERNEST PENNYPACKER 56 FRONT STREET, PHILADEL-
PHIA PA
DEAREST PAPA HAVE MADE AWFUL MISTAKE STOP AM IN
SCOTTISH HIGHLANDS MUST GET OUT STOP CANNOT
BEAR OCEAN AGAIN PLEASE SEND AIRPLANE STOP I
NEED YOU STOP YOUR DEVOTED DAUGHTER

The postman was even less impressed after I realized I had no way to pay him.

As soon as I left the post office, I began to wonder if I'd done the right thing. I hoped so, because the thing was certainly done.

When Ellis returned, I knew he would try to talk me out of going, but since he and Hank seemed intent on leaving me behind anyway, I couldn't see why they shouldn't leave me all the way behind, in the States. I supposed the only reason they'd brought me along in the first place was that Ellis couldn't afford to stash me anywhere else.

I couldn't go back to the inn until I was sure Anna had left, so I wandered around the village trying to find the loch.

The village consisted mostly of row houses and a few freestanding cottages surrounded by stone walls. There were only three stores, and stark reminders of the war everywhere: posters advising to "Make-Do and Mend" along with "Dig for Victory Now!" were plastered on the walls of the Public Hall, and the lone telephone booth—bright red and looking like it was plucked straight from a postcard—was shored up on three sides by sandbags. A group of fast, tiny planes came out of nowhere, zooming overhead in formation and causing me to shriek and duck into a doorway. The only reason I knew we weren't under attack was that the villagers paid no more attention to the planes than they did to me. Not a single person made eye contact with me. I wondered if they all knew I was the Colonel's daughter-in-law.

I came to a school. As I gazed at the children in the playground, I realized that every one of them, as well as all the adults on the street, had a cardboard box like Meg's slung over one shoulder by a piece of string. I thought of Anna's comment about mustard gas and felt suddenly naked.

Most sobering was the graveyard, which contained family stones with the freshly carved names of young men. There weren't many different surnames, and many of the names were identical. I counted three Hector McKenzies and four Donald Frasers, and wondered how many of the latter were connected to the Fraser Arms. Probably all of them, if you went back far enough. Old Philadelphia suddenly didn't seem so old.

There was one stone, still quite new, that I stood in front of for a long time. It was unusual not just because an infant, husband, and wife had all died within two months of each other, but also because the date of the husband's death was vague—only the month and year were engraved on the stone, with a space left for the date. They had died three years before, so I imagined that he, too, was a casualty of war, and that in the chaos the specifics had been lost. There was only one date for the baby. She must have been stillborn, or died immediately after birth. The wife had died six weeks later. Perhaps she'd died of a broken heart. I wondered what it would be like to love that much.

The sky had turned threatening, so I wasn't surprised when the sleet started. I left the churchyard and headed up the road. Not long after, I became so light-headed I had to lean against a wooden fence post until the feeling passed. If I hadn't known better, I might have thought I was pregnant.

The furry white ponies on the other side of the fence came to greet me, pushing their inquisitive noses into my face and giving whiskery kisses for naught. There was nothing in my pocket but a soot-covered, crumpled handkerchief.

Eventually, I walked the long way around to the top of the road where the Fraser Arms was. As I skulked around the bend waiting for Anna to leave on her bicycle, I realized that I'd been all the way around the village and had yet to lay eyes on the loch. On the map, Drumnadrochit appeared to be virtually on its bank.

I'd harbored the hope that at some point in the afternoon I'd see the monster. Not that I had a camera or any way to prove it, and in a way I was glad I hadn't seen it, because it was not a noble wish. I just wanted to see it before Hank and Ellis did, to make them regret leaving me behind—and not just that day, or the day before.

It had always been Ellis and Hank, or Hank and Ellis, long

before our group included Freddie and whatever girl was currently swooning over Hank. It had begun years before that, when they were at Brooks together, and then at Harvard. Even after Ellis and I married, I often felt like an afterthought.

I needed him to comfort me, to reassure me that I was wrong. But he wasn't there. He simply wasn't there.

Chapter Thirteen

Meg corralled me instantly and dragged me into the kitchen to fix my manicure.

"I wondered where you'd gone off to. Just having a wee wander, were you?" she said, pulling two chairs up to the corner of the table.

"Not very successfully," I said. "I never even found the loch. I thought we were right beside it."

"We are, but it's behind the Cover," she said.

"The Cover?"

"The Urquhart Woods. But no one calls them that. It's a dead giveaway that you're an outsider."

"I think my accent already takes care of that," I said.

She spread out a towel, shook a bottle of red polish, and unscrewed the top. As she got to work on my left hand, she explained that while it wasn't officially possible to buy nail varnish, it was sold as "ladder stop" at the drugstore. The idea of using bright red lacquer to stop runs in stockings was so absurd I laughed, and she laughed, too, pointing out that there weren't any stockings to get runs in anyway. And then I felt guilty, because I was wearing a pair at that very moment.

She glanced at my face, then back at my freshly painted fingers, which lay draped over hers. "This color matches your lipstick perfectly."

"I've always worn red."

"Good. 'Red is the New Badge of Courage,' you know. And it brings out your lovely green eyes." She tilted her head from side to side to inspect her handiwork.

Then she sighed. "I'm down to the dregs of my own lipstick. At this point I'm digging it out with a stick, and there's none to be had in Drumnadrochit of any color. I'll have to go to Inverness, although Lord knows when I'll find the time, or the coin."

"I have an extra tube," I said.

"Oh, I couldn't," she said, setting my hand carefully on the towel.

"I insist! And anyway, I'm using your rollers."

"Well, since you put it that way ... You're lucky you can stand sleeping on them," she said, looking up quickly. "Your hair turned out beautifully. Those are some nice victory curls, right there."

I decided that when my father sent for me, I was going to leave all my stockings and makeup behind with Meg.

Dinner was trout, simply done, served with a generous helping of boiled kale and a heap of potatoes. Meg brought me a half pint of port and ginger.

Once again I cleaned my plate, and once again the tall, thin Conall, whom Meg had identified as a Scottish Deerhound, released a disappointed sigh. He'd joined me by the fire as soon as I'd come down, and I was grateful for the company.

It wasn't until Mr. Ross turned the radio on to let it warm up that I realized how late it was, and that Ellis still wasn't back. What had been a fleeting notion the night before returned more urgently, along with all my fear and bafflement. What if he didn't come back at all?

Before he absconded to Inverness, it had never once occurred to me that Ellis might abandon me, but the more I thought about it, the more possible it seemed. If he did leave me, his mother would lobby that much harder for his continued financial support and eventual return to the family seat. A divorce was scandalous, but scandals could be swept under carpets. I could be replaced by a more suitable wife, and the Colonel and Edith Stone Hyde could have grandchildren who were not just three quarters of the right kind, but of entirely the right kind. Upon even further reflection, I realized that the whole purpose of the trip—restoring Ellis's honor—had been mooted the second he was caught in a lie, and that he might very well not want to show his face in Drumnadrochit again. But to leave me behind?

Disappearing without a word was a cowardly way to leave a woman. Beyond cowardly, given that for all he knew I'd been turned out that morning.

When the broadcaster uttered the words "flying bombs," it broke my miserable reverie. Doodlebugs had flattened hundreds of houses in East London, killing 143 people. Survivors were picking through the rubble with sticks, salvaging what they could of their personal belongings, and more than forty-five hundred people were sleeping on platforms in the Underground.

The lumberjacks and the locals, some wearing their uniforms from the Great War, stared at the radio in silent, united resolve.

· · ·

Just after the broadcast ended, Ellis and Hank rushed through the door in a gust of wind and swirl of snow, giggling. Anger flared up in me.

"Darling!" said Ellis, spotting me immediately and coming to kiss me. I turned my face so his lips landed on my ear. His hot liquored breath wafted past my face.

"What kind of a welcome is that?" he said, struggling out of his coat and throwing it over the arm of the couch. He plopped down next to me and looked at my plate. "Good Lord, Maddie. What did you do—lick it clean?"

Hank snapped his fingers in the air and said, "Three whiskeys! Make them doubles."

Mr. Ross ignored him completely. Meg raised her eyebrows and got three glasses from beneath the counter.

"None for me, thank you," I said, lifting my port and ginger. "I'm still working on this."

Hank threw his coat on top of Ellis's and flopped into the chair opposite.

"Where were you?" I asked Ellis.

"In Inverness. Didn't that girl tell you?"

"Her name is Anna. And yes, she did."

"Then what are you upset about? And where are those whiskeys?" he asked, raising his voice and looking around.

Meg appeared with the drinks and slammed them down on the table.

Hank picked his up and took a gulp. "What's on the menu?" he asked. "I could eat a horse."

Meg crossed her arms over her chest. "I could get you a beetroot sandwich, I suppose," she said.

"What did she have?" Ellis said, tilting his head toward my plate.

Meg lifted her chin. "*She* had trout. The last piece, as it happens."

"We have ration books," said Ellis, nodding encouragingly at Hank.

"Yes! Indeed we do," Hank said, leaning over to dig through one of the duffel bags. He pulled out the books and fanned them like playing cards.

"So, what's on the menu now?" he asked, grinning.

Meg snatched them from him and said, "Beetroot sandwiches."

Ellis went stony-faced. "Is this some kind of joke?"

"It most certainly is not," said Meg.

"The hotel in Inverness had beef rissoles. *And* electricity," said Ellis.

"Then I suggest you go back to the hotel in Inverness," she said, spinning on her heel and striding off.

"Fine! We'll have the sandwiches!" Ellis called after her. He threw himself against the back of the couch and drank steadily, tipping the glass to his lips without ever putting it down. When it was finally empty, he set it back on the table.

He looked again at my plate. "It's not like you to overeat. I hope you're not going to make a habit of it."

I was too stunned to reply.

Hank shook his head. "Darling girl, pay no attention. He's sozzled. Here, have a ciggy . . ." He held the case across the table in offering.

I intended to just brush it away, but both our hands were in motion and I somehow ended up smacking it. Cigarettes flew all over. The case bounced off Hank's chest.

The rest of the room went silent. All heads turned toward us.

"Ow," said Hank, examining his chest. He brushed off his sweater and collected the cigarettes. "Maddie, look what you've done. You've broken two."

The landlord crossed the room in long strides and stood in

front of us, hands on hips. He looked at Ellis for a very long time, and then at me, and finally, at Hank.

"Is everything all right, then?"

"You'd better ask her," said Ellis. "She's the one launching missiles."

"Everything is fine," I said quietly, staring at his heavy black boots. I could not look him in the face.

"You're sure of that?"

"Yes," I said. "Thank you, Mr. Ross."

"I beg your pardon?"

"Thank you, yes," I said, thoroughly chastened. "Everything's fine."

After a slight pause, he said, "I'm very glad to hear it."

When he left, Ellis leaned toward me and said, "Have you lost your mind? What is *wrong* with you? You can't go around lobbing objects at people in public!"

"I didn't mean to lob anything," I said, looking desperately at Hank. "It was an accident. I'm sorry, Hank."

He nodded and waved dismissively. "S'all right."

"Well, I don't believe it *was* an accident," said Ellis. "You've been acting like a total bitch from the second we walked through the door."

I caught my breath. Never in my life had anyone spoken to me like that. Even during her tirade on New Year's Day my mother-in-law had referred to me in the third person. And because everyone in the room was still looking at us, they'd all heard.

"Ellis!" Hank hissed, somehow appearing sober. "Get control of yourself."

As I stood, crossed the room, and disappeared into the stairwell, I was fully aware that all eyes were on me, with the exception of my husband's.

.   .   .

This was by no means the first time Ellis had drunk enough to act outrageously—at one party, he'd overturned a full tray of drinks when he felt the waiter was serving them in the wrong order. The frequency of these episodes had increased steadily since his color blindness was diagnosed, but before that night he had never directed his rage at me. I had always been the one who could calm him down and persuade him it was time to go home.

I was doubly sure I'd done the right thing in appealing to my father, and hoped he wouldn't let me down. I also hoped that Ellis would find the monster during my absence, and that it would have the curative effect he was so sure it would, because if it didn't, I couldn't shake the feeling that I'd just had a glimpse of the future.

Chapter Fourteen

At ten the next morning I knocked on Ellis's door, hoping to catch him alone. He wasn't there.

As I descended the stairs, I could see Anna dusting a heavy silver candlestick on the mantelpiece, her face as pinched as if she'd eaten a green persimmon.

I wondered if she'd heard about the scene from the night before. Then I wondered how I was ever going to face any of the customers at the bar again, never mind Mr. Ross.

Hank and Ellis were sitting at a table, wearing layers of heavy wool and hobnailed boots. Bags and equipment were heaped on the floor beside them, along with their coats, hats, and gloves. I couldn't believe it. They were going to leave again.

I sailed past and took a seat by the window.

Ellis joined me immediately. "Darling, what's wrong?"

I tipped my head at the pile of bags by Hank's feet. "Were you at least going to leave me a note this time?" I said, trying to keep my voice down.

"About what?" He glanced over and looked back, surprised. "That? That's our field equipment. We were waiting for you to get up. But I gather from your question you're upset we went to Inverness."

"Without *me*," I said in an urgent whisper. "What if the landlord had thrown me out?"

Anna's duster was poised above the mantel, its feathers quivering. It was perfectly clear she could hear every word.

"I knew full well Blackbeard wasn't going to throw you out."

"How?" I demanded, no longer bothering to whisper.

"I asked him, obviously."

Anna slammed the duster down and stomped into the kitchen.

"You still could have left me a note," I said.

Ellis reached across the table and took both my hands. "Darling, that girl was supposed to tell you. And it's not like I was trying to keep anything from you—Hank and I only realized at breakfast that we needed to get ration books and gas masks immediately or we'd all starve to death, never mind the other possibility. It didn't even occur to me you'd want to join us. We had to beg a ride in the back of a paraffin van. It reeked to high heaven and we had to crouch the whole way. You'd have been miserable." He tilted his head, trying to catch my eyes. "Darling? Is something else the matter? You still look upset."

"Well, I am. Of course."

"About what?" he asked.

"What do you think?"

His face went blank. "Maddie, I have absolutely no idea."

"He doesn't remember a thing," Hank called over from the other table. "One too many libations, I'm afraid."

"You called me a very rude name last night," I said. "*Very* rude. *In public.*"

Ellis frowned. "I would never do that. Surely you misheard."

"I don't think she did," Hank piped up. "I'm pretty sure

everyone in the room heard. Shall I join you, or would you prefer I continue to fill in the blanks by shouting across the room?"

"What did I say?" Ellis asked.

"I don't care to repeat it," I replied.

Ellis squeezed my hands. "Maddie, I'm so sorry. If it's true, I'd clearly had too much to drink—I would never slight you in my right mind. I adore you."

I trained my eyes on the fireplace beyond him, but he took my chin and aimed my face at his. He raised his eyebrows questioningly, beseechingly.

After several seconds, I sighed and rolled my eyes.

"That's my girl," he said, breaking into a wide grin.

"If we're all peachy again, can we get this show on the road? The sun is up, so the clock is ticking," Hank said. "Maddie, darling girl, while you look absolutely stunning, you can't tromp around the scrub in that getup. Didn't you bring something a little more . . ." He stirred the air beside his head with one finger. "I don't know, Rosie the Riveter?"

"Well that's more like it," Ellis said when I came back downstairs.

Hank had gone to a local pier to arrange for a boat, and Anna had returned just long enough to drop plates of drawer porridge on the table.

I glanced down at my dungarees, safari jacket, and utility shoes, and hoped she wouldn't come back out of the kitchen before we left. I felt ridiculous.

"Here," Ellis said, handing me a bright red case made of leather. It had an adjustable strap and a shiny brass buckle. "What do you think? Isn't it pretty?"

"It's very bright," I admitted. "What is it?"

"Your gas mask. The cases have been weatherized, since it

seems to be perpetually raining or snowing," he explained, tapping the lid of his own case, which was dark brown.

I took the mask out to examine it. It was made of pungent black rubber, with a clear plastic window at the top and a strange metal canister capped by a bright green disk at the bottom. Three white cloth straps came from the sides and top of the face and were attached by a buckle.

I had just put it on and was trying to adjust the straps when Hank burst through the door. He stopped just inside and assumed a look of pure astonishment.

"Ellis! You weren't supposed to find Nessie without me!"

I pulled the mask off and stuffed it back in its case. "Very funny, Hank."

"It was, actually," said Hank. "Nobody appreciates me around here. Let's start over. Pretend I just came in. Go on—turn around and then turn back."

When Ellis and I obliged, Hank stepped forward and threw his arms in the air.

"And we are in possession of a mighty sea vessel, ours for the duration!" he announced grandly. After a few beats, he dropped his arms and continued. "All right, maybe she's not so mighty, and maybe it's more accurate to say she's a lake vessel, but I do know she doesn't leak. I took her out for a little test spin."

He clapped his hands in front of him. "Chop, chop, my dearest sourpusses. We're wasting precious daylight. Let the adventure begin!"

Chapter Fifteen

W e walked a few hundred yards north to Temple Pier, a tiny local dock, and set out in a battered rowboat. The plan was to find an accessible piece of land near Urquhart Castle and start surveillance.

When I first laid eyes on the boat and the ladder leading down to it, I balked. Hank and Ellis clearly sensed my apprehension—before I knew it, they'd handed me into it and pushed off, and instead of climbing into the bow behind Hank, Ellis sat next to me in the stern. This left the boat unevenly weighted, and when Hank started rowing, I stayed as close to the middle of the bench as I could, clutching my gas mask case with one hand and the edge of the bench with the other.

The water was eerily black and seemed to move against itself, the top layer gliding across the ones beneath. The bottom third of the oars disappeared with each stroke, and I found myself thinking of what might be lurking down there. I decided to focus on the shoreline instead. It was densely wooded, marshy even, and almost level with the water. Since we were headed south, I realized that it was the Cover, and that the village was right behind it.

"That's the Urquhart Woods," said Ellis, pointing. "Drumnadrochit is straight through there, although you'd never guess."

The banks became steep immediately beyond the Cover and remained so—three to four feet high, with thick scrubby vegetation that reached right to the edge, and trees that seemed to rise straight from the water. We passed two sheep stranded at the brink, bleating and struggling to keep their footing. Their wool was thick and full of twigs, and their skinny black legs bent at odd angles as they tried to gain purchase. Their cries were pitiful, and sounded for all the world like people making fun of sheep.

"How on earth did they end up there?" I asked.

Hank glanced at them and shrugged. "They're not exactly known for their brains."

"Surely we're not just going to leave them there," I said as Hank continued to row. "Ellis?"

"There's nothing we can do about it, darling," he said, prying my hand loose from the bench and holding it on his thigh. "Anyway, sheep can swim. The wool makes them float."

Hank was rowing mightily, and soon the sheep were just tiny dots on the bank. I twisted in my seat, continuing to watch and worry. Even if they got up the bank, how would they ever make their way back through the thorny scrub? I couldn't figure out how they'd gotten past it in the first place.

"Look!" said Ellis, touching my arm to get my attention and then pointing. I turned around and caught my breath.

The castle was on a promontory immediately in front of us—spectacular, massive, and ruined, with a single tower that was missing its roof and much of its face. The surrounding walls and battlements were crumbling and jagged, their stones mottled with lichen and moss.

Ellis watched me take it in and broke into a mischievous smile. "So enlighten us. Tell us everything you know."

The blood rushed to my face. I hadn't read any of the books he'd asked me to.

"You haven't cracked a single spine, have you?"

"I'm afraid not," I said. "But I will. I'll start tonight."

He laughed and patted my knee. "Don't worry your pretty little head. I only got the books to keep you out of trouble on the trip over, although I can't say that was a great success."

Hank snorted.

"Fortunately, I have all the news that's fit to print right here," Ellis continued, tapping his head. "I read everything in my father's library before the Great Purge." He drummed his fingers against his lips. "Hmm, where to start . . . Well, the part you can see from here was built between the thirteenth and sixteenth centuries, and changed hands many times. It was last used by Loyalists in 1689, and when they were forced to retreat, they blew up the guardhouse"—he made sounds like explosions and threw his arms over his head, causing the boat to rock—"so the castle couldn't be used by Jacobite supporters ever again. There are huge chunks of it lying near the entrance."

"Try not to tip the boat, Professor Pantywaist," Hank said. "This particular spot is more than seven hundred and fifty feet deep."

I checked quickly for life belts and, seeing none, resumed my death grip on the bench.

Ellis went on. "For our purposes, the interesting thing about the castle is that it was built on the site of an ancient Pictish fort tied to the earliest monster sighting ever recorded. Saint Columba was on his way here in the year 565 A.D., and several witnesses claim he saved a man who was clutched in the monster's jaws by making the sign of the cross."

I shrank away from the water. "The monster eats people? Why didn't anyone tell me?"

Ellis laughed. "You have nothing to fear, my darling. The worst it's been accused of since is mauling a sheep or two."

Knowing that Anna's cousin had been too traumatized to ever get back on his boat or speak of his experience, I wasn't entirely reassured.

"Here we are," said Hank, using one oar to turn the boat toward a small landing next to the castle. He held the boat steady while Ellis removed his boots and socks and rolled up his pants.

Ellis nodded at Hank, who bared his teeth in a primal roar and dug both oars into the water, pulling so powerfully the veins in his face bulged. He drove us hard and fast toward the shore, and when we hit, I almost came off the bench. The bow lifted, which dropped the stern even further, and I shrieked.

Ellis grabbed a coil of rope and jumped out. The water came up past his knees, soaking his pants to midthigh.

"Shit!" he yelped. "*Cold!*"

Hank laughed as Ellis sloshed out of the water. "Approximately thirty-nine degrees, if I'm not mistaken. Sit in the bow next time, and you'll be closer. Better yet, you can row, Mr. I-Was-on-the-Rowing-Team-at-Harvard."

"Damned right I'll row," said Ellis. "Starting today, on the way back."

He grabbed the bow, hauling the boat toward him. I could feel and hear the gravel scraping against the bottom.

"Works for me," said Hank. "There's a dock at the other end."

"Ha, ha. You think you're so clever, don't you?" said Ellis.

"That's because I am," said Hank. "I keep telling you."

Ellis continued to pull until the boat was solidly grounded.

He wiped his hands on his thighs and said, "That's it. Every-body out."

Hank grabbed the tripod and a couple of bags and hopped off the side.

Ellis reached in for his boots, then helped me climb out.

"At least my socks are dry," he said, glancing at his soaked pants. He was grinning, beaming really, and it was like I'd been whisked back in time.

I was looking at the Ellis I'd met at Bar Harbor—before the war, before his diagnosis, before my own diagnosis, before the rift with his father. The charming, optimistic devil I'd married was still in there, and was apparently just as close to the surface as the Ellis who'd been so awful the night before.

I decided then and there to send a second telegram to my father that rescinded the first. I had to, even though I knew it would infuriate him, because I realized Hank had been right all along.

Ellis *did* need this, and I wanted to be there when he found the monster, to watch his restoration with my own eyes. Just as importantly, I didn't want Hank to be the only one tied to the memories of that glorious day.

Hank set up the tripod and screwed the camera onto it while Ellis spread out a blanket and pulled a variety of things from the bag—beakers, binoculars, compasses, a thermometer, maps, and logbooks. Although I hadn't gone to college, it all looked terribly scientific to me.

I arranged myself on the blanket and looked out over the loch's glistening surface. If Hank was right about how deep it was, I was having trouble imagining it. Were its depths as low as the hills were high? The loch became so deep, so dark, so quickly, it seemed as impenetrable as the fortress beside us once was.

Ellis ran through the plan. "First, we record the temperature of the water. Then we take a sample to see how much peat
is floating at the surface. It affects visibility, and also tells us
how strong the undercurrent is. Then we record surface conditions, weather conditions, wind speed and direction, et cetera.
We'll repeat all of this once an hour."

"And in between?" I asked.

Hank took over. "In between we scan the surface of the
water and watch for disturbances. If you see something, call
'Monster!' We'll confirm its location by compass, and I'll begin
filming. You two keep it in your sights at all times, in case I
somehow lose it in the viewfinder."

There were supposed to be three pairs of binoculars and
three compasses, but one of the compasses was missing. Ellis
gave me one of the remaining two, insisting that he and Hank
could share.

When I finally admitted I didn't know how to use it, I expected some kind of smart-aleck response, or at the very least
an eye roll. Instead, they simply showed me.

"It's easy," said Ellis, guiding my hands. "Turn it, like this,
until the arrow points north. Now, imagine a straight line from
the degrees marked around the edge to the object you're looking at, and read the number next to it. And really, that's all
there is to it."

I successfully confirmed the location of a speck of shore on
the opposite bank, which we decided would define one edge of
my viewing area. I was to start there and scan to the left, slowly,
carefully, before coming back and going just far enough past
the landmark to ensure a little overlap with Ellis. Hank had no
boundaries, which I thought hilarious, but since they hadn't
made fun of me for my lack of technical knowledge, I refrained
from making a joke.

A few minutes after we began, I thought I saw something
and swung my binoculars back. A rounded thing was poking

out of the water, moving steadily, and leaving a series of V's in its wake.

"Monster!" I shouted. "Monster!"

"Where, Maddie? Where?" said Ellis.

I leapt to my feet, pointing strenuously. "There! Over there! Do you see it?"

"Use your compass!" Ellis cried.

"Keep your eyes on it!" Hank ordered, dropping his binoculars and getting behind the camera. He bent over it, peering through the viewfinder, cupping one hand around it for shade.

"I can't do both!" I said desperately. "What should I do?"

"It's okay! I see it!" Ellis shouted. "Maddie, keep your eyes on it. Goddammit, I think we've got it!"

He jumped up and held the compass right next to the camera so Hank could steal glances at it while aiming the lens.

"It's at seventy degrees," Ellis said, coaching Hank. "Still at seventy. Now it's just past seventy. Still moving. Call it seventy and a quarter."

"Got it," said Hank. He began turning the crank handle on the camera, quickly, at least two rotations per second.

I had my eyes locked on the object in the water. It flipped on its back, exposing whiskers and a black nose.

"Oh my God," I said, utterly deflated. "I'm so sorry."

"About what?" said Hank, still cranking away.

"It's an otter."

"Ellis?" Hank said, continuing to film.

Ellis picked his binoculars back up. After a short pause, he lowered them and said, "She's right. It's an otter."

Hank let go of the handle and straightened up. He shaded his eyes with his hand and gazed over the water. "Oh well," he said, sitting down. "Never mind. At least we know Maddie's got sharp eyes."

Ellis recorded the event in the logbook, Hank lit a cigarette, and they passed a flask, which I declined.

. . .

"I'm sorry," I said, after calling the alarm over a duck.

"It's all right," Ellis said with false cheer. "Better to have a hundred false alarms than to miss the real thing."

He duly recorded it. He took the water's vitals again, and we resumed our watch.

"I'm really sorry," I said, after a floating log.

"Never mind," said Ellis. "I suppose it did look a little like a creature's back from that distance."

When I apologized for the jumping fish, Hank said, "Ellis, maybe you could take a quick peek at whatever Maddie's looking at before anyone calls the official alarm?"

"I don't think that's a good idea," Ellis said, clearly dispirited. "Because if it's the real thing, that kind of a delay would give it time to dive down. That's why my father only got three pictures."

I stared at his back.

He really did believe his father. This wasn't just about fixing himself—it was also about vindicating the Colonel. How could I have been so clueless about my own husband? I sat beside him on the blanket, so close our shoulders were touching.

Hank sat next to us and lit a cigarette. "That's all well and good, as long as we don't run out of film," he muttered. "Pass the flask, will you?"

Four and a half hours later, Hank had smoked eleven cigarettes, he and Ellis had finished a third flask, and I had seen a twig, two thrashing ducks, and a second airborne fish.

Chapter Sixteen

When the sun began to sink behind us, Hank declared it a day. They tried to hide it, but I could tell they were both out of patience with me and my false alarms, and I felt terrible for disappointing them. We barely spoke as Ellis rowed back.

I was also anxious about facing everyone at the inn, but there was no avoiding it. I couldn't even slip in unobtrusively because of my Rosie the Riveter getup, never mind my bright red gloves and gas mask case.

It turns out I needn't have worried. I smelled perfume and heard giggling as soon as we cracked the door open, and when we stepped inside, no one gave us a second glance. A crowd had gathered, and this time it included young women.

"Well now, what have we here?" said Hank, casting his eyes around the room.

A dance was about to start at the Public Hall, and the excitement was palpable. Meg and the other girls had pulled chairs over so they could sit together, and were sipping drinks, praising each other's shoes, hair, and outfits, and surreptitiously posing for the lumberjacks, who colluded by pretending they weren't looking.

One girl told how she'd dismantled an old dress her mother had "grown out of" and transformed it into the latest style using a pattern from the most recent "Make-Do and Mend" booklet. Another girl was wearing real stockings, which were the object of much admiration. She extended her leg for the other girls to examine, although there was a great deal of examination from the lumberjacks as well.

"They're lovely," Meg said enviously. "Look at the sheen on them. Are they silk or nylon?"

"Nylon," said the other girl, pointing her toe in various directions.

"Where on earth did you find them?"

"My George sent three pairs from London. He says the girls are stealing them right and left, in plain daylight. Shopkeepers have to store them under the counter."

Meg sighed. "And here we are without a single pair to steal." She turned to a large and ruddy-faced lumberjack sitting at the next table. I realized he was the man I'd seen slipping out of her room. "Rory, next time you're on leave, do you think you can get me some real stockings?"

"And risk being ripped limb from limb by roaming packs of thieving girls?" He flashed a grin. "For you, anything."

Meg turned her leg so she could examine the line she'd drawn. "I suppose I've done well enough with gravy browning and a pencil. But if it rains, I'll have the dogs chasing me again, licking my legs."

"I'll keep the hounds away, canine or otherwise," said Rory, winking. "Go on, girls, have one more drink. My treat."

"Och, but you're an awful one!" said Meg, wagging her finger. "Don't think I'm not onto you. We're all onto the lot of you!"

There were giggles all around as the girls blushed, each

casting a shy glance at a different lumberjack. They cleared out together a few minutes later, laughing and excited, leaving only three older locals perched on stools at the bar.

One twisted around to watch the young men file out after the girls. When the door closed behind them, he turned back.

"Well, I suppose if there's a good time to be a sheep it's when you're a lamb," he said with a sigh.

"Aye," said the others, nodding sagely.

"Say, I don't suppose you want to go," said Ellis, giving me a playful jab.

I tried to smile but couldn't. He'd meant it as a joke, but I would have given anything to be part of that pack of girls making their way to the Public Hall.

I'd never had female friends. My single best opportunity—boarding school—was a complete wash. What happened with my mother ensured I was a pariah before I ever set foot in the place. My next opportunity, the summer I graduated, was no better. It was clear the other girls were simply enduring me in order to gain access to Hank, Ellis, and Freddie, and when I apparently took two of them off the market at once—breaking one's heart and marrying the other—most of the girls dissipated. Hank's sweethearts continued to tolerate me until they realized he wasn't going to marry them, but not one of them had tried to stay in touch after. Violet was the first one I'd felt at all optimistic about, especially since I thought Hank was finally going to let himself be caught.

I felt guilty again about how we'd left her behind.

There was a knock on my door shortly after I'd gone to bed and blown out my candle.

"Who is it?" I asked.

"It's me," said Ellis.

It didn't happen often, but from the tone of his voice I knew what he wanted.

"Just a minute."

I groped my way to the dresser, found the hand towel, and wiped the cold cream off my face. Then I began fumbling with the rollers.

"What are you doing in there?" he said.

"Nothing," I replied. "Just making myself presentable."

"I don't care if you're presentable."

There was no way I was going to get the rollers out in the dark, so I gave up and opened the door.

Ellis stepped in and took my face in his hands, pressing his mouth against mine.

He had shaved and applied cologne, a custom concoction he'd been wearing as long as I'd known him, and although his lips remained closed, I could taste toothpaste. His pajamas were silk.

"Oh!" I said, pulling back in surprise. There was usually no preamble at all.

"What on earth?" he said, patting the sides and back of my head.

Because Lana had always taken care of the serious business of maintaining my hair, all Ellis had previously encountered on my head were bobby pins and a delicately beaded hairnet.

"Rollers," I explained. "I've been setting my own hair. If you give me ten minutes, I'll light a candle and get them out."

"In the middle of nowhere, with no electricity, my intrepid wife still finds a way to be gorgeous," he said. "Hank's right, you know—they did break the mold when they made you."

He pushed the door shut and slipped his arms around my waist.

"After our little misunderstanding, I thought we should make up properly," he said in a low growl. "Also, I was reminded today of just what a good sport you are. You have no idea what it means to me."

He backed me against the dresser and pressed his hips into mine. There was no mistaking his intentions.

"Do you mean for going monster hunting?" I said.

"Yes . . ."

"False alarms and all?"

"Just proves what wonderful eyes you have . . ."

"What about for tolerating Hank?" I asked. "Am I a good sport for that?"

"Positively saintly," he said in a hoarse whisper. He put his hands on my hips and began grinding against me. I leaned my head back, boldly offering my throat. I had never before done such a thing, and when he didn't kiss it, I wondered if he couldn't see it in the dark.

"What about my overactive imagination?" I continued. "And my unseemly appetite?"

"There is absolutely nothing unseemly about you," he said. "Should we light a candle, or just try to find the bed? Is your luggage in the way?"

"No, the way is clear . . ."

"Are you just neater than me or did they put your things away?"

"I think I'm just neater . . ."

"Neater, prettier, quick as a whip . . ."

He guided me backward. When we bumped into the side of the bed, I climbed under the covers and lay against the pillows.

He crawled in beside me, lifted my nightgown, and arranged himself above me. Then he nudged my legs apart with a knee, balanced on one arm long enough to pull down his pajama bottoms, and entered me. After a few pushes, he collapsed, gasping in my ear. A minute later he rolled off.

"Oh, Maddie, my sweet, sweet Maddie," he said, caressing my shoulder.

I wanted to tell him that we couldn't be finished yet, that it wasn't my shoulder that needed attention, but I couldn't find the words. I never had, and I probably never would, because I wasn't entirely sure what it was that I needed him to do.

I lay wide-eyed in the dark long after he'd crept from my bed and gone back to his own.

During my teen years, when my mind turned to such things, I imagined the physical side of marriage would be very different than it turned out to be. Perhaps it was the forbidden novels passed around the dorms at Miss Porter's that set my expectations so high. Perhaps it was the whisperings about girls who had *actually done it* (and anyone who didn't return after a holiday was suspect). Perhaps it was the sight of dreamy film heroes turning their leading ladies into willing puddles of mush with a single, authoritative kiss.

I had high hopes for our wedding night, but it was a complete disaster, with Ellis cursing and thrusting limply while his mother wept theatrically in a room down the hall. I was too innocent to realize it at the time, but I don't think we even managed to consummate the marriage.

Our wedding night may have had extenuating circumstances, but in the months after, when there were none, I remained baffled and disappointed. Either it was over as soon as it began, or else he couldn't finish, which left him extremely ill-tempered. I kept hoping it would develop into something more, something that involved *me*, but it never did.

I thought he must be disappointed too, because the frequency had fallen off the edge of the earth as soon as he had the excuse of my diagnosis, and I never tried to start anything. It was no wonder we didn't have a baby.

Chapter Seventeen

The second day of monster hunting was much the same as the first, except that it was snowing.

I was desperate to get to the post office, but couldn't think of an excuse to slip away. For all I knew a plane was already on its way to collect me.

I continued to see disturbances in the water, but grew reluctant to say anything. Hank could not hide his displeasure at wasting film, and I couldn't stand the look of disappointment on Ellis's face.

The third day was gloomy and dark, and the air was heavy with the threat of rain. Everyone was cranky and cold, and I was even more distressed about not having sent the second telegram.

A few hours after we set up, Ellis realized I wasn't pointing anything out and accused me of not pulling my weight.

Shortly thereafter, I saw a large disturbance very close to the opposite bank and raised the alarm. It turned out to be a swimming stag, which climbed out of the water and shook itself off, right on the landmark I'd found with the compass.

"Wonderful! Fantastic!" Hank cried, throwing his hands in the air. "I've got twenty seconds of crystal-clear footage of a fucking deer. And that's the end of this reel."

He wrestled the camera off the tripod, pulled out the film, and chucked it into the water.

"What the hell are you doing?" Ellis said. "What if we accidentally filmed the monster?"

Hank dug around inside the duffel bag. He pulled out another reel and another flask. "We've filmed plenty of monsters. Maddie's 'monsters,' to be precise," he said, making quotation marks with his fingers before shredding the film's yellow box in his haste to get it open.

"For God's sake, control yourself," said Ellis. "We need the original boxes to send to Eastman Kodak."

"I wouldn't worry. Apparently we're going to have all kinds of empty boxes," said Hank, thrusting the new reel into the camera and then struggling to put the side panel back on. He slapped it twice with the heel of his hand.

"We're not going to have anything if you break the goddamned camera," Ellis barked. "Stop acting like an idiot, and give me the fucking thing. It's not lined up properly."

Hank swung his head around to face Ellis. His eyes were wide, his expression murderous. I thought he was going to throw the camera to the ground, or maybe even at Ellis. Either way, I was absolutely sure they were going to fight.

They stayed that way for a long time, their eyes burning and chests heaving. Then, for no apparent reason, Hank seemed to snap out of it. He reattached the side of the camera, screwed it back on the tripod, and sat down.

Ellis picked up the flask and took a long swallow. He held it out to Hank, pulled it away when Hank reached for it, and took several more gulps himself. When he once again held it out, Hank glared at him for a few seconds before snatching it from his hands.

I was dumbfounded. In four and a half years, I'd never seen Hank and Ellis turn on each other. There had been plenty of bickering and sniping, especially if one of them came up with a quip that hit too close to home, but this was entirely different. They'd nearly come to blows, and probably would have if I hadn't been there.

I was too shaken to keep scanning the surface for disturbances, particularly since my sighting of the stag had caused the explosion. Even so, I ended up keeping my binoculars glued to my face, because Ellis noticed that I'd stopped looking. After that, he spent more time making sure my binoculars were moving than looking through his own.

I couldn't believe that sitting on the bank with a camera at the ready was their whole plan, but despite the scientific trappings and meticulous measuring of conditions, that did seem to be what they had in mind. That, and drinking, and blaming me for doing exactly what I was supposed to be doing.

Finally, I set my binoculars down and said, "Why don't we try something different?"

"What's that?" Ellis muttered with a complete and total lack of interest.

"Why don't we bait it?"

He and Hank lowered their binoculars and turned to face each other. After a moment of silence, they said incredulously, and at exactly the same time, *"Bait it?"*

They burst into peals of hysterical laughter. Hank reached out and grabbed Ellis's thigh, giving it a hearty shake before falling backward and bicycling his legs in the air. Ellis also fell onto his back, hugging himself and stamping his foot.

"Sure," Ellis finally said, wiping tears from his eyes. He looked demented. "We'll string a few sheep up over the water, shall we? Or do you think it prefers children? I'm pretty sure I saw a school in the village."

"Better yet, why don't I just whistle for it?" Hank said, giggling maniacally. "Maybe it will do tricks for us if we offer it a treat?"

"Whistle for it!" cried Ellis. "Of course! Why didn't we think of that before?"

They began howling again, purple-faced, thumping the blanket with their fists.

I clamped my mouth shut and turned away. I'd finally realized what was going on. Although it was barely noon, they were completely sloshed.

An hour later, when the drizzle turned into bullets of water and Ellis and Hank's hysteria had turned back into deadly, drunken purpose, I couldn't stand it anymore.

"I'm going back," I said.

"We can't pack up now," Hank snapped. "There are several hours of daylight left."

"I'll walk," I said, climbing to my feet. My legs were achy and stiff from being folded beneath me. "Where's the road?"

"Right up there," Hank said, pointing over his shoulder. "Turn right. It's only a mile and a bit."

I leaned over to pick up my gas mask. Ellis was watching me.

"Hank, we have to take her."

"Why?"

"Because it's raining."

"It'll be raining on the boat, too," Hank pointed out.

"What if she can't find the inn?"

"Of course she can find the inn. She's a clever girl."

"It's all right," I said. "I'll find the inn."

"Well then," Hank said. "If you're sure."

Ellis was still looking at me.

"It's okay. Really. It's not that far," I said.

Relief washed over his face. "Atta girl, Maddie. You're the best. They broke the mold when they made you."

"So everyone keeps saying." I started up the hill, barely able to bend my knees.

"She's terrific, you know," said Hank. "Best coin toss you ever won. And now I suppose I'm going to be stuck with Violet . . ."

"You shouldn't complain. She's miles better than the mewling, needle-nosed sheep my mother had lined up for me," said Ellis.

I stopped and turned slowly around. They were perched side by side on the blanket, searching the loch through binoculars, unaware that I was still there.

I trudged back to the village with my hat pulled down, my collar turned up, and my hands stuck deep in my pockets. I kept my eyes on the road in front of me, watching the raindrops hit and join others before running off the pavement in rivulets.

I tried various ways of analyzing what I'd just heard, twisting the phrasing in the hope that I might have misinterpreted, and finally concluded that I understood perfectly. I'd been won in a coin toss.

As outrageous as it seemed, when I thought back over our history, there was nothing to contradict it.

We'd all met the summer I left Miss Porter's, when I still hoped to go to college myself. Many of my former classmates were headed for Sarah Lawrence or Bryn Mawr, and while I wanted to be among them, I didn't have a clue how to go about it. I knew better than to expect help from my father, who hadn't even tried to get me into the Assembly Ball, and who had apparently forgotten I was coming home for the summer. A few days after I returned, he left for Cuba, where he spent the summer deep-sea fishing.

Left to my own devices, I packed up and went to Bar Harbor, slipping into the tide of Philadelphians going to their summer houses. My father hadn't opened ours since my mother's *grand scandale*, and going, especially on my own, made me excited and nervous in equal parts. I'd essentially been kept in purdah since I was twelve, and this was my first chance to connect with my hometown peers. I hoped they would accept me, regardless of what their parents might whisper. The girls at Miss Porter's certainly hadn't.

I needn't have worried, because Hank, Ellis, and Freddie took me under their collective wings immediately. They didn't give a hoot about my family's checkered history—indeed, Ellis and Hank had somewhat checkered histories themselves. While they all referred to themselves as Harvard men, Freddie was the only one who'd left with a degree. Ellis was what was euphemistically referred to as a "Christmas graduate"—he flunked out in the middle of his freshman year—and Hank was expelled shortly thereafter for trying to pass off as his own a paper written by John Maynard Keynes. And then, of course, there was Hank's kitchen maid.

Hank was the clear ringleader, a virtual doppelgänger of Clark Gable with a dangerous streak girls found irresistible. Neither the rumors about the kitchen maid nor the plagiarism deterred hopeful debutantes or their parents, because Hank was the sole heir of his bachelor uncle, a Wanamaker who was the current president of the Pot and Kettle Club.

If Hank was Clark Gable, then Ellis was a towheaded, clean-shaven Errol Flynn. He had been on the rowing team during his time at Harvard, and his physique reflected this. His chest was like chiseled marble. He also had a quirky sense of humor I found hilarious—a trait that he, in turn, found adorable.

And Freddie—poor Freddie. Although the men in his lineage had married exclusively beautiful women for generations, he was proof that such planning couldn't guarantee an outcome. His features were asymmetrical enough to be off-putting, and the hair on his crown was already thin. He sported frightful sunburns, and, because of his asthma, was constantly sucking on his Rybar inhaler. I was never quite sure how he ended up being so thick with Hank and Ellis, but he was very kind and he doted on me.

I quickly became their confidante, little sister, and partner in crime, although I was aware that a large part of my appeal was novelty. I was the only girl around who hadn't been paraded under their noses at cotillions, tea parties, and clubs for the last decade, and they agreed unanimously that I was refreshing and modern precisely because my natural spirit hadn't been ruined by grooming for presentation. They toasted my father for neglecting to have me finished, as well as for having the good manners to be otherwise occupied in Cuba.

We spent our days playing tennis, sailing, and dreaming up increasingly outrageous practical jokes. At night we went to parties, built bonfires, and drank ourselves silly.

It was at a beach party, while we were lying on our backs in the sand watching fireworks, that Freddie suddenly popped the question. I was caught completely off guard—I had never even considered him as a romantic possibility—and thought he was joking. When I laughed, his face crumbled and I realized what I'd done. I tried to apologize, but it was too late.

Not a week later, Ellis asked me to marry him. He said that Freddie's proposal had made him realize how much he loved me, and while he didn't want to seem hasty, he couldn't risk another close call. I hadn't realized we were in love, but it made sense. I'd never felt more comfortable with anyone in my entire life—we could talk about anything—and it certainly explained his indifference toward other girls.

The instant I said yes, Hank spirited us away to Elkton, Maryland, the quickie wedding capital of the East Coast, but because of a newly instated waiting period, Ellis's mother managed to track us down. She turned up at the chapel wearing a purple mourning dress, crying hysterically. When she finally realized she couldn't prevent the ceremony from happening, she inexplicably pulled the diamond comb from her own hair and pressed it into my hand, curling my fingers around it.

While this drama was playing out, Hank snickered and Ellis rolled his eyes. They were dressed identically in tuxedos—even the roses in their lapels were indistinguishable—and I remember thinking that either one of them could have been the groom. How right I was.

I'd been won in a coin toss. There had been no duel, no joust. No ships had been launched, no gauntlets thrown. There were no passionate declarations, challenges, or displays about winning my hand—just the toss of a coin.

No wonder the physical side of my marriage was virtually nonexistent, and no wonder Hank was always around. When they'd realized there were Freddies in the world who might actually be serious about me, they'd decided one of them had to marry me just to keep things as they were.

A coin toss, for Christ's sake.

I was soaked through and shaking violently by the time I reached the Fraser Arms.

Anna was sitting at a table with a row of lamps in front of her, cleaning the glass globes with a rag.

"Back so soon?" she said, glancing up.

"Yes," I said.

I closed the door and went straight to the fire. My teeth were chattering, my very bones chilled.

Anna's brow furrowed. "On your own?"

"Yes."

I was aware of Anna watching and girded myself. It was the first time I'd been alone with her since Ellis and Hank returned from Inverness, and I thought I might be in for another tongue-lashing. Instead, she came over and threw another of the mysterious logs onto the fire.

"Get yourself closer," she said. "Your knees are knocking. I'll fetch a cup of tea."

I hadn't realized how cold my fingers were until I held them toward the flame and the feeling began to come back. It was like being jabbed with a thousand needles.

Anna brought a cup of strong, milky tea. I took it, but realized immediately that I was shaking too hard to hold it and put it down. She watched me a few moments longer, then went behind the bar and returned with a small glass of whiskey.

"Get that down you," she said.

"Thank you," I said, taking a sip. The warming sensation was immediate.

We were silent for about a minute before she spoke again. "And they left you to walk back on your own, did they?"

After a pause, I nodded.

She tsked. "It's not my business and I'm usually not one for the blather, but it's weighing on me and I'm going to say it anyway. When your husband and that Boyd fellow went to Inverness, they never asked Angus if you could stay. I wasn't going to say anything, but then he lied straight to your face, and I thought you should know."

I sat in silence, absorbing this. They'd wagered that Mr. Ross wouldn't throw me out if I was on my own, and no thanks to them, they were right. I wasn't just their plaything, their pretty, fake wife. I was their unwitting pawn, theirs to strategically play.

There would be no second telegram.

Chapter Eighteen

After my stag sighting, we fell into a pattern that was as unwavering as it was stultifying. Ellis and Hank left with their equipment every day, presumably rowing to different vantage points around the loch, while I stayed behind and did nothing but grow increasingly depressed about the war and wait for my father to send for me. The weather was so remorselessly foul I didn't even feel like walking.

Hank and Ellis returned each evening obscenely smashed, and arguing incessantly about whose fault it was that they hadn't found the monster. It was like watching a snake try to eat itself from the tail up. One particular night, they arrived so sauced up it was hard to believe they were still on their feet. I was surprised they'd managed to row back, never mind climb out of the boat with all their gear.

Ellis was sure he'd seen the monster and Hank hadn't even tried to film it because *he* was sure it was just another otter, and definitely not large enough to be the monster. Ellis said that maybe there was more than one monster, and although this one might have been a juvenile, it would have been just as useful for their purposes. Hank said he wasn't going to waste film on yet another otter, and Ellis insisted again that it was a monster. An otter, a monster, an otter, a monster—on they went, round and round.

The next morning, I went downstairs and found the two of them sprawled next to each other on the couch. Hank hadn't even gotten dressed. He'd just thrown a robe over his pajamas and stuffed his feet into slippers. He was unshaven and his hair stood in spiky tufts.

Ellis was in even worse shape. It appeared he hadn't made it upstairs at all, because he was wearing the same clothes as the night before. His shirt was untucked and his collar open. His belt and shoes were missing.

Hank pried one eye partly open as I approached.

"Morning, sunshine," he croaked.

"Good morning," I said.

Ellis grunted.

"I'm warning you right now, I'm not rowing today," said Hank. "I'm not even sure I can walk."

"Me either," said Ellis, draping an arm over his face.

They sat in silence for several minutes, not moving even as Anna set cups of weak tea in front of them.

She stood looking at them, and then shook her head. Her gaze moved to me.

"I'll be back with your tea," she said. "It's still steeping."

After she left, Ellis said, "I was thinking, maybe we've worn out that particular vantage point." He neither lifted his head nor opened his eyes.

"Huh," said Hank. "Very possible."

"Maybe we should take the day off and regroup, so to speak."

"I think you're onto something," said Hank.

"Let's reconvene later then, shall we?"

"Absolutely," said Hank. He climbed to his feet, wobbled for a few seconds, then lurched toward the stairwell.

Ellis followed. "Say, do you want to try some hair of the dog?"

"Can't hurt," said Hank.

Anna brought me a cup of strong, sweet tea and returned to the kitchen. I gulped it, collected my things, and headed for the door.

"And what do you think you're doing?" she said, reappearing behind me. "I was just about to start your breakfast."

"I'm sorry. I need to . . . not be here," I said.

"They've gone back upstairs, have they?"

I nodded.

She tutted. "Foolish men. Where are you off to, then?"

"I thought I might go up to Craig Gairbh and have a look at the Big House."

"You canna go there!"

I was stung by her tone. "I was just going to take a peek from a distance."

"You canna go near it at all unless you want to get killed! It's a battle school now, and they train with live ammunition! Many's the morning I see tracer bullets crossing the sky when I'm out milking the cow."

"Oh," I said. "I wasn't aware. In that case, I suppose I'll just wander around."

Anna's outrage fell away. "You stay there a wee moment, and I mean it—no running off on me."

A few minutes later, she was back. She handed me an umbrella and pressed a paper-wrapped packet into my hand. "It's just a bit of Spam in a sandwich. I added some drippings to the bread. You need fattening up. And mind what I said about the estate. There's a reason you don't see any green berets around town. Even the men don't get to come and go—except

Angus, of course, but he knows the grounds like the back of his hand."

I was as lost outdoors as I was inside, but I had to put some physical distance between my husband and me.

We were no strangers to alcohol at home, but he and Hank were now drinking outrageous amounts—dangerous amounts—and I wondered, again, what might happen if they never did find the monster.

Hank would be fine, of course, but Ellis had lost everything. Even if he somehow managed to redeem himself socially, I wasn't sure I wanted to be part of that life anymore, not knowing that my whole marriage—what I'd always thought of as my salvation—was nothing but a pretty, pretty fraud.

And pretty it was: I'd lived in fabulous houses, been driven around in fancy cars, and drunk only the finest champagne. I had a closet of designer gowns and furs. My life consisted of waking at noon, meeting up with Hank and Ellis, and then bouncing from eye-opener to pick-me-up to cocktail to night-cap, and staying out all night at dances or parties before starting all over again the next day. It was full of luxurious trappings and shiny baubles, and that had blinded me to the fact that nothing about it was real.

Growing up as I had, how had I not seen that it was all posturing?

Society's love affair with my fragile, martyred mother came to an abrupt end just after I turned thirteen, when she left a note on my father's desk, secured by a glass paperweight, that informed him she was running off with a man named Arthur.

Seven weeks later, when Arthur was persuaded to return to

his wife by means of social shunning and a few solid turns of the financial screw, my mother also slunk home. She had no choice. Although the money had come from her side, my grandfather hadn't left her in control of it.

My father retreated on an almost permanent basis into his study, even taking his meals there, which left me to deal with her entirely by myself.

She took to her bed, and her weeping became more than I could bear. She was sure that she was the one who'd been wronged, and her indignation was huge—Arthur's lack of chivalry and bravery were incomprehensible. She'd have been happy to live with him in a cave, so passionate was her love, and he'd simply tossed her aside.

When she discovered that the thick letters she sent every day were being returned by the postman and then burned, unopened, by my father, she went off her rocker.

She was furious that Arthur couldn't even be bothered to read the words that pained her so to write. She was furious at my father, for his complete and utter lack of understanding, and also, incredibly, because he, too, couldn't be bothered to read the letters, which she was convinced would move any human being with a soul to forgive her. And she was especially furious at June, Arthur's wife, for allowing my mother's former friends to surround and comfort her.

When none of this worked, she began writing to June instead, warning her that Arthur was feckless and unfaithful— he'd lured my mother in and was responsible for her ruin. She and June had been equally deceived. Couldn't June see how similar their situations were? Those letters were also returned unopened.

In the blink of an eye, my mother had gone from social darling to pariah. It was irrevocable, but she was incapable of accepting that. She showed up at public venues, presumably in a bid to convince people she was still the brave, stoic, tragic Vivian, but no woman would talk to her, and not one man was allowed to.

The injustice of it, particularly when she found out that Arthur was being accepted back into society, pushed her entirely over the edge. She wished my father dead, and cursed her own, consigning him to hell for locking her away from what was rightfully hers. She cursed the servants and fired the housekeeper, whom she suspected of being my father's spy, and whom he immediately rehired. She even cursed me, because if I was going to ruin her figure and keep her trapped in a loveless marriage, I could at least have been a boy.

My mother became essentially housebound, and I became an unwilling confidante. She sought constant reassurance. Was she losing her looks? Was her neck still tight? Because there was a surgery, a thing called a "skin flap," that was supposed to turn back the clock. Did I think she needed one? I did not, but she went to New York and got one anyway. She came back with her face pulled taut and, more alarmingly, full of ideas for the improvement of me.

It was a shame I had not inherited her nose, but there was a surgery that could fix that. I was contrary and worried too much—there was a surgery to fix that, too. It was an easy thing, a simple adjustment of the front part of the brain. I'd be in and out in an hour, and I'd be so much happier. All the best families were having it done. And if somehow that didn't do the trick, there was a promising new treatment in France that involved electricity. It was just that she hated seeing me so unhappy, particularly when a cure was available.

I did not take enough care with my hair, but a permanent wave would fix that. I was not thin enough, but for that, alas, there was no quick fix. I should never put more than the equivalent of three peas on my fork at a time, or one small disk of carrot. I should always leave two thirds of my meal on my plate, and was never to eat in public.

She weighed me regularly, and hugged me if I was lighter. These fleeting moments of affection were enough to keep me drinking my morning "tonic" of apple cider vinegar and eating as little as possible, although occasionally I got so ravenous I would sneak down to the kitchen in the middle of the night and eat an entire loaf of bread. I once ate a pound of cheddar while standing at the sink.

Despite the occasional binge, over the next two years I grew four inches and lost five pounds. My backbone and hips protruded, and there was not—according to my mother—a more elegant neck in all of Philadelphia.

I was desperate to escape. Everyone else my age was already at boarding school, but my mother claimed she couldn't bear to be apart from me, not for a single day, never mind that I hadn't seen her the entire time she was off with Arthur. I had no friends at all. My father wouldn't look at me, and my mother wouldn't stop.

One day, I pulled out the yellow pages and looked up the address of a children's home. In retrospect, stepping out of a hired car in expensive clothing and declaring myself an orphan to the mother superior was probably not the best-laid plan. Certainly I was returned forthwith, and after that was literally a prisoner in our house—the servants were under strict orders to prevent me from going out and to inform my mother if I tried. They had nothing to worry about. I had nowhere to go.

Shortly after my attempt to flee, my father and I met in the hallway, and instead of passing me by and grunting, he stopped. His eyes ran from the top of my head down to my feet and then back, dwelling for an uncomfortable period of time on my hips and chest. He frowned.

"How old are you?" he asked.

"Fifteen next month," I said.

"You look like a damned boy. Where is your mother?"

"In the drawing room, I think."

He pushed past me and stormed away, bellowing, "Vivian? Where are you? *Vivian!*"

When he slammed the drawing room door so hard it shook the walls, I realized that something extraordinary was about to happen. I crept closer, eager to hear. Our housekeeper, Mrs. Huffman, was further down the hall, with her eyes wide and her hand pressed to her mouth. We exchanged a look, agreeing implicitly to eavesdrop. She came up behind me.

There were none of the usual weapons of war: no cool but caustic innuendos, no carefully crafted barbs, and there were certainly no devastating silences. My father's opening salvo was a roar, and my mother's response was to cry hysterically.

I expected her to dash out at any moment, her face buried in a handkerchief, but instead her weeping turned into furious shrieking, punctuated by the sound of things smashing. At the height of a primal scream came the biggest crash of them all—it sounded like a billiards table had come through the ceiling. Mrs. Huffman and I looked at each other in horror, but since the battle raged on, it seemed no one had been murdered.

From him: It wasn't sufficient for her to destroy his reputation by running off with another man? Did her hatred of him really run so deep it now extended to ruining the health of his only child?

From her: She was only looking after my interests, because he certainly didn't. He cared as little for me as he did for her— he'd never loved her, had only ever wanted her money. Was it her fault he was no husband at all? Was it so wrong to want to be loved?

From him: What money? If she was foolish enough to think the proceeds were worth tolerating her antics, she had a vastly inflated view of herself. The principal itself would not be worth the torment of being married to her.

A period of earsplitting cacophony followed, during which they each tried, unsuccessfully, to outshout the other. Finally, my father thundered for silence in a voice so unexpected and frightening he got his wish.

When he spoke again, his voice simmered with determination and quiet fury.

He may have been doomed, he said, but as yet I was not, and since it appeared I was going to be his only child, he would not stand idly by as she starved me to death. I was going to boarding school immediately, tomorrow, as soon as it could be arranged.

The door opened so suddenly both Mrs. Huffman and I had to flatten ourselves against the wall to avoid my mother, who streaked past, her face red and twisted, clutching a handkerchief.

My father emerged a split second later with bulging eyes and a glistening forehead. He stopped when he saw me, and for an awful moment I thought he might hit me.

He turned to Mrs. Huffman. "Pack Madeline's things. All of them," he said, before swiveling on his heels and marching to his study. When he slammed the door, another door, somewhere upstairs, slammed even harder.

Mrs. Huffman and I poked our heads into the drawing room.

It looked like a war zone. Every vase was smashed, every photograph shattered. The curio table was on its side and missing a leg, and, most spectacularly, the grandfather clock lay on its face, its casing exploded, surrounded by splinters of wood, shards of glass, springs, coils, and cogs.

As I surveyed the damage, an immeasurable thrill swelled up within me, the closest thing to ecstasy I'd ever experienced. If nobody smoothed this over, I might actually get out, perhaps even with my nose and frontal lobe intact. For the first time ever, I decided not to go up to my mother, and I prayed—actually prayed—that neither parent would yield.

I did get out. Four days later. But not before finding my

mother submerged in the bathtub, her hair floating around her like Ophelia's, and an empty bottle of nerve pills by her out-stretched hand.

I had broken down and gone upstairs less than an hour after the argument. She had gambled that I would come sooner.

A formation of planes whizzed past, startling me out of my reverie. Meg had told me that "our own fellows" flew by all the time, and that there was nothing to worry about unless the siren was blaring. Nonetheless, it shattered what was left of my nerves.

I walked to the field of white ponies, who once again ap-proached the fence to see if I had anything for them. I un-wrapped my sandwich and offered up tiny pieces of crust, but they yanked their heads back in disgust. Realizing that I'd just tried to feed them part of a meat sandwich, I murmured help-less apologies and then ate the crusts myself. Moments later, I devoured the whole thing.

When I passed the graveyard, a single crow appeared over-head, circling and cawing as though it had a personal griev-ance. It also seemed to be following me. Certainly it was still above me when I reached the entrance to the Cover, and I ducked down the wooded path simply to get away from it. I hadn't gone far before realizing I was being ridiculous, and stopped to get my bearings.

The trees and vegetation were dense, and the ground squelched beneath my feet. I was surrounded by the sound of rushing water, and although the trees were leafless, everything around me was iridescent green, verdant even, with moss cling-ing to the ground and fallen trunks, and dangling in lacy tan-gles from branches.

The forest floor was dotted with beautiful toadstools. They

were tiny and shaped like chalices, their outsides an unremarkable fawn, but their interiors were the most spectacular scarlet I'd ever seen. I picked a few and put them in my pocket. As I did so, I found the compass. It was all I could do to not throw it into the trees.

Before long, I came upon a fast-moving river and followed the path beside it. When it veered sharply to the right, I realized that by ducking and dodging, I could see the loch through the trees.

To get closer, I would have had to cross a stream that was feeding the river. There were stones suitably spaced, but I imagined myself slipping, breaking an ankle, and not being found for days, which was entirely possible if Ellis's and Hank's hangovers lasted more than a day, or if the "hair of the dog" turned into another bender.

The idea of not being found swelled into a frenzied panic when, after forty minutes of trying to find my way out, I realized I was going in circles.

I switched directions. I took different paths. I went back to the loch and used the compass to try to figure out which direction the village was, but the paths were hopelessly twisted and there turned out to be multiple rivers. I was Gretel, on my own, and it was too late to start dropping crumbs, because I'd eaten them.

Maybe Mr. Ross or Meg would notice if I didn't show up for dinner—or maybe they'd just assume I was sleeping one off, like Ellis and Hank. Even if they noticed I was gone, they'd have no idea where to start looking.

What kind of an idiot wanders blithely into a forest?

I was about to sit on a log and cry when I caught sight through the trees of a woman kneeling on the opposite side of the river. She was washing what looked like a rust-stained shirt, rubbing it against a large upright stone. Her hair was tied in a kerchief and her clothes were old-fashioned—a long green skirt made of rough cloth, an apron, and worn brown boots that went up past her ankles.

"Excuse me! Hello!" I cried, stumbling forward.

She stopped scrubbing and looked at me. Her eyes glistened with tears, and when she blinked, a single drop fell into the river. Her lips were slightly parted, exposing a snaggletooth. The whole effect startled me, bringing me to a temporary stop, but soon I was staggering around the winding path, hands on tree trunks, trying to get closer to her.

"Hello! Ma'am? Excuse me! I'm sorry to intrude, but can you please tell me . . ."

My voice trailed off when I came around a bend that should have put me directly across from her. She wasn't there.

I scanned the bank quickly, confirming by the uniquely shaped rock that this was indeed where she'd been. I looked around desperately, listening for the sound of footsteps or crackling branches. There was no sign of her, yet I couldn't figure out where she could possibly have gone, or what I had done to make her flee. It was as though she'd simply vanished.

"Please come back!" I shouted, but the only answer was the sound of rushing water and the cawing of the crow, which was still somewhere above me.

"I'm lost! Please!" I yelled one last time, before sinking to my knees and bursting into tears. I stayed like that for about ten minutes, sobbing like a child.

Eventually, I pulled myself together. I got up, wiped my face with the backs of my gloves, and brushed off my coat, which was muddied from kneeling. Then I straightened my scarf and staggered forward, using the umbrella as a walking stick.

Chapter Nineteen

When I finally found my way out of the Cover, the sight of open sky and the towering, rugged hills made me weep again, only this time with joy and a completely unexpected rush of gratitude to the divine.

Although nominally Protestant, I'd given up prayer many years before. The last time I'd prayed for something, my request had been granted, but the means of my delivery to boarding school had apparently required my mother's death.

Despite my dubious history with God, I was so grateful at being delivered from the Cover that I decided to stop by the church and offer up a small thanks—but only if it still felt right when I got there, and only without asking for anything specific, and only if there was no one else in the building.

I had just climbed the steps when I saw Mr. Ross at the grave I'd found so tragic the first day I'd gone walking, the one with the young family whose members had perished so close together. He had his back to me, but I recognized his broad shoulders and unruly hair.

After a moment he knelt and placed his hand on the granite

marker. He bowed his head and stayed that way for several minutes. Then he put something on the ground, rose, and headed for the gate, where Conall was waiting. He trudged up the road toward the inn with the dog at his hip, never knowing I was there.

I descended the steps and went to the grave. He'd left a handful of snowdrops.

"Willie the Postie came by with some letters for you. I set them by the register," Meg said when I came in.

She was behind the bar holding glasses up to the light and then wiping them with a dish towel.

I hung up my coat and collected the letters. There were several addressed to Hank and Ellis, which I dropped on the counter, and one addressed to me, sent by airmail. I recognized the handwriting immediately. My relief was so great I almost dropped it.

I sat by the fire and tore it open.

January 18, 1945

Dearest Madeline,

I was most surprised to receive your telegram. I can't imagine how you think I could—or would, for that matter—arrange for an airplane to save you from your "awful mistake." Have you any idea what that would entail? Clearly not. I take partial responsibility for that, having shielded you from the realities of life as best I could. You embarked on a most foolish and dangerous endeavor without affording me so much as the courtesy of a discussion, thus depriving me of the opportunity of saving you from yourself—much as you did when you decided to get married behind my back and without my permission.

I had to learn of your most recent hijinx second- or

even thirdhand from cohorts of Frederick Stillman amid rumors of nefarious and, dare I say it, arguably treasonous dealings. Until your telegram, I had no indication that you had even survived the journey. I have taken the liberty of informing the Hydes and Boyds that their offspring also survived, since you did not indicate otherwise.

I wish you had come to me, my dear, but since you did not, I can do nothing for you. I will not bankrupt myself to bail you out of a situation entirely of your own making and that any sane person would recognize as, well, not. Whether you intended it or not, you have once again made my life most difficult.

Most sincerely,

Your Father

P.S. You should probably know that your in-laws are furious, and your friend Freddie has his own fish to fry.

P.P.S. I agree that you should stay away from the ocean. I'm afraid I think you should stay put until the end of the war. I wish you luck.

I stared at the letter long after I finished reading it. He'd written and sent it the same day he received the telegram. I knew that it would be difficult and expensive to arrange for a flight, but it was certainly not impossible. The Germans didn't control the airspace, and military commanders flew back and forth all the time. He'd simply decided I wasn't worth saving, apparently without even taking the time to sleep on it.

I put the letter back in the envelope and tossed it into the fire. Within seconds it was engulfed in flames—white, orange, red—and then finally was just a rectangle of black melding into the charred logs.

I realized Meg was watching.

"Is everything all right?" she asked.

"No. Not really."

She continued to stare at me, but I could not think of a thing to add.

I stayed by the fire through the rest of the afternoon and then into the evening, as the locals filed in and the lumberjacks arrived in groups. I was barely aware of them. I didn't even respond when Conall slunk over and plopped down at my feet.

"You haven't moved in hours," said Meg, bringing me a glass of sherry. "Is there anything I can do?"

"I'm afraid not," I said. "But thanks for asking."

Meg stiffened. "Here they come."

I turned to watch as Hank and Ellis emerged from the stairwell. Although they'd shaved and gotten changed, they looked every bit as sepulchral as they had in the morning.

Meg came over immediately, bringing their mail and a letter opener.

"Two whiskeys," Hank said, taking them from her. "Make them doubles. And keep them coming."

The letters were responses to the advertisement they'd placed in *The Inverness Courier* from people who'd seen the monster and were willing to be interviewed, and the excitement of that—along with the whiskey—brought them both back to life. They consulted their watches and decided that it was not too late to call. Hank waved Mr. Ross over.

"We need to use the telephone," he said.

"It's up the street," said Mr. Ross, stroking his beard.

"What do you mean it's 'up the street'?" said Ellis.

"I mean it's *up the street*," Mr. Ross repeated, folding his arms across his thick green sweater.

"There's a telephone booth just a little ways up the road," I said, not exactly clarifying, but hoping to defuse. "It's not far. I think it takes coins."

"It does," said Mr. Ross, nodding. "Do you need change?"

"You don't have a telephone? You don't have electricity *and* you don't have a telephone?" Ellis said.

"Ellis, knock it off," said Hank. "You're giving me a headache."

Mr. Ross went back behind the bar. Our eyes met a couple of times, and after that I was careful not to look.

I wondered if he'd always worn a beard, and what he'd look like without it. I wondered why he didn't have a wife, for there was nothing wrong with him that a little feminine attention couldn't fix. I wondered what it would be like to be married to him.

I wondered what it would be like to be married to anyone other than Ellis. Had the coin fallen the other way, would I have let myself be persuaded that I was in love with Hank and married him instead? Probably. Either way, I'd have been bamboozled into a marriage as real as the monster tracks Marmaduke Wetherell had pressed into the shores of the loch with his hippo foot.

I was still lost in thought when the policeman arrived, and noticed only because Hank and Ellis fell silent. The tired-looking man, in his mid- to late fifties, stopped just inside the door.

"Bob!" Meg called from across the room. "Bob the Bobby! We haven't seen you in ages. Any news from your Alec?"

"Some. We've had letters. He can't tell us where he is, but he did say he's flying a Spitfire."

"Well, that's something, isn't it?" said Meg. "It's a pally ally you'll be wanting, I assume?"

"I'm afraid not," he said regretfully. "Joanie's had me sign the pledge. Also, I'm here on official business."

"Oh?" said Meg.

The policeman cleared his throat and lowered his voice. "Angus, do you think I might have a wee moment?"

"Certainly," said Mr. Ross, coming around the bar. He joined the bobby by the door.

Hank, who had his back to them, put his finger to his lips. Ellis gave a knowing smirk, and both of them rearranged themselves into better listening positions.

"It's about the ... *incident,*" said the bobby, dropping his voice to a whisper on the final word. "You know normally I wouldn't bother you with such things, but I'm afraid you did throw the water bailiff in the river."

"Aye, that I did. And I'd do it again. He deserved it, speaking like he owned the place."

"I've no doubt, no doubt at all," said the bobby, shaking his head sympathetically. "Only, he made an official complaint up at Inverness, and so I am forced to say something. And there it is. I've said something."

"It's all right, Bob," said Mr. Ross. "I understand."

"Only, could you show just a wee bit more restraint next time?" The policeman held his forefinger and thumb so close they were almost touching. "Perhaps in the future you could just dangle him the tiniest bit?"

"Certainly. Next time I'll just dip his toes. His socks won't even get wet."

The bobby laughed and clapped him on the shoulder. "That's grand, Angus. You know I wouldn't interfere if there hadn't been an official complaint. You know we all appreciate everything you do." He lowered his voice again. "My mother greatly appreciated the bit of salmon the other day."

"Ach," said Mr. Ross, waving him off. "That could have been anyone."

"We know perfectly well who it was."

Our landlord waved again and said, "If your business is concluded sufficiently for the purposes of reporting to Inverness, how about a wee dram on the house?"

"But Joanie's had me sign the pledge . . ."

"Just a wee one. And you know what they say. Always carry a large flagon of whiskey in case of snakebite, and further, always carry a small snake."

"I've not heard that," said the bobby. "Who said that?"

"Some American film guy. Has a potato for a nose. A jowly sort of fellow."

"Well, it's bloody brilliant. But what's wrong with a potato for a nose?"

"Absolutely nothing. And if Joanie finds out, I'll get you an adder. Or throw you in the river. Whichever sounds better at the time, in terms of needing a dram for consolation," said Mr. Ross, draping an arm across the man's shoulders and leading him to the bar.

"Well in that case I don't suppose it would do any harm," said the bobby, a look of relief flooding his face. The men at the bar, the locals, pulled a stool up beside them and welcomed him.

"Poaching," said Ellis, tapping his chin and staring at Hank. "That carries quite a stiff penalty, if I'm not mistaken."

Chapter Twenty

When the siren sounded, I knew instantly what it was. With my heart pounding, I felt my way in the dark to the chair, where I'd laid out my coat and shoes. I was pulling them on when someone flung my door open and hit me in the face with the beam of a flashlight.

"Are you ready?" Meg yelled over the din. She was already zipped into her siren suit, which was made of black-and-red tartan.

"Ready," I called back, hopping toward her while forcing my heel into a recalcitrant shoe.

The siren continued its deafening wail, rising and falling. Hank and Ellis staggered into the hallway barefoot and in their pajamas. Hank was wearing only the bottoms.

"What the hell?" he said, shielding his eyes from the flashlight.

"It's an air raid. Come on! We've got to go!" said Meg.

"To where?" Ellis said, rubbing his eyes and looking confused.

"To the shelter!"

Meg and I pushed past them and ran down the stairs. I heard them clumping after us, cursing as they navigated in the dark.

Mr. Ross appeared at the bottom of the staircase holding another flashlight.

"Come on," he said, waving us urgently toward the kitchen. When we were all at the back door, Meg and Mr. Ross turned off their flashlights.

Meg went out first, and I could see just well enough to follow her. I stumbled and fell to my knees on the frozen earth. Someone—Mr. Ross, I realized immediately—scooped me up and propelled me forward, clutching my elbow with his left hand and keeping his right arm firmly around my waist.

Meg had thrown the burlap flap back and was already inside. Mr. Ross held me by the armpits and lowered me in, handing me to Meg.

"Mind your head. There's a bunk at the back," she said, pulling me in deeper and leading me to it. "There's another above it, so mind your head there, too. When everyone's in, Angus will get a light on."

She sat beside me and leaned in close. I huddled against her and we clutched hands. It smelled damp and earthy, and was terribly, terribly cold.

Outside, the men were shouting. Hank and Ellis were arguing that they'd never laid eyes on the shelter in the daylight so how were they supposed to know where it was or how to get in, and couldn't Mr. Ross shine the light on it for just a moment? He replied that he didn't care what the hell they did or did not know, and to get the bloody hell inside.

My voice came out as a raspy screech: "Ellis! Hank! Get in here! It's two steps down. Climb in backward if you have to, but hurry up!"

"Get in, *amadain*!" Mr. Ross bellowed. "Just get in!"

"I would, if I could just fucking— Hey!"

There was some kind of kerfuffle at the front of the shelter, followed by a thud, and a vile stream of curses from Hank. There was another thud, and this time I heard someone scraping toward us.

"We're back here," I said, reaching my arms out. My hands found the top of Ellis's head, and then his shoulders. He was crawling.

"There's a bunk right here," I said.

"Conall, *thig a seo*!" Mr. Ross yelled, and shortly thereafter, he turned on his flashlight.

The burlap flap was closed. We were all inside. Our breath curled like smoke from our mouths, and Mr. Ross's expression was so fierce that while I knew his eyes were blue, at that moment I would have sworn they were black.

When Ellis saw that the bunk we were sitting on was made up, he grabbed the top quilt with both hands and yanked it out from under us, nearly dumping Meg and me on the floor.

"Hey!" I said. "Was that really necessary?"

"I'm fucking freezing," he said, wrapping himself in it.

"Throw me one of those," said Hank, who was crouched barefoot against the corrugated wall. "I can see my goddamned breath."

"Get it yourself," said Ellis. "I'm as naked as you are."

"Oh, for the love of God," said Meg, and without even thinking I turned to help her rip another quilt loose, this time nearly toppling Ellis. She balled it up and threw it overhand at Hank. He wrapped it around his shoulders and made his way to the back of the shelter, climbing onto the bunk above us.

The wailing of the siren continued.

"You've not got your gas masks?" said Mr. Ross.

I glanced quickly and saw that Meg had brought hers.

"No," I said. "I'm very sorry."

He tossed his into my lap.

My hands shook as I tried to put it on. The smell of rubber was stifling, my area of vision vastly limited, and I couldn't get the straps over the rollers in my hair. Meg pulled her mask on in a single fluid motion and turned to help me.

"Hold still," she said in a muffled voice. "I just have to thread the straps through . . . There's one . . . There's another . . . Wait . . . I've almost got it . . . And there you are. Nice and tight."

The combination of screaming siren and having my head confined sent me spiraling into panic. It was as though I was back on the SS *Mallory* during the U-boat attack. I felt like I couldn't breathe, although clearly I could, because the inside of my mask was so fogged up I couldn't see a thing. When I tried to wipe it from the outside, Meg pulled my hands from my face and held them against her thigh. "It takes a bit of getting used to. Just breathe normally and it will clear up."

I closed my eyes and took deep, deliberate breaths.

"That's it," she said. "In through the nose, and out through the mouth. In, and then out. That's better already, isn't it?"

When I opened my eyes, the window of my mask was starting to clear.

"What about me? I don't have a mask," said Hank, from the bunk above us.

"You'd take one off a woman, would you?" Mr. Ross snapped.

Hank was silent for a moment, and then added, in a tone that could be interpreted as chastened, resigned, or both, "I don't suppose there's any whiskey in this tin can?"

Mr. Ross threw him a look of disgust and turned off the flashlight. The starry sky was briefly visible as he went through the flap. A moment later he returned and switched the light back on. He'd retrieved a rifle and was crouched with it by the opening. Just as I remembered his missing trigger finger, I realized he was holding it by his left side.

"How long is this going to take?" Ellis asked. He was curled into a ball in the corner of the bunk, wrapped in the quilt. "I think I'd rather take my chances inside."

Mr. Ross held his hand up for silence, listening, concentrating.

From far in the distance, over the siren's wail, came the *boom-boom-boom-boom* of large engines.

"Bloody hell," he said, leaping to his feet and pumping the rifle.

"What? What's wrong?" said Ellis.

"A fucking Heinkel."

The light went off and he slipped outside with an untranslatable growl. The booming got closer and louder until suddenly it was right over us and Mr. Ross was shouting—and shooting—at it.

"Thall is cac, Mhic an Diabhail!"

After the second shot, the sound of the airplane changed from a steady set of booms to three followed by a gap. It continued on, limping into the distance.

Mr. Ross climbed back inside the shelter and turned the flashlight on again.

"Did you just do what I think you just did?" said Meg.

He shrugged.

"Did you just shoot out an engine?"

"It doesn't matter if I did. He's got three more."

"But with a rifle?"

"The *shite* was right over our heads. I could have jumped up and touched—"

He was interrupted by a huge explosion in the distance, followed immediately by another—a terrible sound that reverberated across the water and through the glen. I screamed into my mask and grabbed Meg, who gripped me just as tightly.

After about twenty minutes, which felt like twenty years,

the siren rose to its highest pitch and stayed there, before finally dropping off into silence.

"What's that? What does that mean?" said Hank, who remained on the top bunk.

"That's the all clear," said Meg, removing her mask. She was pale. "Sweet Mother of God. I wonder where that was?"

Mr. Ross set his rifle down and simply shook his head.

"Please God they didn't hit anyone," said Meg, pressing her fingertips to her temples.

"Aye," said Mr. Ross, nodding slowly.

I tried to pull off my mask, which wouldn't budge, so I yanked even harder. Meg stilled my hands and got me free. I'd forgotten she'd threaded the straps through my rollers.

Without a word, Mr. Ross shut off the flashlight and left the shelter, leaving the flap open.

"Come on then," said Meg. She and I felt our way to the front and climbed out. I could see Mr. Ross's silhouette as he trudged across the yard toward the inn, Conall at his side. He never looked back.

Meg and I linked arms, feeling our way together across the frozen earth, and trying not to step on the precious winter vegetables. Hank and Ellis followed.

Moments after I reached my room, there was a knock on my door.

"Maddie? Darling?" said Ellis.

"I'm getting ready for bed."

"Maddie, please. I need a pill."

I let him in.

"They're in the top drawer," I said.

Ellis yanked it open and rummaged around until he found the bottle. I could tell from the rattling that he was taking more than one. He kept his back toward me until he'd tossed them in his mouth.

"Do you want one?" he asked, after gulping them down with water from the pitcher. It dribbled down the front of his pajamas. "Fuck," he explained, wiping his mouth with the back of his hand.

"I'm fine," I said.

"You must be shattered. Here, take these." He shook a couple of pills into his hand and held them out to me.

"Put them on the dresser," I said.

I took my coat off, folded it in half, and laid it over the back of the chair. Then I lined my shoes up beneath the chair's edge, where I wouldn't trip over them.

Ellis watched with narrowed eyes. "Were those laid out for you?"

Instead of answering, I smoothed my coat, brushing off the frost.

"They were, weren't they?" he insisted. "That's why you were able to get them on so quickly."

He glanced at the dresser drawer he'd left open, at the clothes that had been folded until he'd messed them up. He stepped across the room and opened my closet, revealing dresses and other items on hangers.

"They've put your things away," he said indignantly. "You should see the state of my room. It's like they're refusing to do it on general principle."

"I put my own things away."

It took him a second to respond. "You did what?"

"I did it myself."

He blinked at me in disbelief. "Darling, you know better than that. What were you thinking?"

He launched into a speech about the dangers of making excuses for the help, and how slippery a slope it was from there to familiarity, and then Heaven only knew where it would end, but certainly not well. If Hank's kitchen maid wasn't proof of that, he didn't know what was. Mrs. Boyd had nearly gotten into a legal pickle sorting that mess out. Maintaining a proper distance was crucial, and he certainly hoped I wasn't . . .

I stared in fascination, watching his tongue undulate behind his teeth. Once, a string of saliva attached itself to his lips and survived the length of a few words before snapping. His nostrils flared beneath his pinched bridge. Deep lines appeared between his eyes, and when he tilted his chin so he could look down his nose at me, I could have sworn I was looking at his mother's head spliced onto his body, a living, breathing cockentrice that had climbed off its platter and spat the apple out of its mouth so it could yammer at me about how surely even I could see that my blurred boundaries not only encouraged the lower classes to be lazy, but threatened the very social structures our lives were built upon.

I realized that he'd stopped talking.

"Maddie?" he said, peering closely at me. "Are you all right?"

"I'm fine," I said, trying to shake the image from my head. "It's just been a long night, and I'd like to get to bed."

His expression softened. "I'm sorry, darling. Sometimes I forget how fragile you are. I shouldn't have scolded you, especially right after . . ."

He left the sentence unfinished, having apparently decided that reminding me of the air raid would send me over the edge.

"Can you forgive me?" He took a step toward me, and I instinctively held up my hand. He stopped, but looked hurt.

I gripped the back of the chair and trained my eyes on the grate. There was no point in telling him that his behavior in the shelter had been a degree worse than ungentlemanly. I wasn't looking for an argument.

"And now I'm the one who's sorry," I said, turning to face him. "I didn't mean to be prickly. I just need to sleep."

"Yes, of course," he said, becoming the epitome of chivalry. "But if you need anything, anything at all, you know where to find me. And make sure you take your pills. Even if you're not having an episode, they'll help you sleep."

As soon as he left, I went to the door and turned the lock. I also slid the bolt.

When I put the pills he'd set out back in the bottle, I was alarmed by how many were missing.

Twenty minutes later, there was another knock.

I turned my back to the door and pulled the pillow up around my face. If I ignored him, surely he'd assume I was asleep and leave me alone.

"Mrs. Hyde?" said Meg.

Seconds later, I was standing at the open door.

"Meg—is everything all right?"

"Perfectly," she whispered. "Except my feet are freezing, and I thought yours might be too, so I brought you a pig."

She thrust a hot water bottle made of stoneware into my arms. It was indeed shaped like a pig, complete with snout.

"Thank you," I said, clutching it. Though it made no sense, I shivered all the more for its heat.

"Best close the door now. I've only brought the two, and I'm not going back for more—not for the likes of them, anyway. I've got to be up and out in less than four hours."

I shook my head in the dark. "I honestly don't know how you do it."

She let out a quiet laugh.

"Me either. No choice, I suppose."

Chapter Twenty-one

When I dragged myself downstairs in the morning, I found Ellis and Hank in unusually good spirits, not in spite of being wrenched out of their beds in the middle of the night, but because of it.

As they revisited the air raid over the breakfast table, the details matured. By the final retelling, Ellis had made sure that everyone else was safely in the shelter before coming in himself, Hank had positioned himself on the bunk above Meg and me to shield us with his own body, and Mr. Ross was barely present.

Anna's demeanor got stonier and stonier as she served and cleared breakfast.

Hank decided he would write to Violet, musing that perhaps the idea of his being in mortal danger would loosen her draconian premarital rules.

"You and she are premarital now, are you?" said Ellis.

"Well, *pre*-premarital, at least," said Hank. "But still, I think I ought to be able to sample the goods. What if I wait

until the wedding night and then find I'm stuck with something subpar until death do us part?"

"*Hank,*" I said urgently.

"What?"

"In case you've forgotten," I continued in a lowered voice,
"you're in mixed company."

"Darling girl, when did you become such a prude?"

"I don't mean me." I cut my eyes over to Anna.

"Oh," he said, furrowing his brow.

He changed the topic to monster hunting, but not before
giving me an odd look. It was perfectly obvious that he hadn't
registered Anna's presence at all.

The front door opened, and a handsome ginger-haired man in
shabby clothing came in. He nodded at Hank and Ellis, set the
two baskets he was carrying on the floor, and turned his attention to the door, swinging it back and forth until he identified
the point at which it squeaked most loudly. He was young
enough to be fighting, and I wondered why he wasn't—not
that I would judge, but I was certainly sensitive to the issue.

"Well, whadya know," Hank said to Ellis. "It's George the
Vannie. Maybe he'll give us a lift again."

"Aye aye, George," said Anna, appearing behind the bar.
"And how are you getting on?"

"You're seeing it. Although it's right dank, the day," he said,
closing the door and carrying his baskets to the bar.

I couldn't help staring. He walked from side to side, almost
like a penguin, swinging his right leg forward from the hip.
The leg was false.

"And what have you got for me today?" asked Anna.

"Paraffin, naturally. Plus a packet from the laundry and
some things from the butcher."

"Well, let's see them."

"There's mutton shanks and some lovely sausages," said George, hauling them out and setting them on the bar. The meat was unwrapped with the price drawn directly on it.

Anna leaned over to sniff it. When she stood back up, she put her hands on her hips.

"And I suppose our sheets are also smelling like paraffin?" she asked accusingly.

"Just pitching in to save petrol," said George. "They'll air out. Put them in the meat locker and they'll be right as rain."

"I'm to put the sheets in the meat locker, am I?" Anna said with a long-suffering sigh. It was apparently a rhetorical question, because she turned and took the meat through to the back.

"Shall I oil the door for you, then?" he called after her. "It screeches like someone caught a cat by the tail."

He craned his neck, peering through the doorway and waiting in vain for an answer. Eventually he gave up.

"Well, I'm off then," he said to the three of us. "Tell her I'll be back to fix the door."

"Say, I don't suppose you're going anywhere near the Horseshoe, are you?" Hank asked.

"I wasn't, but I suppose I could be."

"Same terms as before? Perhaps a little extra for your trouble?"

"I'd be a fool to say no," said George. "Are you ready now, or shall I come back when I've finished my rounds?"

Hank drained his tea and lifted his duffel bag. "Ready when you are. Why don't you drop us off at the telephone and collect us when you're done? We have some calls to make."

Ellis kissed my cheek before he left.

Anna came back from the kitchen and cut the strings on the parcels of sheets. She flipped a few folds open and sniffed the creases.

"Oof!" she said, waving a hand in front of her nose. "I'd hang these out back if it weren't for the snow. Maybe if I leave the quilts off and open the windows for a few hours ... And I suppose it's paraffin pie I'll be making for dinner tonight." She glanced sideways at me. "I can't help but notice you've not gone with them for a week and a half."

"Can you blame me?"

"Not a bit," she replied. "They're that *sleekit* you might turn around and find they've left you at the side of the road."

After a few seconds, I said, "Anna, can you teach me to knit?"

She had started refolding the sheets. She stopped.

"Come again?"

"You once asked if I could knit. I can't. But I want to. I want to knit socks for the soldiers."

"It's not as easy as that," she said, looking at me strangely. "It's difficult to turn a good heel. There are competitions over it."

"What about squares? Surely I could learn to knit squares. Are those also for the soldiers?"

"Mrs. Hyde——" she said.

"Maddie. Please call me Maddie."

"I'm very sorry, but I don't have time to teach you how to knit."

"Then can I help you with the housework?"

She shook her head vigorously. "Oh, I don't think so. No, I don't think that would be wise at all."

"But why?" I pleaded. "When we first got here, you accused me of 'lolling about by the fire,' and it's true. It's what I do all day, every day, and it's driving me mad, but I'm stuck here until my husband either finds the monster or gives up on it. Please—— your load would be lightened, and I'd be so happy to have something to do."

She frowned. "Your husband would never approve, and I don't suppose Angus would either."

"They'll never know. I won't say a word to anyone, and I'll turn back into my usual idle self the second anyone else steps in the door."

Her hands went still, and I knew she was considering it.

"Have you ever made a bed?" she finally asked.

"Yes," I said. "Well, once."

She did a double take, then returned to folding. "I suppose if I change the sheets, you'd only have to put the quilts back on. And Mhàthair did ask me to pick up a few things at the shops this afternoon . . ."

"I can do more than just put the quilts on. I can also put their things away."

She gave a sharp laugh. "Well, that would be an immense improvement. I've fairly given up hope in that regard."

"So have they," I said solemnly.

Her eyes widened. "I beg your pardon?"

She stared at me, daring me to deny it. Instead, I nodded.

"Oh, no, they *never* did think," she said indignantly. "They could *not* have expected . . ."

"Yes, they most certainly did." I raised my eyebrows for effect. "And still do."

Her eyes blazed. "Well, in *that* case, I'll just get these on the beds and leave you to it. Because if you don't do it, I cannot see how it's *ever* going to happen, and if nobody ever does it, I'll never be able to sweep the carpets again."

She scooped the sheets off the bar and sailed away, her bosom hoisted like the prow of a Viking ship.

I don't know if I was more astounded at having talked her into the idea, or at coming up with it in the first place.

· · ·

While Anna changed the sheets, I flipped through the newspaper to see if there were any details about the bombs we'd heard drop. There weren't, but of course the paper would have already gone to press by the time it happened. There was plenty of other news though, and as I read it, my optimism about having found something to do with my days crashed into bleak depression.

The juggernaut that was the Russian army was now only 165 miles from Berlin, and Marshal Stalin had announced that in one advance in Silesia alone they'd left behind sixty thousand dead Germans and taken another twenty-one thousand prisoner. It was a victory for our side, but I could not feel anything but a grim acknowledgment of progress.

So many dead. Only two weeks earlier, I had found the idea of three thousand men killed in a single afternoon nearly impossible to comprehend. The sheer vastness of sixty thousand deaths was even more numbing. It made it almost possible to forget that each and every one of the dead had been an individual, with hopes and dreams and loves now snuffed.

I did not see how this could go on. The world would run out of men.

When Anna came back downstairs, I was sitting with the newspaper open in my lap, staring at the wall.

"You've not had a change of heart, have you?" she said.

"Not at all," I said, forcing a smile. I folded the newspaper and stood. "So besides straightening everything and putting the quilts back on the beds, what else should I do? Fill the pitchers?"

She frowned in temporary bafflement. "Oh, you mean the *jugs*? Don't worry about that. I'll finish up after I've been to the shops."

"It's okay, Anna," I said. "Even I can't mess up filling pitchers—or rather, jugs—and you can check my handiwork when you get back."

She tsked. "Oh, I'm not worried. Well, all right. Maybe I'll have a wee peek, but just for the first few days." She dug a key out of her apron pocket and held it out to me. "Here's the master."

I took hold of it, but it was several seconds before she let go.

I started with Meg's room, which was easy because she was tidy, and worked my way down the hall.

Hank's room was about as I expected. His clothes were mostly out of his luggage and scattered across the floor, and the rest looked like they were trying to make a slithering escape. I piled everything temporarily on the bed and began dragging his trunks and suitcases into the closet.

One trunk appeared to be full of stockings and cigarettes, but when it refused to budge, I dug beneath the top layers and found dozens of bottles of liquor. They were buffered by straw and cardboard, but I was surprised they'd survived the trip. Hank's cache of international currency was so heavy I had to get down on my hands and knees and brace a foot against the bed to shift it, but eventually I forced it into the closet.

I was out of breath. Although the window was wide open, my blouse was sticking to my back, and this was before I had even begun to address the remaining mess.

It felt oddly intimate to be touching things like his socks and pajamas, never mind his underpants, but I soon got into a rhythm. At least he'd thrown his dirty clothes into one pile, so I didn't need to inspect anything too closely in that regard.

Just when I thought I'd put everything away, I caught sight of something under the bed. It was a stack of postcards, and when I picked them up was shocked to find I was looking at a naked woman. She was reclining on a chaise longue with her legs apart, wearing nothing but a long string of pearls and a tiara.

I glanced through the rest of them, fascinated. I had never seen a fully naked body except my own—Ellis had always gotten straight to business with as little displacement of clothes as possible, and always in the dark—and was surprised at how different they were. One lay on her back on a white horse, letting one leg dangle so the camera could focus on the dark area between her legs. Another was on all fours on a picnic blanket, smiling over her shoulder at the photographer. Her legs were parted just enough that her dangling breasts were visible between them, so large they almost looked weighted. Mine were tiny by comparison.

When I came to the final card and realized there was a naked man in it as well, pressed up behind the woman and cupping her breasts, I became suddenly self-conscious and eager to be rid of them. I pulled open the drawer of the bedside table and, as I did, saw a small package labeled DOUGH-BOY PROPHY-LACTIC. I had always thought a prophylactic was a toothbrush, but when I saw the words "for the prevention of venereal disease," I realized it was something quite other. I dropped the postcards inside and closed the drawer. I didn't want to learn anything else about Hank, and was glad that I'd finished his room.

I braced myself for the next, afraid of what I might learn about Ellis.

Although I thought I was prepared for anything, I was wrong. When I opened Ellis's door, I stopped in my tracks, utterly stupefied. It looked as though a bomb had gone off. Clothes of all kinds, including his underpants, were strewn everywhere—flung over the bedposts, the back of the chair, even over the fire irons. There were heaps in corners, under the bed, and in the middle of the floor. His shoes, toiletries, and other sundries were scattered everywhere, and the only thing that had found its way onto the dresser was a slipper.

I couldn't imagine how he'd managed to create such a mess. Then, with a wave of nausea, I realized he'd done it on purpose.

I could see it clearly: every time he discovered that his belongings still hadn't been put away, he'd upped the ante by reaching into the trunks and throwing armloads of anything that came to hand into the air, kicking it all as it fell. How else to explain the toothbrush sticking out of a shoe, or the comb and hair pomade beneath the window? It was brutish, childish, and destructive, and it frightened me.

I started in the far corner and worked my way out. I could think of no other way to approach the mess that wasn't overwhelming.

When I opened his top dresser drawer, I found a photograph of Hank and him standing on the beach at Bar Harbor, their arms slung casually over each other's shoulders and grinning into the sun. Beneath it was a photograph of Hank alone, standing shirtless on the deck of a sailboat with his hands on his hips. His chest glistened, his arms and shoulders were muscled, and he smiled mischievously at whoever was behind the camera. There was no picture of me, although I must have been around.

In the next drawer down, I found several monogrammed handkerchiefs folded into packets. I opened them and counted more than a hundred of my pills. Then I folded them back up and left them where they were. I didn't want him to think that Anna or Meg had taken them.

I had been locking my door only at night but decided to start keeping it locked during the day as well. I wanted to see how long it took him to go through that many pills.

.   .   .

I wondered if anyone other than Anna had seen the condition of Hank's and Ellis's rooms. I hoped not. I could only imagine what she thought of them and, by association, me.

Both of them would come back and see that everything had been put away and think nothing of what the person who'd done it had seen or thought. Indeed, they wouldn't think of the person at all, except perhaps to feel victorious.

Although I'd unpacked my own things after only a couple of days, I was ashamed of how much I'd always taken for granted. I wondered how Emily was faring, and wished I could let her know how grateful I was for everything she'd done for me over the years. I couldn't imagine it was easy being Edith Stone Hyde's maid at that particular moment in time.

When the rooms were all finished and I'd replaced the quilts, closed the windows, and put up the Blackout frames, I slipped a few pairs of silk stockings from my own supply into Meg's top drawer.

Chapter Twenty-two

When I returned to the kitchen, Anna looked at me in surprise.

"Surely you're not finished!" she said.

"I am."

"And you've put all their things away?"

"I have."

"Well, if that doesn't call for a cup of tea, I don't know what does. Get settled by the fire and I'll be right out. I think we deserve a proper *strupag*, don't you?"

"So, are the sheets still smelling of paraffin?" Anna asked, sipping daintily from a teacup decorated with primroses and edged with gold leaf.

She'd brought out oatcakes and jam along with the tea, which was the strongest I'd seen yet, all of it served on fine china. She'd even put a doily on the tray.

"I didn't smell anything," I said.

"Good. Because the wash is not a job I'm keen on doing myself. There's some that won't send it out because they're afraid it'll come back with lice." She harrumphed. "Personally, I'm more afraid of what George will put next to it in that van of his."

"Why on earth would it come back with lice?"

"Because the same laundry facility also does the wash for the men at the Big House and forestry camps. It's mostly old folk and Wee Frees who worry about it, but I suspect the real problem is that sending your wash out smacks of being a luxury. I'm just grateful Mhàthair isn't of that opinion— she's about as strict as they come, being old *and* a Wee Free."

The top log on the fire slid toward us, sending up a cascade of sparks. Anna rose and jammed it back into place with the poker.

"And stay there!" she scolded, watching it for a few seconds before sitting back down.

"That may explain the old woman doing her laundry in the river the other day," I said. "Although it seemed a very odd place to do it."

Anna set her tea down. "I beg your pardon?"

"I got lost in the Cover, chased in by a crow of all things. I thought it was following me."

I was suddenly aware that the atmosphere had changed. I looked up to find that Anna had gone pale. I ran through what I'd said, wondering which part could possibly have caused offense.

"I'm sorry," I said, panicked. "I don't really think that."

Anna continued to stare at me.

I put my tea down, afraid I would spill it. "Please forget I said anything. I have an overly active imagination."

"Who was doing laundry where?" she asked sharply.

"An old woman was washing a shirt in the river. She didn't

answer when I asked for help. Then, when I tried to get closer, I couldn't find her. It was like she'd never— Anna, whatever is the matter?"

She'd clapped a hand over her mouth.

"Anna? What's wrong? Please tell me what I've done."

"The Caonaig," she said hoarsely. "You've seen the Caonaig."

I shook my head. "What's the Caonaig? I don't understand."

"Someone's going to die," she said.

"No, surely not. It was just an old woman—"

"Wearing green?"

I hesitated. "Yes."

"Did she have a protruding tooth?"

I hesitated even longer. "Yes."

"Was she crying?"

This time I didn't answer, but apparently my eyes gave me away.

Anna shrieked and bolted into the kitchen. I called after her, and then ran after her, but she was gone, leaving the door flapping on its hinges. I ran back to the front door, but by the time I stepped into the road, she was receding into the distance on her bicycle.

"What's going on?" Mr. Ross said.

I whipped around. He and Conall had come up behind me in the street.

"She thinks I've seen the Caonaig," I said helplessly.

"And what made her think that?"

"Because I saw an old woman washing a shirt in the river."

He took a sharp breath that whistled through his teeth.

"But how can that mean someone's going to die?" I said desperately. "It was just an old woman. I don't understand."

"Anna still has two brothers at the Front," he said.

Still?

I turned to look down the road, where she'd disappeared.

.   .   .

I went upstairs and hid in my room, but about an hour before Meg usually returned from the sawmill I began to panic. Anna had not come back, and she always started the dinner, which Meg then finished and served to the customers. Eventually, I crept downstairs again, thinking I'd at least better warn Mr. Ross that there would be no food to serve, but there was no sign of him either.

I didn't know what to do, but since I'd somehow managed to cause the problem, I ducked into the kitchen and scoured the pantry for the makings of a meal.

I realized almost immediately that it was hopeless, not only because I couldn't find any of the meat I'd seen delivered that morning, but because even if I could, I wouldn't have had a clue what to do with it. I wasn't even sure how to start potatoes, and in about an hour upward of twenty men would start arriving, each of them expecting to be fed.

When Meg came in the back door, she found me leaning over the butcher's block table, my head buried in my hands. She quickly assessed the situation, her eyes landing on the empty range.

"Anna left early," I said.

"What's happened?"

"I said something to upset her."

"And what was that?"

"I'm not exactly sure," I said miserably. "But I can tell you I didn't mean to do it."

I expected her to grill me, but instead she simply set her coat and gas mask on the chair and said, "Right then. Can you get the tatties going?"

I blinked a couple of times. "Yes. I think."

"You think, or you can?"

"I think."

The truth was, I didn't even know how to slice bread. During my ravenous adolescent raids of the kitchen, I'd torn the bread off in chunks, digging out the soft middle to eat first, and then gnawing at the crust over the sink so I could rinse away the evidence.

Meg told me to fill the largest pot with water, add salt and forty potatoes, and put it on to boil. She stoked the fire herself while instructing me to hurry up about it so my husband didn't come back and catch me where I didn't belong, because she had a feeling that wouldn't go very well.

Then she went out back to retrieve something she called "potted hough," for which she thanked the dear Lord, for she had some on hand and it was served cold.

The bar was abuzz that night with news of the bombing, which distracted somewhat from the mashed potatoes, which tasted as though I'd boiled them in seawater. I also hadn't realized I was supposed to remove the skin or dig out the dark spots, or that the knife was supposed to glide smoothly through before I declared them done, all of which Meg explained to me later. I saw more than one man lift a full fork, examine it with disbelief, and then attempt to fling the potatoes back onto the plate to see how tenaciously they stuck. Poor Meg—although there wasn't a man in the room brave enough to complain, she was assumed to be responsible.

Conall, who'd joined me by the fire as soon as Hank and Ellis arrived, didn't seem to mind how gluey they were. I was convinced that he'd come because he knew I needed moral support, so to thank him I began slipping him tiny bits of mashed potato on the end of my finger, which he gravely licked. At one point, I thought I saw Mr. Ross watching when I had a potato-dipped finger extended in offering. Apparently Conall thought so too, for he stared straight ahead and ignored it until his master's attentions were elsewhere. Only then did he tip his head toward me and let his tongue sneak out the side of his mouth.

Since the bombing hadn't made it into the paper, people were adding their own bits of knowledge to the general story. Hank and Ellis listened with great interest.

Two bombers had flown down the Great Glen from Norway, targeting the British Aluminium plant in Foyers, a village several miles down the other side of Loch Ness. One night guard had been killed when the blast threw him into the plant's turbine, and another died of a heart attack.

When someone shared the news that one of the Heinkels had gone down in Loch Lochy almost immediately after, I gasped and looked at Mr. Ross. He finished pulling a pint and slid it across the bar to one of the locals as though he hadn't heard.

"Well, whadya know," said Hank, his voice betraying a sliver of respect. "He shot down a bomber with a fucking rifle. I wonder why he's not fighting?"

"That's a very good question," said Ellis. He twisted in his seat and said, "Say, bartender, my friend here has a question for you."

"Don't!" I whispered, utterly appalled.

"Why?" he asked.

"Because it's none of our business," I hissed. "And he's the landlord, for goodness' sake, not the bartender. Can't you show a little respect?"

But it was too late.

"And what would that be?" asked Mr. Ross.

"You're pretty good with a gun," said Hank. "Why aren't you at the Front?"

The room went silent. Mr. Ross simply stared at Hank.

It was Rory who finally spoke. "That's funny," he said slowly. "We've been wondering the same about you."

"Medically unfit," Hank said, as though it were all a joke.

"You look healthy enough to me."

"I have a condition called *pes planus*," Hank said.

"Do you now?" said Rory. "Is that Latin for yellow belly?"

Hank jumped to his feet. The lumberjack also rose, but slowly. He was clearly more than a match for Hank.

"Hank, *sit down*," I pleaded.

"And let him get away with calling me a coward?"

"If the shoe fits," said Rory.

"Ellis, are you going to just sit there and let him call us cowards?" Hank said, outraged.

"He wasn't talking to me," Ellis muttered.

"As a matter of fact, I was," said Rory. "Have you got some fancy diagnosis for lily liver too? *Planus lilicus*, perhaps?"

"I have protanopia," said Ellis. "I can't see color. And for your information, I tried to enlist twice."

"The lot of you should mind your own business," said Meg, coming out from behind the bar.

"It *is* my business, if he calls me a coward," said Hank.

She threw him an exasperated look, gave up, and turned to the lumberjack. "You can't fight him, Rory. You heard what he said. He's got a medical condition. You can't go around beating up invalids."

Hank opened his mouth to protest, and Ellis whacked him on the side of the leg.

"They don't look sick," said Rory.

"Well, you don't always, do you? George the Jannie looked just fine until he dropped dead of a weak heart. You can't fight a man with *pes planus*. You might kill him on the spot."

Rory stared at Hank for a long time. He finally returned to his seat. "I suppose you're right," he said with a sigh. "It would be like kicking a puppy, wouldn't it?"

"Of course I'm right, you daft fool," said Meg, slapping him on the arm. He responded by slapping her bottom. She whipped around and pointed a finger in his face, but he just laughed and blew her a kiss. She glared at him and sailed back behind the counter.

As the rest of the men returned to their conversations, Hank and Ellis sat in silence, both of them ashen.

Chapter Twenty-three

Anna showed up the next morning and served breakfast as though nothing had happened. I wondered whether she'd decided that the deaths in Foyers had satisfied the Caonaig's ghoulish requirement.

I watched her surreptitiously, hoping that the fragile thing that had sprung up between us hadn't changed and that she'd still let me help with the rooms, but I had to wait to find out because Ellis and Hank were still there.

Neither of them said a word about their rooms having been put straight. Instead, they sputtered indignantly about why everyone thought it was all right to judge them when clearly Blackbeard was as fit as anyone else except for his missing digit, which just as clearly didn't prevent him from shooting a gun. They said all this right in front of Anna, as though she didn't exist, and I cringed with embarrassment. She was at the far end of the room, sweeping the hearth with a broom made of sticks. She acted impervious, but I knew she wasn't.

I had almost given up hope of them ever leaving when George the Vannie showed up.

"I've oiled yon door for you," he said, glancing bashfully at Anna and swinging it back and forth. "Yesterday afternoon when I came back."

"That's very kind of you," she said, without looking at him.

He stared openly for several seconds, and from his stricken expression I could tell he was in love with her.

"Well, I'll be waiting outside then," he said to Ellis and Hank.

"We'll be right out. Oh, say, do you still have a compass?" Ellis asked, turning to me. "We're missing one."

"It's in my right coat pocket," I said. "Hanging by the door."

He went over and rifled through it.

"When did you go into botany?" he said, looking into his palm. He came back and dropped a handful of the red and fawn toadstools on the table. "Throw these out. They look noxious."

There was a flurry of activity as they got on their coats and hats and gathered their equipment. When the door finally closed behind them, the only sound was the rhythmic swish of Anna's broom against the stone floor.

I wanted to start a conversation and figure out where things stood, but even though Hank and Ellis had left, their presence lingered like a cloud of soot.

Anna finally glanced up and said, "Those are elves' cups you've got there. They're not poisonous, but they're also not tasty. They dry well, if you want to keep a bowl in your room."

"I'll do that. Thank you," I said.

"So what *is* wrong with them?" she asked.

I didn't have to ask what she meant.

"Hank is flat-footed and Ellis is color-blind."

She raised her eyebrows. "I see."

"It's true. He can't tell red from green—it's all just gray to him. He didn't even know before he tried to enlist. There's absolutely nothing he can do about it, but people don't believe it.

They think he's making it up. That's why we're here—he thinks that finding the monster will force people to recognize he's not a coward."

"Does he now?" she said, and went back to sweeping.

For a moment, I could think of nothing to say. I realized I was finished making excuses for either of them.

"I suppose you've heard what they said to Mr. Ross last night."

"To who?"

"Mr. Ross. Angus."

She laughed. "Angus is a Grant. What on earth gave you the idea he was a Ross?"

"The sign," I said. "It says A. W. Ross. And then on our first day here, you told me that he ran the place . . ."

"He *does* run the place, but the proprietor is Alisdair. Angus is just holding down the fort until Alisdair gets back from the Front." She leaned the broom against the wall and put her hands on her hips. "Have you thought that all along?"

Someone knocked on the door, a solemn, slow rhythm.

Anna frowned. "Well, I don't like the sound of that. Not one bit."

She wiped her hands on her apron and answered the door. Willie the Postie was on the doorstep, holding his hat in his hands. His face was gray.

"And for what reason are you knocking, Willie?" Anna said in an angry voice that did nothing to mask her fear. "The door's not locked. Come in then, if that's what you're wanting. I haven't got all day."

"I'm very sorry, Anna," he said without moving. "But you need to go home."

"What are you on about? I see nowt in your hands but your hat."

"You need to go home," he repeated quietly. "I've just delivered a telegram."

Anna's knees buckled. She reached for the doorframe.

I shoved my chair back and rushed to her, grabbing her by the waist.

"Your parents need you," Willie said. "Go to them."

She caught his wrist, gripping it so tightly her knuckles turned white.

"Which one was it?" she said frantically. "Tell me that much."

"Anna—"

"Was it Hugh or was it Robbie?"

Willie's mouth opened, but it was a few seconds before he spoke. "'Twas Hugh," he finally said, lowering his gaze.

She dropped his wrist and twisted free of me. She took a step backward, shaking her head, her eyes wild. "You're wrong. It's not true! It'll be like Angus! You'll see!"

Willie shook his head helplessly. "Anna . . ."

She took flight, bursting past him and out the door. When I tried to follow, Willie caught my arm.

"Let her go," he said.

He was right. I had no business intruding. When he realized I wasn't struggling anymore, he loosened his grip.

I craned my neck past the doorframe and saw Anna pedaling furiously away, her bicycle jerking from side to side with the effort, her hair flying in the wind.

She'd left everything behind—coat, hat, scarf, and gas mask. If I'd known where the croft was, I would have taken them and left them on the doorstep, but all I knew was that it was somewhere between the inn and the castle.

I searched for the master key, eventually finding it on a hook under the bar. Then I made up the rooms, moving through the tasks like a robot. When I was finished, I went back and did them again.

I lined the toiletries up at exact intervals on the dressers. I wiped the mirrors clean. I picked the wax off the candleholders and smoothed the surfaces of the quilts. And when there was nothing left to straighten or polish or dust, I went to bed.

I stayed in my room that evening, despite Ellis's insistence that I join him for dinner. I could tell from his tone that he was in a foul mood, and when I stopped responding, his entreaties turned into accusations of mental instability. He threatened to send for a doctor if I didn't come out.

I did not, and a doctor never appeared.

Hours after everyone else had gone to bed, I continued to thrash, twisting the quilts around my feet and punching my pillow, trying to find a position that would finally allow me to rest, but nothing helped, because it was not my body that refused to go still. My throat was so tight I could barely swallow, and my eyes welled with tears.

I knew with absolute certainty that if I'd gone upstairs right away, my mother would still be alive. But if I hadn't gone into the Cover and seen the Caonaig, would Hugh also still be alive?

I crept downstairs and sat by the fire, which had been dampened with a layer of ash.

When Mr. Grant found me, I was on the floor in front of the grate, hugging my knees to my chest. I didn't hear him coming, or even notice the light of the candle.

"Is everything all right?" he asked.

I jerked around, pulling my nightgown over my ankles in an attempt to hide my bare feet. My cheeks were slick with tears.

"What's wrong? What's happened?" He held the candle closer and looked me over.

The lump in my throat had grown even larger, and it was

difficult for me to speak. When I did, my voice was strangled. "I did it, didn't I?"

"Did what, lass?" He set the candle on the low table and knelt beside me, searching my eyes with his. "What have you done?"

"I've killed Anna's brother."

"And how do you figure that?"

"I saw the Caonaig—I didn't want to see her, but I did, and then when I told Anna, she knew right away what it meant. I thought she was just being superstitious, but it turns out she was right. If I'd just stayed out of the Cover, if I hadn't let that stupid crow chase me in, her brother would still be alive."

"Oh," he said, letting the word slide out on a long exhale. His expression melted into one of pity and sadness. "No. No, lass. He would not."

"But I saw the Caonaig—"

"You didn't do anything. It was the godforsaken war."

"But Anna's already lost at least one other brother. How much loss are people supposed to bear?"

He shook his head. "I'm afraid I don't know. It seems there's nothing so good or pure it can't be taken without a moment's notice. And then in the end, it all gets taken anyway."

I looked wildly into his face. "If that's the case, what's the point of even living?"

"I wish I knew," he said with a wry half smile. "For some time now, that's been a source of great mystery to me."

I looked at him for a few seconds longer and then burst into tears—colossal, heaving sobs that wracked my shoulders.

Before I knew what was happening, he'd wrapped his arms around me and pulled me to him, breathing heavily into my hair. I scrabbled onto my knees and tossed my arms around his neck, pressing my open, sobbing mouth on the pulse that beat so strongly in his throat.

Chapter Twenty-four

It was an innocent embrace, I told myself for the thousandth time, hoping that I would eventually believe it. For hours after I returned to my room the night before, I lay in the dark wishing he was there with me. I wanted him to hold me, I wanted to fall asleep in his arms. I was aware of wanting more, too.

Despite being up most of the night, I got up early and waited at my door until Hank and Ellis were in the hallway. Then I joined them so we could all go down together. I was incapable of facing Angus—I could no longer think of him in formal terms—on my own. Even the thought of seeing him in the company of other people left me light-headed.

When the three of us went downstairs, he was standing by the front door talking with a very old woman in a language both guttural and burbling. When he glanced at me, I thought my knees might give out.

I couldn't look at him for fear of giving myself away.

The air was so electrically charged I was sure Hank and

Ellis would pick up on it, so I also couldn't look at them. That left no one but the crone, who stared at me as if she were plumbing the deepest recesses of my mind and unearthing all kinds of terrible things.

"This is Rhona," said Angus. "She'll be here until Anna gets back. She doesn't speak English." And with that, he left.

"And the stellar service continues," Ellis muttered, leading the way to our usual table. "What are we supposed to do? Learn Gaelic? Play charades?"

"Why not?" said Hank. "It's always porridge anyway, and I can mime that." He put his hands to his throat and pretended to choke.

"Don't tell me you're getting used to this," said Ellis.

Hank shrugged. "At least they've started putting my things away."

Ellis harrumphed. "Talk to me when they start ironing the newspaper."

Rhona served our breakfast in dour silence and otherwise ignored us completely. I wondered if she was the wife of the old man who'd blown our cover the first day. Even if she wasn't, it was clear she disapproved of us as much as he did.

She was ancient, with a dowager's hump and bowed legs. Her hair was white, her clothes black, her complexion gray. She smelled like wet wool and vinegar and, as far as I could tell, wore a perpetually sour expression. Her upper lip and chin were lightly whiskered, her face so weathered that her eyes appeared as mere slits under the weight of her lids. Even so, I caught an occasional flash of piercing blue—usually as I was fighting off the memory of being held by Angus, or despairing of Anna's brothers, and wondering how two such disparate thoughts could coexist in my brain.

"Maddie?"

Ellis was looking at me. His forehead was crinkled, and I

realized he'd said my name at least twice, but I'd heard it from a distance, as though through a tunnel.

"Darling? Are you all right? You seem ... I don't know, shaken, or distracted, or something. Are you having an episode?"

"No. Nothing like that. I just didn't sleep well."

"Why not?"

"I was thinking about Anna's family. I was here when she got the news about her brother."

"What about her brother?"

"He was killed in action," I said. "He's at least the second brother she's lost."

"Ah," he said, smiling sadly. "I suppose that explains why you wouldn't come down last night. But I'm afraid these things happen, my darling. *C'est la guerre.* How are you now? Should I have sent for a doctor after all?"

I could only shake my head.

He patted my hand and turned his attention back to Hank.

I stared at him for a long time. If he wanted to end his search for the beast, he need look no further than a mirror.

I collected my things and escaped as soon as Hank and Ellis left with George, whom they'd apparently hired full-time, petrol restrictions notwithstanding. I wondered how fast Ellis was going through his remaining money. Perhaps Hank was already supporting us.

After I got outside, I was free of Rhona's penetrating glare, but found myself yet again with no destination, no goal, and no purpose on a day I desperately needed to be occupied. However, even if we'd shared a language, I wouldn't have had the nerve to ask Rhona about doing the rooms. She clearly despised me. Once again, I'd been lumped in with Hank and Ellis.

My brain was fevered, my system overwhelmed. My glass had been filled too full, too fast. The Caonaig, the death of Anna's brother, my embrace with Angus, never mind finally recognizing the sheer callousness of my husband—

Even after he'd shanghaied me into a war, even after I'd realized our entire marriage was a sham, even after I'd watched him go below deck to avoid seeing the wounded on the SS *Mallory*, I had never believed him to be as cold-blooded as he'd just revealed himself to be. I'd always assumed his avoidance of all things war-related was guilt over not being able to serve, but now I realized that he just didn't care.

Even if he didn't think of Anna as quite human, had he never considered the fate of George's leg? Apparently not, since he'd interpreted my distress as a symptom of fragility.

I thought of the moment Angus pulled me to him, gripping me tightly, not at all as though I might break, even as I was sobbing into his neck. We clung to each other as though life itself depended on it, and maybe it did.

I looked up with a gasp.

It'll be like Angus, Anna had said, her face twisted in grief, less than a minute after laughing at me for getting his name wrong.

Was it possible?

I marched down the street, keeping my head down— especially when the lace curtain in a front window shifted by the width of a finger, as nearly all of them did.

If red was the new badge of courage, I was certainly a shining beacon of bravery, with my stupid red gloves and my stupid red gas mask case. I shoved my hands in my pockets and encountered the last of the elves' cups, which I flung to the side of the road for the crime of being red.

Red, red, everywhere. I wanted to be gray.

I found myself back at the headstone, staring at its etched granite as though I could force it to reveal its secrets.

AGNES MÀIRI GRANT,
INFANT DAUGHTER OF ANGUS AND MÀIRI GRANT
JANUARY 14TH, 1942

CAPT. ANGUS DUNCAN GRANT,
BELOVED HUSBAND OF MÀIRI
APRIL 2ND, 1909–JANUARY   , 1942

MÀIRI JOAN GRANT,
BELOVED WIFE OF ANGUS
JULY 26, 1919–FEBRUARY 28, 1942

I knew how many men in the village had the same names—
I'd seen it myself on the other gravestones, and I knew that
Willie the Postie was called that to distinguish him from Willie
the Joiner and Willie the Box because every one of them was a
Willie MacDonald—but I couldn't shake the image of Angus
putting snowdrops on the grave.

*It seems there's nothing so good or pure it can't be taken with-
out a moment's notice,* he'd said, and there was nothing so pure
as an infant. Was it possible he'd returned from the war only to
find that everything he loved had been snatched by cruel fate?

I thought back to the night we'd arrived in Scotland. When
I realized it was the third anniversary of the child's death, I
was afraid I might break into pieces after all.

I was afraid that if I went back to the inn I might take a pill, so
I headed down the A82, knowing that somewhere between the
village and the castle was the McKenzies' croft.

Small houses dotted the hillside and I stopped briefly in
front of each, wondering if Anna and her parents were inside.
Eventually I reached the castle, and knew I had passed
them.

The ruined battlements looked very different than they had when we'd approached them by water. There was a large dry moat around the castle, full of high grasses and scrubby weeds, and I lifted my coat and tromped down, across, and up the other side, ignoring the thorns that snagged my hems.

Directly beside the entrance was a massive chunk of stone—or stones, really, because they were still stuck together with mortar, still rigidly holding right angles. It looked like someone had torn a large corner piece from a very stale gingerbread house and flung it to the floor.

I paused beneath the arched entrance, where the drawbridge had once been, imagining all the people who had passed in and out over the centuries, every one of them carrying a combination of desire, hope, jealousy, despair, grief, love, and every other human emotion; a combination that made each one as unique as a snowflake, yet linked all of them inextricably to every other human being from the dawn of time to the end of it.

I walked through it myself and went straight to the tower. Within its gloomy interior, I found a winding staircase, and climbed the worn steps carefully. They were so narrow I had to brace my hands on either side.

I stopped on the second floor to look out, but pulled back immediately.

Angus was standing at an arched gate that led down to the water. He stayed for a long time, staring at the loch, which was as flat as if it had been ironed. Then he leaned over, picked up his gun and a brace of rabbits, and turned around. I ducked further into the shadows, although there was no reason—he plodded straight to and through the main gate without ever looking up.

· · ·

The light snowfall turned into a flurry, and before I knew it, turned into a blizzard. I had no choice but to return to the inn—to stay in the tower would mean freezing to death.

Rhona was neither upstairs nor in the front room, and although I had been desperate to get away from her just a few hours earlier, my need for a cup of something hot now made me just as desperate to find her. I hoped I would be able to pantomime what I needed, and that she'd be receptive to interpreting. I took a deep breath and entered the kitchen. When my eyes landed on the big wooden table and the freshly skinned rabbits upon it, I stopped.

Angus was standing shirtless at the sink with his back to me, washing his arms.

I knew I should leave, but I couldn't. I was rooted to the spot, watching the rhythmic, alternating movements of his shoulder blades as he cupped water first in one hand and then the other, sloshing it up past his elbows to rinse off the soap.

I don't know what gave me away, but he whipped his head around and caught me watching.

Despite my heart being lodged in my throat, I couldn't look away. After several seconds he straightened up and—without breaking eye contact—turned slowly, deliberately, until he was facing me.

His chest and abdomen were a network of thick, raised scars—red, pink, purple, even white. They were not puncture wounds. Someone had jammed a serrated blade into him and ripped through his flesh, over, and over, and over.

I stared, trying to comprehend.

"Oh, Angus," I said, covering my mouth. I rushed a few steps toward him before coming to a halt.

He smiled sadly and raised his palms. After a few seconds, he turned back to the sink.

I reached a hand out as though to touch him, although a

good fourteen feet still separated us. The illusion was there, though, and I let my quivering, outstretched fingers graze his shoulder. When I realized what I was doing, I bolted to my room.

I took my pills out and put them back no fewer than three times. I did not know what to do with myself, and ended up pacing between the bed and the window, turning on my heel as precisely as a soldier.

Had he answered my suspicion about the gravestone? Had he been assumed dead and somehow survived? And what in God's name had happened to him? I couldn't imagine, and yet I couldn't stop imagining.

Chapter Twenty-five

Ellis thumped on my door as soon as he and Hank returned, demanding I join them for a drink. I tried to plead an upset stomach, but once again he threatened me with a doctor, saying that this time he really meant it.

As we walked toward the staircase, Ellis bounced off a wall. He was utterly soused.

We took our usual spot by the fire. His and Hank's initial excitement at interviewing eyewitnesses had gone sour after only three days and was compounded by Ellis's anger at not being able to view the site of the bombing, despite having traveled all the way around the loch to get there.

He relived their outing from the comfort of the couch, sputtering about "pulling rank" and "having someone's head" and other such nonsense. Eventually, his rant segued into the interviews themselves. He held his notebook open, stabbing it with a finger.

"Two humps, three humps, four humps, no humps . . . Horse head, serpent's head, whale-shaped, coils. Goddamned white mane, for Christ's sake!" He threw his arms up in frustration. "Scales on another. Eyes of a snake, eyes at the ends of antennae, no eyes at all. Crossing the road while chewing on a goddamned sheep. Gray, green, black, silver. Dorsal fin, flippers, all arms, no limbs, tusks. Tusks, for the love of God!"

He glared at me as if I'd made the offending observation. When I didn't respond, he turned back to Hank.

"Vertical undulation. Flaring nostrils. Otters. Deer. Lovelorn sturgeon. Giant squid. Rotten logs exploding from the bottom. The only thing we haven't heard is fire-breathing with wings."

"I'm sure we will," said Hank. He was leaning back with his legs crossed, blowing rings of smoke.

"How can you be so calm about this? How the hell are we supposed to figure out what's true when so many of them are obviously lying to us?"

"We should stop paying them, that's how," said Hank. He successfully blew a smaller smoke ring through a larger one. He leaned forward and poked me on the knee. "Maddie, did you see that?"

"I did," I said.

So did Angus, who was watching from behind the bar.

"If you'd learn to smoke, I could teach you all kinds of tricks," Hank continued. "Watch this——"

He exhaled a vertical loop before sucking it back into his mouth.

"*Hank, for God's sake!*" said Ellis. "Get back on topic. If we don't pay them, they won't meet us."

"And if we do pay them, they'll lie. If people are willing to meet with us just to tell their story, they're more likely to tell the truth." Hank turned to me. "What do you think, darling girl?"

"I really don't know," I said. "I can see both sides, I suppose."

"What was that?" Ellis said, swiveling toward me. "Would you please repeat that?"

"I said I really don't know."

"No, you don't," he said, "and yet you're always offering opinions."

I decided to ignore the insult and poked through the remainder of the pie. I was looking for pieces of rabbit, because I didn't care for the mushrooms. Unfortunately, they were the same shade of brown.

A fully formed thought crashed into my head, a *coup de foudre*. I put my fork down and looked at Ellis, feeling my eyes grow wide.

He had decided upon sight that the elves' cups were noxious, but there was absolutely nothing noxious-looking about them other than their red interiors.

"Stop gaping," Ellis said. "You'll catch flies."

"Ellis!" Hank snapped. "What the hell is wrong with you? That's *Maddie* you're talking to."

"If you'll excuse me," I said, setting my napkin by my plate and rising.

Ellis scowled and shook his head.

"Shall I walk you up?" said Hank, rising quickly.

"No thank you. I'll be fine on my own."

"Yes, of course," he said, although he came around the table and touched my elbow. "Maddie, he doesn't mean it. He's just being a knucklehead. He's under a lot of stress."

"Stress," I said. "Yes, of course."

I tried to wrap my head around the enormity of what I suspected. If I was right, not only would it prove Ellis immoral on a completely different scale, it would also negate the entire purpose of this foolish, arrogant venture. Finding the monster wouldn't restore his honor, because he had no honor to restore.

Over the course of the night, I became convinced.

He hadn't crashed cars because he couldn't tell if the light was red or green. He'd crashed cars because he was drunk. Likewise, it was no coincidence that the dresses and jewelry he bought me were almost exclusively red. He knew it set off my green eyes. And the only reason I could think of for him buying me a bright red gas mask case was that it matched my gloves.

The thing I found most abhorrent was that he'd made such a show about trying to enlist a second time, then acted so devastated when they'd turned him down again. The entire spectacle was designed to garner sympathy, which—incredibly—he seemed to think he deserved. It was a production worthy of my mother.

I made sure I was the first one down the next morning, bringing my coat, gas mask, and gloves with me. I set the gloves on the table and waited. I was usually the last one down, so I didn't know who would arrive first.

To my relief, it was Ellis.

"Good morning, darling," he said, kissing me on the cheek. "You're up early. Big plans?"

I was momentarily shocked by his cheer. I wondered if he even remembered the previous night.

"Just tromping around the countryside," I said, trying to match his tone. "I wish I had my watercolors."

"Your paintings would be entirely washed away by the rain." He pulled a logbook out of his duffel bag and opened it.

I fingered my scarlet gloves, flattening the thumbs carefully against the palms.

"Yes, I suppose you're right," I said. "Which reminds me, I'm so glad you got a weather-resistant case for my gas mask. I'm sure a cardboard box would have dissolved by now."

"Nothing but the best for my girl," he answered.

"But I *am* curious why you got this color."

"To match your gloves, of course. Say, what do you suppose a fellow has to do to get some breakfast around here?" He craned his neck, searching for Rhona.

"But my gloves are green," I said.

"No they're not, they're red."

"No," I said, slowly. "They're green."

He looked down at the gloves, and then lifted his gaze until it was locked on mine.

"Well," he said, just as slowly, "you told me they were red."

"Did I?" I said, still playing with the gloves. "That must have been another pair. These are green, and it's a rather odd color combination. I feel a bit like a Christmas wreath."

I looked up. He was unblinking, his expression cold as granite.

"Anyway," I continued, "if you find yourself back in Inverness, I could use a new pair. These ones have water stains all over them. And this time I *would* like red—did you know there's a saying, that red is the new badge of courage?"

Hank appeared beside me. "What's up, kids?"

"What color are these gloves?" Ellis demanded.

"What?" said Hank.

"Maddie's gloves. What color are they?"

"They're red," said Hank.

Ellis stood so suddenly his chair legs belched against the stone floor. He tossed his logbook into the duffel bag, pulled the bag onto the chair, then yanked the coarse-toothed zipper so hard it took him three tries to get it closed. He threw me a final searing glare and stormed outside.

After a couple of seconds, Hank said, "Christ. You two aren't falling apart on me, are you?"

Instead of answering, I stared into my lap.

He pulled out a chair and sat. "Is this about last night? He was just being stupid. He's under boatloads of stress. If the Colonel doesn't forgive him, he's seen the last cent he's going to until we find the monster. And even then, the Colonel still has to forgive him."

"You underestimate the powers of Edith Stone Hyde."

"I hope so, because he sent her a letter yesterday morning. That's why he got so snockered last night."

I was shocked. "He wrote to her? What did he say?"

"Well, he didn't show it to me, but I assume he threw himself on her mercy and begged for divine intervention with the Colonel."

"I had no idea he was going to write to her."

"He didn't want you to worry."

"Because I'm so delicate?"

"Because he wanted to protect you."

"Well, he has a funny way of showing it."

Hank sighed. "If you're talking about last night, they're just words, Maddie. You know he didn't mean any of it."

"I don't know anything anymore. I don't think he even remembers. He's taking my pills and washing them down with liquor."

"What are you talking about?"

"I just told you."

His eyes met mine with something like comprehension.

"When did this start?"

"He's always helped himself, but it's really ramped up since we got here."

"I had no idea." He stared into space. After what felt like an eternity, he took a deep breath and slapped his thighs. "All right. Don't worry, darling girl. I'll straighten him out."

"It's too late," I said.

"I'll straighten him out," Hank said firmly.

When the front door clicked shut behind him, I whispered, again, "It's too late."

Ellis returned to the inn that night sober and courteous to a fault. His calm exterior and placid expression were too calm, too placid, and I wondered whether he was masking terrible hurt or terrible anger.

I began to second-guess myself.

If he really was color-blind and I'd accused him of faking it, I was no better than all the other judgmental people. But if he was faking it and knew I'd found out, I was as lethal to him as a loaded gun.

If the Colonel discovered that Ellis had lied to shirk duty, he'd disown him immediately and permanently, and there would be nothing Edith Stone Hyde or anybody else could do about it.

Either way, I'd made a mistake and was going to have to fix it.

When Ellis laid eyes on me the next morning, his expression confirmed how critical it was for me to get things back on an even keel. The second he saw me, his jaw clenched and he stared at his logbook.

I hated what I had to do, and hated even more that I knew how. I would be drawing directly from my mother's playbook.

"Good morning, darling," I said, joining him. "Where's Hank?"

He made a great show of licking his finger and turning the page.

"Sweetheart, please tell me what I've done," I said. "You

left in such a hurry yesterday, and then you barely spoke to me at dinner. I know I've done something, but I don't know what."

He continued to look down at the book, pretending I wasn't there.

"Except that's not true," I said miserably. "I do know why you're angry. It was my pitiful attempt at a joke, wasn't it? Ellis, *please* look at me."

He lifted his face. His expression was glacial, his eyes hard.

"My joke about the gloves," I went on. "I was trying to be funny, not make fun of you. But I should have known better than to joke about your condition. It was awful of me."

He had no reaction at all. He simply stared, his lips pressed into a grim line.

I had no choice but to barrel on, because I had no other plan.

"I thought if I told you my gloves were green, you'd think Hank had pulled a prank on you by picking the wrong color case for my gas mask, but then it all went wrong. As soon as I saw your face I should have stopped, but I was so far in I kept going and tried to turn it around instead. It's all so stupid—I really do need new gloves, and I was just trying to come up with a clever way of asking. It was the vaudeville in me trying to come out, but I'm no star. I'm meant to be a supporting act. So rest assured that yesterday's performance marked both the debut and finale of my solo career in practical jokes."

He finally spoke. "Not vaudeville. Burlesque."

My cheeks burned. "Yes. Of course. It's just we don't usually call it that."

"My mother always said that blood will out. I wish I'd paid attention."

My mouth opened and closed a couple of times before I

could respond. "I suppose I deserved that, after what I said to you."

He laughed once, a short, harsh bray.

The two of them didn't return to the inn that night or the next, so I had no idea if Ellis had bought my story about the gloves. They left no note or any other indication of where they had gone.

Chapter Twenty-six

When Anna finally returned, five days after learning of Hugh's death, she accepted my condolences and otherwise simply carried on, although there was a heaviness in her step that hadn't been there before. She let me resume doing the rooms, for which I was very grateful, because I'd been losing my mind trying to stay out of Rhona's way and had no idea what I'd say to Angus if I found myself alone with him.

The crone apparently shared Anna's view about picking up after others, because Ellis's dirty socks and underpants lay exactly where he'd stepped out of them three nights before, and his pajamas lay in a crumpled heap in the corner. Hank had at least tossed his clothes onto the chair.

Of the hundred pills I'd initially found in Ellis's room, only thirty-six were left.

Hank and Ellis returned that night. When they came through the door, I took a deep breath, steeling myself.

"Darling!" said Ellis. He swooped over and kissed my cheek

before sitting next to me on the couch. He stank of paraffin oil, but not liquor.

"Did you miss me?" he asked.

"Of course," I said, trying to read his face.

Hank plopped down on one of the chairs opposite. "You'll never guess where we've been."

"She doesn't care about that," said Ellis, rubbing his hands together. "Quick—get her prezzie!"

Hank dug around in one of the duffel bags and handed Ellis a thin gift-wrapped box, which he solemnly presented on the palms of both hands.

I pulled off the satin bow and lifted the lid. A pair of red kid gloves lay inside, on tissue paper flecked with gold.

The blood drained from my face.

"What do you think? Do you like them?" he asked.

"They're beautiful," I said.

"More importantly, what color are they?"

"They're red," I said in a near-whisper.

"Good," said Ellis, smiling broadly. "That's what Hank said, too, but I never know with you two jokers." He held a hand over his head and snapped his fingers. "Bartender! Two whiskeys. Actually, just bring the bottle."

Angus glared, but pulled out two glasses. Meg picked them up and tucked a bottle under her arm, her expression conveying every word that didn't come out of her mouth.

The gloves were a message, obviously, but what did they mean? Had I managed to convince Ellis that I still believed he was color-blind? Or had he interpreted my desperate soliloquy as a promise to keep his secret? Or was he actually color-blind?

Over the course of the evening, Ellis drank almost a whole bottle of whiskey, but he remained—at least outwardly—jovial.

He kept a proprietorial hand on my shoulder or leg the entire time, and it was a constant struggle to keep from shrinking away. I stole occasional glances at Angus, whose face was unreadable.

I'd been back to the graveyard twice since seeing his scars, and had myself mostly convinced that he was the Angus on the stone, the one who'd lost everything in the space of six weeks.

I thought often of our embrace by the fire, and wondered if he did, too.

They never told me where they'd been, and I didn't ask. Despite Hank's promise to straighten Ellis out, they fell right back into their old pattern of returning to the inn plastered and then continuing to drink until they were both in a stupor. Judging from his fast-diminishing stash, Ellis was also gobbling pills. By my estimation, he was taking anywhere from eight to ten a day.

On the night I knew he'd run out, he knocked on my door and asked if he could have one. After popping one into his mouth, he shook more into his hand and slid them into his pocket. From what remained, I figured he'd taken about fifty, enough to last him five or six days.

We achieved a tenuous kind of normal. Ellis seemed to have completely forgotten about the glove incident, and while he was consistently drunk, he never tipped into a rage.

Every day he looked for a letter from his mother, and every day it didn't come. He began to say he didn't need her anyway—he was more certain than ever that when he found the monster, he would clear both his and his father's names, and that the Colonel would welcome him back with open arms and checkbook.

Finding the monster in Loch Ness was all he cared about.

He remained as ignorant as ever about the monster facing the rest of the world.

I began to iron the newspaper, in the hope that he—or Hank—might start to read it. They did not.

Although there was no question that it was selfish and cowardly to blinker themselves against the chaos and horror, there were times I almost understood.

At the end of January, the Red Army had liberated a network of death camps in Auschwitz, Poland, and the details that trickled out over the days and weeks were so excruciating I fought a very real urge to remain ignorant myself.

Hundreds of thousands of people—perhaps many, many more, because the reports were often contradictory—had been interned and killed, most of them simply for being Jewish. They'd been rounded up and transported in cattle cars, and assigned to either death or hard labor as soon as they climbed out. Death was by gas chamber, and the chambers and crematoriums ran night and day. Many of those spared immediate death died anyway, from illness, starvation, torture, and exhaustion. There were rumors of a mad doctor and unthinkable experiments.

When the SS realized the Red Army was closing in, they tried to destroy the evidence. They blew up the gas chambers and crematoriums and set fire to other buildings before retreating on foot, forcing tens of thousands of starving inmates— every last person who was capable of walking—to march further into Nazi territory toward other death camps. The only people they left behind were those they were certain were dying. They shot people randomly as they retreated.

Even the hardened soldiers of the Russian army were unprepared for what they found: 648 corpses that lay where they'd fallen, and more than seven thousand survivors in such terrible condition they continued to die despite immediate rescue efforts.

They discovered that the SS had burned the infirmary with everyone inside it, 239 souls in all. One of the six storage buildings the SS had not had time to destroy was filled with tons—literally tons—of women's hair, along with human teeth, the fillings extracted, and tens of thousands of children's outfits.

I despaired of humanity. Although the Allies were making progress, I thought maybe it was too late, that evil had already prevailed.

Chapter Twenty-seven

With Anna weighed down by fresh grief and my own days as available as ever, I took it upon myself to expand my household duties, although I kept to the upstairs so I wouldn't get caught.

I began sweeping the bedroom carpets with the witchlike broom, which turned out to be made of dried heather, and then, since I was sweeping anyway, did the hallway to the top of the stairs. Less than a week after Anna's return, I was doing the entire upstairs on my own, polishing the doorknobs, trimming and filling the lamps, gathering laundry, changing the sheets—even scouring the sink, tub, and toilet with Vim powder. Meg repaired my manicure as necessary, so while my nails were shorter, they were as flashy as ever, and Ellis remained none the wiser.

I grew bolder, and one day decided to sweep all the way down the stairs, since that was where the carpet ended. Too late, I heard the clicking of Conall's toenails and a moment later was face-to-face with Angus. I was on the bottom step, in

an apron, clutching the broom. I froze like a deer in the middle
of the road.

A sudden widening of his eyes betrayed his surprise.

"Good afternoon," I said, after a few beats of silence, trying
to act as though we found ourselves in this situation all the
time.

He frowned. "And how long has this been going on?"

"A while," I said, feeling the heat rise to my cheeks. "Please
don't blame Anna—it was entirely my idea. I just wanted to
help."

The corners of his mouth twitched and a twinkle crept into
his eyes. He laughed before continuing on his way, shaking his
head and followed by a visibly confused Conall.

I sank down on the stair, light-headed with relief.

I had been restricting my efforts to the upstairs only for fear
of getting caught, but since Angus apparently didn't mind,
I began to help in the kitchen as well. I always brought my
coat, gloves, and gas mask with me, so that if Ellis and
Hank returned early, I could slip out the back and return by
the front, pretending I'd been on a walk. This was Meg's idea,
and Anna objected vehemently. She was adamant that it was
bad luck for a person to enter and leave a house by different
doors.

Although I was close to useless to begin with, I was a willing student and they were patient with me. I soon learned how
to scrape, not peel, carrots and potatoes, and how to cube turnips. After my first brackish mishap, I learned how to properly
salt water for boiling, and not just how to slice bread, but how
to do it to wartime standards—vendors weren't allowed to sell
bread of any kind, even National Loaf, until it was stale enough
to be sliced thinly. Anna confessed her suspicion that National
Loaf was not made of flour at all but rather ground-up animal

feed, and I thought she was probably right. It would explain a lot about the dense, mealy bread that was commonly referred to as "Hitler's Secret Weapon." It was rumored to be an aphrodisiac—a rumor many suspected had been started by the government itself to get people to eat it.

I learned that all tea was loose leaf and steeped more than once, and also that the strength of a guest's tea was directly related to Anna's feelings about the person. At that point, Hank and Ellis were drinking hot water with a splash of milk.

I discovered that in addition to Anna's many personal beliefs—she couldn't see a crow through the window without running outside to see how many there were and then analyzing what the number meant—there were all kinds of universally accepted sources of bad luck. One of them explained why I hadn't been able to find any meat the day Anna thought I'd seen the Caonaig and run off before starting dinner. It was considered unlucky to store it inside, and so it was kept in a ventilated meat safe out back. I also discovered that Angus was responsible for the contents of many a meat safe.

In the hill just beyond the Anderson shelter was a tall, drafty dugout, which he kept stocked with venison, grouse, pheasant, and other game, hanging it until it was tender. Anna and Meg took what was necessary for the inn and wrapped the remainder in newspaper, which Angus then left on the doorsteps of families in need, delivering the packets at night so no one would feel beholden.

I'd already figured out that Angus was poaching—how else to explain the visit from Bob the Bobby, or the ample supply of game?—but I wasn't shocked, as I once might have been. My education at the hands of Anna and Meg included enough history that I understood the policeman's reluctance to enforce the law, and also that it reflected the prevailing attitude.

It started the day I asked Anna what made a croft a croft instead of just a farm, and got an unexpected earful:

"It *is* a farm," she said indignantly, "only not quite big enough to support a family. *That's* the definition of a croft."

Meg shot me a glance that said, *Well, now you've done it,* and she was right.

Although the events Anna spoke of had taken place nearly two hundred years before, she railed on with as much outrage as if they'd occurred the previous week.

She said that in 1746, following the Battle of Culloden—the final, brutal confrontation in the Jacobite Rising—the Loyalists forced an end to the clan system so the Jacobites could never rise again. They seized their traditional lands and dispersed clan members, banishing individual families onto tiny tracts and expecting them to become farmers overnight. The former communal hunting grounds were turned into sheep farms and sporting estates, and anyone caught hunting on them was subject to severe penalties. The aristocratic shooting party's right to an undepleted stock was held to be more important than feeding the starving.

But it didn't end there. Beyond the physical displacement and the abrupt, forced end of the clan system was a methodical attempt to wipe out the culture. Speaking Gaelic became a crime, and the first sons of clan chiefs were forced to attend British public schools, returning with the same upper-class accent my father-in-law had affected during the heady days of his celebrity.

I imagined the Colonel strutting around in his estate tweeds with his smug sense of superiority on full display, and realized that the loathing Rhona and Old Donnie felt for him—and all of us by association—ran far deeper than anything he'd done personally.

"And *that's* why the taking of a deer is a righteous theft," Anna said, wrapping up with a decisive nod. She had unknowingly repeated Meg's words from the day she showed me the Anderson shelter, and I finally understood.

The taking of a deer was a righteous theft because it was taken from land that was stolen.

Because of their overlapping shifts, I spent the first part of each day with just Anna and the latter part with just Meg, and during these times, our chitchat sometimes turned to confidences.

From Meg, I learned that Anna's brother Hugh had stepped on a mine and what could be found of his remains had been buried in Holland. The other brother she'd lost, twenty-one-year-old Hector, had been hit in the chest by a mortar bomb during the D-Day landings. His body was never recovered, although a fellow soldier had paused long enough to grab his identification tags.

From Anna, I learned that Meg had lost her entire family—both parents and two younger sisters—four years earlier in the Clydebank Blitz. Five hundred and twenty-eight people were killed, 617 injured, and 35,000 left homeless during two nights of relentless air raids that left a mere seven out of twelve thousand houses intact. Meg had been spared only because she'd already joined the Forestry Corps and was in Drumnadrochit.

I kept hoping one of them would offer some information about Angus's background, enough to confirm or refute my theory about the gravestone, but they didn't, and I couldn't ask for fear of giving myself away. I was fully aware that my desire to know wasn't based on curiosity alone.

Chapter Twenty-eight

Meg told us the young women at the Forestry Corps were so excited about the upcoming Valentine's Day dance that they had been reprimanded twice for their lack of concentration around the huge, engine-driven saws. I couldn't blame them. Several of the girls, including Meg, expected to be presented with rings, making their engagements official.

As the day grew closer, the lumberjacks' remarks became increasingly ribald. The night before the dance, one of them said something so off-color it turned Meg into a redheaded fury. She leaned over Rory, who flattened himself against his chair, and scolded him harshly, even as he protested—correctly—that he hadn't said a thing.

"But you did nothing to stop him, did you?" she said, still holding a finger in front of his face.

He glowered at her, but his arms hung slack off the sides of his chair.

When she spun and flounced off, her red curls bouncing, the older men at the bar gave somber nods of approval, and the rest

of the lumberjacks—who understood that Rory had been reprimanded for all of them—went on their best behavior.

Hank leaned in toward Ellis and held a hand up to the side
of his mouth so his voice wouldn't carry.

"Who's the tough guy now?" he snickered.

Ellis was too distracted to be amused. Not twenty minutes
before, he'd excused himself and gone upstairs, only to return
looking pale. I knew exactly what had happened. He'd tried my
door and found it locked.

When I did the rooms that morning, I'd noticed he was
down to five pills. I knew he must be desperate to get more and
wondered why he didn't just come out and ask me, like he always did. Maybe he didn't want to ask in front of Hank, I didn't
know—but whatever the reason, I was grateful because I
couldn't have helped him anyway. I'd flushed the rest of the
pills down the toilet.

On the day of the dance, Meg, Anna, and I went to special effort to dress up the front room because we knew girls would be
coming in. We put linens on the tables, and Anna created something called "coalie flowers." She blamed the lack of real flowers on both weather and the war, and instead put four or five
pieces of coal in glass bowls, added water, salt, and ammonia,
before finally pouring a mixture of violet and blue ink over
them. It was a complete mystery to me how this alchemy would
result in anything resembling flowers, but they were "bloom-
ing" within the hour.

We didn't have enough to put on each table, so we decided
that Meg would herd the girls toward the tables that had them,
and steer the men—who wouldn't appreciate them anyway—
elsewhere. The job was Meg's by default, because Anna would
have gone home by then, and I, of course, would be waiting by
the fire for Ellis and Hank.

The coalie flowers were not our only efforts. Among the three of us, we'd managed to come up with enough eggs and sugar to make two glazed Bundt cakes, which were resting in the dead center of the wooden table in an attempt to keep them out of Conall's reach. The beast himself was sprawled across his master's bed, watching keenly. He was tall enough to reach anything he liked if we turned our backs, but there was no chance of that. We would have protected those cakes with our lives.

Meg and I had given up our egg and sugar rations for the week, which were enough to make one cake, but then Anna's hens went on a laying spree. Because they lived on a croft, the McKenzies got chicken feed instead of egg rations, so their supply was sometimes iffy, but on this occasion the hens came through like champs. Each of the dance-goers was going to get a proper slice, instead of just a taste.

As Anna prepared to leave, hours later than usual, her mood deflated.

"I don't remember the last time I had cake," she said, looking longingly at them.

"Don't you worry," said Meg. "We'll put aside the very first slice, and it will be lovely and thick, too."

"Thank you," Anna said, still sounding glum. "I suppose I'll be off then. Have a grand time—and mind you, I want to hear *all* the details tomorrow."

Anna's parents were staunch Wee Frees, and she wasn't even allowed to wear face powder, never mind attend a dance. Music itself was not allowed, except on Sundays, and then it had to be for the sake of worship only, and sung unadorned. The senior McKenzies were so strict they confined their cockerel under a bushel basket on the Sabbath so he wouldn't get up to anything untoward with the hens.

I understood Anna's melancholy, because I also wished I

could go to the dance, although that would require an alternate universe in which Ellis didn't exist.

At least I'd be able to witness the prelude. I was particularly looking forward to seeing the reaction to the cakes, since I'd had a hand in making them. Although I'd only cracked the eggs and stirred the batter, I'd never been as proud of anything in my life.

Because we didn't trust Conall with the cakes, I stayed in the kitchen to guard them while Meg went upstairs to get ready.

She returned looking like a Valentine's Day dream, in a figure-hugging dress printed with tiny red hearts, her hair carefully arranged, and lips painted into a vermilion cupid's bow. Her high-heeled shoes were made of red suede, with pretty lace-up fronts. They had to be brand-new—I couldn't imagine suede surviving a single day in that climate.

I also noticed she was wearing stockings, and a smile crept across my face. She followed my gaze, blushed, and smiled back.

"What do you think?"

"I think Rory will be knocked off his feet," I said. "I think you'll be the belle of the ball."

"Well, at least I won't have to worry about so-and-so over there trying to lick the gravy browning off my legs."

Conall's tail slid back and forth.

It was my turn to get dressed for dinner, but I hesitated. I knew I wouldn't have another chance to talk to her alone, and I wanted to say something about her imminent proposal. I found myself tongue-tied, probably because I was distinctly unqualified to offer advice in the marriage department. Eventually Meg saved me.

"Now go on," she scolded, flicking her fingers toward the

door. "Make yourself up properly. Tonight, more than ever, beauty is your duty! Even if it's wasted on your pair of Boring McBoringtons over by the fire, the others will notice. And your dress had better be fancy. And it had better be red, especially tonight! Remember, red is the new badge of—"

"I know! I know!" I said, cutting her off with a laugh. "I'll wear red! And good luck tonight! Not that you'll need it!"

I sprinted off before she could reply.

I made up my face as though I really were going to a party, and chose a red taffeta poodle dress that didn't look expensive, because it wasn't. I'd bought it myself, off the rack, before Ellis took control of my wardrobe.

Finally, I used an eye pencil to draw a shaky line up the back of each leg. I wanted to fit in, not stick out, and that night, especially, I didn't want to steal anyone's thunder.

By the time Ellis and Hank came through the front door, their cheeks flushed with the elements and whatever else, the other side of the room was filling up.

"Well, would you look at that," said Hank, coming to a halt.

The mood was electrifying. The girls, all impeccably groomed, were admiring the cakes, which had been presented but not cut. The lumberjacks also made noises about the cakes, but were really admiring the girls. I couldn't help wondering which ones were expecting rings.

Meg was standing next to a table of girls from the Forestry Corps. She leaned over to point out how the coalie flower had transformed since Anna conjured it into being, but I knew exactly what she was really doing. It took but a moment.

"Wait—those are real seams!" squealed one of the other girls. "How on earth did you get your hands on stockings?"

The lumberjacks murmured surprise, as though they weren't already looking at Meg's legs. Having been given an excuse, they stared openly, hungrily.

"Oh," Meg said, shrugging coyly. "They magically appeared." She turned her ankle to better display the back of her calf.

Hank and Ellis watched all this from just inside the door. Finally, Hank dug an elbow into Ellis and they launched themselves toward the fire.

Ellis tripped on the edge of the rug and fell forward, catching himself on the back of a chair. He navigated his way around it, clutching it all the while, and dropped onto its seat. His eyes were bloodshot, his forehead was shiny, and I was shot through with dread.

Hank was so busy looking at Meg that he planted himself squarely on the arm of the second chair before tumbling sideways into it, leaving his head hanging over one upholstered arm and his legs dangling off the other. After a few seconds of stunned surprise, he hauled himself upright.

Ellis looked me up and down. His eyes narrowed. His lip curled in disgust. "What's this?"

I knew he meant my cheap dress and lack of stockings, but I feigned ignorance.

"They're going to a dance," I said. "It's Valentine's Day."

"It's what?" said Hank. "Oh shit. I should have sent something to Violet."

"No, I meant this . . . *getup*," said Ellis, waving the back of his hand toward me. "It's like a combination of scullery maid and streetwalker."

I clamped my mouth shut. There was no point in explaining why I was dressed the way I was. There was no point in doing anything at all, except keeping quiet and hoping the moment would pass.

"Well, *I* think she's a sight for sore eyes," said Hank, still fixated on Meg. "If I'd known she'd be so excited about a pair of stockings, I would have given her a dozen. I'd have given her as many as she wanted. In fact, there's no telling what I might give that girl. With that face and figure, she could come up in the world, like Maddie's mother." He swung his head briefly toward me. "No offense, darling girl."

"Don't take up with trash, Hank," said Ellis, still staring at me. "Blood will out. It always does."

"What?" Hank asked vaguely. He was back to gazing at Meg's calves.

"You can't make a silk purse is what," said Ellis.

"No, those are definitely silk. Look at those gams. I bet they're a mile long. They deserve nothing less than the finest silk . . ."

"Hank?" I said desperately. I waved, trying to get his attention. *"Hank!"*

He glanced quickly and said, "You look nice, too, Maddie. Definitely a silk purse."

"So, Maddie, this silk purse of yours," Ellis said with deadly purpose, "is it red, or is it green?"

Adrenaline blasted from my core to my extremities.

"I beg your pardon?" I said.

"It is *red,* or is it *green?*"

"It's a fine brocade, a veritable smorgasbord of color," said Hank, still completely oblivious to the parallel conversation.

"Maddie? You didn't answer me," said Ellis. The corner of his right eye began to twitch.

"I can't," I said, looking into my lap.

"And why's that?"

"Because you were right."

"About what?"

"About everything."

"Say it!"

"Fine! There's no silk purse! There's only a sow's ear!"

He gave a bitter laugh. "Submission is a color that suits you, my dear. You should wear it more often."

"I suppose you would know," I said, before turning toward the bar.

Meg was serving slices of cake to an admiring audience. Rory had still not arrived, and while she was putting on a brave face I could tell she was wilting.

"I'd have some of her cake, oh yes indeed," Hank said with a low whistle. He swiveled suddenly in his seat. "Say, kids—I just had a crazy idea! Let's go to the dance—it'll be like the servants' ball at Christmas. You two lovebirds can do your own thing, and I . . . well, I might just find a pretty little lovebird of my own. To tide me over, so to speak."

He beamed expectantly at us. When neither of us answered, his smile fell away. His eyes darted suspiciously between us.

"Oh, come on," he groaned, before glancing at the ceiling in despair. "Are you two at it *again*? Let me guess. Ellis said something totally stupid, and now you're not talking to him. Hell, you're not even looking at him. Is this what marriage does to people? No wonder I want nothing to do with it. Neither one of you is an ounce of fun anymore." He sighed and turned back toward the bar. "Now that one over there, *she* looks like an ounce or two of fun . . ."

Chapter Twenty-nine

At eight on the nose, twin brothers from Halifax dropped to their knees and presented matching engagement rings to their sweethearts. When the blushing girls said yes, the remaining lumberjacks burst into song, serenading the brides-to-be with "O Canada." No sooner had they started than old Ian Mackintosh nipped across the road and returned with his pipes, striking in and accompanying the young men as they followed up with a heartfelt rendition of "Farewell to Nova Scotia."

Ellis sipped his whiskey steadily and continued to stare at me like he wanted me dead.

Halfway through "A Ballad of New Scotland," I could stand it no longer and rushed upstairs, locking myself in my room. I leaned against the door, panting.

Not two minutes later, with the pipes still blaring on the main floor, I thought I heard something and pressed my ear to the door. Ellis was swearing and stumbling in the hallway and sure enough came straight to my room. When he found the door locked, he began to pound it.

"Maddie! Maddie! Open the *goddamned door*!"

"Go away!"

I dove onto the bed, pulling my knees to my chest.

"Open the goddamned door! I'm fucking serious!"

I knew he was using the side of his fist because of the way the door jumped in its frame. I wished I could light a candle so I could see if it was in danger of giving, but my hands were shaking too hard to strike a match.

"Maddie! If you don't open the goddamned door right now, I swear to fucking God I'll break it down—do you hear me?" he roared, renewing his assault.

I curled into a ball and pressed my hands to my ears. I couldn't scream for help—there was no possibility anyone would hear me over the booming of the pipes—but where the hell was Hank? Surely he'd noticed we'd both disappeared, and surely he'd been at least vaguely aware of the state Ellis was in.

Over a period that felt like centuries, the thumping slowed to an uneven staccato and, finally, stopped altogether. I heard a soft clunk as Ellis slumped against my door. He began to weep.

"Maddie? Oh, Maddie, what have you done? You're my *wife*. You're supposed to be on *my* team. Now what am I supposed to do? What the hell am I supposed to do?"

His fingernails scraped against the wood as he slid to the floor. He continued crying, but that, too, eventually petered out. A few minutes later, all I could hear was my own ragged breath.

Just as I began to believe he was out for the night, I heard shuffling on the carpet, then a pause.

I held my breath.

A terrible, primal scream preceded a massive blow to the door, followed by another, and then another, as he repeatedly rammed it with his body.

When the wood started to crack, I scrambled off the bed, fumbling in the dark until I found the grate and the fire irons.

Then I crouched behind the chair, clutching the poker and crying.

There was another tremendous blow to the door, and the clatter and thud of a body falling, followed by copious swearing.

Then I heard Hank. "What the hell do you think you're doing?"

"*I need to talk to my wife!*"

"Get up, you moron," Hank said calmly.

"*I need! To talk! To my!*" Ellis huffed and puffed, but could not seem to come up with the final word.

"You can't even stand up. Let's get you to bed."

"I need to talk to her," Ellis insisted, although he sounded suddenly out of steam. He moaned, then began sobbing again.

I crept over to the door, still clutching the fire iron.

"Good Lord," said Hank. "You're a complete mess. Give me your hand."

Ellis mumbled something incoherent.

"No, you didn't dislocate your shoulder. If you had, I wouldn't be able to do *this*."

There was a sharp holler of pain, followed by whimpering.

"See? But if you had dislocated it, you'd have fucking well earned it for being a knucklehead. Give me your hand. All right, upsy-daisy. Now, give me your key and *don't move*."

There was a crash against the wall right outside my door.

"Jesus. Can you at least *try* not to fall over while I get your door open? Do you think you could handle that?"

Ellis was drawing heavy, wheezing breaths, so close it sounded like he was in the room with me.

The door to his bedroom opened, and Hank came back.

"All right. One foot in front of the other."

After a few seconds of clunking and shuffling, I heard the violent screech of bedsprings. It sounded like Hank had tossed Ellis into his room from the doorway.

"Stay put," said Hank. "If you don't, I swear to God, I'll tie you to the bed."

The door shut, and a moment later there were three polite raps on my door.

"Maddie?" said Hank.

"Yes?" I said, still crouched with the fire iron.

"Are you sitting by the door?"

"Yes."

"Are you okay?"

I didn't answer. My heart was thumping so hard I was sure he could hear it, and I was shaking uncontrollably.

After a pause, he said, "Okay, I get it. You're mad at me, but what was I supposed to do? Knock the bottle from his hand?"

"Yes."

He sighed, and I heard him scratch his head. "Yeah, you're right. This won't happen again, I swear. By the way, I locked him in. Want the key?"

"No. You can have it."

"Get some sleep," he said. "He won't be bothering you again tonight. And Maddie? I really am sorry."

He waited awhile before going away, hoping, I suppose, that I'd tell him it was okay.

But I couldn't. Things weren't even remotely okay, and with Ellis out of pills, they could only get worse. Why, oh why, had I flushed them?

When Ian Mackintosh's pipes finally stopped, the gathering downstairs exploded with applause; they cheered, whooped, and stamped their feet until the whole building shook.

Within minutes, the younger crowd had gathered in the street and gone on to the Public Hall, but even after they left, the men who remained at the bar—the older men, the locals—

spoke and laughed in raised voices, excited by their participation in the impromptu *cèilidh*.

I made my way to the window, still in the dark, pulled out the Blackout frame, and opened the sash.

I heard accordion and fiddle music coming from the Public Hall, along with laughing, singing, and animated conversations, including a few that sounded like arguments. Despite the icy air, I knelt by the window and rested my head on the sill, listening.

I felt a terrible pang of longing. Less than half a mile away, young people—people my age, people in love—were planning futures together, futures that would include all the perks of truly loving each other: intimacy, passion, children, companionship, even though there were sure to be trials along the way. Some of the couples might even end up mismatched and miserable, but at that particular moment they were as happy and joyful as the rest, and no matter how mismatched or miserable they turned out to be, I could almost guarantee that none of them would end up with a marriage like mine.

Footsteps came up the road, and I heard a man and a woman talking. They stopped at the house opposite the inn, and went silent for what I could only assume was a good-night kiss. He whispered something, and she went inside, giggling. He waited a few seconds after the door closed, and then whistled as he headed back down the road.

Eventually, I replaced the Blackout frame, and went to bed.

"You *liar*! You *whore*!"

A man's angry shouting jolted me awake, and I initially thought Ellis was back. Then I heard Meg crying and realized the man was Rory. They were in the hallway.

I jumped out of bed and lit the candle on my dresser. Then I stood with my ear to the door.

"I swear by everything that's holy, I'm telling you the truth—"

There was a smack, followed by Meg's sharp cry.

I grabbed the fire iron, which was still leaning by the door.

"You worthless, lying slut! Tell me who he is! *Tell me!*"

"There *is* no one else," she pleaded.

"Then why can't you tell me where you got the stockings?"

"I *did* tell you, Rory—"

"You want me to believe they 'just magically appeared'? What kind of a fool"—another smack, another cry—"do you take me for? What else has he given you, or did you earn them? Is that it? Have you turned professional? What's your price, then? What does a pair of stockings buy a man?"

"Rory, for the love of God—"

"Is it that flat-footed bastard? I've seen how he looks at you. What room is he in? Tell me! *Tell me!*"

When Meg screamed, I yanked my door open and rushed out. The only light was coming from the candle behind me, but it was enough for me to see him haul back and punch her in the side of the face. She dropped to her knees, clutching her cheek, sobbing. She was completely naked. He was in an open shirt and underpants.

"Stop!" I cried. "She's telling the truth!"

He glanced over his shoulder. Our eyes locked. He turned deliberately back to Meg, grabbed a handful of her hair, and kicked her full force in the ribs. The sound of the blow was a terrible muted thud. She made an *oof* noise as the air was forced out of her.

"*I gave them to her!*" I shrieked.

He kicked her again, still holding her by the hair, then tossed her aside. She collapsed and made no effort to move, like an unclothed porcelain doll dropped in a nursery. As he pulled his leg back to deliver another kick, I raised the poker and tore down the hallway.

Before I could get there, Angus charged out of the stairwell and in a single motion had Rory pinned against the wall by his throat, dangling him so his feet were above the ground. Rory's hands swatted at and finally grabbed the hand around his throat, but he didn't make a sound. Angus's other arm remained at his side, his fingers splayed.

"What the fuck is going on?" said Hank, peeking out of his room with a candle. When he saw, he ducked back in.

I dropped the poker and rushed to Meg. She was conscious, but barely. I dragged her toward her room and crouched beside her, wrapping my arms around her, shielding her nakedness. She whimpered and covered her head with her arms.

There was a rhythmic thumping across the hall. I looked up, expecting to see Angus throwing punches. Instead, he continued to dangle Rory with one hand. The thumping was Rory slapping the wall behind him with open palms. His eyes bulged and his tongue protruded, and while the light was faint, his face was clearly not the right color, and getting darker quickly. The slapping got slower, and finally ceased. A wet patch appeared on the front of his underpants, and urine trickled down his leg, over his foot, and onto the floor.

It felt like an eternity, but it was probably only a few seconds later that Angus dropped him. He crumpled to the floor and remained utterly still. I was sure he was dead, but after a few seconds he jerked violently and clutched his throat, gasping for air. It was a terrible sound, grating and rasping.

Angus stood beside Rory, hands on hips. He was in blue striped pajama bottoms, but no shirt. Not a one of us was properly covered, least of all Meg, and it made the horror of the moment somehow more real.

Angus poked Rory with his foot. "I don't suppose I need to tell you what will happen if I ever find you darkening my door again," he said.

Rory writhed on the floor, drawing ragged, scratchy breaths, and still grasping his throat.

"I'll take that as a no," said Angus, leaning over and lifting Rory by the armpits. He turned and threw him into the stair-well.

I held my breath during the series of bangs and thuds as Rory fell down the stairs. I was sure I'd just witnessed a murder, but moments later I heard the front door open and then click quietly shut.

Chapter Thirty

Angus scooped Meg out of my arms as though she weighed nothing.

"Pull back the bedclothes," he ordered, sending me scrambling across the floor. "And you," he said to Hank, who'd appeared in the doorway with a candle, "bring that in and light the others."

Angus laid Meg on the bed and drew the covers over her pale, naked form. She rolled onto her right side, crying quietly. Her left cheek was bloodied, her eyelid ballooning. Blood trickled from her nose, and her lip was split.

"Where else did he hurt you, *m'eudail*?" Angus said softly, sitting on the edge of the bed. He stroked the top of her head as though she were a child. She just wept.

"He kicked her in the ribs," I said. "Hard."

Angus swung his head around. "And what were you doing out there? You could have been hurt as well."

"I was going to kill him."

He stared at me for several seconds.

"I'm going to get Dr. McLean," he said, standing up.

"There's a first aid kit in the kitchen. It's tucked in behind the—"

"I know where it is," I said. "I'll get it."

Angus nodded and turned to Hank, who had by then lit the other candles.

"You—fetch some logs from the peat stack downstairs and get a fire going in here. And light the hall lamps. It's going to be a long night."

I ran down the stairs, feeling my way in the dark to where I knew there was a flashlight. I located the white metal tin with the red cross and knocked down the soap flakes in my haste to grab it. As I sprinted back upstairs, I passed Hank on his way down.

I sat on Meg's bed, flipped open the lid, and soaked some cotton wool with iodine.

"Oh, Meg, I'm so sorry. This is going to sting," I said, before dabbing the gash on her cheek. She didn't so much as flinch.

Her left eye had shut completely in my short absence—the flesh above the socket had expanded and rolled over, creating a grotesque new lid. A trickle of blood ran from the corner of her mouth to the pillow, and, with a fresh wave of horror, I wondered if she'd lost any teeth.

Hank returned with an armful of logs.

"I have to get some compresses," I said. "She's swelling badly."

I got two large metal bowls from the kitchen and took them out back, leaving the door wide open. I fell to my knees on the frozen ground and scooped up snow, throwing it into one of the bowls and punching it down until ice crystals formed and tore at my knuckles. When I couldn't pack it any harder, I ran back inside, pausing just long enough to kick the door shut with my bare foot. I paused at the sink to fill the second bowl with water, set it on top of the first, and dropped a pile of clean rags into it.

When I appeared in the doorway with the stacked bowls,

Hank turned his head, but otherwise didn't move. He'd managed to get a small fire going and stood awkwardly in front of it.

"Hank, the hall lamps," I said.

He sprang into action.

I set the bowls on the bedside table, wrung out a cloth, and draped it across Meg's forehead. I folded another and laid it on her cheek, right under her eye.

Then I sat beside her, stroking her tangled hair and making shushing noises until I realized my fingers were sticky with blood. When I investigated, I found that a chunk of her hair was missing, leaving a patch of bright red scalp exposed.

I cleaned that as well, before covering it with yet another cold cloth. Meg didn't react to any of it.

As I waited for Angus to return with the doctor, there was nothing I could do but sit with her, swapping out the compresses when they were no longer cold and watching the water turn pink. I'd never felt so helpless in all my life.

Dr. McLean banished everyone while he examined Meg, so the rest of us went downstairs to wait. As far as I could tell, Ellis had slept through the entire thing. That, or he was dead, but I saw no reason to check. If he was dead, he'd still be dead in the morning.

Hank and I sat by the dampened fire. Angus lit a lamp and paced. He'd pulled on a sweater before heading out into the night, but I knew Hank had already seen his scars. They were impossible to miss.

When Dr. McLean finally emerged from the stairwell, I leapt to my feet.

"How is she?"

The doctor set his bag on the floor and adjusted his glasses. "I've given her morphine, so for the moment she's comfortable, but she's taken a very serious beating. Do you happen to know the brute responsible?"

"Aye," said Angus. "And he's taken a wee beating himself."

"Will she be all right?" I asked.

"She has a concussion, a great number of contusions, bruising of the spleen and kidney, and at least three cracked ribs. She lost the top molars on the left side, and the bicuspids are loose, although they might take hold again."

"We need to call an ambulance," I said. "Surely she needs to go to the hospital."

"Ordinarily I'd agree," said Dr. McLean. "But under the circumstances, if there's any possibility she can be cared for here, I think that would be preferable."

"What circumstances?" asked Angus.

"The hospital is in Inverness," the doctor explained, "which is suffering from a fuel shortage and an outbreak of respiratory illness. Chest congestion is the last thing the poor girl needs with cracked ribs, so I'd strongly prefer not to expose her. But if you do keep her here, you'll need to watch her very closely."

"What do we do?" I asked.

After a pause, I realized everyone was staring at me. I turned to Angus.

"I know you're busy elsewhere during the day, but between Anna and me, I'm sure we can manage. Maybe Rhona can come back for a while."

"Maddie," Hank said slowly. "Are you sure you know what you're doing?"

"I know exactly what I'm doing . . . Angus?"

It was the first time I'd addressed him by his Christian name in front of anyone else. He looked hard into my eyes.

"Maddie . . ." Hank said in the background.

"Please," I said to Angus. "The doctor said she'd be better off here, and I'll hold up my end. I promise."

He turned to Dr. McLean and nodded. "She'll stay here."

. . .

Hank sat quietly as the doctor gave instructions for Meg's care.

We were to watch for signs of shock—paleness, a drop in temperature, a weak or rapid heartbeat. If that happened, we were to call an ambulance immediately, because it meant she was bleeding internally. Also, because of the concussion, we were to wake her once an hour for the next twelve hours to check her mental acuity.

"I would normally have you compare her pupils at the same time, but I'm afraid that won't be possible with the swelling. However, each time you wake her, she must take five or six deep breaths to ward off pneumonia. If she can manage to cough, all the better. She will not want to, but it's critical. I left morphine on the dresser. With your experience in the field, I assume you're comfortable administering it?"

"Aye," Angus said grimly.

"Good. Well. Unless you have any other questions, I'll be off."

He picked up his bag and went to the door. Angus walked with him.

"And the animal who did this—you say he's been dealt with?"

"For the time being," said Angus. "But if you should happen to be called out to one of the lumberjack camps tonight, may I recommend you take your time, or perhaps even a wrong turn?"

"Aye," the doctor said. "With the Blackout, it can be very difficult to find your way in the dark. One might even say impossible on a night such as this. I assume you'll be paying a visit to the commanding officer tomorrow?"

"That I will," said Angus. "And I may well pay a visit to the man himself."

The doctor nodded. "Under the circumstances, I can't think of a single reason to try to dissuade you. Good evening, Captain Grant."

Hank looked up sharply, and my heart began to pound.

I was right. It was him—he was the Angus on the stone.

Chapter Thirty-one

Although my heart was racing from learning the truth, the rest of me was bone weary. We all were, and slogged back upstairs in single file—I followed Angus, Conall followed me, and Hank brought up the rear.

I stopped cold when I saw Meg. I hadn't thought she could look any worse.

"Dear God," I said, creeping closer to the bed.

The doctor had stitched up the cut on her lip, as well as the gash that ran vertically down her cheek. The latter was terrible to behold—a makeshift black zipper, encrusted with blood, and indisputable proof that she'd be permanently scarred. I wondered if the missing teeth would hollow out her face, and hoped to God she wouldn't lose the others. Despite all this, she appeared to be in a deep sleep.

Hank cleared his throat. He lingered in the hallway, just beyond Meg's door.

"So, do you need me to grab more logs, or . . . ?"

What he was really asking was if he could go to bed, and I hated him for it.

"We'll manage," said Angus.

Hank hung around a few seconds longer before disappearing. I could only imagine what he'd tell Ellis in the morning, but there was nothing I could do about it.

When Angus went to get more ice, I retrieved a quilt from my own room, pushed the chair around so it faced Meg, then settled into it, tucking my feet beneath me.

"You should go to bed," Angus said when he came back. "I'll sit with her tonight and Anna can take over in the morning."

"I'd like to stay, if you don't mind."

"I don't mind, but unless I manage a wee bit of rearranging, you'll probably be on your own in the afternoon."

"That's all right."

He stoked the fire, then crouched against the wall. I snuck a quick peek. He was studying me.

"So you were going to kill him, were you?" he asked.

"I meant to, yes."

He gave a soft laugh. "You surprise me, Mrs. Hyde."

"Maddie. I'm just Maddie. Anna and Meg have been calling me that for weeks, except when my husband is around."

He looked at me for a very long time, and I wondered how much he had figured out.

"I'm afraid it's time," he said forty minutes later.

Meg was difficult to rouse, but we finally managed it by calling her name and tapping the backs of her hands. Angus asked if she knew the date. She replied that it was Valentine's Day and began to cry.

It was her fault, she mumbled through broken lips. Rory had been in his cups, and she should have known better than to be coy about the stockings, never mind scolding him the night before. He was a good man, really he was—she was moving to

Nova Scotia with him after the war. She'd seen the "Welcome to Canada" film just the week before, along with all the other girls who were going to marry lumberjacks when the war ended.

"Hush now, *m'eudail*," said Angus.

"What if he doesn't come back?"

Angus and I exchanged glances.

"You've got to take some deep breaths now," Angus said. "Only five, but they must be deep."

"I can't," she wept. "You don't understand. It hurts."

"You've got to, Meg," I said. "It's doctor's orders. You don't want pneumonia, do you?"

Angus and I helped her roll onto her back and held her hands, counting aloud as she valiantly filled and emptied her lungs. Her cries were heart-wrenching, but as soon as we counted to five, she turned onto her side and drifted off.

"Thank God for morphine," Angus said. "She probably won't even remember we woke her."

"How long before her next dose?"

"Not quite four hours. I'll give it to her just a wee bit early to stay ahead of the pain. It's better than trying to catch up to it."

As he sat back down, I wondered if he was speaking from personal experience.

"What will happen to Rory?" I asked.

"There's no saying. But I can tell you this—he'll never lay a finger on her again."

The fire danced in his brilliant blue eyes, and I knew Meg would be safe from Rory forever, even if she didn't want to be.

With everything else that had gone on that night, it was hard to believe that Ellis was still locked in his room, quite possibly tied to the bed. I wanted to crawl across the floor to Angus and tell him everything. I wanted to ask him about his own family. I wanted to feel his arms around me, and to wrap mine around him. I wanted to feel the blood coursing through his veins as he vowed to protect me, because I would believe him.

Just after we woke Meg for the third time, we heard Anna moving about downstairs.

Angus climbed to his feet. "Well, I suppose I'd better let her know what's happened. Then I have to step out for a while—I have a wee bit of business to take care of."

A few minutes later, Anna raced up the stairs and into the room. When her eyes landed on Meg, she burst into tears. I rushed around the bed to hug her.

"It's evil, Maddie, that's what it is," she said, crying into my shoulder. "Pure evil. What kind of a monster would do such a thing? To our poor, sweet Meg, of all people. Meg, who has no kin at all."

"I don't know," I said helplessly. "I really don't know."

When Anna calmed down enough that I believed she'd remember the doctor's instructions, I left to get some sleep.

As I walked down the hall toward my room, I noticed that the door was ajar. I had been in a rush when I got the quilt, but the daylight behind it gave me pause. I clearly remembered replacing the Blackout frame after eavesdropping on the dance.

I crept up to the door and gave it a little push.

My room had been completely torn apart. The dresser drawers were wide open and empty, the top one yanked out completely. Everything I'd kept inside—my personal littles, slips, nightgowns, stockings, and books—had been flung randomly about the room. My dresses, trousers, and sweaters had been ripped from the closet, and the suitcases and trunks I'd kept stored behind them had been hauled out, opened, and overturned. Even my cosmetics case had been dumped, and then hurled with such force that one of the bronze hinges from the tray stuck out to the side like a broken wing.

Someone touched my shoulder. I spun around, flattening myself against the wall.

It was Ellis, of course. His face was gaunt and his complexion yellow. The expression behind his red-rimmed eyes seemed vaguely conciliatory, solicitous even.

"Maddie?" he said, inching forward and cocking his head. He forced his parched lips into a smile. "What have you done with the pills, Maddie?"

My mind spun, but I couldn't hide what I'd done. I couldn't magically conjure up more.

"I flushed them," I said.

His wheedling façade was replaced in an instant by fury.

"You did *what*? When?"

"I don't know. A while ago."

"What in the hell possessed you to do such a stupid thing? *Jesus!*"

"You did," I said.

He looked dumbfounded.

"Oh my God. Oh my God," he said quietly, to himself. He ran a shaky hand through his hair and began gasping for breath.

I moved sideways, feeling the wall behind me and trying to find my door. My fingers found and curled around the edge of the doorframe.

He raised his face abruptly, looking at me with stricken eyes. "What the hell happened to you, Maddie? When did you become so hell-bent on destroying me?"

My mouth opened and closed, but I couldn't find an answer.

He turned and launched himself down the hallway, weaving from side to side and banging into the wall when his legs failed to straighten.

I slipped into my room and bolted the door. Then I collapsed on the bed and surrendered immediately to a deep, dreamless sleep.

When I woke up and realized that almost nine hours had gone by, I rushed back to Meg's room. It was well past the time Anna usually returned to the croft, and close to the time hungry customers began to arrive.

She was curled up in the chair with my quilt over her legs, as I had been earlier. I paused at Meg's bedside, gazing down at her battered face.

"How is she?" I whispered.

"Angus gave her some morphine just now, so she's out again. He says we don't have to wake her up anymore. Alas, he also says that when she is awake, she still has to take deep breaths and try to cough."

I sat on the floor beside the chair, with my legs stretched out and crossed at the ankles. "I'm sorry I slept so long. I can take over now. Has anyone done anything about dinner?"

"There's no need. Angus tacked a sign to the door saying 'Closed Due to Illness'—illness, for goodness' sake."

I could only shake my head.

Anna sighed. "It must be very bad indeed since the doctor didn't give her castor oil. Before anything else, you get a dose of the castor oil. I don't even see that he's left a tonic—he always leaves a tonic. How is she supposed to recover without a tonic?"

She looked at me as though I should know. When I raised my hands to indicate that I didn't, she sighed again.

"Rhona's got a soup going downstairs and I'm sure Mhàthair is mixing up all kinds of tea right at this very moment, but Angus says we're not to give her anything until Dr. McLean says it's all right."

A quiet moan rose from the bed. We sprang to our feet.

Meg moved restlessly beneath the bedclothes. Anna wrung out a cloth and mopped her brow, then dabbed her lips with something from a small jar.

"Lanolin," Anna whispered. "We've no shortage around here. Unfortunately, it does leave you smelling a bit like a sheep."

Meg went still again. Anna and I returned to our spots and stared into the flames. They were hypnotic.

Anna finally broke the silence. "Are you cold? Do you want the quilt?"

"I'm all right, thanks. It's toasty in here. I don't think I've been this warm since I got to Scotland."

"I suppose your house in America is very warm."

"Temperature-wise, sure," I said.

Anna peered sideways at me. "Is everything all right? Only I couldn't help but hear the racket earlier, with your husband shouting and stumbling about the way he was."

"No, not really," I said. "Things are actually pretty dismal."

After almost a minute of sneaking expectant glances, Anna broke down. "I don't mean to stick my nose where it doesn't belong, but sometimes it can help to unburden yourself." She turned deliberately away, presumably to ease my confession.

I hesitated, but not for long. "I think I'm going to get a divorce," I whispered.

"A divorce!" Anna's head whipped around, her eyes so wide I could see the whites all the way around. "You'll be like Wallis Simpson!"

I recoiled. "I certainly hope not. I only plan on getting the one—if I can even figure out how."

As Anna reflected on this, she turned back to the bed. Her eyes remained huge.

"I shouldn't have said anything," I said. "I've shocked you."

"No," she said, shaking her head vehemently.

As a silence swelled between us, I plunged into despair. I couldn't stand the thought of Anna not liking me anymore.

"You think I'm awful, don't you?" I asked.

"Don't be ridiculous," she said. "It's plain to see how he treats you. It just hadn't occurred to me there was anything you could *do* about it."

I thought of the cockerel confined under his basket on Sundays, and realized that divorce was probably not an option in Glenurquhart.

"Does he know?" Anna asked.

"No, and I have to keep it that way for now, because after I tell him, I'll have to live somewhere else. If I can find somewhere else."

"Oh aye," she said, nodding. "I can imagine it would be miserable indeed to remain under the same roof once you've broken the news."

I looked at Meg's swollen, bloodied face, and thought of the cracking sounds the door had made as my enraged husband threw himself against it, trying to get to me.

"I'm worried it might be worse than that."

Anna's eyes flew from me to Meg and then back again, widening in understanding.

We looked hopelessly at each other, then resumed staring at the fire. It cast long shadows that danced all the way across the ceiling before turning sharply down the far wall, like they were following the folded crease in a piece of paper.

Although in the scheme of things I'd said very little, I'd probably said more than I should have. But I wondered if what I'd told her might have set the tone for a few more confidences.

"Anna," I said, "I know it's none of my business, but will you please tell me what happened to Angus? I know he's the one on the gravestone, the one who didn't die. But I know nothing else."

She frowned and blinked, studying me as she considered my request.

My face began to burn. I'd made a mistake, asking about things I had no right to know. I turned toward the opposite wall, filled with shame.

Behind me, Anna sighed heavily.

"Well," she said, "you won't hear it from him, because he doesn't talk about it, and while I'm not one for the blather, it's not what you might call a state secret, so I don't suppose he'd mind."

I'd imagined a million scenarios since the headstone first caught my attention, but none was as tragic as the truth. The only body beneath it was the infant's.

"Mhàthair helped deliver her, in this very room," said Anna. "It's almost certainly the last time there was a fire in the grate. The wee mite lived only a few minutes, God rest her soul. That was nearly the end of Màiri right there. Then, a month to the day later, the telegram came saying Angus was also gone. I was here when Willie delivered it. It's still in the lockbox downstairs. It came on Valentine's Day, of all days."

"When did you find out it wasn't true?"

"Too late for our poor Màiri."

The very first time I saw the grave I'd wondered if Màiri had died of a broken heart, and it turned out she'd done just that. Two weeks after hearing that Angus was dead, she walked to the castle, through the Water Gate, down the slope, and into the loch. The frantic fisherman who saw her do it could not row fast enough to reach her, and her body was never found.

When Anna told me this, my heart twisted. I realized I'd seen Angus at both graves.

"Had they been married long?" I asked.

"They'd been sweethearts for years, but they only wed when the war broke out and Angus joined up. It had that effect on a lot of people."

"My God. They weren't even married two years."

"Aye. The war has cut short a great many things."

She fell silent, and I knew she was thinking of her brothers.

"Did they have much time together before Angus shipped out?" I asked.

"Here and there. It wasn't until April of 'forty that the fighting really heated up, and it wasn't long after that that Angus was injured the first time."

As Anna recounted what happened, I was struck not just by what she was telling me, but also by how well she knew it. Then I remembered the size of the village and how huge a tragedy this was, even in an age full of tragedy.

During the Battle of Dunkirk, Angus had gone back into the line of fire not once, not twice, but three times to rescue other members of his unit, despite having taken shrapnel in the thigh. His courage attracted the attention of higher-ups, and when he recovered, he was invited to join the newly formed Special Service Brigade.

Only the toughest made it into Winston Churchill's "Dirty Tricks Brigade," the elite and deadly group he formed for the sole purpose of creating "a reign of terror down the enemy coast." They trained at Achnacarry Castle, by then known as Castle Commando, under the fifteenth Lord Lovat, who based his techniques on the small commando units that had impressed his father during the Boer War.

Angus and other potential commandos were dumped off at the train station in Spean, seven miles away, given a cup of tea, and then left to their own devices, in full battle gear, in whatever weather, to find their way to the castle. If they made it, they spent six grueling weeks training with live ammunition, being pushed to the brink of physical exhaustion and beyond, as well as learning all the ways you could kill a man even if you didn't have a weapon.

Angus was shipped off after a leave of only a few days, which was nonetheless long enough to leave Màiri with child. Nine months later, he was grievously wounded—gutted, essentially—during hand-to-hand combat in France, collapsing only after slitting his opponent's throat with the edge of his metal helmet.

As Anna spoke, I could see it all in my head, unfolding relentlessly. I'd dreamed up countless versions of what had happened, but this was worse than any of them. I saw Angus doubled over, struggling to remain upright, using one arm to try to hold in his internal organs while slashing out with the other to fell the enemy soldier. I saw Angus collapsing, sure he was dying, his eyes open and trained on the blue sky, his thoughts on his wife and the child that was due at any moment, and may well have already been born.

Angus was hauled to safety by members of the French Resistance, but nobody knew for a long time—his ID tags had been torn off and lay somewhere among the rotting bodies that littered the cobblestone streets. The fighting was so fierce the corpses could not be recovered for more than a week, rendering them grossly bloated and unrecognizable.

He had remained on the brink of death for weeks. It was a miracle he survived at all, but five months later, against all odds, he made his way back to British territory.

"My God," I said, when Anna paused. "And then he found out his wife and child had both died."

"Aye," said Anna. "There was nothing anyone could have

done about the child, but he blames himself to this day for what happened to Màiri."

"That wasn't his fault," I said.

"I know that, but he feels responsible anyway, like he should have been able to find a way to get word back, even though he was lying right *gralloched* somewhere in a French cellar. He hasn't touched the waters of the loch since. He'll only fish in the rivers. In fact, he won't set foot through the Water Gate."

"Other than that, has he recovered? I mean, physically?"

"He's strong as an ox—I've seen the man haul a deer down the hill on his shoulders, Harris-style. The only reason he's not back at the Front is because they need him at the battle school. Only a commando can train a commando, so that's what he does, up at the Big House, most of the time. The rest of the time he's keeping us all fed."

"Do you think he'll go back to being the gamekeeper? I mean, after the war?"

Anna shook her head. "No. The old laird died, you know. Only a few months ago, but it was a long time coming. He never recovered from the loss of his son, the poor man."

I remembered Bob the Bobby's warning with a sinking feeling. There were no hunting parties at the estate—for obvious reasons—so no rich person was being robbed of a trophy head, and Angus was supplementing the diet of every last family in the village. It was a true case of righteous theft, and I hoped the new laird would have a change of heart. After everything else Angus had been through, it seemed beyond cruel not to let him go back to being the gamekeeper after the war. It was clear he knew and loved the land.

"Well," Anna said wearily, "now that I've blathered your ear completely off, I should probably get going. I'll fetch you a cup of tea first."

"Anna?" I said, as she got to her feet.

"Aye?"

"Thank you for filling me in," I said. "Even if it isn't any of my business."

"Oh, I don't know. I'm starting to think of you as one of us now."

A lump rose in my throat. I thought that might be the nicest thing anyone had ever said to me—and meant.

Chapter Thirty-two

When Anna brought the tea, she also handed me the newspaper.

"Since she'll probably just sleep, I thought you might want something to pass the time."

After Anna left, I checked on Meg, laying a hand across her forehead and watching the rise and fall of her rib cage. Except for her ravaged face and the blood that matted her copper curls, she looked as peaceful as a sleeping child.

I settled into the chair with the newspaper.

IT WON'T BE LONG, NEARING THE END, and GERMANY'S AP-PROACHING DOOM, blared the headlines, although the articles themselves revealed a far grimmer reality.

There was a report from a war correspondent who was traveling with the Seaforth Highlanders as they fought along the Western Front, describing "scenes of utter devastation"—of soldiers trying to clear minefields in torrential rains, of abandoned towns that contained only shells of buildings, of corpses piled high along both sides of the road. In another article, the very same battle was characterized by a stiff-lipped field marshal as "going very nicely although the mud is not helping it."

There was an article about the respiratory illness that raged through Inverness, as well as the fuel shortage. A recent cold spell had caused such a sharp rise in consumption that the municipal authority, the source of the city's firewood, ran out completely. Despite suggestions that emergency fuel supplies in the North should be made available to people in dire distress, nothing had been done about it. One government fuel dump alone had more than seven hundred tons of coal and a thousand tons of timber, yet the sick and elderly in Inverness had nothing at all to put in their grates or stoves.

Sprinkled among reports that the Red Army had killed more than 1,150,000 German soldiers in just over a month, and that Tokyo had been bombed again, and that two days of raids conducted by the Allied Forces had reduced the city of Dresden to rubble, were advertisements for the Palace Cinema on Huntly Street announcing two new movies, *You Can't Ration Love* and *The Hitler Gang,* which would be shown three times a day, and for vitamin B yeast tablets, because "Beauty Depends on Health." A purveyor of effervescent liver salts promised its product would "gently clear the bowels, sweep away impurities, and purify the blood." A circumspect warning about venereal disease admonished that its rise was one of the "very few black spots" on the nation's war record, although it wasn't offering advice on what to do about it.

Perhaps the most absurd juxtaposition of all was of a statement issued by Field Marshal Montgomery, declaring the war to be in its final stages, which was set immediately next to an article about a horse pulling a milk cart that had bolted while the driver was setting milk on a stoop. The horse made a mad dash "along Old Edinburgh Road and down the brae" as milk bottles "flew in all directions." It failed to take the corner at High Street and crashed, cart and all, through the front window of Woolworth's. While "badly cut about the shoulder," the horse was rescued by a policeman and several soldiers, and was expected to make a full recovery.

The sheer scope of detail and information, as well as its seemingly random placement, was proof to me that the world had both gone mad, yet remained the same as it ever was.

Mass killings were described right next to information about laxatives. Cities were bombed, men slaughtered each other in knee-deep mud, civilians were blown to pieces from stepping on mines, but horses still spooked, people still went to the cinema, and women still worried about their schoolgirl complexions. I couldn't decide if this made me understand the world better or meant I'd never fathom it at all.

Dr. McLean came in the late afternoon and said that while he was no longer worried about her concussion, Meg was by no means out of the woods. We were still to watch carefully for signs of shock. He encouraged us to try to get some sustenance into her, although he also warned that we should be gradual about it. He nodded approvingly when I told him that Rhona was downstairs at that very moment working on a soup.

When he left, I followed him downstairs and went into the kitchen. He'd wakened Meg for the examination but followed it with an injection, and I wanted to get something into her before she slipped back out of reach. As soon as Rhona saw me, she ladled out a bowl of rich, fragrant broth and held it out to me with gnarled fingers.

"Thank you," I said.

She returned to the soup, her back so stooped her face was nearly parallel to the steaming liquid. Her white hair was pulled tightly into a bun and parted in the center, showing almost an inch of pink scalp. I couldn't even hazard a guess about how old she was. She could have been anywhere from seventy to ninety, perhaps even older.

I managed to get only a few spoonfuls into Meg before the morphine pulled her away from me.

At three minutes before nine, Angus brought an armful of logs upstairs.

I hadn't heard him come back. As far as I'd known, I was alone in the building. I then wondered what Ellis and Hank were up to, because to my knowledge they also hadn't returned. Perhaps they'd gone elsewhere after seeing the sign on the door.

Angus dropped the logs by the grate, brushed off his hands, and went to Meg's side.

"How is she?" he asked.

"A little better," I said, before relating the events of the doctor's visit. "She had a tiny bit of soup earlier. She's been stirring for about half an hour, so I've been trying to get her to sip some water."

"What time did Dr. McLean give her the shot?"

"Around five."

"Then she's due. That's why she's restless."

I sat in the chair, watching as he administered it. This was the first time I'd laid eyes on him since Anna told me what had happened to him.

He filed a groove into the neck of one of the glass ampoules, snapped the top off, and filled the syringe. Then he wrapped a length of rubber tubing around Meg's arm, slid the needle in, and slowly depressed the plunger. After, he stood at the side of the bed, looking down at her.

"You should go," he said, glancing at me. "Get some rest while you can."

"You're the one who should sleep. You were up the entire night."

"If I'm not mistaken, I wasn't alone."

"Yes, but I slept for nine hours after Anna came. I can easily last until morning, although I can't give her morphine. If you go to bed now, you'll get almost four hours before she's due again, and then you can go right back to bed."

He put his hands on his hips, considering.

"Please," I said. "I insist."

His eyebrows shot up. "You insist, do you?"

"I promised last night that I'd hold up my end, and it's clearly your turn to sleep," I said, nearly tripping over my tongue in my haste to explain. "That's all I meant."

"I rather preferred it when you were insisting."

I glanced at him. He was grinning.

I lifted my chin, trying my best to channel the headmistress at Miss Porter's. "In that case, I'm afraid I really must insist that you get some rest."

He laughed quietly. "Well, when you put it like that, I suppose I have no choice."

He eventually did go down to sleep, but not before replacing the bowl of ice, stoking the fire, and extracting a promise that I would get him if I needed anything else—or even if I just changed my mind about going to bed—and that in any case, he'd be back in just under four hours.

I curled up in the chair, which was deep enough that I could fold myself sideways and end up almost horizontal. It was only when I tucked the quilt under my legs that I realized I was still barefoot, still wearing the nightgown I'd donned the night before, and therefore had paraded around like that all day—in front of the doctor, in front of Rhona, in front of everyone.

Getting dressed simply hadn't occurred to me. Although I was embarrassed, at that moment I was also relieved. Keeping an overnight vigil would almost certainly be more comfortable in a nightgown.

Apparently, it was too comfortable.

The fire let out a loud snap and jolted me awake. A red ember sat on the carpet in front of me. I leapt from the chair, grabbed the poker, and pushed it onto the stone flags.

After a quick scan of the room showed that nothing else was on fire, my eyes landed on Meg. I looked and looked with rising fear, because I could not see any movement beneath the quilts.

I was at her bedside in an instant, hovering in blind terror. Her face was gray, her mouth slack. Her right eye, the one that wasn't swollen shut, was slightly open, displaying a sliver of white. I laid a hand on her rib cage, trying to discern movement, but my hand shook too violently for me to tell. I pressed three fingers to the side of her throat, seeking a pulse.

"Meg?" I said, and then again, loudly, "Meg?"

I grabbed the hand mirror from her dresser and held it in front of her mouth. It jerked wildly despite my best efforts to keep it steady, but it was aimed at her face at least part of the time and I never saw so much as a hint of fog.

Seconds later I was stumbling down the stairs in the dark, feeling my way along the walls, and screaming, *"Angus, Angus!"*

We ran into each other in the doorway to the kitchen. He caught me by my upper arms to steady me. "What is it? What's wrong?"

"She's not breathing—"

He sprinted past and was thumping up the stairs before I even had a chance to turn around.

By the time I found my way back, he was sitting on the bed holding two fingers against the inside of her wrist.

I crept over, breathing heavily, too afraid to ask.

After an unbearably long time, he laid her hand down and felt her forehead.

"Her pulse is steady," he said. "She's a little hot, if anything. Probably from the fire. Shock has the opposite effect."

I covered my mouth to contain a cry of relief.

"Oh, thank God! Thank God! I fell asleep and then when I woke up she wasn't moving, and I thought. . . ." I sucked air through my steepled fingers before finishing in a whisper. "I thought I'd let her die."

"You didn't, lass. Everything's all right."

My vision filled with swarms of gnats, then disappeared completely.

The next thing I knew, my forehead was resting on my knees and I was looking at the folds of my nightgown.

I was on the floor, and Angus was propping me up. He had an arm beneath my legs, lifting my knees, and the other behind my shoulders.

"Stay as you are until the blood comes back," he said, when I tried to lift my head.

"I'm sorry," I said. "I don't know what happened."

"You fainted is what happened," said Angus. "You went down pretty hard. Are you hurt?"

"I don't think so. I'm sorry."

"Don't apologize. There's nothing to be sorry about."

Sweat broke out on my brow and upper lip, and the buzzing in my ears grew louder. A wave of nausea ran through me.

"Oh God, I think I'm going to be sick."

He grabbed the stacked bowls from the bedside table and set them on the floor next to me.

I was horrified at the thought of vomiting in front of him, but for a while it seemed inevitable. Eventually, mercifully, the feeling passed.

"I'm all right now," I said.

"When did you last eat?"

"I'm not sure," I said. "Yesterday, I think. Although I had a cup of tea earlier."

"Well, that will do it. Where did you put the first aid kit?"

"It's under the bed."

A minute later I was nibbling the small square of emergency chocolate. As soon as it was gone, I folded the foil wrapper and said, "I think I can walk now."

"And I think you should wait another minute or two."

He took a facecloth from the bowl, wrung it out, and held it against my forehead. After a moment, I took it from him and wiped the front and back of my neck.

"I think I really am all right now," I said.

"Then let's get you to bed."

He stood and offered me his hands. As he pulled me to my feet, I crumpled. He caught me with both arms and held me upright.

"Steady, there. Do you need to sit back down?"

"No," I whispered, leaning heavily against him. "I'm fine."

"Take your time. Just let me know when you're ready."

When I finally thought I could control my legs, I said, "I'm okay now. Really, this time."

"All right," he said, keeping a firm grasp on me. "One foot in front of the other. I can't grab a candle, but I know the way. I won't let you fall."

"You should know something," I said as he steered me into the darkness of the hall.

"And what's that?"

"There are a few things on my floor."

"What sorts of things?"

"Mostly clothes. My husband was looking for something this morning."

Angus supported me into the pitch black of my room and through the flotsam.

"Here you are, then."

I sank onto the bed and against my pillow. As Angus found and pulled the covers up over me, his hands grazed the top of my foot, my throat, my chin.

"I'm really sorry, Angus," I said, after he wrapped me into a cocoon.

"For what? You couldn't help fainting."

"No, for promising I'd look after Meg and then falling asleep."

"Don't *fash* yourself."

"But now you're not going to get any rest at all."

"I got a couple of hours, and I'll grab a few more winks here and there. But I'm afraid there is something that *I* must insist on."

"What's that?"

"No more skipping meals. I can't have all of you out of commission at once. The inn doesn't run itself, you know."

His words caused a bittersweet lump in my throat, my second of the day.

Although I couldn't see a thing, I knew exactly where he was. I could feel his presence, and for a moment I thought he might reach for me. I held my breath and lay absolutely still, waiting, hoping, yet also fearful.

When nothing happened, I said in a cracked voice, "Angus?"

"Aye?"

For a short time I thought I might say something, even though I didn't have a clue what, but the silence rose and overwhelmed me, a vast, oppressive thing that billowed around me until I was sealed within it.

"Thank you for helping me back to my room," I finally said.

"I'd best get back to Meg now," he said. "Sleep well, Maddie."

A few seconds later, the door clicked shut behind him, and I was left gasping in the dark.

Chapter Thirty-three

The next day, I stopped long enough to gather some clothes off the floor and get dressed before rushing to Meg's room. I was still trying to smooth the wrinkles from my skirt when I got there.

"Sorry I'm so late," I said, batting at the creased material. "I guess I really did have some sleep to catch up on, but with any—"

I glanced up, expecting to see Anna. Instead, I found an old woman with peppery hair sitting in the chair. She was knitting up a storm: *clickity-clickity-click* went her needles, which were fed by an endless strand of yarn that coiled out from a carpet-bag beside her. A sock was forming beneath them.

She peered at me over the top of her wire-framed spectacles. "I suppose you'll be the one from America, the one Anna's been talking about. Maddie Hyde, is it?"

"Yes. That's me."

"I'm Mrs. McKenzie, Anna's mother, but the folk around here call me Mhàthair. You might as well too. When it comes right down to it, we're all Jock Tamson's bairns."

I moved closer to Meg. "How is she?"

"Taking a bit of soup when she's awake, and also sipping tea."

"One of your teas?"

"Aye. I've left some more with Rhona. Try to get as much of it down her as you can. It's for the bruising and swelling, and will only work for the first couple of days. Then I'll bring another."

Mhàthair's needles never stopped moving, even when she was looking at me. I stared in fascination at the partial sock.

"Where's Anna?"

"At the croft. She'll be back later. Angus said you'd had a rough night, so I stayed on a wee bit to let you rest."

"Thank you."

"And now you're to get yourself down to the table. You've nowt on your bones at all. I've seen bigger kneecaps on a sparrow."

It seemed Angus had told everyone about my fainting spell, because minutes after I sat down, Rhona shuffled out of the kitchen with a plate of scrambled eggs, a large slice of ham, and a heap of fried potatoes. She set the plate down, pointed at it, and then pointed at me.

She had just gone back into the kitchen when Hank and Ellis breezed through the front door. They were smiling, freshly shaven, and enveloped in a cloud of cologne. Ellis looked preternaturally pink and healthy—it didn't seem possible given what he'd looked like the day before.

When they headed toward me, my heart began to pound. I felt like my mother-in-law's canary, trapped in its evershrinking cage.

"Good morning, darling girl," said Hank, plopping himself onto a chair. "Did you miss us?"

"Morning, sweetie," said Ellis, kissing my cheek.

Bile rose in the back of my throat. I couldn't believe he thought we could go back to pretending nothing was wrong. Even Hank should have realized that things were too far gone, but he barreled on with whatever silly game he was playing.

"So did you?" Hank asked.

"Did I what?"

"Miss us? You know—because you love us and we spent the night at the Clansman? Don't tell me you didn't notice." He blinked at me expectantly, then dropped his jaw in outrage. "Oh my God. You *didn't* notice. Ellis, your wife didn't even notice we were missing."

"I *did* notice."

"But you didn't miss us?"

"I'm sorry. I was a little busy," I said.

"Busy *sleeping* is what we heard," Ellis said with a grin. "We swung by to collect you in the afternoon, but the girl—not the injured one, the slow one from the kitchen—said you were having a nap. Apparently you needed it. You still look a bit peaked."

I'm sure I did—I hadn't done my hair and face in two days. He, on the other hand, looked like the picture of health. I didn't understand how that was possible. Had he come across someone with nerve pills at the Clansman? Certainly something had happened to restore the apples to my husband's cheeks.

"You didn't miss much," Hank said, lighting a cigarette. "Its only advantage over this dump was that it was open and we were starving. But wait—what's this?" He looked at my plate in wide-eyed amazement. "Ellis, maybe we should have stayed here after all. I haven't seen a breakfast like this since we were on the right side of the pond."

"Looks good," said Ellis, reaching over and helping himself. "Anyway, darling, go pack a few things and slap on some war paint. We're going on a road trip."

"We're what?" I said.

Hank also snagged some potatoes, popping them in his mouth.

"Oh, wow," he said. "These are really good." He licked his fingers and reached for more.

"Anyway," Ellis continued, "we're going to Fort Augustus. One of the old farts at the Clansman last night told us the abbey there has manuscripts that describe the very earliest sightings of the monster. Apparently one of Cromwell's men saw it around 1650—he recorded seeing 'floating islands' in his log, but since there are no islands on the loch, the only possible thing he could have been seeing was the monster—maybe even several of them, which is interesting for all kinds of reasons. There are also Pictish carvings of the beast, which probably contain clues as well. There's obviously some pattern we haven't figured out yet, and it could be something as simple as migratory—it's a bit like code breaking, very complicated, but we're definitely circling it. In fact, we're so close I can practically taste it."

I stared, unable to believe he'd just compared what they were doing to code breaking, or anything else related to the war.

"I can't go," I said.

"Why not?"

"Because I have to look after Meg."

Ellis leaned back and sighed. "Darling, you *can't* look after Meg. But if it makes you feel any better, we can hire a nurse."

"But I promised Angus—"

Outrage flashed across his face. "*Angus?* And when, exactly, did Blackbeard become Angus to you? Good Lord, Maddie. I can't even remember how many times I've warned you about getting friendly with the help."

"Fine. I promised *Captain Grant* that I would help look after Meg."

Ellis's expression switched from indignation to painfully aggrieved. He tore his eyes away. "That was uncalled for."

"How was that uncalled for?" I went on. "He *is* a captain. Which means he's a commissioned officer—hardly 'the help.'"

"Regardless of rank, he's a poacher and a common criminal, and I don't understand why everyone around here, including, apparently, my own wife, seems to think he's such a hero," he said.

"Because he *is* a hero. You know nothing about him."

"And you do?" he asked.

I stared straight ahead, at the far wall.

Ellis leaned forward and clasped his hands on the table, donning the insufferable face he always did when he decided my opinions were a result of mental frailty.

"I understand that you care about Meg and want to make sure she recovers," he said patiently, "but there's absolutely no reason you have to do it personally."

"But I do. She's my friend."

"She's not your friend. She's a barmaid."

"Who happens to be my friend."

Ellis hung his head and sighed. After several seconds, he looked back up.

"I know you're in a delicate state right now, but I wish you could see what is really happening."

"I'm not in a delicate state. I'm *fine*."

"But you're not fine, darling," he said. "You threw out your medication, you're having delusions, you're forgetting your station in life—please don't misunderstand, I'm not blaming you. I know it's not your fault. These are all symptoms of your condition. But these people *will* take advantage of you, if they haven't already, and as your husband, it's my duty to protect you. There's a hospital in Fort Augustus, quite well known, actually . . . I thought maybe you could check in for a while, just until you're back on an even keel."

With a bone-deep sense of dread, I realized he was planning to have me locked up. He hadn't just come up with a solution that would provide him with endless pills, he'd also come
up with a solution that would dismiss anything I might say
about his color blindness—his behavior in general—as a fig-
ment of my diseased imagination. As an added bonus, he would
appear to be a loyal, martyred husband, deserving of pity and
respect.

*Poor, poor Ellis, saddled with mad, mad Maddie. The things
he must have borne, and he never once let on. Such a shame—it
was a love match, you know, against his parents' wishes, and then
to have her turn out like her mother . . .*

Everyone would shake their heads, demonstrating the appropriate level of sadness, while simultaneously feeling the
thrill of vindication, because they'd all known it was inevitable.
And then, one by one, the matrons of Philadelphia high society
would make pilgrimages to the mansion on Market Street to
snivel condolences at Edith Stone Hyde, who would hold up
admirably, while secretly reveling in having been proved right.

I wondered if Ellis pictured me locked safely in the attic
during all of this, like the crazy first wife of Mr. Rochester,
except drugged into submission.

The icing on the cake, the sheer beauty of his plan, was that
I'd still be alive, so he wouldn't even have to marry again. It
would be Hank's turn to put on a show. Poor Violet. I wondered
if she'd slip as naïvely into the role as I had, and if she'd ever
recognize it for what it was.

But Ellis's otherwise masterfully crafted solution had one
enormous flaw: unless the Colonel forgave him, he would not
be present at his mother's side to lap up sympathy. Without the
Colonel's absolution, he still had nothing. Ellis had more at
stake than ever in finding the monster.

There was an *Aroogah!* from the street.

"That's George. We should go," said Hank, getting up.

"Please come with us," Ellis said, looking me right in the eyes. "I'm begging you."

Aroogah!

"Ellis, we have to go," said Hank.

"Darling, please change your mind," Ellis entreated.

I shook my head.

After a pause, he climbed to his feet.

"I hate leaving you like this, even if it's only for a few days. But if you won't come, I have no choice. One way or another, we have to wrap this thing up so we can go home and get a fresh start."

"Your plan won't work," I said quietly. "They won't lock me up, because I'm not insane. I never have been."

He smiled sadly. "I'll see you in a few days, darling. Take care of yourself."

A few days. I had only a few days to come up with some way of extricating myself from this tangled mess, because despite my bravado, I wasn't at all sure he couldn't have me committed. And he certainly wouldn't let me divorce him—the proceedings would reveal all kinds of things he'd do anything to keep under wraps.

In the late afternoon, during one of Meg's waking moments, she asked for a mirror.

Anna and I exchanged glances.

"Why don't we give it a few days?" said Anna. "Give Mhàthair's tea a chance to do its work."

"I want to see," said Meg. "I already know it's going to be bad."

Anna looked at me in dismay, and I shrugged my shoulders. I didn't see how we could refuse.

"Well," Anna said, "in that case, let's get you tidied up a bit."

She worked at loosening and wiping away the yellowish crust that continued to ooze from the cuts around Meg's mouth and eye. I got my hairbrush, which had softer bristles than Meg's, and ran it carefully over her hair, taking pains to avoid the raw area, trying gently to encourage a wave or curl to form. Anna stood in the background, chewing her nails.

When I handed Meg the mirror, she looked into it and turned her face from side to side. She lifted her fingers to her ruined cheek, tracing the outline of the stitched-up gash, before hovering over the deep new hollow. Then she set the mirror on the bed and wept.

Chapter Thirty-four

Two days later, Dr. McLean decided to replace Meg's morphine with a bright red tonic.

As he put the syringes in a box with the remaining morphine, he paused and knitted his brow. He pushed the ampoules, both empty and full, around with his finger.

"Well, that's very odd," he finally declared. "I would have sworn I brought more than this. There should be four left. You've not accidentally double-dosed her, have you?"

"I should think not," replied Angus, with more than a little affront.

"No, of course not," said the doctor, shaking his head. "I must have miscounted."

A knot formed in the pit of my stomach. I knew exactly where they'd gone, and why Ellis had looked so improbably healthy.

. . .

When Anna saw the tonic, she nodded in satisfaction. To her, it indicated that everything was just a little more right with the world.

To Meg, it meant she could no longer sleep through the pain. Additionally, Dr. McLean insisted that deep breathing was no longer enough. Now Meg also had to get up and shuffle the length of the hallway twice a day to ward off blood clots.

Meg bore this bravely, but it was clear that every step was agony. Anna and I would flank her, holding her elbows, and giving encouragement. When we got her back to her room, we'd help her into the chair, where she'd sit stiffly until she felt up to the task of lying back down, because lying down required using the muscles in her abdomen and back. Lifting, laughing, coughing, breathing—all of it caused pain.

Rhona had been a constant presence since the morning after Meg's injury, and she and Mhàthair made continuous adjustments to the soup we spooned into her. We consumed it as well, and its ever-changing nature was a source of mystery to me. One time, a pile of tiny lime-green leaves appeared on the corner of the big table in the kitchen. I fingered them absentmindedly, thinking they might be mint. They turned out to be the first spring shoots of stinging nettle, and I had to sit for hours with my hands submerged in a bowl of snow. This amused Anna and Meg no end, although Meg finally called an end to the merriment because she couldn't bear the pain of laughing anymore. What they didn't notice was that my laughing had turned to crying.

There was no getting around it—a few days meant three, four at most. My grace period was almost up.

Four days turned into five, and then six, and there was still no sign of Ellis and Hank. I almost wished they'd return just to get it over with, because a bolt of terror ran through me every time the front door opened.

Nights were even worse. My brain turned and turned, robbing me of sleep, yet I couldn't come up with a single solution. I had no money at all, either in a bank or on my person, so even if I'd known how to bribe my way onto another freighter, I didn't have the means. I also had nowhere to go at the other end.

Although there was no longer any need, I continued to sleep in Meg's room. I was afraid that Ellis would come back and look for me in mine.

On the seventh day, when Rhona began assembling game pies, I realized Angus was reopening the inn.

I didn't see how he could. Even if Rhona prepared all the food, Meg was weeks away from being able to carry trays, and Rhona was simply too frail. Angus couldn't possibly serve and clear tables as well as tend bar.

When I came downstairs, he had the front door propped open and was taking down the sign, collecting the tacks between his lips.

"Is everything all right?" he mumbled, glancing at me.

"Yes. Everything's fine. I just wanted to ask something."

"Ask away."

"I notice you're reopening the inn, and I wondered if I could help. It's too much for one person, and Meg says she'll be all right on her own for a few hours, as long as I leave her with a book."

Angus spat the tacks into his hand and shut the door.

"And what do you think your husband would make of that?"

"He'd hate it. In fact, he'd forbid it. But he's out of town."

"I had actually noticed that," he said with a quick laugh. "But for how long?"

"I'm really not sure," I said. "I thought he'd be back a few days ago."

"And if he were to come back and find you behind the bar?"

"There would be a scene, but I'm afraid that would be the least of my worries."

Angus dropped the tacks onto the nearest table and looked at me.

"Maddie, is there something I should know? Because I can't help if I don't know."

I wanted to tell him, but there was nothing he could do.

There was a long silence as Angus continued to stare at me, his hands on his hips, his expression stern.

"It's complicated," I finally said, "and when it comes right down to it, I don't think anyone *can* help me."

"You're sure, are you?"

I nodded and said, "I'm pretty sure, and in the meantime, I'm trying not to think about it. So what do you say? Can I distract myself by helping with the dinner service?"

"I'd be grateful for the help," he said, his voice still serious. "And if you change your mind and want to tell me what's going on, you know where to find me."

A few minutes before six, when I was expected downstairs, I paused at Meg's door. I'd helped her move to the chair a little earlier, when she'd decided to read. Apparently sitting ramrod straight was more comfortable than being propped up in bed.

"I'm going down now. Do you want me to get you anything first? Touch up your tea, or move you back to the bed?"

She looked at me over the spine of *Died in the Wool*, then set it facedown in her lap.

"Is that what you're wearing?"

"It was," I said, glancing down at myself. I was in a navy

blue dress that I hoped would be forgiving of stains, and shoes that were low enough that I probably wouldn't trip.

She tsked and frowned. "You look like you've come from a funeral, for goodness' sake! You're supposed to lighten their mood, not darken it—change into something more appropriate, and then come back."

"But they'll start arriving any minute," I protested.

"Angus can pull pints while you make yourself presentable," she said firmly. "At least you've done your hair and makeup," she added in a mutter, returning to her book.

I stood in front of my closet and considered my options. I picked out a periwinkle rayon dress with a pleated skirt and matching belt, and a pair of shoes whose heels were high enough to lengthen my calves, but that I hoped would not hinder my balance or speed.

Moments later, I stood in Meg's doorway with my hands on my hips.

"Will I do?" I asked.

I meant it rhetorically, but she ran a critical eye over the whole of me, from my hair to my toes and back again.

"Turn around," she said, stirring a finger in the air.

I obliged, even as I heard the first customers arrive.

"The lines up your legs are a little crooked," she said. "But otherwise, you'll do nicely."

Although I had visions of china crashing to the floor and dinners sliding into laps, I was not a complete disaster. It was certainly awkward: everyone who came in was clearly taken aback at finding me behind the counter. I'm not sure they quite realized what was going on until they saw Angus tutor me on pulling pints and measuring drams, and I was the one to deliver them. In the moments between orders, I didn't know what to do with my hands, or even where to look. I felt like I'd been thrown naked onstage and forgotten all my lines.

When the curious and mischievous among them began placing orders with me directly, they addressed me as Mrs. Hyde, even though Angus was openly calling me Maddie. It was a strange night for names all around, because when the lumberjacks finally began to trickle in—they usually arrived in a raucous crowd—they were subdued and addressed Angus consistently as either Captain Grant or Sir. I thought they must be testing the waters, to see if they were still welcome.

Willie the Postie was the only one to make a direct comment. He came to a dead stop just inside the door when he saw me. Then he marched up to the bar.

"What's this, then?" he said, looking me up and down. "Are my eyes deceiving me?"

"What'll it be then, Willie?" said Angus, ignoring the question. "The usual?"

"Aye," Willie said, continuing to eye me suspiciously.

I got so that I could pull a pint without half of it being foam, and tried to remember what Meg did when there was a lull. I topped up the water pitchers, took empty glasses back to the kitchen, and wiped the bar until my wrists ached, but what Meg did that I couldn't was chat and flirt and anticipate orders.

There was not a single local who didn't ask after her, although they did it individually and discreetly. It was clear they knew what had happened, although Rory's name was never spoken. Angus simply said that while she was improving, she was still feeling poorly, and that he'd pass along their good wishes. To a one, they responded with serious nods and expressions that underscored a wordless rage.

The lumberjacks did not ask, and their discomfort increased

as the night wore on. It seemed to me they were trying to figure out if they should leave, and probably would have been
relieved to do just that.

Conall was at his usual place by the fire, and by his hopeful
look I realized he expected me to join him. His eyes followed
me wherever I went, and over the course of the evening—
when it finally dawned on him that I wasn't coming to
sneak him bits of my dinner—he lost faith and dropped his
head on the stones. It was all I could do to not take him a
little something. We had a pact, and I felt terrible about breaking it.

When all the tables and stools were occupied, and I was
running back and forth between the front room and the
kitchen, the hours began to fly. Before I knew it, everyone had
eaten, I'd cleared the tables, and hadn't broken anything. I'd
spilled just two drinks, and only one of them had landed on a
customer—the piper, Ian Mackintosh, who was entirely gra-
cious about it.

When nine o'clock rolled around, and Angus tuned the
wireless to the nightly broadcast, I paused in the doorway to
listen.

The Red Army was drawing ever closer to Berlin, and had
cut railway lines and roads that led to the city. Dresden may
have already been reduced to rubble, but the Allied Forces continued to bomb Germany "night and day," in the words of the
announcer. British troops had taken Ramree, an island in
Burma, and an important battle had begun on Iwo Jima, an
island close to mainland Japan.

I slipped away before I could hear the number of casualties.

Rhona had the dishes stacked next to the sink, and I stood
beside her to help. She seemed to have shrunk over the course
of the evening, and was moving even more slowly than usual.
If we'd shared a language, I'd have suggested that she rest her
feet and let me do the dishes.

Conall had slipped in behind us, and when the last plate was washed, he heaved a heartbroken sigh and collapsed by Angus's bed, as though my cruelty had deprived him of the energy to even jump up.

If I'd done the dishes on my own, I would have let him lick a few.

After everyone left, I took a bowl of the latest incarnation of soup upstairs, along with a half pint of beer.

"Knock, knock," I said, although Meg's door was open. "I brought you a little something."

She'd made her way back to the bed and lay facing the far wall.

"Unless it's morphine, I don't want it."

I put the bowl and glass down and sat next to her. She'd lost what little color she'd had earlier in the day.

"What happened? I thought you were feeling a bit better."

"I was," she said. "I think I overdid it."

"I brought you some soup. Do you want to move back to the chair?"

"No. I think the chair is what did me in." She raised herself onto an elbow, slowly, haltingly. It was painful to watch. "Just stick a pillow behind me. So, how did it go downstairs?"

"I think it went fine," I said. "I only doused one person."

I held the soup under Meg's chin and fed her half a spoonful. She winced, manipulating her jaw carefully. Earlier in the day, Rhona had added finely diced pieces of potato and leek, along with a few other vegetables.

"Do you want me to pick the vegetables out?"

"No. I can mush them around. I just have to be careful."

"Have a sip of beer," I said, putting the soup down and handing her the glass. "Someone wise once told me that it builds blood."

"Maybe she wasn't so wise after all," Meg said with a wry smile. She took a swallow and gave it back. "So, when I asked how it went, what I really meant was . . ."

She fell silent. After a few seconds, she leaned back and closed her eyes.

I finally comprehended what her earlier surge of liveliness and corresponding collapse had been about.

"No, he didn't come, and I don't think he will. I don't think he'd dare."

She nodded and blinked. Her eyelashes were moist.

"I'm so sorry, Meg."

"Aye," she said, sniffing. "I suppose I knew that, and I suppose it's for the best, but God help me, in spite of everything, I still love him. It's not something you can just turn off."

I held her hand.

"So you really don't think you can fix things up with your husband?" she asked.

A sickening feeling spread through me. "I beg your pardon?"

"Anna said you were getting a divorce. Please don't be angry—it's just she's never met a divorcée."

"She still hasn't! And she probably won't, because I'm not getting one!"

"You're angry!" Meg said with a sudden sob. "I shouldn't have said anything."

"No, no, no, don't cry," I pleaded. "I'm not angry, exactly, but I *am* a little alarmed. How many other people do you think she's told?"

"Possibly Angus, but I doubt it. She swore me to absolute secrecy."

Angus. My heart lurched at the thought.

"Anyway, I'll tell her tomorrow you've changed your mind, and that will be the end of it. Was it just a rough patch then?"

"No," I said. "It's definitely permanent."

"It might come around again. You never know. You must have loved each other at some point."

I shook my head. "I thought we did. But no, I'm afraid not. His affections have always been elsewhere."

Chapter Thirty-five

I was curled in the chair when the air-raid siren started its wail. There was no warning, and almost no warm-up—it went from silent to deafening in a matter of seconds.

"Oh God, oh God," I said, jumping to my feet and looking wildly around. Meg's siren suit was stashed under the chair. I grabbed it, then stood helplessly at the foot of her bed. I had no idea how to wrestle her into it. Angus and Conall showed up seconds later, before I had a chance to try.

"Put that on yourself," said Angus, when he turned the flashlight on me and saw what I was holding. "And grab the gas masks."

"The two of you go," Meg cried. "I can't make it."

"The hell you can't," said Angus. He thrust the flashlight at me, then scooped Meg up along with all her bedclothes and carried her away.

I pulled on Meg's siren suit, grabbed our gas masks, and clumped downstairs.

A hazy bit of moonlight revealed the shelter's squat outline, and I ran ahead, holding the flap back while Angus climbed in with Meg. Then Conall slunk in, and I followed, letting the flap fall shut behind me.

I turned the flashlight on and leaned it up against the wall. Angus, stooping because the ceiling was so low, made his way to the bunks at the back and laid Meg on the bottom one. She turned on her side, writhing.

"Give me her gas mask," he said, crouching beside her. "And get yours on as well."

He slipped Meg's over her battered face. She whimpered and curled up even tighter.

Angus reached beneath the bunk and pulled out a roll of brown canvas that was labeled FIELD FIRST AID. He unfurled it, revealing a variety of surgical instruments and containers strapped to the interior. A moment later, he was injecting something into Meg's arm.

"What was that?" I asked, kneeling beside him. "Was that morphine?"

"Aye, a Syrette. A preloaded syringe. I jostled her something fierce getting her in here, and I see no reason she shouldn't sleep through this." He glanced back at me. "I said get your mask on."

I was struggling with the straps when Angus twisted on his heels and did something to the back of my head. I reached up to investigate. He'd secured the place where the straps converged with a safety pin.

Several aircraft screamed overhead, one after another. I shrieked and covered my head. Angus threw his arms around me and I clutched him in a death grip, turning my face and digging the canister of my gas mask into his shoulder.

"Those are Spitfires—just Spitfires. There's nothing to fear," he said. "Let's get you up top. I've still got to get my gun."

I gripped the edge of the upper bunk and he gave me a leg up, as if helping me mount a horse. I struggled to find my way under the covers, but the gas mask made it nearly impossible to tell what I was doing.

"I'll be right back," he said, ducking away. I cried out, even tried to grab him, but a moment later he was gone. As even more aircraft zoomed overhead, I burst into tears, blubbering inside my gas mask.

The gun must have been in the dugout, because he was back almost immediately.

"It's all right," he said, crouching by the flap. "It's just more Spitfires."

The siren was relentless, rising and falling, rising and falling, and after a few hours I grew numb to it, lulled into a stupor.

I lay on my side, watching Angus the entire time. He kept his head slightly down, listening carefully. Each time a plane roared overhead, he shouted over to me, telling me what it was. I didn't know the difference between a Lockheed Lightning and a Bristol Blenheim, but decided that if Angus wasn't outside shooting at it, it probably wasn't going to drop a bomb on us. I grew so inured to the siren's wail I was startled when it finally went steady, shrieking solidly at its highest note.

When it tapered off and fell silent, Angus set his gun down.

"That's that, I guess," he said, climbing to his feet.

He made his way toward the back of the shelter and dropped out of sight to check on Meg. A few seconds later, he reappeared, folding his forearms on the edge of the bunk and resting his chin on them. His face was right in front of the clear plastic window of my mask, and I realized he'd never put his on. He hadn't even brought it out. His arms had been full.

"You all right then?" he asked.

I started to kick my way free of the covers.

"Stay put," he said. "Meg's asleep."

"We're spending the night out here?" I asked, my voice muffled by rubber.

"Aye, what's left of it. It will be easier to navigate by the light of day, and I don't want to manhandle her again." He tapped the window of my mask. "You can take that off, you know."

When I removed it, he took it from me and leaned over to put it back in its ridiculous red case.

"Are you warm enough up there?" he asked.

"Yes, but where will you sleep?"

"I'll nip inside and get a quilt."

"Why don't you take the top bunk, and I'll move down with Meg?"

"No. She's curled up, and it would take some doing to rearrange her. We'll stay as we are."

"There's enough room up here for both of us," I said.

He popped back up. Our eyes met, and this time there was no separation at all, no plastic windows, green canisters, black rubber, or anything else that might have disguised my words. I had no idea how they'd come out of my mouth.

He smiled, and the skin beside his eyes crinkled.

"I'm sorry," I said, aware that my cheeks were blazing.

He held two fingers to my lips, then slid his hand around until he was cupping my cheek.

I gasped and turned into his hand, pressing my face against it and closing my eyes. When I opened them again, he was staring right through me. His eyes were as penetrating and startling as the first time I'd seen him.

"Hush, *m'eudail*," he said. "Everything's all right."

He pulled his hand free.

"Where are you going?" I cried.

"Back in a jiffy," he said, slipping out of the shelter.

He'd left the flashlight on. Conall was sitting by the entrance, his head bowed like a gargoyle.

Angus returned with a quilt, which he wrapped around himself. He crouched against the wall by the entrance and turned off the light.

"Good night, *m'eudail.*"

I reached up and traced the area of my face where he'd touched me.

Chapter Thirty-six

On the ninth day, I began to wonder if something had happened to Ellis and Hank, and if so, would anyone know how to find me. On the eleventh day, it dawned on me that they might not be planning to return.

It started out as magical thinking, but I soon convinced myself it wasn't that outlandish: Ellis had no home or money to return to, whereas Hank had all the money in the world, and would continue to have it wherever he was. They could change their identities, go somewhere exotic, find an opium den by the sea, leave the whole mess behind. I knew I was part of that mess, but if they really had run off together, never to return, why would they care what happened to me? Maybe they'd found some fondness for me after all, and had decided to set me free.

Of course, I wouldn't really be free until I managed to make it legal, but the idea shone as brightly as a sliver of light beneath a prison door. I was sure Angus would let me stay on until the end of the war—I worked as hard as anyone—but it was more than that. I felt at home at the inn, even welcome.

I couldn't bring myself to think beyond the war, when the proprietor came back. My dearest hope, my deepest desire, was the one thing I couldn't let myself think about at all, in case I started to believe it was possible, because I knew it wasn't.

On the twelfth night of my husband's absence, I moved back into my room.

It was mid-afternoon, and Anna and I were up in Meg's room. We were making ourselves scarce because Rhona was concocting yet another soup, this one with a base of mutton shanks and barley. Between them, Rhona and Mhàthair appeared to have laid out an exact plan for Meg's recovery based on soup and tea. There were now four big pots simmering on the range, and they filled the entire building with an irresistible aroma.

Apparently it was not irresistible to Meg.

The three of us were sprawled on her bed playing Hearts when she wrinkled her nose and asked what the stink was. I told her about the new soup.

"Not Scotch broth!" she wailed. "I haven't had real food in two weeks!"

Anna and I glanced at each other. This was the first time Meg had shown an interest in *any* food since her injury—real or otherwise.

"I'll be right back," said Anna, leaping into action.

She returned shortly with a bowl of porridge and a coddled egg, both of them swimming in butter.

"I hope you enjoy it," she said, handing the egg to Meg and putting the other bowl on the table. "Because when Rhona tells Mhàthair, I'm done for."

"Why?" I asked.

"Because their prescription of the day is cock-a-leekie, and no doubt I've undone all their good work."

"This is marvelous," said Meg, her mouth full of egg. "I don't suppose there's another?"

"I'm afraid not, but I'll bring an egg a day from now on."

"And if the hens don't cooperate?" I asked.

"I'll pick them up and squeeze until an egg pops out," Anna said, making strangulation gestures with her hands. "And if that doesn't work, I'll remind them what happened to Jenny."

"Who's Jenny?" I said.

"The hen in the soup. She stopped laying. Do you want to know the name of the sheep in t'other?"

"No! I most certainly do not!" I said.

"Elsie," said Anna. "She was a fine ewe. She'll also show up in potted hough, mutton hot pot, and haggis. Oh, we'll be seeing Elsie for quite some time."

"Stop!" I said, holding my hands over my ears. "I'll never be able to eat again!"

"City folks," Anna said, shaking her head. "You never even met Elsie . . . I can see your cards, you know, when you tip them like that."

"Behave yourselves, the both of you!" Meg said, trying unsuccessfully not to laugh. "My ribs—remember?"

"Sorry," Anna said in a singsong voice. "It's not my fault if some people can't—"

There was a knocking on the door downstairs, a solemn, familiar rhythm.

The three of us froze.

My mind began to race. Meg had already lost everyone, Angus had already lost everyone—

"Robbie," Anna gasped, leaping from the bed. I scrambled after her, and had just caught up when she yanked the front door open.

Willie the Postie was on the doorstep, holding his hat along with a telegram.

Anna slid silently to the floor. I dropped down beside her, wrapping my arms around her.

"Anna!" Willie said quickly. "It's not for you."

"What?" she said, looking up at him with shocked eyes.

"It's not Robbie," said Willie. "The telegram is not for you."

"Oh," she said.

"Mrs. Hyde," said Willie, "I'm afraid it's for you."

I climbed to my feet, confused.

"My deepest condolences," said Willie, handing me the telegram.

Anna got up and closed the door, even though Willie was still standing there. I walked to the couch and sat down. Anna sat next to me.

The telegram was from a lawyer. My father had choked to death on a piece of steak fourteen days earlier. The lawyer was sorry the notification was so late, but my whereabouts had been somewhat difficult to discern. I was to confirm whether this was indeed my current location, and if this was where I wished details to be sent.

I set the piece of paper in my lap and looked blankly across the room.

My father had died on the night Ellis tried to beat down my door, the night Rory nearly killed Meg—

It was also the anniversary of Màiri receiving the telegram that turned out to be the end of her.

"Maddie?" Anna said in a hushed voice.

I handed it to her.

"Oh, Maddie," she said after reading it. "I don't know what to say. I'm so sorry. I'm so very, very sorry. Is there anything at all I can do?"

"I think I need to be alone for a while."

"Of course. Whatever you want."

As I stood, she laid her hand on my arm.

"That was Valentine's Day," she said, her eyes opening wide.

"I know," I said. "It must be cursed."

I walked slowly along the A82, stepping aside to wait as an impossibly long line of moss-colored military vehicles rolled past. They were lumbering and square-faced, the first dozen or so with tarps tied over their loads, and the rest transporting soldiers. Men from every vehicle leaned out the open backs, hanging by one arm, to whistle and make catcalls. More than a few made vulgar comments, but there was no way I could escape their attentions. I was trapped at the side of the road.

I turned to face the oncoming vehicles, because then I didn't have to see the men's leering expressions. The drivers also looked at me, but they were behind glass, so I couldn't hear what they said. Finally, I saw the end of the line.

In all, twenty-eight vehicles had driven past. I wondered how many of the young men would come back alive from wherever it was they were being sent.

I kept walking.

The clouds were an intense gray, surging and changing, and appearing in some places to roll out of crevices in the hills themselves. It was astonishing how little it took for the same landscape to take on a completely different cast. The hills, with their fields and forests, were alternately bleak, looming, rugged, or majestic, depending on what the sky above them was doing. At that moment, they looked aptly funereal.

It must have seemed strange to Anna that I did not cry. Perhaps she thought I was having a delayed reaction. I considered the possibility, but dismissed it almost immediately.

I wondered if he'd been eating in his study when the meat lodged in his windpipe, or if he'd gone back to taking his meals in the dining room. Had he made any noise, or was he completely silent? Perhaps he'd turned purple and staggered around, trying to summon help. Perhaps he'd simply fallen facedown into a spinach soufflé. I pictured these scenarios with morbid curiosity, but not sorrow, and definitely not grief.

Although his letter to me had removed all doubt, I think I'd always known that he didn't love me, and apparently his lack of affection had engendered the same in me. There'd been a dearth of affection all around.

My mother certainly hadn't loved me, despite her extravagant claims. Her affections, such as they were, vaporized entirely during the seven weeks she was on the run with Arthur and returned, redoubled, only when she was forced to go back to my father.

Ellis had also never loved me. At least, not as a husband should love his wife, and recently, not at all.

I reached the castle. Although I hadn't consciously chosen it as a destination, I climbed up and through the dry moat and across the interior grounds without hesitation. I found myself standing at the opening to the Water Gate.

I picked my way down the hill, which was steep enough that toward the bottom I ended up in a graceless gallop to keep from losing my balance.

In the scrub to the side of the landing, there were dozens upon dozens of cigarette butts. I was heartsick at the thought of Hank and Ellis setting up on the very spot from which Màiri had stepped to her death—drinking, smoking, and swearing, oblivious to everyone but themselves and their future fame.

I stepped forward, as Màiri once had, until my feet were at the water's edge. I took another step, just a little one, so that the soles of my shoes were submerged. I watched the water swirl around them, then looked up at the loch itself, black and rolling, endlessly deep.

What had Màiri's thoughts been as she walked in? When it

was too late to turn back, when the water closed over her, had she regretted it or felt relief, believing that she was about to be reunited with her husband and child? I opened my mind, trying to channel her. I wanted to know what it was like to experience a love so deep you couldn't bear to exist without it.

I felt her then—I felt Màiri and the cavernous depths of her grief, and had an overwhelming urge to keep going, to walk into the loch. Her anguish was boundless, her sorrow without end. I was drowning in it. *We* were drowning in it.

I closed my eyes, lifted my arms, and let myself fall.

A deep rumbling started in the water, like something was rising, followed by a great *whoosh* as it broke the surface. I opened my eyes, still falling—no way to stop then—and saw two blades of water curling from the edges of a channel that was being cut, but by what? Something was obviously racing across the surface of the water, but it looked like nothing was there. Before I could make any sense of it, the thing struck me in the abdomen, folding me around it and knocking me backward.

I landed away from the water's edge, banging my head so hard my peripheral vision filled with tiny, sparkling stars. Although the wind had been knocked out of me, I staggered to my feet.

The surface of the loch was smooth, the stones on the landing dry. There was no sign even of a dissipating wake.

I scrambled up the hill, grabbing tufts of grass to speed my ascent. Only when I reached the top did I pause to catch my breath. I leaned against the inside of the ancient arch, periodically looking back at the loch, and trying unsuccessfully to calm myself.

Chapter Thirty-seven

If Willie the Postie was surprised by my disheveled state when I entered his post office and asked about the possibility of making a transatlantic phone call, he didn't betray it. It was, after all, mere hours since he'd delivered the news of my father's death.

He explained that overseas calls were by radio only, and that the equipment was at the Big House.

"Thank you," I said, putting my gloves back on.

"And where do you think you're going?" he demanded, angling his eyebrows fiercely.

"To the Big House," I said.

He raised a hand. "I'm afraid that's absolutely out of the question. The equipment is strictly for military use, no exceptions. It's not like a telephone box, you know. And anyway, you can't just go mucking about on the grounds of a battle school."

"No. Of course not. I wasn't thinking."

"You'll be sending a telegram then?"

I cast him an embarrassed look. "I would, but I'm afraid my situation hasn't changed."

"Ah," he said, nodding. "Under the circumstances, I think I can overlook the fee."

"Thank you," I said. "That's very kind. I'll do my best to keep it short, but I'm afraid it might end up being rather long anyway."

"I quite understand," he said, preparing to take my dictation.

And I think he did understand, right up to the part where I asked the lawyer to please let me know what was involved in getting a divorce and whether I could do so from Scotland, and to please respond by either telegram or airmail, since I wished to settle both matters as quickly as possible.

Willie understood that part too, but it was a different type of understanding, one not tempered by empathy. His entire bearing hardened.

Despite the warnings, I couldn't help myself. I had to see Craig Gairbh.

I had no illusions about getting inside the Big House. I just wanted to lay eyes on the place. It was where Angus had lived before the war, and still spent his days. It was where he "took" the game and fish so many villagers depended on to supplement their rations. It was where the Colonel had made such a nuisance of himself, all those years ago, causing the international scandal that eventually led to Ellis and Hank deciding we had no choice but to find the monster ourselves. It was the nucleus of everything.

There were no signs to direct me, although there were posts with holes in them where signs used to be, so I walked the periphery of the village until I found a dirt road that led into the forest. Because of my experience at the Cover, I took a moment to note where the sun was, as well as the relative positions of the hills, before winding my way in.

Ancient rhododendrons began dotting the side of the road, the tips of their droopy leaves pulled toward the earth by the weight of snow, but already bearing buds for the coming spring. In one clearing, a constellation of purple crocuses poked defiantly through the crusted ice.

About three quarters of a mile in, I caught my first glimpse of the house. I could see it only in bits and pieces, because the road was still twisting its way around, and many of the trees between the house and me were coniferous. Still, I got an immediate sense of its scope.

I hurried around the bend to see more. The road grew wider and the thicket beside it disappeared, turning quite suddenly into a formal approach lined by hundred-year oaks. I stayed back, in the shadow of the woods.

I was no stranger to large houses, but this was enormous. From counting windows, I could see that the center of the house had at least four main stories, and the end towers even more. I could not begin to count the chimneys—I started at one end and lost track at sixteen, before I even reached the center. Semicircular staircases with stone balustrades approached the main door from both sides, and another row of balustrades graced the roof's parapet.

This was no house. This was a castle.

The entire front garden—or what had been the front garden—was enclosed in barbed-wire fencing and crammed with row upon row of corrugated metal shacks. They looked like Anderson shelters, only much larger. An enormous stone fountain, dry of course, rose from the center.

The fountain looked to be from the Baroque period, with three or four human forms kneeling under an enormous vessel. I crept up behind a large yew to get a better look, and tripped on an exposed root. I fell forward, catching myself on the tree's rough trunk. Only then did I see the sign nailed to it, directly above my hand. It was bright red and triangular, with a white skull and crossbones on top, and a single word across the bottom:

MINEFIELD

I froze. My right foot was still partially on the root, leaving me precariously balanced. With my hand still firmly planted on the trunk, I looked down, studying my feet and the ground around me, wondering if there was any way at all of knowing where a mine might be buried.

A spurt of gunfire crackled in the distance, underscored by male voices: bellowing, primitive, and fierce.

I hadn't moved—was still standing with one foot teetering on the root and my hand braced against the trunk—when another round of gunfire went off, answered by a volley from a different, much closer location.

I think I screamed. I'm not sure. But certainly my careless attitude toward live ammunition had been replaced by sheer terror. Tracer bullets at night were one thing. Minefields and machine guns were quite another.

I was carrying my red gas mask case and wearing my red gloves, which would either make me visible enough that no one would shoot me accidentally, or else would make me an easy target.

Guided by sheer instinct, I twisted away from the tree and leapt toward the road in long strides. My feet landed in a thick carpet of leaves three times before I reached it, and each time I was sure I was going to be blown to smithereens.

When I found myself safely back on the road, I went completely still. I wondered if I'd been walking in a minefield the entire time, and how the hell I was going to escape.

As shots continued to ring out in the forest around me, my eyes lit on tire tracks. I hopped into a rut and stayed carefully within it, placing each foot directly in front of the other. By the

time I passed the last of the ancient rhododendrons, I was running flat out. My gas mask bounced behind me, hitting me in
the back with every stride.

I stumbled out of the woods and onto the street, my legs
pinwheeling as though someone had shoved me from behind. I
went straight over the white painted curb and crashed into the
low stone wall beyond it.

I leaned against it, doubled over and wheezing, as a red cow
with very long hair and even longer horns gazed placidly at me,
chewing its cud.

Meg was standing by the end of the bar when I burst through
the door and slammed it behind me.

"Maddie! Whatever's the matter?"

I peeled off my gloves, but my hands were shaking so hard
I dropped them. When I leaned over to pick them up, my gas
mask slipped off my shoulder and landed on the floor with a
thunk.

"Leave them," Meg said. "Come sit."

I left everything and wobbled over to the couch. I sat on the
very edge and reached up to feel my hair, which was plastered
to my forehead and neck.

Meg looked anxiously at the door. "Why were you running?
Is someone chasing you?"

I waved vigorously, still out of breath. "No, no—it's nothing
like that. Don't worry."

She looked at the door one more time, then sat gingerly
beside me.

"Then what is it?"

"Nothing," I said.

"It's clearly *something*. You're all worked up. Wait here—
I'll get a glass of water."

"Please don't get up," I said. "What are you doing down here, anyway? You're not supposed to exert yourself."

"I'm hardly exerting myself. I needed a change of scenery, so I brought down the crossword puzzles you gave me. Stay where you are. I'm fetching some water, and I'll have no arguments about it, either."

I gulped it down noisily as soon as she handed it to me, not even lowering the glass when I had to pause for breath. When it was empty, I set it down and wiped my mouth with the back of my hand.

"Thank you," I said, glancing over in embarrassment. I found Meg gazing at me with a combination of sympathy and sadness.

"Anna told me about your father," she said quietly. "I'm very sorry for your loss. It's perfectly natural to be rattled. You never know how you're going to react to news like that."

"It's not my father," I said. "I don't care about my father."

Meg watched me for almost a full minute. I realized how awful what I'd just said sounded, and wondered if she thought me heartless.

"Then what is it?" she inquired carefully.

I let out a desperate, nervous laugh. "I'm not sure I should tell you."

"Rest assured, I'll not be judging," she said. "I'm hardly in a position to cast stones."

"You're going to think I'm crazy."

"Well, I won't know until you tell me."

I leaned in closer. "I was attacked by the monster today."

Meg's eyes widened. After a brief pause, she said, "You were *what?*"

I threw myself against the back of the couch. "I knew you'd think I was crazy! I didn't believe in any of this supernatural stuff before I came here. Then the Caonaig came for Anna's brother—there was never any doubt in Anna's mind that she'd come for Hugh, and she was right. And that damnable crow, signaling sorrow and chasing me into the Cover. And today, the monster—it rose straight out of the water and attacked me!"

Meg stared at me for several seconds, then got to her feet. "I think we could both use something a wee bit stronger."

She poured two small whiskeys and brought them over.

"*Slàinte,*" she said.

"*Slàinte,*" I said, clinking my glass against hers.

"All right, then," she said. "How about you go back to the beginning?"

I didn't know how far back she wanted me to go, so I started at the actual beginning, blurting out everything and barely pausing for breath. Everything, from how I felt nothing about my father's death because he had been completely indifferent to my existence, to my mother starving me for years, to her plans for fixing my nose and scrambling my frontal lobe, to the suicide attempt that I was supposed to foil, to discovering that Hank and Ellis had tossed a coin to see who had to marry me and now had abandoned me completely, to my belief that Ellis wasn't color-blind after all, to realizing I was crushingly in love with Angus, to my alarming experience at the bottom of the Water Gate, to sending a telegram to the lawyer asking how to go about getting a divorce, and, finally, to wandering into a minefield because, for whatever reason, the Big House held some kind of gravitational pull I couldn't resist.

In the dead silence that followed, I realized what I'd done.

"Oh God," I said, clapping my hands to my face.

"If you're talking about Angus, it's hardly a surprise," Meg said. "I've seen how you look at him."

I turned away, panting through steepled fingers.

"And I've seen how he looks at you, too," she added quietly.

My heart either skipped a beat or took an extra one.

I lowered my hands and turned back around. She was staring straight into my eyes.

"Go back a wee bit. Tell me exactly what happened at the water's edge."

I told her again. "And then, just as I was about to hit the water, it was like a boulder of air exploded from the surface, knocking me backward. I know how crazy it sounds, but it's the God's honest truth, even though I can't explain any of it."

Meg nodded knowingly, solemnly. "Aye. But I can. It wasn't the monster, Maddie. If it had been, it wouldn't have pushed you away. It would have dragged you in."

I shook my head. "But then what—"

"It was Màiri," Meg said. "She died three years ago today, at that very place. She entered your head and your heart to see if you'd be true to Angus, and when she saw that you would be, she pushed you to safety. Maddie, she gave you her blessing."

Chapter Thirty-eight

In the space of one day, I'd gone from thinking that no one in the world had ever loved me to thinking that the man I was hopelessly in love with might feel the same way about me. It was more than just that, though—the ghostly intervention gave me hope that we were meant to be together. After the Caonaig, I was no longer inclined to ignore such a message.

Meg wanted to return to work that night, just to lend a hand, but Angus was having none of it. I had to agree—she'd only just had her stitches out, and I still caught her wincing when she thought no one was looking. Still, I was sorry she wasn't going to be there, because I felt in need of moral support.

A few minutes before six, when I took my place behind the bar, Angus came up beside me and laid a hand on mine. "I heard about your father. I'm very sorry for your loss."

"Thank you," I said, looking up at him. "And I, for yours."

He nodded slowly, and that was it. He knew I knew everything.

As the evening wore on, I watched Angus's face, hoping for

a sign that Meg's words were true. But he was understandably preoccupied, his expression unreadable.

It was clear that the local men also remembered the anniversary, for they placed their orders solemnly and with diffidence. The only chatter was at the tables of lumberjacks, some of whom had brought their fiancées.

At one point, when I was sprinting into the kitchen with a stack of empty plates, I ran straight into Angus. He caught my elbows to steady me.

"You all right?" he asked.

"Yes," I said, in a pathetic attempt to sound casual. "Not sure about the front of my dress though."

He stared down at me, his eyes intense and unblinking. For the longest time, neither one of us moved.

When he finally stepped around me and returned to the front room, I dropped the stack of plates onto the table and leaned against it.

When the front door opened and closed for the last time, and Meg had gone to bed, I crept down the stairs as quietly as a cat.

I had prepared myself like a bride, brushing my hair until it was soft, rubbing scented lotion into my hands and elbows, and donning a long white nightgown—modest, but with lace at the neck and on the ends of the sleeves.

The fire had been smoored, and cast but the faintest glow. The flagstone floor was cold beneath my feet, and I almost lost my nerve. I stood with both hands on the bar, gathering courage.

If I turned back, it would be like nothing had ever happened. If I kept going, I would be stepping into the great unknown.

Maddie, she gave you her blessing.

I slipped into the kitchen, and felt my way along the wall

until I found one of the carved wooden doors that slid shut in front of his bed. In the darkness, I couldn't tell if they were open or closed. I let my fingers crawl along the wood until I reached the far edge.

The doors were open. I was standing right in front of him.

I found myself in a beam of blinding light, and jumped backward. When Angus saw it was me, he leaned the flashlight against the wall so it was aimed at the ceiling instead, then swung his legs around. He was wearing blue striped pajama bottoms and an undershirt, just as he had on the night of our arrival.

"What's going on? Is everything all right?" he said, rubbing his eyes.

"Everything's fine," I said, blinking quickly. The flashlight's glare had left two white spots in the center of my vision.

"Then what is it?"

I dropped my gaze and bit my lip. After the better part of a minute, when the blind spots had mostly gone away, I forced myself to look up again. He was watching me with obvious concern.

"What is it, *m'eudail*?" he asked gently.

I steeled myself. "Angus, there's something I want to . . . no, something I *need* to tell you. Something important." I swallowed loudly and looked directly into his eyes. "I know the situation is unusual and that under any other circumstances none of this would make sense, but nothing about our circumstances is normal, and I've come to realize that . . . that there are . . . that I have . . ." I clapped my hands over my mouth to stifle a cry. "Oh God! I'm so sorry! I've never felt so stupid in all my life!"

In a flash, he was up and I was in his arms. "Hush, *m'eudail*, you don't have to say a thing. I already know."

"But how can you know if I can't even manage to tell you?" I sobbed.

AT THE WATER'S EDGE 319

"Because I just do," he said. His heart went *thumpity-thumpity-thump*, inches from my ear.

Eventually he pulled back, keeping his hands on my shoulders. He stared into my eyes, and held my gaze until there was nothing on earth but his face. When he put his hands on my cheeks and leaned toward me, my legs almost abandoned me. I closed my eyes and let my lips part.

He kissed my forehead.

"*M'eudail*, you're grieving," he said quietly. "You're vulnerable. This is not the time for such things."

I don't know how I made it upstairs. Certainly quickly, and certainly not gracefully, and when I finally reached my bed, I blubbered shamelessly, burying my face in the pillow.

There was a quiet knock on the door. Even though my sobs had subsided into quiet weeping, my ignominious retreat had certainly been loud enough to wake Meg.

"It's not locked," I said.

The door opened, and the light of a candle cast long shadows at the far end of the room. Judging by its silhouette, the chair was almost as tall as the ceiling. I lay facing it, my knees folded nearly to my chest, my face and pillow wet with tears.

"Sorry I woke you up," I mumbled.

"I'm not," said Angus.

I jerked my head off the pillow and looked behind me. He was standing in the doorway, holding the candle.

"May I come in?"

I pulled myself upright, sliding backward until I was against the headboard. I sniffed and wiped my face with shaking hands.

He set the candle on the dresser and crossed the floor to the bed.

"Forgive me," he said.

I stared at him, trembling. Fresh tears rolled down my face.

He sat on the bed and ran a thumb across my cheek. I held my breath and closed my eyes.

"Forgive me," he said again.

When I opened my eyes, I was looking directly into his.

"I was wrong, *mo run*—this is exactly the right time."

He shifted closer and began kissing the tears from my cheeks in a slow, tender dance that moved from one side of my face to the other. Finally, when I thought I couldn't stand it any longer, he put his lips on mine.

They were warm and full and slightly parted, and I felt the quickness of his breath behind them. He kissed me over and over, with increasing urgency, his beard brushing against my skin. His hand slid down my neck and into my nightgown.

I gasped, and he stopped.

With his hand cupping my breast, he searched my face for a signal. It was a moment of excruciating sweetness, of torturous rapture, of exquisite need. It was unbearable.

I leaned forward, tugging at his shirt. He stood and pulled it over his head. I knelt on the bed, yanking at my nightgown.

"Wait," he said, and this time I was the one who stopped.

He removed my nightgown, slowly, reverently.

I had never felt so exposed, yet I didn't want to cover myself. The candlelight flickered behind him, and his breathing grew even heavier as his eyes traveled my body, resting without shame on my breasts and hips.

"*Mo run geal og,*" he said. "So beautiful."

He untied his pajamas and let them drop to the floor. I caught my breath. I obviously knew the anatomy, but other than statues, I'd never seen a naked man, never mind an aroused one. Angus seemed to sense that and paused, giving me a chance to look.

Finally, he knelt on the bed and put a hand behind my neck, supporting my head as he guided me backward.

Moments later, when he was poised above me, he looked deep into my eyes and said, "You're sure, *mo chridhe*? For this cannot be undone."

"Yes," I whispered. "I am completely and absolutely sure."

When he sank into me, I was so lost my body began to quake. I wrapped my arms and legs around him, holding on for dear life.

The next morning, it took me a moment to realize I wasn't dreaming. The candle had long since burned out, so we were in cave-like darkness, side by side, our naked bodies pressed together. He had one arm under my pillow and the other across me, his hand resting between my breasts. I lay very still, with my hands on his forearm. When he stirred, I clasped his hand to my heart and ran my fingers up his arm, marveling at our different textures. Although he was still asleep, a pulsing nudge intensified until the length of him was pressed against my back.

I rolled over and pulled the sheets down, kissing his chest and tracing his scars with my lips and fingers. When I finally worked my way up to his mouth, he took my face in his hands and pressed his lips against mine, parting them so we shared the same breath. A moment later, he lifted me across him like I weighed nothing, setting me down so my knees were on either side of him. I put both hands on his abdomen to brace myself, more than a little shocked to find myself straddling him.

He reached up and ran his thumbs over my nipples. I sucked in my breath and almost didn't let it out again.

"Maddie, *mo chridhe*," he said.

"Angus—oh my God," I said in a broken voice. "I don't know what to do."

"You do, though. Let yourself come to me."

I lowered my hips slowly, and stopped breathing altogether when I felt the tip of him pressing against me.

"Angus—"

"It's all right," he said, stroking my face. "*Na stad.* I'm right here with you."

He held himself steady while I took him into me, slowly, slowly, sliding down until he was buried so deep our hips met, then lifting myself up until I was afraid I might lose him, then sinking back down until we were joined again. I leaned forward and put my hands on either side of his head, breathing hard into the pillow beside his face.

He had his hands on my waist, and his hips rose a little higher each time I sank down, pushing himself deeper and staying there longer. I felt his blood pounding, as if our nerve endings had merged.

My legs were shaking violently, and just when I thought I was going to lose control entirely, he reached up and clasped my hands, intertwining our fingers, and guaranteed it.

The contractions overwhelmed me, so unexpected and intense I cried out, and he held my face, covering my mouth with his, pressing into me, faster, more urgently. When I felt his own surrender, I was shot through with an ecstasy so intense I thought my heart might actually stop.

After, as we lay in each other's arms, he stroked my hair and back. My face was buried in his neck, and every breath I took was suffused with his scent.

"Well," he said, kissing me. "I'm afraid that while I'd love to stay here forever, duty calls."

I caught his wrist. "I love you, Angus Grant. With all my heart, I love you."

He leaned over and gave me a long, lingering kiss.

"And I, you, *mo chridhe.*"

Chapter Thirty-nine

Meg knew exactly what had happened the second she laid eyes on me. She said nothing, just smiled in a knowing manner. It didn't help that I blushed and looked at the ground, or that I was wearing a turban because I hadn't set my hair.

I finished the upstairs chores at about the same time Anna finished the downstairs, and the three of us wound up around the kitchen table having a *strupag*.

Anna had spent the last few afternoons clearing rocks from the tatty beds at the croft, and was suffering from a stiff back.

"It's the buckets of stones," she explained. "They weigh more than buckets of milk, and you're always picking them up and putting them down, and then leaning over to collect even more . . . It's murder on the back, I tell you. I'll look like Rhona when all is said and done."

"Of course you won't," I said, although not as convincingly as I wished. Crofting sounded like a very hard life indeed.

"Stand up and lean over the table," Meg said. "I'll work those knots out for you."

Meg stood behind her and massaged Anna's back, digging her thumbs into the areas just above Anna's hips.

"I'll come help with the stones," said Meg. "Many hands make light work."

"I should think not," Anna said with righteous indignation. "Dr. McLean has not cleared you for any type of work yet, especially not clearing rocks."

"Well, I can't just do nothing, can I?" said Meg. "I'm sick to death of Maddie's crossword puzzles and their fiendish American spelling—why would anyone put an *e* in whisky, for goodness' sake? Anyway, Dr. McLean is going to clear me for work any day now, which probably means I'm already perfectly capable."

"Maybe I can help clear stones," I said.

Anna and Meg looked at me, deadpan. A couple of seconds later, they burst out laughing.

"And get your hands dirty?" Meg practically crowed.

"I get my hands dirty all the time!"

"I didn't see you offering to help clean the range this morning," said Anna.

"You didn't ask," I said. "And for your information, I was upstairs scrubbing the toilet. I didn't see you offer with that, either."

"Oh go on," said Anna. "We're just having a little fun."

"I know that!" I said, laughing. "Don't be silly!"

Anna narrowed her eyes and looked me up and down. "You're in a very good mood this morning . . ."

The front door opened, and after a few seconds it closed. Anna glanced at the clock.

"That'll be Willie with the mail," she said in a panic. "And here I am all covered with soot and oven blacking!"

"Grab a cloth and clean yourself up," said Meg. "I'll stall him."

Willie was expected to pop the question at any moment, having already asked permission from Anna's father.

It was a mystery to me what the attraction was—it was easy to see why Willie was attracted to Anna, but what did Anna see in Willie? He had always struck me as an angry, orange gnome who was quick to judge and was also a good twenty years older than she was, but apparently she was madly in love with him. I supposed there was no accounting for Cupid's aim. I felt sorry for poor one-legged George, though.

Anna ran to the sink and began scrubbing her face. I followed to make sure she didn't miss a spot.

Meg returned, pale as beeswax.

"It's not Willie," she said.

"Then who . . . ?" I asked.

Meg looked despondently at me, and I knew.

"Dear God in Heaven," I said.

Meg stepped forward and squeezed my hands. "He's not asked for you yet—when he does, I'll tell him you've gone walking."

"No," I said quietly. "I'll go out. There's no point in delaying the inevitable."

"What are you going to tell him?" Meg asked.

"I have no idea."

"At the very least, wait until Angus comes back."

I shook my head.

Meg watched me for a beat, then nodded. "All right, but I'll be standing right here with the heaviest saucepan we have, should you find yourself in need of assistance."

I pulled my apron over my head and hung it on a peg. Then I walked through to the front room, my legs seeming to move of their own accord.

. . .

Ellis and Hank were settled by the fire in their usual places, as though they'd never been gone at all. Ellis sat on the couch with his back to me, and Hank sat in one of the wing chairs. He stood at once.

"Maddie, darling girl!" he said, raising his arms in welcome. When I didn't respond, he dropped them and frowned. "What's the matter? You look like you've seen a ghost."

"I feel rather as though I have. What are you doing here?"

Ellis shifted around to face me, draping his arm across the back of the couch. "That's an odd question. We're staying here, of course."

"Well, no, in fact, you haven't been."

"You knew we were going away," said Ellis.

"You said you'd be gone a few days," I said. "It's been two weeks."

"Thirteen days," said Hank. "But who's counting?"

"I was," I said. "I didn't think you were coming back."

"Oh dear—you didn't think I'd abandoned you again, did you?" said Ellis. He raised an eyebrow and turned to Hank, adding, "I told you she has quite an imagination."

My knees buckled. A moment later, Hank and Ellis were steering me toward the couch.

"What's the matter? Are you having an episode?" said Ellis.

"Get her a glass of water," said Hank.

"I can't," Ellis replied. "There's no one behind the bar."

"Then get a glass and find a sink!"

"You mean in the kitchen? What if the hag's in there?"

"Then use the bathroom, for Christ's sake!"

Ellis glanced at Hank in a wounded manner, then went behind the bar for a glass. After pausing at the door to the kitchen, he changed his mind and went upstairs.

Hank perched on the low table in front of me. He leaned forward, resting his forearms on his thighs.

"Darling girl—what's going on? Talk to me."

"There's nothing going on," I said, although my voice betrayed me.

"It's not nothing, obviously. And if you don't tell me what's going on, he's going to think you're having an episode."

I couldn't help laughing. "He always thinks I'm having an episode. I don't care anymore."

"You don't mean that," said Hank.

"Oh, but I do."

"Fuck," Hank said. He glanced quickly at the stairwell. "Look, I think you should know that Ellis has been making inquiries. Actually, more than inquiries. Arrangements."

"So, he's really going to try to have me locked up, is he?"

"No, he's going to have you treated."

I was shocked into momentary silence.

"Treated?" I asked in a hollow voice, although of course I already knew.

"Given the severity of your symptoms, the physician he spoke to thought a permanent cure was the best solution. You wouldn't even have to stay in the hospital."

You'll be so much happier, my mother had said. *An easy thing. In and out in an hour.*

"And what did Ellis say to the doctor to make him think that?"

"Well, for starters, that you flushed your medication—"

"I flushed the pills because Ellis was eating them hand over fist. I've had one pill in my life. *One. Pill.* He's always been the one who took them. Hank, you *know* that."

"You've lost all sense of social structure, you're showing signs of paranoia—"

"*Paranoia?* Really, Hank?"

"—and you've begun having delusions."

I stared at him and began nodding. "So that's what this is really about."

"What?"

"As if you don't know. I'm sending a telegram to the Colonel this very minute."

"Saying what?" Hank asked.

"That Ellis isn't color-blind! That he lied to get out of service!"

Hank went slack-jawed. "Maddie, my God! Of course he's not faking it. That's a terrible thing to say!"

"Oh, please," I said. "How stupid do you think I am? You obviously planned it together, finding conveniently invisible ailments to keep you out of the war."

"What are you talking about?"

"Flat-footed? Please."

Hank sputtered in outrage. "I *am* flat-footed. I've been wearing custom shoes my entire life!"

"You're each as bad as the other. I've had it." I stood up.

"Maddie, stop—"

He said it with enough conviction that I did.

"Don't do it," he said.

"Why? There will be no point in having me treated once everyone knows the truth."

"Because it's *not* the truth, and this is exactly the type of rash behavior Ellis is worried about. You get something in your head, and then you act on it without any regard for consequence, no matter who it damages. If you send a telegram to the Colonel, Ellis will just have you treated sooner rather than later—it's all been arranged, he only has to make a phone call—and then for good measure, he'll probably have Blackbeard hauled off as well."

"Angus? Why?"

"Because of exactly that. The unsuitable familiarity. Ellis is sure he's been taking advantage of you, so he stopped by the courthouse to check the penalty for poaching. It's two years in prison per offense, by the way."

I sat back down, slowly.

"So if it's a phone call away and there's nothing I can do, why are you even telling me?" I asked.

Hank sighed. "I don't know. I guess because it *is* a phone call away. To warn you, I suppose, so you can try not to set him off. I was initially against the whole idea, but I have to be honest—Maddie, you're scaring me. Do you realize what you just accused me of? What you just accused Ellis of? It's like you consciously came up with the one thing that would hurt us the most. That's not like you. The Maddie I know wouldn't do that."

Ellis came thumping back downstairs.

"Here," he said, pressing a glass of water into my hands.

I pushed it back at him, spilling some onto his pants.

He set the glass on the table and gazed at me with exaggerated concern.

"Darling, you look rattled. Do you need a pill? I picked some up while we were gone. Found a very nice doctor, top of his field."

And then I knew it was true. I could see it running behind his eyes like a ticker tape—the false and self-serving concern that he would eventually convince himself was genuine, his enormous and growing satisfaction that I was, indeed, acting hysterically, along with his rewriting of history, so that he'd only ever done what was necessary for my happiness, because it was all he'd ever cared about—

It was like he was channeling my mother. I realized how much now hinged on my behavior, and did my best to channel her too.

"No, I just have a bit of a stomach bug," I said. "I've been queasy all day. If you'll excuse me, I think I'll go lie down for a bit."

"Do you want me to come with you?" he asked, using the same unctuous tone.

"No. I'm sure I'll be fine."

"Maddie?" he asked. "Were you in the kitchen just now, when we came back?"

"Yes," I said, forcing a brief smile. "I was looking for something to settle my stomach."

"Ah," he said, nodding. "Of course."

"I'll come down at seven, shall I?"

"Only if you feel up to it," he said. "Try to get some rest, darling."

I rose in as dignified a manner as I could, and somehow made it up the stairs.

Meg showed up within minutes.

I opened the door, then collapsed facedown on my bed.

"What's going on?" she said, closing the door. "You should have spoken louder. We couldn't hear a thing."

"Bolt that, please," I said.

She locked the door and sat beside me. "What happened? Did you tell him you were ending it?"

"No."

"Why not?"

"Because I can't," I said miserably. "I have to reconcile with Ellis, or at least pretend to."

Meg jumped off the bed and spun angrily toward me. "*What?* How could you? Do you have any idea what this will do to Angus? Does he mean that little to you?"

"No, he means that much to me!" I whisper-shouted. "And if I ever do have a chance at a future with him, I'd like my brain intact!"

Meg stared at me for a while, then sat back down.

"I don't think I follow," she said.

"Do you remember when I told you my mother wanted me to have a lobotomy?"

"Yes," she said doubtfully.

"Do you know what a lobotomy is?"

"No, not exactly."

"They put a tiny spatula up through your eye socket into the front part of your brain and then twirl it around a bit—and that's exactly what my husband is going to have done to me the next time I do anything to upset him."

Her mouth opened in horror. "But surely he can't do that!"

"It appears he can, since he's got it all arranged. I was diagnosed with a nervous ailment a few years ago, and my mother was entirely nuts. Ellis sold the doctor on the idea without the doctor ever laying eyes on me. All Ellis has to do is make a phone call, and they'll come cart me off."

"Dear Lord in Heaven," said Meg. She got up and walked stiffly to the chair.

"And you didn't tell him you asked about a divorce . . ."

"No, thank goodness. If I had, the ambulance would already be on its way."

"And he doesn't know about you and Angus . . ."

"He suspects something, but certainly not the full extent of it."

She slapped the arms of the chair, startling me. "Then *why*?"

"Money, of course," I said. "And the *really* stupid thing is that I brought all of this on myself."

"No," she said, frowning. "How could you have?"

"I was stupid enough to let him know that I don't believe he's color-blind. If I tell his father, he'll cut him off without a penny. So he's come up with a plan that lets him dismiss anything I say as crazy talk—and, of course, if I were ever foolish enough to open my mouth, he'd make the phone call and take care of the problem. The only thing I can do is try not to upset him until I figure something out."

"No, *this* is what we're going to do," Meg said firmly. "We're going to get you out of here. Anna's family will have you, I'm sure of that. Angus will spirit you over later."

"It wouldn't work. He'd find me."

"We'll make sure he doesn't."

"He'd find me and have the rest of you arrested for kidnapping. And, of course, I'd be delivered to a hospital in the back of an ambulance and come back drooling. Drooling, but ever so obedient."

"But you can't just sit around waiting for it to happen!" Meg said angrily. "It makes no sense!"

"You don't understand. *He'd find me.* There's too much money involved—his own family's fortune is big, but sooner or later he's going to find out that *my* father is dead, and there's an *obscene* amount of money at stake there."

Meg fell quiet for long enough that I finally turned back to her. Her pale eyes bored through me. She sighed and turned away from me, staring into the empty grate.

She obviously knew there was more to it, but what could I tell her? That there was nothing anyone could do to save me that wouldn't land Angus in prison for life? That his fate lay in the hands of my volatile, feckless husband, and in my attempts to pacify him?

After more than a minute, she began tapping a finger against her chin.

"Well," she said, "it's just possible there's another way."

For the first time since flopping on the bed, I pulled myself upright.

"What? What is it?"

"Fiddlehead stew is a delicacy around here, very tasty indeed, especially with a few drops of malt vinegar. Of course, you have to be very careful not to cook it too late in the season or you risk bracken poisoning . . ."

Her eyes cut sideways at me, to see if I was following.

"But I suppose if the shoots were just a *little* bit iffy—maybe a week or two older than someone might usually use them, an inexperienced cook might decide they were still safe. And then somebody else might see the pot boiling, and—knowing that it was too late in the season to be cooking fiddleheads—come to the conclusion that someone was boiling up a batch of insecticide for the vegetable garden. And to be helpful, she might throw in a few rhubarb leaves."

I blinked a few times.

"I don't think I can do that," I finally said.

"Do what?"

"Kill him," I whispered.

"Heavens no," Meg said sternly. "It would be an unfortunate case of kidney failure, a tragic misunderstanding."

"Even if we make this . . . mistake," I said in a strained voice, "Angus is still going to think I betrayed him. At least until I figure something out."

"I don't see how that's to be avoided, since you won't hear of being removed from the situation. If you won't let him do anything to protect you, we certainly can't tell him—if he thought for a moment you were being threatened, he'd take matters into his own hands, and then we'd have a body to dispose of, and not from anything nearly as neat and tidy as kidney failure. I can't guarantee that he won't take matters into his own hands anyway."

"What if he stops loving me in the meantime?"

"I don't imagine you have to worry about that," Meg said. "But I also don't see that you have much choice, since you won't be talked out of doing nothing. Seeing you with your husband *will* crush him—that much I know."

Chapter Forty

I could barely breathe when I descended the stairs that night, and as I crossed the small distance to the nook by the fire, I felt like I was climbing the platform to a guillotine. I wondered if Hank had filled Ellis in about our chat by the fire and my ill-advised accusations. I tried to convince myself that he wouldn't say anything—he knew what was at stake. He couldn't possibly hate me that much, even if it turned out he was flat-footed.

I tried to read Hank's face as I approached the couch, but he was giving nothing away. Ellis patted the cushion next to him.

"Sit, darling! I was beginning to wonder if you'd show up."

"I'm sorry about earlier," I said, flashing him a quick, forced smile before taking my seat. "I'm sure that wasn't the welcome you were hoping for."

"Don't be silly," Ellis said. "I should have sent word that we were going to be staying away longer. Is your stomach any better?"

"A bit."

My attempt at an about-face probably would have been

more convincing if I'd asked him about the trip and what
they'd discovered about the monster, but I knew enough about
what else they'd been up to that the conversation would have
required a level of artifice I couldn't possibly sustain. For the
moment, I was just going to have to blame my lack of curiosity
on an upset stomach.

Angus was watching the three of us intently, his face an
inscrutable mask. I couldn't look directly at him—didn't want
to give Ellis any reason to notice him at all—but in my peripheral vision I saw the way he clunked glasses down on the bar,
the way he grimly went about his business.

I couldn't imagine what he thought. He must have known
that things weren't as they seemed, but he also must have wondered why I didn't just tell him what was going on. I wanted to,
desperately, but I was as good as shackled. Either he'd go to
prison for life, or he'd kill Ellis and hang for it.

To a man, the locals were as stony and speechless as Angus,
and when Willie the Postie came in, he took his seat without so
much as a glance in our direction—it was as though Hank and
Ellis had never been gone, and the last thirteen days hadn't
happened.

I was careful to avoid eye contact with the lumberjacks,
who were clearly baffled at seeing me back in my old role as
Mrs. Hyde. I sent up a silent prayer that none of them would
let on that I'd been working behind the bar, because I knew
with absolute certainty that if anything would send Ellis off to
the phone booth, that was it.

Fortunately, the lumberjacks were much more concerned
with Meg than with anything that was happening by the fire.
Earlier in the afternoon, Dr. McLean had cleared her for work
at the inn, although she could not yet return to the sawmill.
She was painfully thin and moved carefully, but she'd made
herself up and donned a bright dress, determined to carry on as
usual. From the right, she was as gorgeous and perfect as ever.

From the left—well, seeing her from the left made me want to cry.

"Shame about her face," said Hank, lighting a cigarette. "She was a real looker."

"Can't say I noticed," said Ellis. "But she's definitely a wreck now."

I wondered if the night he'd tried to break down my door ever crossed his mind, or if he had any idea what he'd planned to do if he'd succeeded.

When Meg set our plates in front of us, Ellis asked, "Is this beef?"

"Venison," she replied.

Ellis shot Hank a gleeful look.

I hated him. Oh, how I hated him. It seethed inside my belly like a squirming snake.

A quarter of an hour later, an old man in a ragged uniform stumbled in and announced with drunken flourish that he'd just seen the monster.

Willie snorted. "Here we go again," he said.

"Are you doubting me, then?" the man asked incredulously.

"Oh, heavens no. What possible reason would we have to doubt you?" said Ian Mackintosh. Chortles ran down the length of the bar.

"Well, if that's how it's going to be, I'll just take my custom elsewhere."

"You'll be walking the two and a half miles to the Clansman, will you?" said another.

"Well, I'll not be staying where I'm being insulted, that's for certain!"

Willie's orange eyebrows shot up. "You'll be lucky to make it home, from the looks of it."

The old man harrumphed and turned to leave, staggering toward the door.

Ellis and Hank exchanged glances. Ellis leapt up and rushed over.

"Excuse me, sir," he said, touching the old man's elbow, "I couldn't help overhearing. Would you care to join us? We'd be delighted to hear about your experience."

The man ran his rheumy eyes over Ellis, spent a moment concentrating and weaving, then poked him in the chest.

"I know you. You're the . . . I know who you are," he said, struggling to form the words. "I heard you were in town. Do you know, I met your old man. Nice chap. Very generous, if I recall."

"Yes, that runs in the family," Ellis said brightly. "Do come sit." He swept an arm toward the fireplace, as though inviting the old man into our drawing room.

"Well, I don't mind if I do," said the man.

"Bartender?" Ellis said, snapping his fingers over his head. "Bring the gentleman whatever he wants."

I cringed. I could only imagine Angus's reaction, and it took every ounce of my self-control not to look.

Ellis took the old man's arm and parked him in the chair beside Hank. After introducing the three of us, he took a seat and leaned forward, rubbing his hands together. "So, enough about us. Tell us about you."

"The name's Roddie McDonald," he said. "And I should have known better than to say anything in a room full of skeptics." He cast a disparaging look back at the bar, then leaned in to confide. "This isn't the first time I've seen the monster, you know. I told your father about the other time. And very grateful, he was." He nodded knowingly. "Your father . . . he was a colonel, wasn't he? How is the old devil? He was in the Great War, like me . . . only now we're supposed to call it World War

One." He looked down at himself. "This uniform . . . I wore it in the Battle of Liège, you know. It's the Home Guard for me, this time around. Too old, they say . . ." He looked directly at me, cupped a hand around his mouth, and said in a loud, wet whisper, "Just shows what they know. I'm as much of a tiger as I ever was."

He winked, and like a scene from a *comédie grotesque,* Hank and Ellis threw their heads back and howled. Roddie looked alarmed, then just confused, and then he joined in, exposing rotting teeth and the gaps between them. I shrank into my seat.

"I'll just bet you are. Can't keep a good man down!" said Hank. He stopped laughing and cleared his throat. "Now, start at the beginning and tell us everything."

Although it was perfectly obvious that Roddie had come to the inn with financial gain in mind, I sensed immediately that something more was going on. He claimed to have seen the monster at the Water Gate, which should have upset Hank and Ellis since that was exactly where they'd been setting up shop, but they displayed not so much as a ripple of displeasure. Instead, they were attentive and encouraging, dazzling in their conviviality. I imagined them in tuxedos, holding court in some mansion on Rittenhouse Square.

Roddie clearly relished the audience, making wild expressions, inflecting dramatically, and illustrating with his hands. "Then, with no warning at all, the surface began to boil and churn, and suddenly the neck and head rose straight out of the water, not fifty yards away!" Roddie shook his head in wonder. "Oh, it was a sight to behold . . ."

"The neck was long and curved, was it not?" said Ellis.

"Oh, aye," said Roddie, nodding. "Like a swan's. Only much, much larger. And its eyes—"

"Were they prominent?" Hank asked. "Round and dark? Like a creature of the deep?"

"Oh aye," Roddie said, nodding again. "It had a fearsome

look about it, like it wouldn't think twice about carrying you off."

"How big was the fin on its back?" asked Ellis.

Roddie cackled and slapped his thigh. "And how were you knowing it had a fin?"

"We've been doing some research," Ellis said, glancing at Hank, and I suddenly understood. Interviewing doctors and visiting the courthouse was not all they'd been up to while they were away.

"Indeed, it did have a fin, and that alone was at least four feet long . . ."

In due course, Roddie confirmed that the monster's body was "dark olive, with signet brown on the flanks, and a sort of speckling on the belly." He'd gone from claiming he'd seen the head and neck of the beast from a distance of fifty yards to describing its whole body.

"Excuse me, darling," I said. "I think I'm going to head up now."

Ellis looked at me with surprise. I couldn't remember the last time I'd called him "darling," and was sure he couldn't either. It was all I could do to force the word past my lips.

"But you haven't touched your dinner," he said.

"I'm sorry," I said. "I'm still a little queasy. I'm sure I'll feel better after a good night's sleep."

"Of course," he said, rising. "I'll walk you up."

"No, please stay." I laid a hand on his arm. "This is important. Get as many details as you can. The sooner you flush the beast out, the sooner we can go home, and then everything can get back to normal."

He watched with a curious expression as I bade good night to Roddie and Hank, and then continued to watch as I rounded the couch and headed for the stairwell.

He was not the only one watching. I nearly crumbled under the weight of Angus's scrutiny.

. . .

As soon as I closed the door, I threw myself on the bed. The scent of Angus lingered on my pillow. I buried my face in it and cried.

Hank and Ellis either had built a model or were planning to, and because of the description they'd coaxed out of Roddie, I knew exactly what it would look like. If they'd already built it, they would obtain their footage in a matter of days, and arrange to go home. But first, Ellis would have my brain scrambled, because he would be returning triumphant, with clear footage that confirmed the Colonel's pictures.

Father, son, and bank account would be reunited, and Ellis would not let anything on earth get in the way of that—especially something of as little consequence as me.

Chapter Forty-one

I spent the night tossing and thrashing, twisting the quilts until they were a tangled pile. Every time the chimney whistled or the window rattled—every time I heard anything at all—I was sure Angus was coming to me, and then what would I do? Tell him everything, and hope to God he'd come up with a solution that hadn't occurred to me? Or just hope to God that what I told him wouldn't make him go straight down the hall and murder Ellis?

Eventually, I couldn't stand it anymore and snuck down to the kitchen, feeling my way along the wooden doors of his bed until I reached the seam where they met. He'd shut himself in.

I leaned my forehead against the crack, thinking that he must know I was there—I felt his presence behind the doors as strongly as I felt the heart beating in my own chest, and even if he didn't sense me in the same way, surely he'd heard the shushing of my fingers running along the wooden panels, or the tiny clicks as the doors pushed against their tracks under the weight of my head.

If he did know I was there, he gave no indication. It was just as well, I told myself. Nothing could save me, and there was nothing I could do to Angus but harm him. I pressed my lips against the wooden door in a silent kiss, and crept back upstairs.

I heard Ellis and Hank talking downstairs the moment I stepped out of my room, and took a few breaths, steeling myself.

Being my mother's daughter, placating them should have come easily even if it was the last thing I wanted to do. Instead, I felt nauseated, lethargic, numb. It was as though my brain had already been compromised and nobody had bothered to tell me. I wondered what the procedure was like, and if I would retain any memories afterward. I wondered if I would be able to form new ones.

Anna was sitting by the fire, polishing a full set of silverware that was laid out on a length of felt. She glanced up when I passed, making brief eye contact, and I wondered what Meg had told her.

"Good morning, my dear," said Ellis, standing and pulling out a chair.

"Good morning, darling," I said.

When I uttered the endearment, a flash of surprise crossed Ellis's face, just as it had the night before. Hank looked up and said nothing. His empty expression terrified me.

"You're obviously feeling better," Ellis said, sitting back down. "You look like Rita Hayworth going on safari. Got plans?"

"Yes," I said, smoothing my dungarees over my thighs as though they were made of the finest silk. "I thought I'd come with you today."

"Really? Why?"

"Because I haven't seen you in ages," I said. "I've missed you."

Hank and Ellis exchanged glances.

"This is probably not the best day for you to come along," Ellis said.

"A girl could take that the wrong way, you know," I said. "I promise I won't make you waste any film."

"The weather's terrible," Hank said.

"He's right," said Ellis. "Have you seen what it's doing outside? The sky is gray as far as the eye can see. No chance of it clearing up."

Either they were ready to mount the hoax, or Ellis had already pulled the trigger and the ambulance was on its way.

Angus walked out from the kitchen, saw me at the table with Hank and Ellis, and spun on his heel with a disdainful bark.

Ellis stared after him. "I honestly think he's the most unpleasant man I've ever met."

Meg poked her head out from the kitchen. "Will the three of you be joining us for dinner tonight? Only we're having a fine stew, and we've some proper bread for once."

"Don't we always join you for dinner?" Hank asked with an amused smirk.

Ellis rolled his eyes and shook his head.

"Yes—when you're here, that is," said Meg, "but this is a local specialty and we've only the one good loaf for dipping—fluffy and white, and baked just this morning. There won't be anywhere near enough for everyone. Come down early, or I'll bring it up, because the rest will be getting beetroot sandwiches on National Loaf."

"Why the special treatment?" asked Hank.

"Think of it as a welcome back," she said, before disappearing.

"I think that lumberjack may have knocked a screw loose," said Hank.

Ellis laughed. "I think she always had a screw loose."

A local specialty.

I wish I could say I dismissed the thought out of hand, but if my suspicions were correct, Meg was cooking up, quite literally, the only solution to my problem.

Could I let her? Could I live with myself?

I wondered if Rhona and Mhàthair were out foraging, or if they were already in the kitchen.

Hank and Ellis had just begun to gather their things when the front door opened and Willie the Postie came in. He walked over to the fire.

"Good morning," he said to Anna. "It's a right *dreich* day."

"Aye, that it is. I wish I could spend the whole of it by the fire," she said, sighing. "But the fields don't plow themselves."

"You canna plow today—you'll be *drookit*!" Although he assumed an angry face, I knew enough about his feelings for Anna to recognize this as a display of affection.

"I've a raincoat. If I get too wet, I'll go in."

"Make sure that you do," he said, nodding sternly. "I've some letters for your guests. Well, a letter and a telegram, anyway."

"They're right over there," Anna said, tilting her head at us as though Willie wouldn't otherwise find us.

"And which one of you is Mr. Boyd?" he said, coming to the table.

Hank held out his hand, and Willie slapped a letter into it.

Even if the handwriting hadn't been impeccable, and even if it didn't still carry the faintest hint of Soir de Paris, the pale lavender of the Basildon Bond envelope would have given her away.

"Oh dear. It looks like my little songbird has finally tracked me down," Hank said. He slid a knife beneath the flap. "Probably begging me to come home. Well, it won't be long now, and then I suppose I'll have to slide a ring on that pretty little du Pont finger of hers."

As Hank pulled out Violet's letter, Willie handed me the telegram. He held my gaze for long enough that I knew he was trying to tell me something. I took it with great reluctance.

"Well, go on, open it," said Ellis.

I was motionless, clutching the telegram. I hadn't thought the situation could get any worse, but apparently I was wrong. Ellis was about to find out that my father was dead, and also that I'd asked about getting a divorce.

Hank unfolded his letter and began reading.

"Well, if you're not going to, I will," said Ellis, snatching the telegram from my hands.

I covered my eyes. There were a few seconds of silence while they both read.

"What the hell? Your father died?" said Ellis. "Why didn't you say anything?"

"Oh my God," said Hank in a hollow voice.

"Oh my God!" shouted Ellis, slapping the table. "Holy shit, Maddie. We're richer than Croesus. We're richer than Hank! But only because you're not a boy, and thank God we don't have a boy, or we'd have had to name him after your grandfather, surname and all, just to access the interest, and then the whole damned thing would have gone to the kid on his twenty-first birthday. But it seems your grandfather wasn't looking quite far enough ahead. Ha! You outwitted a robber baron, my brilliant, barren princess. Now we can buy our own house on Rittenhouse Square—the Colonel be damned!"

"She's left me," Hank said quietly. "She's fucking well left me . . ."

I peeked through my hands. Hank was pallid, gaunt. Ellis

was leaping around the room like an idiotic leprechaun. He'd left the telegram on the table. I picked it up and read it.

He was right. I got everything free and clear, but only because I was the sole heir. If there had been a male anywhere in the picture I would never have seen a cent, unless the male in question was my own son, in which case I would have been destitute the moment he came of age. The lawyer suggested we meet in person once I got back to the States, but there was no mention at all of a divorce. I realized that was what Willie was trying to tell me—that the telegram was safe to read in front of my husband.

I set the telegram on the table and looked up. Hank had me locked in his gaze. He looked puzzled. His eyes were wet.

"She's dumped me, Maddie," he said, shaking his head. "She's going to marry Freddie. I don't understand. How could she do this to me?" His expression switched abruptly, and he slammed the table. "Freddie! Damned Freddie! This must have been his plan all along! He wanted me out of the way so he could steal Violet out from under me! I'll kill him, Ellis—I swear, I'll kill him!"

He leapt up from the table as well, and suddenly Ellis was in front of him holding him by the shoulders.

"No, you won't kill him," Ellis said calmly and slowly. "We're going to get our footage, and then we're going to go home, and then we'll be world famous, and then you'll steal her back. That's what we're going to do."

Hank stared into Ellis's eyes for a long time, huffing and puffing like an enraged bull.

"Let's get the hell on with it then," he said.

"If you put it that way, I suppose I don't have much choice, although I was enjoying a moment with my lovely, rich wife," said Ellis. He put his coat on, then kissed me on the cheek. "Goodbye, my gorgeous golden goose. See you at dinner."

When the door shut behind them, I was too stunned to

move. Apparently so was Anna, who sat on the couch holding a serving spoon in one hand and a polishing cloth in the other.

Meg came through from the back, shaking her head in disgust. She went to the window and peered out at an angle, watching them walk away.

Chapter Forty-two

See you at dinner, he'd said.

I stayed at the table grappling with the concept, trying to parse it into something that wasn't cold-blooded murder. I tried to look at it from a purely rational point of view, as simply having to make a choice between organs—my brain or his kidneys. But it wasn't just his kidneys. It was his life.

I tried to look at it as self-defense, but it wasn't. If I allowed it to happen, it would be an execution, and a preemptive one at that, because he had yet to commit the crime.

I couldn't do it. Despite everything I stood to lose, I just couldn't sit by and watch him be poisoned.

I had only just come to that conclusion when the door burst open, hitting the wall behind it.

Two policemen strode in. A dark paddy wagon was parked in the street beyond them, and through the rain, I made out the words INVERNESS-SHIRE CONSTABULARY painted on its side.

These were no Bob the Bobbies—their uniforms were crisp navy with satin stripes running down the sides of their pants, their pointed helmets emblazoned with silver insignia. Truncheons and handcuffs hung from their black belts, and when they came to a stop, water rolled off their slick uniforms, forming puddles around their heavy boots.

"Good morning, ladies," said the taller one, nodding at us.

I almost couldn't breathe. Ellis had done it. He'd actually done it.

Was it because he hadn't liked the way Angus looked at us the night before? Had I not been convincing enough in my role as doting wife? Perhaps he'd returned from the trip already determined, and there was nothing I could have done anyway.

"And how can I help you gentlemen?" Meg asked.

I had to warn Angus, couldn't believe that I hadn't already—

"We're looking for Angus Duncan Grant," said one of them. "I believe he resides here?"

"He does for the moment. And what are you wanting with him?" asked Meg.

"Just a quick word is all."

He sounded so pleasant, so polite, so matter-of-fact. It was hard to believe he was about to destroy Angus's life.

"I'll let him know you're here," said Meg.

I stared after her as she went into the kitchen, and when I jerked back around, both policemen were watching me. I was sure they'd seen the panic in my eyes.

"Good morning, Officers," said Angus, coming around the front of the bar and sitting on one of the tall stools. "I hear you'd like a word?"

Conall came with him, flopping down at his feet. The dog looked relaxed, but his eyes darted.

"Mr. Grant—"

"That's Captain Grant," Anna said, from over by the fire.

The policeman nodded at her, then looked back at Angus. "Captain Grant, my name is Inspector Chisholm, and this is Sergeant MacDougall. We've had a report up at the courthouse about someone poaching on the grounds at Craig Gairbh."

"I'm afraid I wouldn't know anything about that," said Angus.

"The report named you as the perpetrator," said Inspector Chisholm, "and a quick summary of the evidence seems to suggest it's true. We took a wee stroll around the property, and couldn't help noticing that there's a well-stocked dugout in the hill behind. Two red deer, a pheasant, and a capercaillie hanging, if I'm not mistaken. I don't suppose you'd care to tell us how they were obtained?"

"I took them from the hills," Angus said. "As I'm sure you've *jaloused.*"

"And that includes the grounds at Craig Gairbh?"

"Aye," said Angus, nodding.

"Well," said Inspector Chisholm, raising his eyebrows. "I can't say I was expecting that. Your honesty is refreshing, but all the same, I'm afraid we're going to have to take you in."

"I don't think that will be necessary," said Angus, remaining entirely calm. He folded his arms over his chest, then stretched his legs out in front of him, crossing them at the ankles.

"I'm afraid I have no choice," said Inspector Chisholm. "The law is very clear on the matter."

"And who's leveled the charges then?" said Angus. "Because it certainly wasn't the laird."

"And how would you be knowing that?" asked Inspector Chisholm.

"Because I think I'd remember doing it," said Angus.

I was utterly confused. Judging from their faces, the policemen were as well.

"I beg your pardon?" Inspector Chisholm finally said.

"I don't think I can level charges against myself, and at any rate, even if I could, I'm fairly certain I wouldn't want to."

"You're telling us you're the laird."

"Aye," said Angus, nodding. "These three months. Son of the previous laird's late brother. Closest surviving male relative."

I couldn't grasp it. I turned to Angus. "But that night Bob the Bobby came in—he gave you a warning for poaching," I sputtered.

"That wasn't for poaching," he said. "That was for throwing the water bailiff in the river."

I stared into his eyes as I realized what all this meant. Then I leapt to my feet.

"That bastard. That *rat* bastard! I can't *wait* to tell him!"

"Maddie?" said Angus. "What's going on?"

"It was Ellis! He made the report! He was threatening to have you thrown in prison if I didn't turn back into his perfect society wife." I stopped suddenly. "And then he followed through. My God, the hospital is probably on its way for me right now."

"Hospital? What hospital?" Angus demanded.

"Meg can tell you. I have to go," I said, rushing past the officers to grab my coat.

"Maddie, *stop*!" said Angus. "Don't go anywhere. I'm coming with you."

"I'm sorry to interrupt," said Inspector Chisholm, "but could we trouble you for a wee bit of proof about this claim of yours before we all go about our business?"

"That can wait," said Angus, striding toward the door. "Conall, *trobhad! Crios ort!*"

The dog scrambled to his feet, trotting to catch up.

"I'm afraid it cannot," said Inspector Chisholm, reaching out and snagging Angus's upper arm. In an instant, Angus had swung around and was holding the other man's wrists parallel to his ears. Their faces were inches apart.

Sergeant MacDougall stepped forward with his hand on his truncheon.

After a few seconds, Angus released Inspector Chisholm, who straightened his sleeves and stared belligerently.

"I'll get your proof, and you'll be on your way," said Angus. "Meg, get the lockbox. I'll get the key. And Maddie, don't go *anywhere.*"

When he turned around, I took the opportunity to duck into the rain.

There were a number of things I wanted to say to Ellis— and Hank—before anyone else got there.

I ran for as long as I could, then continued at a jog, and by the time Urquhart Castle came into view, had slowed to a stumbling walk.

The sight of it gave me a second wind, and I sprinted down and then up the slopes of the moat, through the gatehouse, and across the scrubby weeds until I was at the top of the Water Gate.

Hank was on the shore, leaning over his camera with a rain-coat tented over his head. Ellis was in the boat, which was half in the water. For a moment I thought he was preparing to get out, but then I realized they'd already unloaded their duffel bags, and the rope was coiled in the bow. He was heading out onto the water.

I hurtled down the hill, and before either one of them knew what was going on, leapt into the bow of the boat. I landed on my knees in collected rainwater and smashed my rib cage against the bench.

When I lifted my head to scrape the wet hair away from my face, I found Ellis staring at me in open-mouthed shock.

"Maddie! What the hell?" he said.

Hank came out from under his raincoat. "Jesus Christ! What the hell are you doing here? We told you this wasn't a good day."

Past the bench, on the bottom of the boat, was the miniature monster, with its curved neck and prominent eyes, its long fin and olive-green body.

I launched myself across the bench and grabbed it.

"Is this the reason?" I said, waving it over my head.

"Maddie, put that down," Ellis said through gritted teeth.

"Gladly." I threw it over his shoulder, as far from the boat as I could. It lay bobbing on its side, and I laughed. "My God, it doesn't even work."

Ellis just stared at me.

Hank sighed dramatically. "Ellis, grab that thing, will you? We're running low on plastic wood. Maybe you could work on controlling your wife while you're at it."

Ellis picked up the oars and began rowing toward the model, his eyes fixed on mine.

"Hey, *Hank*!" I shouted, my voice cracking with the effort. "I want to talk to you! This business of controlling me. Does that include having my frontal lobe turned into a soufflé?"

Hank rolled his eyes. "For crying out loud, Maddie. He just wants you to stop acting like a lunatic. If you can manage that, he's not going to do anything."

"That's not what you thought yesterday. What's changed since yesterday?"

"He's just frustrated—we're all frustrated!—and we're all saying things we don't mean, including you. *Especially* you. But we're about to get out of this hellhole, so could you please just try to hold it together for a few days longer?"

"Was he frustrated when he called the courthouse? Because two policemen from Inverness came about half an hour ago to arrest Angus."

Hank looked up sharply. "Ellis? Is that true?"

"Why the hell are you asking him?" My voice, overtaxed, came out in broken shards. "Do you think he's suddenly going to start telling the truth? He lied about being color-blind to get out of the war, for Christ's sake!" My words echoed back to me, bouncing off the hills on the opposite shore.

Ellis stepped over the middle bench. I saw his closed fist coming at my head, and the next thing I knew I was lying in water at the bottom of the boat, my vision filled with starbursts.

"Jesus Christ, Ellis!" Hank shouted. "What the hell is wrong with you?"

I lay huddled in the bow, waiting for my sight to return.

"Get that fucking thing back here right now! Ellis, I mean it! *Get back here!*"

"Gonna have a quick word with my wife first," Ellis called over, almost cheerfully.

"Ellis, if you don't bring that boat back this very second—"

"There isn't much you can do about it, is there?"

I hauled myself up on my elbows, my head wobbling. We were a dozen yards from shore. Ellis was sitting on the middle bench, staring at me, smirking.

"So it's true," I said.

"I don't know what you're talking about."

"You can see color."

He shrugged. "So what? It doesn't matter."

"*It doesn't matter?*"

"No one else will ever know. But don't fret about your appointment, darling—the facilities are quite luxurious."

"*Ellis!*" Hank bellowed from shore.

"Once I get off this boat," I said quietly, "you're never going to see me again, except maybe in divorce court. You've got nothing left to hold over me."

"Oh, but I do. You're incapacitated, which makes me your legal guardian. All I have to do is call the hospital."

"The hospital can't take me away if they can't find me, and they won't."

"*Ellis! Turn around!*" Hank roared.

"Oh, and by the way, Angus couldn't be arrested for poaching at Craig Gairbh because he is the *Laird* of Craig Gairbh," I continued. "I suppose that makes you cousins of some sort, although I fail to see a resemblance."

We locked eyes, as if seeing each other for the first time. The water lapped against the side of the boat, which was starting to bob.

"Ellis!" Hank bellowed. "For God's sake, *turn around*!"

"Leave us the hell alone, Hank! I'll bring the boat back when I'm good and ready!"

"*Look!*" Hank screamed, and his voice was so guttural, so uncontrolled, we couldn't help ourselves.

He was filming furiously. He stuck his other arm out from under the raincoat just long enough to point. "Over there! It was long and black and curved. It came up for just a moment— the wake has to be at least sixty feet long! Holy shit! This is it! I'm getting it! I'm fucking getting it! Ellis, this is going to be fucking *spectacular*!"

Ellis's expression shifted and he twisted in his seat. I grabbed the edge of the boat and leaned over to look. Something large, dark, and rounded was moving quickly beneath the water. By the time I realized it was rising, it had rammed the bottom of the bow and flipped me into the air.

My mouth and nose filled with water before I fully comprehended that I was beneath the surface.

The cold was shocking. Thousands of bubbles, both big and small, rushed past me. It was air escaping from my clothing, and since I knew the bubbles must be going up, I must be facing down. I bucked instinctively in an effort to right myself.

The bubbles slowed, which meant that my clothes were becoming saturated. My one and only thought was to get free of my coat, but while I could bring my hands together in front of me, my fingers were too cold to obey. I could find the buttons, touch the buttons, even feel the thread that kept them attached to my coat, but could do nothing at all about unfastening them. Eventually, my hands drifted helplessly away.

I looked up at the surface and, as though through thick, wavy glass, saw Ellis standing in the boat holding an oar. It sliced through the surface and came to a stop against my chest.

With enormous force of will, I managed to bring my hands back in front of me and locked my fingers around its shaft, just above the blade. I kept hold of it and, after what seemed like an eternity, wondered why I wasn't moving toward the boat. Bewildered, I looked up and saw Ellis's determined face through the millions of tiny strands of peat in the water.

He wasn't saving me. He was making sure I stayed under.

I tried to push the oar away, but it was futile. He moved it to the center of my chest and pushed me deeper still, until a final stream of bubbles escaped my nostrils. My consciousness flickered, the surface receded, and then there was silence.

What happened next was like being sucked into an inverted waterfall. An arm swooped firmly around me and I was propelled upward, exploding through the surface with a deafening crash of waves. Then I was being hauled through the water, quickly, from behind.

"Hold on, *mo gràdh,* I've got you," Angus said directly into my ear. His free arm backstroked steadily, his legs pumped furiously beneath us. I tried to take a breath, but my chest wouldn't budge. I couldn't even lift my hands to hold onto his arm.

My eyes drifted shut, and I fought to keep them open. One moment, I saw clouds churning and rolling above me looking for all the world like a living thing; and the next, nothing.

Clouds, nothing. Clouds, nothing. And finally, just nothing.

Chapter Forty-three

The next thing I was aware of was Angus's mouth covering mine, followed by me vomiting water. He flipped me onto my side and a spasm ripped through my rib cage, sending another stream of water flying from my nose and mouth. I drew a hoarse, gurgling breath—my first since going under.

Angus pulled me into a sitting position and wrapped his coat around me.

"What the hell?" said Hank, ducking out from beneath his raincoat tent. "Jesus Christ—what happened? Maddie, are you okay?"

"No, she's not okay," Angus barked. "She's half-drowned and frozen. Give me your coat."

Hank struggled out of it and thrust it at Angus. "What happened? I didn't even see her go in." He looked at me again. "My God, her hands and face are blue."

Angus wrapped me in the second coat and scooped me into his arms.

"I'm taking her to the corn-drying kiln," he said. "It's the intact room in the opposite wall. Run as fast as your legs will carry you to the first white house to the north. It's the McKen-zies' croft. Tell them what happened and have them send for the bobby. He'll bring his car."

As Angus carried me through the Water Gate, holding my head against his shoulder, I looked back at the loch.

Ellis was still in the boat, paddling like a madman with a single oar. The other was floating away from him.

Hank returned with Mhàthair, the two of them bustling in with armfuls of quilts and blankets. Before I knew it, Mhàthair had replaced the coats and swaddled me like a baby, depositing me on the edge of the ancient kiln and then sitting right next to me, pulling the edges of her own coat as far around me as they'd reach. I leaned against her, quaking with the cold, alter-nately drawing shallow breaths and coughing violently.

Angus wrapped a blanket around his drenched clothes like a kilt and paced. Each time I was wracked by coughs, he rushed over to prop me up so Mhàthair could thump my back.

Hank crouched against the wall, pale. After a while, he climbed to his feet.

"I suppose I'll go see if I can get that fool back on dry land," he said.

"If I were you," said Angus, "I'd grab my camera and leave that *amadain* right where he is."

"I know that was a pretty rotten trick he tried to pull on you, but surely you don't want him to drown out there," Hank said.

"I would like nothing more," said Angus, "although I ex-pect he'll find his way back, if only to take care of the evi-dence."

"If you mean the camera, I think it's pretty well protected by my raincoat."

"I do indeed mean the camera. But it's not the rain it needs protecting from. In addition to anything else you might have captured on film was your friend's attempt to murder his wife."

"What? No. That's ridiculous." After a slight pause, Hank jerked around to face me. "Maddie, is that true?"

I managed to nod.

He stared at me for a few seconds as understanding dawned. Then he turned and marched out the door.

From my perch on the kiln, I had a perfect view of the Water Gate. Hank crashed through the weeds, paused beneath its arch, and looked down at the landing. Then he bellowed like a wild animal and tore down the hill. There were several minutes of angry shouting, amplified by the water but none of it comprehensible.

When Hank reappeared, he was changed. He plodded back to the kiln room with his face pointed at the ground and his shoulders slouched. His arms didn't even swing. He looked like an upright corpse.

He slid down the wall until he was crouching against it. He looked at the floor between his legs, resting his forearms on his knees and letting his hands dangle. They were bloodied and scraped.

"He made it back before I got there," he finally said. "He threw the camera in the loch."

The rest of us remained silent.

He looked at me, his eyes bleak. "You tried to tell me and I didn't listen. I thought I knew him. Can you ever forgive me?"

I remained huddled against Mhàthair, not even attempting a response.

"No, of course you can't," Hank continued. "I can't make it up to you, I know that. But I really didn't know—I don't even know when he found the time to slip off to the phone booth. We're almost always together. But I swear, if he called the hospital as well as the courthouse, I won't let them take you anywhere."

"You!" Angus sputtered. "You won't even get a crack at the *bastart* who's fool enough to show up trying to take Maddie away. Someone's brains will get scrambled, I promise you that. And I'll scramble the whole of that coward at the bottom of the slope, brains and all, while I'm at it. He'd better hope Bob the Bobby locks him up right quick, before I get the opportunity."

Hank watched Angus while he spoke, then dropped his head again.

When Bob showed up, Angus carried me to the car, and Mhàthair and Hank followed. No one suggested we get Ellis.

As we drove back to the inn, Bob said, "So you're telling me there was photographic evidence of the attempted murder, but it's gone?"

"Aye," said Angus.

Bob turned to Hank, who was in the passenger seat, staring out the side window. "And you're saying you didn't see a thing?"

"Just the monster," Hank said despondently.

"But you were *right there*!" Bob slapped the steering wheel twice for emphasis.

"I was focused on filming."

Bob glanced at him a couple of times in exasperation, then sighed. "Well, there's one eyewitness, and fortunately the intended victim is still around to testify. I can certainly arrest him based on that."

We reached the inn and pulled up in front of it, the gravel crunching beneath the cold, hard rubber of the tires.

Bob twisted around in his seat, watching as Angus lifted me from the car.

"I'll fetch Dr. McLean," he said, "and then I suppose I should go collect the pathetic *creutair*. I canna remember the last time I had someone in my holding cell." He sighed again. "I suppose I'll be expected to feed him."

As soon as Angus carried me up the stairs, Anna, Meg, and Mhàthair wrested me away and banished him with orders to get himself properly dried off.

In short order, there was a fire roaring in my grate, they'd dressed me in a heavy nightgown, and placed me under so many covers I couldn't move. They tucked stoneware pigs by my feet, and Mhàthair—after pressing her ear to my chest and shaking her head—disappeared for a while and returned with a steaming, smelly poultice that she shoved down the front of my nightgown. She put crushed garlic between all of my toes and wrapped my feet. When she replaced the quilts, she laid an extra one, still folded, across the bottom of the bed, weighing me down even further.

I withstood it all without protest. When I wasn't coughing, my lungs rattled. I was too weak to move, and lay with my eyes aimed vaguely toward the fire, drifting in and out of a fitful trance, reliving what I'd thought would be my final moments— the weightless, almost leisurely rolling in the water, the deafening *whoosh* of bubbles bursting up from all around me, the knocking of the oars inside the oarlocks. The first moments, when I tried to figure out how to survive, and the final moments, when I accepted that I would not.

Ellis had recognized an opportunity to get rid of me and seized it without a second's hesitation. My inheritance, his inheritance, his dirty little secret—all of it could be secured at once, with only a minute or two's effort.

Ellis would deny what he'd done, of course, touting my mental condition as proof that my testimony was unreliable, and saying that Angus had misinterpreted what was going on. He would probably even frame himself as a thwarted hero, claiming he'd been seconds away from hauling me into the boat, and that Angus's interference had subjected me to being in the water even longer.

I wondered how he'd explain the missing camera, or Hank's version of events, because while he might be able to cast doubt on my testimony, that was not true of Hank, and I doubted very much that he would be easily quieted.

Was it really the monster we'd encountered? We'd never know. Because of Ellis, no one would ever know.

Chapter Forty-four

My fitful trance was actually hypothermia, according to Dr. McLean, although, with an appreciative nod toward Mhàthair, he declared me sufficiently warmed up to be past danger in that regard. However, he said I had pseudopneumonia from taking in water, and the important thing now was to prevent it from turning into real pneumonia, which could turn deadly in a matter of hours. He pulled a bottle of bright green tonic from his bag and set it on the dresser.

"This contains an expectorant. We want her to cough everything out."

"What about castor oil?" Anna said anxiously.

The doctor shook his head. "I'm afraid it won't help."

Anna sucked the air through her teeth in despair.

Over the course of the night, my temperature rose and fell, and I went from boiling to freezing in the space of seconds. I was wracked by terrible coughing fits, and in between, felt my lungs crackle whenever I took a breath. I was at the complete mercy of my body.

I would clutch the covers to me, begging for someone to throw more logs on the fire. Then I'd kick the covers away from me, sometimes managing to hurl them to the floor. Mhàthair replaced them every time, calmly, gently.

She was in and out with poultices, alternating onion-and-vinegar mash with mustard plaster. When the unbearable heat rose in me, I flung them away. She replaced them in the same composed manner she did the bedclothes. She hovered in the background, doing mysterious things, seeming more like a pair of competent hands, a set of nimble fingers, than Mhàthair the actual person.

Angus never left my side. When I was sweltering and crying for ice, he mopped my brow and dribbled tiny bits of water onto my tongue. When my body bucked and heaved from the cold, he tucked the covers around me and stroked my face. There was not one moment the entire night when I could not open my eyes and immediately find his face.

At one point, in the wee hours of the morning, when I was so wracked by fever that my jaw was clenched and aching, Angus laid a hand on my forehead and looked up in alarm.

Mhàthair also felt my forehead, then rushed from the room. Angus stripped the bedclothes back and held my limp body forward as he pulled my nightgown over my head. Then he wrung out cold facecloths and lay them all over my clammy skin.

A few minutes later, Mhàthair came back, and I found myself propped up between them, being forced to sip some kind of tea. It was full of honey, but not enough to mask the bitter taste underneath. As they eased me back onto the bed, I was already slipping into a darkness as deep as the loch. The moment before everything disappeared, a pretty young woman with sad eyes appeared in front of me. She was floating, with her gown and hair billowing around her. It was Màiri—I knew it instinctively. She mouthed something to me and lifted her arms, but before I could make out what she was saying, she—and everything else—faded away.

The next thing I remember was waking up and not being sure where I was. I blinked a few times, and found myself looking into Angus's blue eyes. He'd pulled the chair up to the bed.

Mhàthair reached over from the other side and laid a hand on my forehead.

"The fever's broken, thanks be to Heaven," she said. "She's come through."

Angus shut his eyes for a moment, then lifted my hand and kissed it.

"Never scare me like that again, *mo chridhe*. I thought I'd lost you, and I've lost enough to the loch already."

Although my fever had broken, I was in no condition to get out of bed. The coughing alone was exhausting, as well as agonizing.

Anna was knitting by the fire and I was resting my eyes when there was a rapping on the doorframe.

"Knock, knock," said Hank. "Are you receiving visitors?"

"I should think not," Anna said sternly. "Not when she's in this state."

"I'm sorry. I didn't mean to be glib. Please, Maddie—may I have a word? Alone?"

"She's recuperating, you fool," said Anna. "Whatever it is can wait."

"It's all right," I whispered. My voice was nearly gone from all the coughing.

Anna stared at Hank for a couple of seconds, then held up the splayed fingers of one hand. "Five minutes," she announced. "And not one minute more. I'll be in the hallway."

She set her knitting on the floor and sailed out, throwing Hank a searing look as she passed.

He hovered uncomfortably, fidgeting, as though he didn't know what to do with his hands. I was afraid he might light a cigarette. Finally he walked around the bed to the chair. He plopped into it, crossed his legs, and stared at the mantel.

"Did he really try to drown you?" he finally asked. "I mean, are you positive?"

Only after the words were out did he look at me. I stared straight at him. He dropped his gaze and took a deep breath.

"Look," he said. "I know this doesn't change what happened, but I've decided to send a telegram to the Colonel. I'm going to tell him Ellis was lying about being color-blind. There are tests, you know. He can't fake it forever."

After a pause, I said, "What for? Revenge?"

"Because he deserves it! Because in addition to what he almost managed to have done to you medically, he tried to kill you! And he destroyed the footage! And he cost me Violet! He's cost me everything, probably even you!" He dropped his head and pressed his fingers into the corners of his eyes, as though he were about to cry.

I watched him, unmoved.

"He didn't cost you Violet," I said. "You were just as terrible to her as you were to me."

He quit trying to cry and looked up. "I beg your pardon?"

"I know everything, Hank."

"Well, apparently I don't. What are you talking about?"

"Were you heads or tails?" I asked. "And more importantly, did you win or lose?"

His eyes went wide and unblinking. He stared at me for a long time. "Jesus, Maddie. I don't know what to say."

"I think I'd prefer it if you said nothing at all."

Anna came back into the room.

"Bob the Bobby is downstairs," she said. "He says he needs

to speak to both of you right away, and since it can't wait and Maddie can't come down, he's asked me to check if it's all right for him to come up to the bedroom, even though I was very clear that it's not at all proper, and I wouldn't be a bit surprised if you said no."

"It's all right," I said. "He can come up."

I tried to remain calm, but was shot full of adrenaline. What if he'd come to tell us that Ellis had slipped away?

Angus and Anna led Bob into the bedroom.

He stood at the foot of my bed, holding his cap.

"Mrs. Hyde," he said, nodding a greeting. "Are you feeling a wee bit better, I hope? Angus tells me you were quite poorly overnight."

"Yes, thank you. I think I'm on the mend," I said, although the effort sparked a fit of coughing. I rolled onto my side, and Anna rushed over to thump my back.

Bob waited until I was finished and Anna had propped me up again. "I'm very sorry to intrude like this, but I'm afraid a situation has arisen."

"What type of situation?" asked Angus, and from the way his face clouded I saw that he'd jumped to the same conclusion I had.

"It's not what you're thinking," Bob said. He gazed at his shoes for a moment, then looked Hank square in the face. "Mr. Boyd, was there any kind of . . . altercation down at the shore?"

"Sure, I knocked his block off."

"But was he . . . conscious when you last saw him?"

"He was a little worse for wear, but definitely conscious. Mewling and obstreperous, even."

"Yes, well," said Bob, twisting his cap. "I'm afraid that when I went back to make the arrest, I found the suspect deceased."

Angus was by my side instantly, his hand on my shoulder. I reached up and clasped his fingers.

"What? How?" Hank demanded.

"He appears to have drowned in two inches of water," said Bob. "I've never seen anything like it. He was facedown at the water's edge. The rest of him wasn't even wet."

Hank laughed bitterly. "He was probably playing possum so you'd leave—he's not above doing that, you know."

"There's no question that he's dead. The body's already at the morgue in Inverness. So the question now becomes how it happened."

Hank's expression grew panicked as the implication sank in. He leapt from the chair.

"My God, you can't think I killed him!" he said. "He was staggering around when I left, I swear! He must have fallen in after. I boxed his ears! That's all!"

He swiveled to face me, his eyes desperate and his fists clenched. "Maddie! Tell him! For God's sake—you *know* I wouldn't kill Ellis! *Tell him!*"

"It's true," I said. "Hank would never kill Ellis. They're two parts of the same person."

Hank stared at me, stricken.

Bob rubbed his chin for a while, thinking. "Well, given the situation—and it is indeed a first for me—I suppose I could file it as an accidental drowning . . . Assuming there are no objections on the part of the family?"

He looked at me inquiringly. After a few seconds, I dipped my head in assent. Angus squeezed my shoulder, and I clutched his fingers even more tightly.

Bob took a deep breath. "Under the circumstances, I'm not sure what the right thing is to say. And while I know this is all very sudden, I'm afraid you're going to have to start thinking about final arrangements. Please let me know if there's anything I can do to help, anything at all."

"Thank you," I said quietly.

After Bob left, Hank headed toward the door, moving like a sleepwalker.

When his bedroom door clicked shut, I looked up at Angus. I knew something was coming, but nothing could have prepared me for the bloodcurdling scream that rang through the building. I threw my arms around Angus's waist, waiting as the dreadful keening subsided into wild crying.

Angus held my head against him and stroked my hair. "And what about you, *m'eudail?* Are you all right?"

I nodded. "I think so. I don't suppose I would have wished this on anyone, but my God . . ."

"It's all right, *mo run geal og.* There's no need to explain. Not to me."

I took his hand and pressed my cheek into it.

Down the hall, Hank continued to rage and grieve, but there was nothing any of us could do. There was not a soul on earth who could have comforted him, because he was worse than heartbroken. He'd been cleaved down the middle.

Chapter Forty-five

In the end, I sent Ellis home to his mother. I didn't want to attend the funeral, and suspected I wouldn't be welcome anyway.

Two days after Hank flew off with Ellis's body, Angus slipped into my room and my bed. He lay beside me, balanced on an elbow, stroking the hair away from my throat. He fingered the neck of my nightgown.

"Take that off ..."

When I lay back down, he leaned over and whispered directly into my ear. "I want to marry you, *mo chridhe*. To make this official just as soon as we can."

He planted tiny kisses on my neck, working his way down. When he was almost at my collarbone, he took a small piece of my flesh between his teeth. I gasped, and every hair on my body stood on end.

"That's assuming you'll even have such a rough dog as myself," he said, continuing his descent. He kissed his way to my left breast and ran his tongue over my nipple. It tightened into a little raspberry.

He raised his head. "Although I suppose I didn't phrase it exactly as a question, that last comment of mine does require an answer . . ."

"But of course!" I said. "I want to be Mrs. Grant as soon as . . . oh!"

His mouth was once again on the move.

"Actually," he said between kisses, "you'll be the Much Honored Madeline Grant, Lady of Craig Gairbh."

The thing he did next left me unable to respond at all—at least, not with words.

We decided to wait a few weeks for the sake of propriety, but for all intents and purposes we were married from that moment on. Angus spent every night in my bed, although he slipped downstairs before dawn so as not to offend Anna's sensibilities.

The news from the Front made it clear that the war in Europe couldn't last much longer. City after city either surrendered or was liberated, and the Germans were driven ever deeper into their own territory. They were surrounded on all sides. They had also run out of men to recruit. They began drafting boys as young as ten from the Hitler Youth, and reenlisting any soldier who had only lost his leg below the knee.

From there, it all fell like dominoes, beginning with a hit close to home. President Roosevelt died on April 12, and Harry S. Truman became the 33rd President of the United States.

Three days later, British forces liberated a complex of concentration camps at Bergen-Belsen and, according to an article in *The Inverness Courier,* found "thousands of starving men, women, and children, naked bodies lying four feet high stretching a distance of 80 yards by a width of 30 yards, cannibalism rife, disease and unspeakable cruelty rampant." General Eisenhower implored members of the British House of Commons to come see "the agony of crucified humanity" for themselves, because "no words can convey the horror."

On April 16, the same day the Russians began yet another massive offensive, a desperate Adolf Hitler issued his "Last Stand," in which he ordered troops to arrest immediately any officer or soldier who gave orders to retreat, regardless of rank, and if necessary to execute them, because even if they were in German uniform, they were probably drawing Russian pay. He told his forces, "In this hour the entire German nation looks to you, my soldiers in the East, and only hopes that by your fanaticism, by your arms, and by your leadership, the Bolshevik onslaught is drowned in a bloodbath."

Twelve days later, Mussolini and his mistress were executed by firing squad after trying to escape to Switzerland. Their bodies were then hung upside down on meat hooks in the Piazzale Loreto. A woman approached and cried, "Five shots for my five assassinated sons!" before pumping another five bullets into Mussolini's already-battered corpse.

The next day, April 29, American forces liberated Dachau, the first of the German concentration camps to be erected, and among the last to be liberated. Upon their approach, the Americans encountered thirty coal cars filled with decomposing bodies. Within the camp, they found approximately thirty thousand emaciated survivors, who continued to die at the rate of several hundred a day, because their systems were too weak to take nourishment.

On April 30, the Russians took Berlin and raised the Soviet flag over the Reichstag. Deep in their bunker, with the battle raging above them, Adolf Hitler and Eva Braun poisoned themselves and their dogs, after which Hitler shot himself in the head.

.   .   .

We huddled around the radio that night, every one of us breathing through our mouths. It was almost too much to believe. At long last—after more devastation and cruelty and callous disregard for human life than any of us could have possibly dreamed up—the hostilities appeared to be over. They were, in fact, although it wasn't made official for another week, when all remaining German forces surrendered unconditionally.

When Victory Day was finally declared, the collective jubilation became chaos. People ripped down their Blackout curtains and set them on fire in the streets, sirens blared and church bells rang, victory parades turned into wild impromptu parties, people whooped and danced and sang, strangers made love in bushes off to the side of the road, bonfires raged, and bagpipes called out triumphantly from every hill the whole night through.

At ten the next morning, Angus and I got married. The day after that, Anna and Willie did the same.

Chapter Forty-six

A few weeks after our wedding, I noticed that Angus had quietly had the gravestone with his name on it replaced with one that didn't. This time, it was I who knelt and traced the names of Màiri and her baby, leaving behind the handful of bluebells I'd just gathered from the Cover.

Knowing I'd paid homage to just one grave, I continued on to the Water Gate, picking more flowers on the way. After placing them at the water's edge, I stared across the loch's shiny black surface, and wondered what, exactly, had happened to us out there. Was it Màiri? Was it the monster? Or was it something else entirely?

The monster—if there was one—never revealed itself to me again. But what I had learned over the past year was that monsters abound, usually in plain sight.

When Angus asked if I was ready to see my new home, I said that yes, of course I was, as long as he was entirely sure the army had removed all the land mines. He roared with laughter when I told him about my escapade, and told me that there weren't any mines in the first place—the signs were there to keep civilians out, as well as to keep the commandos in. The live ammunition, however, was real.

"What do you think?" he asked, when we rounded the bend and reached the oak-lined drive. The Nissen huts and barbed wire were gone, so it was the first time I'd seen the Big House in its entirety.

Angus's arm was around my shoulder, and he watched my face expectantly.

"Oh, Angus!" I said, skipping ahead of him. "It's magnificent! Is it locked?"

"I don't think so," he said, and then laughed as I ran ahead.

The double doors were huge and studded with brass. The entranceway was draped with carved boughs and vines, starting above the pediment and reaching almost to the ground. Just above that was an enormous coat of arms, and way up at the top, over a frieze of rearing horses flanking a shield, was a clock tower in a cupola that Angus told me was added in 1642. Each window was graced with a carving, and forty-foot Corinthian pillars ran up the wall between them.

When I walked through the front doors and found myself looking up at a vast, multistory gallery, I caught my breath. Generations of larger-than-life Grants glowered down at me from the oak-paneled walls, the frames that contained them separated by gilt curlicues. Most of them had ginger hair; all of them had Angus's striking blue eyes.

There was not one room on the main level that didn't have intricate plasterwork on its ceiling, and most were either painted or trimmed with gilt. Every detail was exquisite— from the ornate chandeliers to the medieval tapestries to the "cabinet of curiosities" that once belonged to Louis XIV. The upholstered furniture seemed oddly shabby until Angus told me that it dated from the early 1700s, and that all the velvet was original.

I tried to imagine the Colonel's reaction when he first stepped inside all those years ago. When he looked up at the portraits of his relatives, did his fantasies of finding the monster grow to encompass fantasies of becoming the laird? During his stay, as he harassed servant girls and adopted his upper-crust accent and commissioned estate tweeds, did he secretly ascertain how many male Grants stood between him and the title?

There was no doubt in my mind. Ellis probably had too.

Although the war was over, Europe remained in chaos: there were food shortages and transportation crises, a staggering number of refugees streaming from city to city, mass surrenders of German troops, hundreds of thousands of freed prisoners, as well as innumerable wounded soldiers who now faced the prospect of trying to rebuild their lives.

I'd never forgotten the wounded men on the SS *Mallory*, particularly the soldier who had caught my gaze and held it. He opened my eyes, awakening me to a reality I had somehow managed to avoid until that point. While Hank and Ellis carried on without a care in the world, it was men like the burned soldier, Angus, and Anna's brothers who sacrificed everything to save the rest of us. I wanted to give something back.

When I told Angus what I had in mind, he folded me wordlessly into his arms.

And so the plans were laid. For the next few years, the Big House at Craig Gairbh would be a convalescent hospital for injured soldiers.

Epilogue

Within two months, hospital beds and portable screens lined the halls and ballroom. The East Drawing Room became a surgery, and the Great Hall a burn unit. We moved into the servants' quarters on the top floor with Conall, and before long, Meg joined us, having decided to become a nurse.

The patients both crushed and amazed me. I watched as a forty-seven-year-old sergeant, newly blind and learning to find his way around with a cane, first fingered the petals of a peony, and then leaned over to bury his face in it. I held the hand of a boy who was not yet twenty as he cried in frustration after donning his prosthetic limb for the first time. I cheered from the sidelines during the frequent wheelchair races in the Great Hall. The library became a game room. One indomitable soldier, twenty-two years old, whose spine and left arm had been shattered, had one of us wheel him into the library each morning, then spent the rest of the day defeating anyone who dared take him on at chess.

I rooted for these men, and hundreds like them, as they passed through our lives and our home. It was a comfort to me to see them taking solace in the garden, or cooling in the shade of the fountain.

Meg was a great favorite with the soldiers, and she married a young corporal, who was also from Clydebank, the following Valentine's Day—an event that Angus and I had to skip for the happiest of reasons. I went into labor the night before, and just like that, Valentine's Day was redeemed.

Two of our children were born during that time, to the great delight of the soldiers. After all the horror, death, and despair, the babies were the truest possible affirmation of life.

Life. There it was. In all its beautiful, tragic fragility, there was still life, and those of us who'd been lucky enough to survive opened our arms wide and embraced it.

Author's Note

A nd now for the usual caveats about writing fiction based on real events:

I've appropriated some parts of the history of monster sightings. In particular, I transformed the "Surgeon's Photo" into the "Colonel's Photo," and reimagined the Royal Observer Corps sighting completely. The British Aluminium plant at Foyers was indeed bombed during the war, but at noon rather than at night, and in February 1941 rather than January 1945. Similarly, while I tried to stay true to all other facts about the creation of the Special Service Brigade, Achnacarry Castle did not become Castle Commando until 1942.

While I did not fictionalize any of these, the facts and numbers associated with some of the battles and certainly the death camps are inaccurate in the book because I had to base them on the information that would have been available to my characters at the time, which was limited to the nightly BBC broadcast and what was reported in *The Inverness Courier*. The real numbers and full truth took years to come out, and, as we now know, are even harder to comprehend than those that so horrified Maddie.

Acknowledgments

I don't know if writing drives people crazy or if crazy people are driven to write, but I could not possibly have written this book without the help of the following non-crazy people, to whom I am forever indebted:

My husband, Bob, my Rock of Gibraltar—without your unwavering support and belief, none of this would have been possible, and I certainly would not be able to continue.

To my sons, Benjamin, Thomas, and Daniel, who are delightful and incredibly well-adjusted young men in spite of having me as their mother.

To Hugh Allison and Tony Harmsworth. It was as though some invisible hand guided me to you. Experts each on Scotland during World War II and the Loch Ness Monster, your willingness to answer my endless questions over the years was nothing short of heroic.

To Hugh's family members, who invited me in by the fire and made sure (for better or worse) that the level in my glass never went down: Hughie and Chrissie Campbell, Donnie and Joan Macdonald, Jock Macdonald, and Alasdair Macdonald—

thanks to each of you for your hospitality and for sharing your memories and mementos with me.

To the people who lived in Glenurquhart during the war and were generous enough to share their experiences: Duncan MacDonald, Angus MacKenzie, Jessie (Nan) Marshall, William Ross, and Bonita Spence.

To Lady Munro of Foulis, for graciously inviting me to Foulis Castle to discuss her experiences in the WAAF, and for allowing me to prowl around the castle's original kitchen with my camera.

To Siobhan McNab, for her timely and thorough archival work; to Fiona Marwick, from the West Highland Museum in Fort William; and to Sheila Gunn for providing Gaelic translations.

To my trusted critique partners: Karen Abbott, Joshilyn Jackson, and Renee Rosen, each of whom has talked me off the ledge at least once, or, if I've already fallen over, pulled me back by my bungee cord. I can no longer count how many books we've collectively survived.

And a very special thanks to Emma Sweeney, my wonderful agent; Cindy Spiegel, editor extraordinaire; Michael Taeckens and Jennifer Grant for too many reasons to count; and last but not least, to Gina Centrello and the wonderful team at Random House—Jennifer Garza, Nicole Morano, Tess Nellis, Jessica Bonet, Leigh Marchant, Erika Seyfried, and Annie Chagnot.

All of you have the patience of Job, a keen understanding of the creative process, and provided an unfaltering but gentle hand in guiding my book toward its finest form. Life threw me a number of curve balls over the last few years and I am grateful beyond words that you stuck with me.

At the Water's Edge

Sara Gruen

A READER'S GUIDE

A Conversation with Sara Gruen

Interview by Brandi Megan Granett

Sara Gruen, author of the new release *At the Water's Edge*, shared some insight into her writing process and what led her to set her latest novel at the edge of Scotland's Loch Ness during World War II.

Brandi Megan Granett: How did the story for *At the Water's Edge* unfold for you? What drew you to writing it?

Sara Gruen: I had a long-standing fascination with the Loch Ness Monster, starting when I was twelve and first visited Urquhart Castle and was convinced I was going to see it, and a random news article rekindled my interest. The idea of incorporating my favorite castle in the world with the looming prospect of the monster was irresistible, so I booked research trips without having any idea of what my story would be. Ultimately, it came to me in a rush when I was standing at the Water Gate in Urquhart Castle (a location that has great importance in the book), and I spent the rest of the afternoon stomping around the castle dictating ideas into my phone. That day was definitely one of the highlights of my writing life!

BMG: Both Jacob in *Water for Elephants* and Maddie and Ellis in *At the Water's Edge* suffer a sort of fall from grace at the start, losing access to a once guaranteed future. What do your stories say about making life your own?

SG: In the broadest sense, almost all stories begin with an upheaval of some sort, because normal people doing normal things does not a good story make! I think the stories that appeal to us as readers are those in which people have to examine what's really going on in their lives, or face a huge change in circumstances, and then see what they do going forward. In the case of *At the Water's Edge*, Maddie and Ellis both face enormous changes in circumstance and their understanding of life as they know it, and react in nearly polar opposite ways to the truths they find.

BMG: What roles do travel and research play in your writing? When does imagination come in?

SG: I love the research part. One of the best things about this job is that I get to find something that fascinates me and that I hope will be fascinating to others, and then I completely immerse myself in it for a few years. It happens in different ways for different books, but in this case the location came first, and after a few weeks of full immersion in the Highlands, the story came to me. It happened while I was standing at the Water Gate, and all the little amorphous bits that were floating around in my brain started to take shape, so I sent my guide back to his car and spent the rest of the afternoon stomping around the castle dictating ideas into my phone. That's one of those writing moments you hope and dream will happen, but very rarely do. I still have the files on my phone. They're taking up a huge amount of space, but I can't bring myself to delete them.

BMG: Your books draw richly on the history of the times; in *At the Water's Edge*, World War II frames the narrative. What do you think it takes to accurately portray a time period?

How do you balance telling the story and setting the historical scene?

SG: For me, I need to take an almost obsessive approach to research. When I'm at the writing stage, I pass through a kind of creative portal every day and feel like I'm really in that other world I've created, and so it has to exist right down to the trowel marks in the plaster, and I'm a stickler for detail. The saying "the devil is in the details" is absolutely right.

BMG: This is your fifth book; what have you learned about your writing process as you gained more experience? What stayed the same for you and what has changed?

SG: I've realized that I can't structure my work time and progress quite as rigidly as I would like to. For my first couple of books, I aimed for (and got, even if it nearly killed me) two thousand words a day. Then I moved to two thousand words a day or eight hours, whichever came first. Now, I feel like if I show up for work and put in an honest day, I've done well. Because I can't force the creative process. Sometimes I am typing as fast as I can all day, and have to drag myself away because there's more to be done, and other times I stare glumly at my open file all day, which is okay, because I've come to realize that when I can't get any words out, it means there's something I need to figure out and change in the storyline, and even if my fingers aren't busy, my brain is.

BMG: Out of all the characters you created, who is your favorite and why?

SG: Before this book, I would have said Rosie, but now I have to say Maddie. She changed so dramatically from what I imagined her to be—coming to life in the way that characters do—and she was so willing to look at things that she had never examined before, in an open-minded and big-hearted way, and she showed courage and resolve in a situation that was utterly impossible, and became increasingly so.

BMG: I read that you needed an Internet-free zone to write *Water for Elephants*. Zadie Smith spoke about using a computer program to block herself from the Internet while writing her novel *NW*. How do you keep yourself from going down the rabbit hole of cyberspace?

SG: I wrote a large chunk of *Water for Elephants* in a walk-in closet, because at that time we didn't have Wi-Fi and it prevented me from obsessively checking my email, shopping on eBay, and basically blowing an afternoon watching cats in boxes on YouTube. Then I used Zadie Smith's method—I know the program she's talking about—but I found a workaround, and so that ended up being no help at all. And just in case she ever reads this, I'm not going to say what that workaround is because I do not want to be single-handedly responsible for the delay of a new Zadie Smith book.

Questions and Topics for Discussion

1. The novel takes place during World War II. Is the war setting a distraction or does it contribute to the success of the novel? Would changing the time frame change the meaning of the novel? How did the austerity of the times affect Maddie, who was used to a life of luxury? Have you ever discussed what things were like during the Great Depression and World War II with family members who lived through it? What stories did they share with you?

2. "What I learned over the past year was that monsters abound, usually hiding in plain sight." Monsters come in all different forms in *At the Water's Edge*. What are some of the monsters in the novel? How are they different from what you might expect?

3. Throughout *At the Water's Edge*, Maddie transforms from a woman who is spoiled, naïve, and helpless to one who is brave and capable. What and who are the major influences that led her to change? What are the biggest lessons Maddie learns throughout the course of the novel?

4. Discuss the novel's ambiguity concerning the supernatural. How does Sara Gruen blend mystical elements into the narrative's realism? Did Ellis and Hank find the Loch Ness Monster after all?

5. Do you think Maddie and Ellis were ever truly in love? What did you think of Ellis? Did you sympathize with him?

Did Ellis change as a character in the course of the novel or did the changes all take place within Maddie?

6. How did you feel about Hank? Did he evolve during the course of the novel or did his character remain the same?

7. The idea for *At the Water's Edge* came to Sara Gruen during a visit she took to Scotland. She became fascinated with the ruins of old castles, the wild beauty of nature, and Scottish history and folklore. Discuss the role that the landscape and atmosphere of Scotland plays in the novel.

8. Discuss the evolution of Maddie and Angus's relationship. What were some of Angus's qualities that Maddie grew to most admire? At what point do you think she realized she loved him?

9. *At the Water's Edge* explores humanity at its most base, as well as its most noble. Can you give some examples of both from the story? In the end, what kind of statement do you think Gruen makes about human nature?

10. Before she goes to Scotland, Maddie only has Ellis and Hank as friends. How do the female friendships she develops in Scotland shape her in new ways?

SARA GRUEN is the #1 *New York Times* and *USA Today* bestselling author of *Water for Elephants, Ape House, Riding Lessons*, and *Flying Changes*. Her works have been translated into forty-three languages and have sold more than ten million copies worldwide. *Water for Elephants* was adapted into a major motion picture starring Reese Witherspoon, Robert Pattinson, and Christoph Waltz in 2011.

She lives in western North Carolina with her husband and three sons, along with their dogs, cats, horses, birds, and the world's fussiest goat.

saragruen.com

ABOUT THE TYPE

This book was set in Walbaum, a typeface designed in 1810 by German punch cutter J. E. (Justus Erich) Walbaum (1768–1839). Walbaum's type is more French than German in appearance. Like Bodoni, it is a classical typeface, yet its openness and slight irregularities give it a human, romantic quality.

Chat.
Comment.
Connect.

Visit our online book club community at
Facebook.com/RHReadersCircle

Chat
Meet fellow book lovers and discuss what you're reading.

Comment
Post reviews of books, ask—and answer—thought-provoking
questions, or give and receive book club ideas.

Connect
Find an author on tour, visit our author blog, or invite one of
our 150 available authors to chat with your group on the phone.

Explore
Also visit our site for discussion questions, excerpts, author
interviews, videos, free books, news on the latest releases,
and more.

Books are better with buddies.
Facebook.com/RHReadersCircle